TORN CLOUDS

The Angel of Forgetfulness sometimes forgets to remove from our memories the records of the former world, and then our senses are haunted by fragmentary recollections of another life. They drift like torn clouds above the hills and valleys of the mind, and weave themselves into the incidents of our current existence.

Attributed to The Nazarene

TORN CLOUDS

JUDY HALL

BOOKS

Winchester, UK
Washington, USA

Copyright © 2004 O Books
46A West Street, Alresford, Hants SO24 9AU, U.K.
Tel: +44 (0) 1962 736880 Fax: +44 (0) 1962 736881
E-mail: office@johnhunt-publishing.com
            www.o-books.net

U.S.A. and Canada
Books available from:
NBN,
15200 NBN Way
Blue Ridge Summit, PA 17214, U.S.A.
Email: custserv@nbnbooks.com
Tel: 1 800 462 6420
Fax: 1 800 338 4550

Text: © Judy Hall 2005

Design: Graham Whiteman Design, Halifax, Canada
Text: Set in Celeste
Cover design: Krave Ltd., London

ISBN 1 903816 80 7

A CIP catalogue record for this book is available from the British Library.

Printed in the USA by Maple-Vail Book Manufacturing Group

contents

acknowledgments

Whilst the characters in this book are fictitious – except for those who bask in the spotlight of history (and even then I have taken liberties with their lives) – and many of the past life memories included here are my own, I have incorporated the fruits of over thirty years regression therapy. Inevitably, I have borrowed snippets of experiences and facets of personality and woven them into the characters who people this book. No one character is based wholly upon anyone I know – living or dead. I'd like to thank all my clients and participants on my workshops from whom I learned so much and borrowed a little.

Jenni Davis has been a wonderful support, her generous copy editing tightened up the initial manuscript, and her sadness at the outcome of Megan's past life affairs brought about the hope of a new relationship freed from the strings of the past.

Dr Robert Jacobs accompanied me on my many trips to Egypt, dealt with Pharaoh's revenge, sat patiently by whilst I walked in the past, and never tired of discussing the myths and my ideas for this book. His encouragement made it possible to go on writing.

John Anthony West's *Traveller's Key to Ancient Egypt* helped me to look beyond the surface meaning of the myths and sites, and was an invaluable guide to the esoteric nature of the sacred places of Egypt as was Alan Richardson's *Inner Guide to Egypt*.

The chapter headings in this book are taken from "One Hundred Names and Epithets of The Goddess Sekhmet" contained in Robert Masters' *The Goddess Sekhmet: The Way of the Five Bodies* (Amity House, New York 1988), a book that arrived in my life shortly after I made my own deep connection to the goddess at whose wish the arts were born. It was the Lady Sekhmet who insisted that this book should be written.

The Laments of Isis and Nephthys in Chapter 16 were adapted from *The Burden of Isis*, one of the *Wisdom of the East* series published in 1910, translated from the Berlin Papyrus 1425 by James Teackle Dennis, a book that, for me, catches the essence of the ancient ritual poetry.

sa sekhem sahu

"Tell me, exactly why are you pouring beer over the lion goddess's head? It's not a sight you see too often in the British Museum." A face peers quizzically at me over the shoulder of my Lady.

My heart thrums as I turn to the man stepping out from behind the great black basalt statue. As his laugh echoes down the gallery lighting up the gloom, the stranger's sky-blue eyes crinkle at the edges. His long chestnut curls gleam in disarray and, high on his cheek, a crescent moon-shaped scar glows white. It's alright, this casually dressed stranger poses no threat to me. Smiling, I turn back to my task.

Quickly I offer bread to my Lady's mouth.

All honor to Sekhmet, Sa Sekhem Sahu.

As I turn back to the tall stranger, a sudden shaft of sunlight catches the golden amulet at his throat and my hand moves instinctively to touch my own. As I finger the cool stone at its center, my heart insists that it cannot be coincidence that he too is wearing my Lady's emblem.

"Ere, I told you, you can't do that feedin' the lion stuff in 'ere. It's not the bleedin' zoo." The grumpy old attendant mutters again as he starts towards us.

"Oh yes, we can. She just did." My new-found friend grins. "But I think we'd better go to the coffee shop so you can tell me why. Shall we?" Courteously he gestures towards the door. Will he take my arm? No, not yet, he's too impatient to do that now.

His long stride propels me down the corridor, urging me past the bookshop and into the formica and chrome interior I have come to know so well. Tingles dance up my spine. Why do some of the best, and worst, moments of my life happen here? And what am I to tell him? Can I really say ... no, surely not, he'll think I'm mad. But then again, he is wearing that amulet – and the mark of Hathor. My leaping heart insists he's going to be important in my life so he'll need to understand. Come on, Mecky, deep breath: "It's a long story, and you might not believe me. I still don't quite believe it myself when I look back on all that's happened to me over this last two years." I can hardly meet his eyes. What if ...

"Why not try me and see? I'm very open minded, and utterly intrigued. I'm John Bellingham by the way, but everyone calls me Jack. Pleased to meet you." As his hand grips mine electricity flashes between us: "Damned chrome, it always gets me that way" – No, it's not the chrome but perhaps now is not the time to tell him.

"And you are ...?"

"Megan, Megan McKennar, but call me Mecky."

"Well Megan McKennar, Mecky, why don't you grab that table over there by the potted palm and I'll get us some coffee, then you can tell me all about it." With a cheerful grin, he takes his place in the queue. It's that table again, but this time, I know, it will be different.

chapter 1.

The Lady of the Flame

It began with a dream:

Eyes. Burning. Fearsome. Reaching into my soul. Beckoning. Demanding. Calling to me across time. *"You are mine. Come!"*

Streaking through night. Thirst beyond measure. Below, rusty shale. Ahead, blood-red ground. Stalking. Leaping. Hanging, poised to strike. Swooping to a pomegranate lake. Drinking without ceasing. Blood. The essence of life. A lioness staring back at me. Dissolving in amber eyes ...

Heart pounding, my head shooting off the pillow, I'd fumbled for the light still feeling hot, fierce breath on my face, the blood-lust in my veins. Seeing those eyes, hearing that supernal voice.

What was a lioness doing in this stark white bedroom with those little patches of paint dabbed on every wall? The colors had looked good in the day but at night they were different, cold and lifeless while I needed something warm and gentle on the eye, especially if I was going to continue waking before dawn like this. A streetlight outside the window meant it was never totally dark, but there were deep pools of shadow, even with the light on. Was she hiding behind those pictures I hadn't hung, or the crates I hadn't yet unpacked but had quickly draped with a silken lilac throw? Was she elsewhere in the flat, maybe in that tiny sitting room that had felt so cozy before I moved in?

Who was she? This being who summoned me across a vast distance, to whom I owed total obedience, the wondrous presence who haunted my dreams.

I needed to find her. At once! But why?

To reclaim my soul, to redeem my life. It sounded so dramatic, and yet I knew it was so.

How could I find her? She was out there somewhere. Waiting. Calling.

I'd hurried out of my lonely bed and left my flat, forgetting breakfast and the potions that would cool my raging blood.

Crossing Museum Street, I had found myself in a travel agents. Reaching out at random, a brochure had fallen open. On the page before me serene sails hung on green water backed by russet sand and an infinite sky. A haunting face, flawless beauty marred by a lost eye stared out at me with haughty disdain. Who was she, this queen from another time? What were her secrets, did she too know unbearable pain and loss, or was she cushioned by her rank? I supposed I'd never know, but I could walk her land. Exhausted, I fell into a chair.

"This one please. A week, as soon as possible. I must go now."

"Just a moment, madam." Peering intently at the screen in front of her she muttered, "Now then, let's see ..." Her computer buzzed and she looked up, a professional smile plastered on her face: "Tomorrow? We could do tomorrow."

"That's fine, yes, thank you." Thank goodness she was filling in the form, my hand was shaking much too much. Quickly I handed over my Visa card, I was on my way.

From high above, I could see a vast body laid out in rocks and sand. At its center, a pulsating artery, carrying its lifeblood between narrow bands of green. A living, breathing being: Khemet, the Land of Egypt. The dying sun sent its rays out across the lapis sky. Russet, grape, and pomegranate painted the void. Tiny white houses and stately mud-brick walls filled my view and passed tantalizingly out of sight. Craning my neck, there was a glimpse of a vast golden mass, glowing as the sun god left the world to face his enemies in the night. A blood-red lake appeared, and moved on. Where were the squawking women? Then everything was gray and green, camouflaged jets and tanks waited on the ground like tethered birds of prey.

There. Was that the shadow of a lioness waiting to pounce? See, there, behind the military bunker at the head of the runway. Stealthy in the fast fading twilight, blending effortlessly into the sand, the last rays of the sun lit up her tawny mane. It was She. Surely, it must be her.

Stepping off the plane, heat and an indefinable aroma hit me like a wall. It was utterly foreign and yet I was home. That smell, so familiar, but I'd never been further than the South of France. The feel of soft night approaching raised my hopes. Waiting to pass through the dirty glass doors, I was a traveler returning home after a long journey. Was this anything to do with my dream? As we came in to land it had been like déjà vu, passing over the blood-red ground and deep purple shadows as so many times before. That glimpse of a lioness, what was that? Surely there were no lions in Egypt now? And yet one haunted my dreams.

Someone pushed me forward, ramming a suitcase into the back of my knees. The queue had moved on. Gathering my sparse belongings together with my wandering thoughts, I was disgorged into a dingy hall. The terminal was hot, fetid, heaving with people. Individual cells in a vast body.

An ancient, hook-nosed man bent under the weight of a huge refrigerator strapped to his back. How could he carry it? How had he got it on a plane? More men appeared, equally loaded.

"They are coming home from Saudi," someone explained. "They work there for years."

Exiles returning, just like me.

Serene pockets eddied within the whirling hubbub, white-robed holy men, murmuring the Koran. My informant pointed, discreetly:

"Pilgrims returning from the Hajj. They will go home and paint the story on their houses for everyone to see." He turned away to reclaim his wife.

Standing in line, moving towards the lone policeman dealing with the passports of "Non-nationals," my sense of time was blurred. As we landed, there was that remnant of sunlight, luminous across the desert. Now beyond the window blackness assailed my senses. And the people, those robes could be biblical. Was this my dream, or a film set I'd wandered into? There may be a fatal weakness in my blood but I was tingling with electricity. With hardly time to pack, it felt like part of myself had been left behind. Or was it here, waiting?

Suddenly an imperious hand beckoned, an irate policeman with hostile eyes, gun prominent on hip, blocked my way until I presented my passport. His aquiline nose and predatory mouth reminded me of a vulture and I was sure he would happily feed on my decaying flesh. Barely glancing at my passport, he sternly waved me back.

"No visa, no entry. Go."

Now what. To have come this far, they couldn't turn me away, surely? If only Greg were with me ... no, stop right there, Mecky, I told myself, ask the policeman what to do:

"What can I do?"

He was so angry, my knees were shaking again.

"Go" he said waving imperiously, "back, you cannot come. Visa."

Coldly he reached behind me for a handful of burgundy passes impatiently thrust forward. These were clearly acceptable because a family bulldozed past without a word to me.

What now? Did he mean return to England? People pushed past until my head spun and I hit a wall.

"There's no need to worry, my dear," a courteous gentleman with eccentric hair came to my rescue. "You should have gone over there – see that man in the far corner. If you change your money with him, he'll sell you a visa. It's Ramadan, you know, that policeman hasn't had a thing to eat since five a.m. Now he has to stamp all these passports before he can break his fast. I'll give him a chocolate bar and he'll soon cheer up."

Before I could thank him, he turned away and was swallowed by the crowd.

My visa was issued from an ancient tin box, my money changed, and the passport stamped by a man with the sweetest smile. This time the policeman waved me past with barely a glance. Squeezing through a gap in yet another queue, I grasped my bag and staggered through a door into a cacophony of sound, and more intoxicating smells. Soft hands reached out to take my case. Everywhere there was the chorus:

"Welcome. Welcome. First time in Egypt? Welcome, welcome! Welcome to Luxor." Quickly followed by: "Baksheesh, you have baksheesh? It is end Ramadan, I must buy food for my family."

"Take no notice of these rogues," my savior with the eccentric hair quietly advised. "They have plenty of money. Save your baksheesh for those who need it."

Baksheesh? What was baksheesh? How silly, I didn't know the language, I should have bought a phrase book.

"Money," said the old man: "If you give them an Egyptian pound or two they'll probably grumble and try for more, but secretly they'll be well pleased. Keep your small coins for the children, and remember to say 'Imshee' firmly. It means go away and is one of the most useful words for dealing with those young rogues." He smiled again, and turned away.

Imshee, I must remember that. Would it work with rogue cells in the blood?

A harassed-looking young woman in a bright red coat and a skirt too short for her legs spotted me. Waving a clipboard, she demanded:

"Mrs. MacKennat? Come on, we're all waiting for you. This coach here. Climb aboard and we'll be on our way."

Why did people get my name wrong? It was correct on the ticket, why not on her list? Should I say something? No, better let it go.

Out of the dusty window, there was such vibrant life. People shouting and laughing. Children waving: "Hallo, hallo." Cars and lorries hooting, and headlights glaring. How could anyone see? Impossibly loaded taxis dodged emaciated donkeys. After the third near-miss had left me grasping my seat, I focused my attention away from the road.

Faded color-washed houses sat under tall green palms and sulfuric light. There was dust everywhere, and smiling faces. To one side, a lake gleamed. Mysterious. Numinous. Its edges shrouded in reeds. Headlights caught the dancing plumes. It felt so light. So *happy*.

Beyond, a floodlit statue sat headless in regal splendor amid the dust and dirt. Discarded bottles at his feet glinted like ancient jewels. Who was this king of ancient time? What kind of life did he have that he remained imprinted on the land?

And on my heart.

A mud-brick wall and a high gate shimmered in moonlight. My fluttering heart thudded with anticipation.

"Here," says the voice. "Come to me here."

The coach pulled up, and willing hands helped me down.

"This way. Welcome, welcome. Leave luggage here." They ushered me through the wide glass doors.

The hotel was cool and friendly. The vast foyer lined with comfortable seats. A bar, to one side, was thronged with suited and bespectacled men and women in bright colors. Were they local? Somehow I didn't think so.

A smiling face waited to register me. Again the murmured refrain:

"Welcome, welcome to Luxor."

Everyone seemed genuinely pleased to see me. As there were few tourists, my request for a quiet room was swiftly fulfilled. I was asked if I wanted to be in the garden, or to have a Nile view? Hesitating, I put a hand to my aching head.

"Why not look both?" His patient face smiled widely as he handed over keys and called forward a young boy to carry my luggage.

We passed through dusky gardens redolent with the scent of incense, and heavy perfumes of the night; a symphony of insects played as we walked. A shady place with all those trees, the pool was wonderfully inviting under the tall palms, despite the darkness. The room was remote, an open veranda let in the night breeze as we headed towards number 122. A nice room, the furniture dark and sparse but it was quiet there. It needed redecorating, but it would be okay.

"You want see other room?" The boy picked up my bag again. I tried to resist, I was so tired but he ushered me out of the door. "No problem, we come back if you not like."

Back we went, and up. The lift creaked, taking forever, a slow stairway to heaven. The boy turned on the lights, slowly put down my small bag, showed me the balcony and the fridge, fussed and lingered. Oh yes, baksheesh. Smiling, I handed him a few notes to be rewarded with the widest grin ever. Flashing white teeth and rolling sleepy brown eyes, he murmured again:

"Welcome, welcome to our land."

The room was plain but spotlessly clean. The large double bed was made up with crisp white sheets, and there was a small armchair and the ubiquitous TV. The bathroom had a suspicion of plumbing in the air. Opening the balcony door, the smell was musky and heady as the night. I was so pleased I'd come. Glancing at a river of light sliding by far below, hearing the faint honk of cars, I drew the curtains against the night and, exhausted, plunged into sleep.

Awaking early, I was too restless to unpack, too highly charged to eat. The echoes of the muezzin exhorting the faithful to prayer drew me to the window. Below me, cars hooted and called. The sky turned red and reflected in still green waters as the sun jumped into being. A spreading crimson stain divided the land. The Nile. Lifeblood of this arcane place. Ra had risen and reclaimed night. It was day once more. Hurrying, I went out into the day.

The street was already hot. Which was the way back to that mud-brick wall? Was it left or right? There was the widely flowing river, but was my destination upstream or down? Which way to the airport? Walking at random, overwhelmed by beauty all around, I hesitated. There, a golden temple sat serenely in the sun. Here white sails glided on fading pink water. Beyond, purple cliffs transmuted to gold. Did we pass this way before? Shopkeepers plying their wares were insistent, demanding:

"Only look. No charge for looking" as they smiled brightly, white teeth and pink gums bright against the dusky skins.

Offering. "Tea, mint tea. Sit awhile."

Hands reached out imploringly. Shrugging them off, I rushed on impelled by the need to be with Her. Taxis hooted imperiously, but failed to catch my eye. Where was she? Indeed, who was she? Why did she call me? Was I losing my mind? Had all those drugs done something to my frazzled brain, or was it a "senior moment," as mother used to say. Surely not-quite-forty was a little young for one of those?

Away from the main street, everywhere there was heat and noise. And new smells. Cats, drains, goats. What were a mother goat and her kids doing foraging on a city doorstep? Behind a half-closed wooden door, cooking pots bubbled, children babbled. A waft of hashish drifted like a scented ghost on the warm air. Nothing seemed real anymore.

Rushing here and there, my heart beat faster. Down an alley, dark eyes peered from behind a black veil. The stench was appalling. Rotting vegetables and what looked like a dead cat. Eyes stinging, I veered away, took another road. Were those really dressing gowns they were wearing in the street?

Everything was the same back there, so many houses, so many narrow streets, so many faces. Who could I ask? Who could I trust? You heard such awful stories. Terrorists, there were terrorists here. Fear was rising metallic in my mouth. My heart pounded, my knees wanted to run, somewhere, anywhere. Of their own volition ...

People stared as I stumbled through the uneven streets, now pushing my way through bright market stalls. More pungent smells, heavy spices, burnt sugar caramelizing the air. A huge inverted wok spun spider webs of sugar. My head spun stars and lightning flashes. Live chickens pecked in tiny cages, huge cauliflowers balanced gracefully on heads set on impossibly slender necks. So much color. Hands reached out to me, importuning:

"Look, only look."

My head was bursting. This was all too foreign. Why did I ever think I belonged here? The contrast between that stark hospital room and the exotica that surrounded me was too much. My body was weary. Was I going to die there in the street? Was it foolish to come alone like this? Whatever impelled me?

"Help me," I implored Her. "Show me the way."

A bell jangled, a sharp crack stung my ears. Startled, I turned. Dark eyes laughed down at me:

"Hey madam, you want caleche? I take you temple Karnak. I am Khaled, I look after you. See, English friends."

He held out well-thumbed photographs and a scruffy letter with a familiar stamp. Climbing up the high step, I sank gratefully into cool leather. The horse's hooves clipped the tarmac. The driver's words washed over me like a litany:

"... musee ... hospital ... moskee ... good papyrus, cheap price ..."

From an open window, children's voices, chanted.

"School for small children. My son ..."

Dogs barked loudly, rousing me from my stupor.

There were excavations, a causeway lined with ram-headed sphinxes. Beyond the gray brick wall, here She was:

"Khaled, please, stop, you must stop." Seeing me try to scramble precipitously from the carriage my driver slowed down and explained:

"Temple Mut closed. Maybe later." He shook the reigns and we moved off again.

"Yes, yes." My heart sang. We turned into a wide, tree-lined square, and stopped outside a mud-brick booth.

"I wait you here. Caleche 72. You buy ticket there."

Clutching my ticket, I passed between lines of sphinxes. Long, repetitive images glimpsed from the corner of my eye. They were strange, eerie, in the early light. All angles and shadowed planes. Did that one move? Was I walking forwards or backwards? Everything was in soft focus. Was it the heat haze shimmering over the sun-washed stones? The veil of dust that hung suspended in the air, whipped by a rising wind. What was it that made my feet float lightly over the ground? My head swim ever so slightly? Fasting? The fatal weakness in my tainted blood? Or was it this magical place?

My scalp prickled. I felt so *alive* ...

Strange that. So alive. My body may be wasting away, my strength gone, and yet I tingled all over. Life was bursting through my veins. It felt like a transfusion of new blood. Healthy cells were racing around my body, engulfing the invader and the poisons administered to drive it out. My hearing was sharpened, my eyes brightened. My senses tuned anew.

Poles and banners swung above me in the freshening breeze. Horns blew, raucous noise assailed my reawakened ears.

Passing through huge entrance doors with their cedar and bronze decoration, all was shadow. A soft brown hand with tender pink palm reached for my ticket, and waved me on.

Stepping forward, I stood transfixed. It was so quiet and still. My eyes were dazzled, time was suspended. A shimmering, shining sea of white danced before me. A vast courtyard, walled by giants rising out of solid stone. The heat was unbearable as it struck my face. Hands held out before me, I felt I was swimming through light.

I reached a vast papyrus swamp set out in ochre flutes. Columns floated upwards, keeping creation in place, holding chaos at bay. All around their stepped bases, a vast moon calendar tracked celestial light. How did I know this? What ancient astronomer priest whispered in my ear?

It was cooler and dimmer now. Sunlight was slanting down. Dust motes hung in liquid light. Murmuring voices and cadences of prayer lingered like an echo of ancient times. Incense was sharp in my nostrils. Entranced, I sank to my knees at the base of a statue, resting my head on the outstretched arms.

"No, madam, no. Come, see." A blue robed man pulled at my arm.

Shaking off the insistent hand, I rose aimlessly, going where my feet would. Adrift in the swamp, at last I sought a refuge.

Turning, an entrance beckoned, ahead lay dry grass and dusty stones but the inviting shade of a palm tree enticed me beyond the wall. Assailed by rushing wind and gritty air, I hastily covered my face, scarf pulled low over my stinging eyes. A policeman approached. Was it forbidden here? About to apologize and retreat, I recoiled as he took my arm.

"Sekhmet," he said: "Come." He tugged me urgently towards a path.

Sand was whipped up all around us, dervishes whirling under the hot sun. Blocks of stone lay haphazardly, their outlines blurred, reflecting heat. The air scorched my head, searing my lungs and drying my skin. Water, I had no water. My thirst rose, I turned back ...

"Come." Impatiently, he pulled my arm.

Unresisting, I followed.

"You come see Sekhmet." Smiling, he led me by the hand. "First time in Egypt?"

Dumbly, I nodded.

"Welcome. Welcome. How many children?"

Numbly, I shook my head, rising tendrils gripped my belly. Don't go there! How could I explain? It was impossible.

"No," I murmured, "None."

"Five," he said proudly, pointing to himself. "Two boys. Three girls. You have stilo?" He made the motion of writing: "For the school."

"No, nothing, sorry. I didn't know ..."

"No matter," he told me. "It is hard with many children in school. We are poor country. Books and pens are expensive. I want my children to be educated. In Egypt we are proud of our young ones. They are our way forward."

Sand whirled around us faster now, caught on the rising wind.

We passed through an archway with strange pictures on the

wall, written in shadow. What story did they tell? A glimpse of Doctor Benu Bird, and a hairless head, ears cocked, and there, was that a lioness? It was too late. We were past. Men glided forward, long robes sweeping the sand gently, scarves expertly twirled around heads. They beckoned, silent fingers to lips:

"Ssh ..." Looking furtively over their shoulders, they ushered me into a tiny courtyard.

It's alright, I'm with a policeman, I reassured myself foolishly, but an atavistic fear had me in its grip. My drumming heart shook my body.

A gate was opened and I was pushed into a dark place. Panic rose in my chest, my heart leapt and surged, I could not breathe. Air, I must have air. Helplessly, my arms flailed and my outstretched fingers touched warm stone.

"Moment. Moment ..."

The scuttling and rattling sounds did nothing to reassure me but suddenly sunlight reflected from a flattened tin can dazzled my eyes. On a plinth, a tiny statue sat before a chipped and battered potter's wheel. The great creator had been reduced to this? If only I had an offering to make. Why? What hold did he have on me? And how did I know who this anonymous being was anyway? My head spun stars to match the smoke-blackened ceiling above me. Robed women moved like wraiths around a cooking fire, tending to small children. How could anyone have moved in here, lived in this god-haunted place? Perhaps they thought their Christian symbols would protect them? Was I going mad?

Suddenly a stream of camera-bedecked Japanese tourists issued from a recessed doorway and disappeared into dust.

Dumbstruck, I awaited my fate. A heavy door was unchained revealing only blackness. Taut with terror, I was unable to move.

The door swung back.

"Come, come." They gestured me forward: "The blessing of Sekhmet."

Dimly I made out a tall, majestic form.

The door closed and a shaft of sunlight pierced the gloom. It illuminated a face I knew so well, it had haunted my dreams and drawn me here to her temple. The proud, leonine head sat atop a sensuous woman's body, her breasts bared. The face was powerful like a lion, compassionate like a woman. The slim beam of light falling sharply from a hole in the roof illuminated her magnificent black basalt figure. Shining out from the surrounding darkness, she was awesome. She must be nearly eight feet tall. Her eyes drew me forward and I wanted to fall to my knees, to prostrate myself full length on the dirt floor, to worship her, but the guardian took my hand and pulled me upward. On tiptoe, I could barely reach her imposing forehead. He moved my hand from her head to mine. Energy surged up my spine. Light flashed across my eyes. As my hand was moved to her breast, the light faded. I felt myself slipping, sliding away. Falling into nothingness ...

chapter 2.

The wrath of Ra

A rushing wind. An all-seeing eye plucked and thrown down. Fierce, burning rage.

"Go. Kill. Destroy the ungrateful wretches who mock their creator. Show them the vengeance of the god, your father, Ra."

Flying across the desert, burning thirst only blood can assuage tears at my heart. Plunging, I drink my fill. Drawing in the life of the land. Consumed by the blood-lust, I travel the length of Khemet, killing all in my path. In vain does my father call me back:

"Spare my children, I only wanted to punish those who mock my old age."

Unheeding, I run on, Sekhmet, Lady of the Bloodbath. I am The Wrath of Ra, nothing can stop me now. My being is a pure cleansing flame burning in the night, a fever in the blood of Egypt. For seven years I roam the land, reveling in the slaughter. The earth is stained red, the great river runs ruddy and bejeweled. For humankind, terror stalks by day and by night.

"It is a plague on our land," says one.

"No, no, the Day of Judgment is come. We are doomed, Anubis is awaiting the harvest of hearts," responds another.

The river squeezes itself between high walls. Inundation high, water whirls and tosses, seeking escape. Aswan the beautiful. The jewel in the crown of Egypt. To one side, a lake glows redly before me. I swoop down. Frightened women run squawking. Here is more blood than in their puny frames. I drink it dry. But – what is this? My head swims. My senses blur. I have been tricked! This is not blood! It is beer laced with deadly mandrake root; colored with ruby pomegranate, the food of the dead. Tasting my own death, I plunge into oblivion. How can this be? I am goddess. Immortal. Invincible. I am She. Night takes me. Whirling, black, stars without number.

A chattering baboon woke me. He had me by the tail and was hauling me along, chuckling to himself as he recounted his silly tales. Sand was in my nose and ears, and my tongue had picked up a coating of grit as the end scraped the ground. The indignity of it.

Clutching my head, I staggered to my feet. Oh, the pounding, the heaving. My husband Ptah was fashioning me afresh on his potter's wheel. He breathed my *ka* back into my body. If this was life, let me embrace death. Let me travel to Amenti.

"What is this, what has happened, who am I?" I asked the silly fellow.

"You are She, you are Sekhmet, the Lady of the Flame" he replied.

Awareness came, and with it remembrance. The killing spree was over. The pure flame extinguished. I was emptied, purged. I dared not count the cost in human suffering, in lives lost.

"How can I live with the knowledge of what I have done? There is nothing for me now." I wept tears of blood. For humankind and, if I am honest, for myself as well.

Tenderly Thoth, god of wisdom – for the chattering baboon

was none other than he – took my hand. Talking all the while, filling my empty spaces with his unquestioning love, he led me home.

Quietly, mindful of my aching head, he reminded me of our creation, and the wrath of my father Ra:

"Many of my moons ago, a young god played alone in the void. Bored, he sought for companions but there were none. Idly as young men do, he grasped his great member. Seed spurted.

The whirling cosmos stilled. Matter took form. The wholeness shattered in half. Shu and Tefnut were created.

Uniting, they procreated.

Twins.

Beings who even while they were in the womb cleaved together so great was their love.

Angrily Shu tore them apart. Thrust them into the void. Geb became the earth. Nuit the night. His backbone formed the mountains, her eyes the stars. From her breasts the milky way flowed.

Geb ached for his mate. His hungry organ reached upward. Nuit strained towards him. The sky trembled, the earth heaved. But they could not be one.

Tearfully Nuit begged me to help her. For we had been close, she had sought consolation but to no avail. Nothing could heal her but her soulmate. With sly cunning, I asked Ra for the feared dark-moon days of my lunar cycle to be gathered together. Thus I won for Nuit a brief span of time in which she could conceive and birth her children.

Time slipped by.

No longer potent, Ra wearied of riding the sun chariot through the void each night. Apopep, the serpent of chaos, grew in strength as the nocturnal battle to birth order each day lost its savor. These were the most dangerous of days, the dying end of the year.

Ra was by now a senile old man, drooling into his beer. He mourned his lost unity – and his lack of power. Crotchety and cantankerous, he issued his orders. Humankind laughed and mocked his efforts to rule. The old order was passing away. The god and his creation grew apart. The divine order was lost. There was a cancer in the body of Egypt.

Angered, Ra set you loose.

In time, he came to regret his unthinking rage, but you had grown strong feeding on the dark power of life itself. You lusted to destroy man. Your own sex, more subtle and schooled in the ways of guile, prepared for you the lake of potent beer. Your rage was stilled. Dying, you were born again with new sight."

"Will I ever be forgiven?" How could I bear this guilt and pain?

"You must seek forgiveness in yourself." He patted my arm gently as his wise eyes held mine.

"How must I do this?"

"To honor the strength of Sekhmet, once in every year, at its dying end, a festival will commemorate your headlong flight through the land of Egypt. Offerings will be made to the three hundred and sixty five statues of your majesty in the inner sanctum of your sacred temple of Mut. The forces of pestilence, the miasmas of death and sickness, the fear of hunger, and the demons from the Otherworld will be held at bay until Ra can birth again with the rising flood."

Tamed by Thoth's loving kindness and gentle words, I sought refuge. Ever a shape-shifter, I assumed the bovine form of my sister Hathor. The great Nile flooded and cleansed the land, fertilizing the earth beneath.

Time passed. The seasons changed. Contented now and at peace, I grazed the sweet pastures by the river, wanting nothing more. My milk nourished the golden land. There was much rejoicing. The body of Egypt was tranquil, the fury forgotten, its work done.

But what was this?

Music and singing assailed my ears. Dancing maidens came to lead me in procession. They decked me with flowers, made offerings of gold and precious jewels. The Great Lady was at their head. She was silent, withdrawn, apprehensive even. The dark days approached once more. Chaos threatened to breach the harmony of Ma'at. Her potent magic must transform my destructive powers at this the weakest moment in the defense of The Land.

"Come my Lady, come," she urged me "we have work to do."

As we approached the great temple of Mut, the doors opened silently. Before me, images of my leonine self replicated a thousand times. Here I was worshipped. Here my transformation took place. No longer destroyer, I was Sekhmet, the beloved. The Healer.

The procession wended its way between the black granite forms. Sistrums rattled, harps thrummed. At length we reached the Holy of Holies. The inner sanctum. Repository of the mysteries. Shawms reverberated. The ebony doors swung open. My dark-haired maidens fell back, afraid to look within.

I enter into that place of nothingness. A vast whirling emptiness. Breathing deep, rushing out through infinite space. Following the milky road to the abode of the ancient ones. Comets flash. Stars veil their light to mark my passing. The great cosmos turns on its axis.

Everything is stripped away.

Still now...

The universe contracts, blood surges, life goes on. I am standing in my own heart. Touching oneness within, and unity without. Opposites. A surgeon's scalpel, a mother's loving touch. My death-dealing destructiveness is necessary to my husband Ptah as he breathes life into the forms he makes on his potter's wheel. Each soul he incarcerates into matter needs my healing touch.

One cannot be without the other. In each ending is the beginning, and each beginning carries the seed of its end. The eternal round.

And beyond that illusion of duality? Much of what is revealed cannot be told here. Part of an infinite continuity of souls rolling across time itself, I perceive the creator bringing life into existence in the vast depths of my being.

Unity beyond measure.

Separating again, I become aware that we, the gods and goddesses of the most ancient land of Egypt are but aspects of the One and the Other.

Gentled now with love, I swelled with power. No more hiding behind the meek and mild Hathor for me. I was She. Death and Life. Strength and gentleness. Roaring mightily, I shed the cow's horns and became lion once more. A rushing wind blew open the sanctuary doors.

Transformed, I leapt ...

My white-robed priestesses laughed with joy and patted me gracefully – but with the respect and awe such a magnificent lion commands.

I was come home. Reconciled. Honored. I was Sekhmet ... She.

chapter 3.

Lady of Enchantments

Hands reached out to lift the heavy leonine mask from my shaven head. At my feet, a bloodied pool spilled from the golden goblet I'd let fall.

The luminescent eyes of Suten held me.

"It was well done. Stand fast."

I could not take my eyes from him. Here was the Lord of my Heart. My Beloved. He turned to present me to the crowd.

"It is finished. The Lady Mek'an'ar did well for us. Khemet's fertility is assured. Sa Sekhem Sahu."

Prostrate forms spread among the tall columns, tailing back into the murky gloom, shaven skulls gleaming. Priests and priestesses bent low in reverence. What lay beyond those shadows? The presence of the gods grew strong.

Priests, priestesses, and gods alike had come to see me, Mek'an'ar, Beloved of Sekhmet, High Priestess of the temple of Mut at Thebes, enter into the goddess and embody her form. They partook of the sacred drama that I am.

A trumpet sounded. Heads rose. A great shout went up.

"The goddess is risen. All honor to Sekhmet. Sa Sekhem Sahu."

Together we rose and mounted the steps to the roof of the temple. Here the sacred instruments were offered to the rising Sun, statues uncovered to receive its blessed rays. Ra, potent and rejuvenated, young once more, poured his life-giving energy onto the waiting world. It was the birth of the New Year. His temple was reborn.

Quickly servants brought food and drink to assuage the long fast. Gallons of beer to honor our lady. Sweet dates and honey cakes to entice our palates. Spiced pigeons and macerated duck to lend us strength. An abundance of vegetables donated their life to invigorate ours. All day the celebrations continued. Statues and instruments were returned to their places, offerings made. Having satisfied the gods, mortals may turn to their own pleasures. Feasts were laid out in the temple, singing and dancing wove their hypnotic spell. Lamps were lit. The great doors thrown open. The crowd spilled over into the courtyards. Soon, couples made their way into the forgiving dusk. On this day, priest and priestess united on neutral ground, honoring the Lady of the Place of the Beginning of Time.

Light-headed still from the narcotic cup the priests had handed me hours before, I looked around. My Lord was still at my side. Silently he commanded:

"Come!"

He led me over the quiet ways to the hidden temple. Food was laid out in the ante-chamber before Ptah. Offering it up, we ate and drank our fill.

Carrying a feast for our Lady we passed into her hallowed presence. A bed fit for Suten and his consort had been prepared before her and she would watch over the rites that night.

Her black basalt figure shone softly in the lamplight. Taller than my Lord, she looked on us with pride. Reverently the sacred herbs were strewn, the oils anointed, food placed in her mouth, a libation of beer poured. The honor of the goddess was satisfied.

In the silence, my Lord took my hand and touched it once to the top of her head. Then to mine own head. My soul took flight and made a bridge to the higher realms. Then to the forehead, lighting up my inner vision. To the heart, uniting all three in the eternal love. To the solar plexus, taking us beyond human emotion. And to the point below the navel where creation begins. Finally, we came to the base from which all things grow. As he touched my *kat*, the kundalini rose, her sacred power flowed into me. I reached out for him.

"Gently," he whispered, "we have the night."

The bed enveloped us in its warm embrace. Sumptuous silk caressed my skin. My Lord kissed me lightly on each eyelid. Such a soft, delicate caress like the wing of a humming bird brushing across them. Gently he explored my flesh, his fingers awoke each cell. Fire rose through my body. His tender touch fused with the energy flowing from the newly awakened land. The great river flowing through my blood pounded and surged as it flooded and receded. I cried out for him but he stilled my urgent call:

"Slowly," he whispered, "we must go beyond time."

Stroking me until I could bear it no longer, he attuned my body to his rhythm. Tenderly and with awe I touched the sacred flesh before me. God and man, Suten of this ancient land and holder of a great mystery.

Breaking off, he turned to pour a goblet of blood-red wine. Standing, he offered it to My Lady, touched it to her lips:

"Sa Sekhem Sahu" and, with infinite slowness, streamed a libation across my aching flesh. Its coolness did nothing to calm my need for him. Kneeling, he licked the ruby stream from the hollow between my breasts down to my *kat*. Tongues of fire moved up my spine. When he moved back and kissed my lips, the sweetness of the wine could not mask the unique taste of my love.

My Lord knelt between my legs. As he raised my heels to his shoulder, his great member approached. Tantalizingly he halted, just touching the entrance to my inner chamber. As I drew breath a shuddering flash passed through my body. The Goddess had entered my flesh. I too was sanctified.

When Pharaoh moved into me, God and Goddess were united. Our love-making was slow, we savored this moment knowing that it would fortify The Land and bring fruitfulness for the coming year. He scarcely moved but each infinitesimal motion was magnified a thousandfold, transmitted throughout my whole being. My *kat* pulsated, energy radiating out as he advanced and withdrew and yet, paradoxically, seemed not to be in motion. It was as though the gods were moving through us.

Enraptured, an age passed. Ecstasy almost unbearable. Suspended in sensuality, wrapped in love. The kundalini rose again and again, each flame passing higher up my spine, each rise taking me further, igniting my soul. As the flame rose inexorably, our pace quickened, moving together in perfect unison, we were the land of Egypt and its gods. We were held within the mystery.

The Goddess inhaled.

The earth rested on its axis.

Rising, rising. Far out beyond the earth. Stars revolving within stars. Two beings in perfect harmony. Nuit and Geb united at last.

The cosmos held its breath.

"My love, my great and dear love."

My Lord cried out with joy as our climax shuddered through all creation. He electrified the sky, the stars took up his call.

My orgasm shook the earth and all its children. Geb and Nuit joined again, primordial wholeness restored.

Life was renewed.

The Goddess exhaled.

Falling, falling into profound peace and stillness. A sacred space so deep nothing could touch it.

We drifted quietly, languorous, satiated. Savoring this moment of time together bathed in the afterglow of a love so profound nothing could break it.

The watcher on the walls called the hour before moonrise. Soon, morning would come. Quietly the priestesses drew away from the drunken, satiated priests. Sadly, without speaking, I left the Lord of my Heart to join my sisters. Like wraiths in the night we slipped out of the southern gate and passed over the torch-lit causeway. Bullfrogs chorused their joy from the canal banks. The dark waters rippled gently as we walked. We processed into our own temple precincts and followed the path to the womb-enclosed lake, the birthing place of Mut.

As we reached the reed-shrouded steps on the far side, each took her appointed place along the banks. Letting white robes fall, chanting the office, we entered the lake as Hathor spread her blessed rays upon the sacred waters, casting light over dark depths. Facing the moonrise, murmuring the mother's words of power, we were purified by the silver water's fall, fertilized by the light of the moon.

Sanctified, we rose reborn.

Our ritual year began anew.

Clouds of sweet smelling frankincense wreathed the temple

and crept into our dwellings as the young priestesses twirled the censers around the old stone walls. It was time to purify our space against the pestilences borne on the breeze and carried by small creatures. To guard against the inhabitants of the unseen world around us. This purification ceremony kept us healthy in body and soul.

In my chamber set high above the temple to catch the cool night breeze, memory tugged at the corners of my mind. Another reality beckoned. I pushed it away. Not now, not when I felt so much at peace. So well.

I slept.

Standing in my accustomed place to greet the dawn, the susurration of the morning all around me, the sacred lake grew weed-choked. The walls, the steps, decayed. The statues lay all but buried in marram grass. The great temple buildings were gone. What was there in that dead landscape for me? My place was here with my people, within these living walls, the heart chakra of the body corporeal of Khemet, the land of Egypt. Following the immutable rhythms of birth, death, and rebirth. Honoring She. Idly I scratched under the heavy wig that covered my shaven head. The heat was melting the cone of perfumed wax that lay beneath the plaited hair. Its musky scent surrounded me, the silken flow cooled my blood. As I began the chant to welcome the morning, for a moment it felt as though my hair had already grown back.

For the space of seven moons I stayed in my temple. Dreaming, healing, laughing, and loving. Yes, loving. Suten had a temple beyond our sacred lake. It honored him and his gods. When he was in Thebes, he went there to pray in the dark of the night ...

... and when he had finished, slipped out of the side door and across to the white stone kiosk at the side of the lake. Here plump cushions were laid, voluptuous silks caressed the stone benches, and furs were spread upon the floor. This was our place. No one disturbed us here.

Whenever possible, the Lord of my Heart entered the temple precincts to walk with me in the cool of the evening light. The Suten and his high priestess had much to discuss. Quietly he took my arm:

"For some time now, the portents have been disturbing. The omens are dire. The astronomer priests at Karnak are predicting a coming together of two of the heavenly bodies in the constellation of the Great Red Hippopotamus. They fear it signifies a cataclysm of cosmic proportions."

"My seers too foresee a time of trouble. I fear invasion. What will you do, Lord of my Heart?"

Suten scratched his head, pushing aside the heavy uraeas crown. Wrinkles on his forehead spoke of the burden he bore.

"The ancient records have been consulted and warnings posted throughout the two lands. The watchers are out on our boundaries. I can do no more." His grave young face no longer sparkled with delight at the world, but his eyes softened as he looked at me: "Pray for me sister-lover of my heart."

"My priestesses and I will petition our Lady to save the land."

The life of the temple continued.

But what was this? The birds fell silent. The temple cats skulked inside. In the distance, a jackal howled. A hot, insistent wind rose. The rushing, sand-clothed air roared. The sky turned livid yellow, deep orange, flamed red, and faded to dull black as the sun died. Buildings disappeared. We ran for cover as stinging sand raked granite nails over our delicate skin. Huge branches fell to the ground. The banners were torn from the walls. The roofs howled.

For the space of half a day, the fierce gale raged. Roiling sand filled the air like the beating wings of a vast beast. The biting wind tossed and roared like a lioness devouring her prey.

Anxiously my priestess cried:

"Is our Lady abroad again, running amok?"

"Has her father Ra set her loose, what have we done?"

"Can the Lady Mek'an'ar save us? Why was she not warned?"

"Has one of the other gods been angered beyond bearing?"

"Is it a plague on the body of Egypt?"

"Has Osiris come to judge the living and the dead?"

Praying incessantly, we made offerings of expiation. The sand was in everything. The bread gritty, the beer gravelly. My eyes were bathed in hot coals.

The light of the sun was out. Ra had withdrawn his face from his creation. Celestial battle raged.

And then, when we were sure the end of the world was come and our soft voices rose in strident, clamorous calls for aid, suddenly everything was still. We prostrated ourselves before our Lady. We dared not look on the face of the Goddess as the light changed into deepest, bloodiest red. Hearts beating wildly, we waited.

Silence.

Slowly I raised my head and began the chant of honor for the Lady. As I watched, the leaden sky turned orange and brilliant yellow, outlining the great statue of Sekhmet that stood invisible before me. A shaft of light from the re-born sun broke through and lit her fierce eyes. Compassion dawned. We were saved.

Everywhere priestesses swept. Wabets scurried with jars of water. The holy places had to be cleansed. Sweet smelling censers were swung in every corner, not merely to perfume the air. We must flush out the scorpions and serpents who took refuge from the storm, and purify and appease the spirits who were disturbed. Everything must return to normal. My Lady's house must be in perfect order.

Suten came to bid me a formal farewell, the iridescent blue war crown on his head:

"Our enemies have invaded the body of Egypt. I must take my leave of my High Priestess, Beloved of Sekhmet and Keeper of my Heart. I must go."

My heart breaking, I steeled myself not to reach out before my priestesses. There was no time to be alone. For a moment he looked deep into my eyes:

"We will meet again. Three and a half thousand years must pass in the Other World before we can be reunited. But I will come for you."

"The Blessing of our Lady be upon you and guide your hand Lord Suten. May our enemies be vanquished. May the gods bring you victory."

The Lord of my Heart mounted his war chariot and sped away without another word.

Be still, frantic heart.

Head held high, I passed into the temple to feed and wrap my Lady for the night. Reverently I closed the doors of her shrine. She would sleep now. Leaving a rush light burning before her, I implored the goddess:

"Keep him safe, let him return to me. Bring us together again." Silently, I heard her response.

"It will be so."

Foolishly I assumed it would be months, maybe even a complete revolution of Ra. Longer would be too much to bear. How could I accept that the Lord of my Heart saw further than I? That the separation would be immense. Eternity would unroll before we would be reunited. Again, memory tugged but I thrust it away.

That night, the tears flowed as I faced the sacred lake. There was no moonlight that night. It was one of the dark days of Thoth. Isis' face was veiled. A flame of anger passed through me.

"Why, why me? Why must I be of temple and my beloved Ibi of court?"

Silently I questioned my Lady. The tender name from our shared childhood jolted through me. It was given to few to know the intimate name of the Suten. The secret name of the god. To know it was to hold his life in my hand. "Why cannot we be together? I am as high born as he, a fitting wife and it was promised. We share the *per aa*, the royal blood."

I seemed to hear my old nurse whispering to me as she did when I was a child:

"We each have our own talents, our unique pathway to flow. We cannot all be the same. If we all walked the same path, the earth would tip over with our weight. We'd fall off. Remember child, walk in your own shoes. Be as the goddess made you. You who are called to Sekhmet from birth ..."

That was all very well, but I was with child. I may need my Lord's protection as well as my Lady's.

As my anger faded, I felt the murmuring certainty of the temple ritual take over and order my life. I was soothed by the evening call and the raised voices of my priestesses chanting thanks for the day and prayers for the night to come. My heart opened. Life continued. I was present at the difficult birth, and I accompanied the dying to Amenti. In teaching the novices, retelling the ancient stories, a certainty grew, this was my life. I heard dreams and saw visions unfold.

The Great Round proceeded unchallenged.

A messenger arrived:

"Suten has won a great victory in the North. The Land is safe, our enemies vanquished."

My heart rejoiced. Khemet was safe once more. But then:

"Suten is wounded. He will be brought by barge to Thebes. The journey will take many weeks."

My heart grew heavy, I was filled with foreboding.

Four more moons had passed and it was time to make ready again for the Great Festival of Reconciliation. The priests came for me. But how could this be when the Lord of my Heart had not yet reached my side?

I was bathed in lotus flowers, perfumed, and bejeweled. Hair fell to the floor as the razor touched my most intimate places. Robed in finest linen, shaven head gleaming, I was purified by the long fast. My priestesses and I made our way to the great Hypostyle Hall. A blood-red moon hung pregnant in the sky. Nuit was birthing her babies. Soon it would be my turn.

Once again the mask of Sekhmet was placed upon my head. I ascended her throne.

The narcotic cup was handed to me by an anonymous priest hidden behind the mask of Ra. Only his eyes were visible, glittering black and predatory in the braziers' flickering light. Shining with a hungry gleam. Who was he, this stranger who had usurped my Lord's role? He wasn't clothed in the lion skin that signified he too had made the journey with My Lady. He had not run amok in the reaches of the night. He had not borne the initiation that fitted him to be my guide. He had not been where I had to go. How could I bear this? How could I rebirth the world without my Lord at my side? How could I overcome the demons of the night, the forces of pestilence and death? How could I turn my Lady's awesome power to healing light? What about my unborn child?

The alien priest spoke the words of power, their echoes reverberated around the sacred walls, magnified a thousand times. They pulled me outwards ...

"No, no," I cried despairingly clutching my bulging belly.

Too late.

The rushing wind began again. A fire in my blood. The goddess was released ...

chapter 4.

Bountiful one

Soft murmuring roused me, gentle hands lifted me. A pool of blood at my feet, but no, it was only Coca Cola spilled by my shaking hand as a guardian sought to aid this heat-struck traveler from a cooler clime. Pulling my scarf down, for a moment it felt like I was still wearing a coiled and plaited wig. I smelt the perfumed cone of wax that melted beneath it. And yet, it was illusion. But there was hair, new grown. Soft like down but undoubtedly my hair where none grew before.

"Can I be of any assistance here? Oh, it's you again. Are you alright, my dear?"

My eccentric-haired friend from the airport peered anxiously down on me.

"Yes ... I think so, the heat ..."

Helping me to my feet, he said:

"I think you need refreshment, I know just the place."

Courteously he offered me his arm. Patting my hand reassuringly, he guided me out of the temple: "This way. Don't try to talk."

Words were beyond me. My head was spinning and trying to think was difficult enough. What had happened to me? Was it an hallucination? It couldn't have been. It was real, I was there, and could still feel the child in my belly, taste the foulness of the cup, see those greedy priestly eyes boring into mine, holding me fast. Still remember what it was like to be loved by Pharaoh, feel his touch setting me on fire. But why did I call him Suten? It wasn't his name, more like a title. My body knew the strength of the lioness racing over the ground, avidly drinking the hot blood.

God, how awful. To drink blood with such relish. This was far worse than the dreams. At least when I dreamt it wasn't *me*. I was seeing Her. This time it was me, I was Her. It couldn't simply be the heat, I must be losing my mind. People who went crazy sometimes thought they were someone else, they had strange fantasies, didn't they? What was the difference between them and me? They believed it was true. So did I, but I could have been making it up. If they could believe they were Jesus or Napoleon, they could think they were an ancient Egyptian. But this was me, I recognized myself. The experience was *mine*. I wasn't crazy. Was I?

How could I relive my past? Step back in time. I believed it utterly, and knew it couldn't be true. How could it be, how could I have lived thousands of years ago there in Egypt, been a priestess in love with Pharaoh, carrying his child. I'd felt that baby kicking, moving inside me. But I'd never carried a child like that so how would I know how it felt – when I ... no, stop right there. Don't think about that. And then dying so dramatically. It sounded like something from an old movie or one of those novels you found at airports. What was it my schoolteacher had called it, an overactive imagination? My heart hurt, I still felt my beloved Pharaoh's loss. Why did he leave me?

I told myself to think about something else. Gazed around for a distraction. It was quiet there in the ruins. Almost like time itself was listening. The past was close. It was no wonder people stepped back in time, or hallucinated, or whatever. Get a grip, Mecky, I said sternly, focus on something real.

We walked down a dusty path lined with stiff furls of marram grass and the occasional carved block. Remnants of other temples, no doubt. There was a gray mud wall in the distance. The wind had dropped, but there were still eddies and that gritty taste in the air. My friend's silver hair ruffled and shone like a punk halo. From time to time he ineffectually scraped at it, to no avail. As though discovering it for the first time, he spotted the hat he was carrying and tamed the wayward hair with a flourish. Catching my sideways glance, he asked:

"Do you like it? I saw it in the Cairo Bazaar and thought it would be fun. A genuine pith helmet. Burton would have worn one of these on his journey to the source of the Nile and I expect Howard Carter had one on when he opened Tutankhamen's tomb. It must have been quite a sight." Grasping the hard brim, he gave a little flourish and then settled the hat on his head once more.

Was he talking about Carter or the tomb? Not that it mattered. Smiling, I nodded. On anyone else a pith helmet would look ridiculous but on him it was perfect. It matched the knee-length shorts and besocked legs. He was like one of those Victorian explorers.

From the corner of my eye, I saw a familiar figure excised in stone, its head thrusting forward.

"Dr Benu Bird." I did not realize I had spoken aloud.

"Oh, you know about the benu bird?" smiled my new friend.

"Well, no ... He reminds me ... One of the guardians said ... Could you ..." It was difficult to string words together, was I making any sense? He didn't look too worried about me, so it must have been okay.

"Certainly. It will be my pleasure. The benu bird migrated here from Heliopolis, which is in the north. It was rather like a phoenix. The benu was said to return to the temple to lay an egg before it died. In the heat of the sun, the egg would split and the benu bird would be reborn. Resurrection we would call it, rising from the dead. The Egyptians were hot on that sort of thing." One eyebrow rose as his eyes quizzed me.

"Resurrection? Didn't they believe in reincarnation?"

"Yes, but for them it was something to be avoided, many of the rituals were intended to prevent reincarnation into a physical body, they showed the soul the way forward into Amenti, the afterlife. Oh, look, ahead of us ..."

A lake. Green, with strange amorphous shapes in its bubbling depths and a stand of palms, arms spread in welcome.

"The sacred lake," he murmured with reverence. "The priests used to set Ra's barque afloat here each morning at sunrise."

For a moment, hope rose. But it was nothing like my lake. This one was hard-edged and square. Masculine. Mine was soft-edged and womb-like. It must have been my imagination. Taking my arm, my friend steered me into the deep shade of an awning and pulled out a rattan chair. Removing his hat and forking through his hair, he said:

"Sit, be comfortable, my dear. As it is Ramadan there will not be much on offer, but I expect there'll be tea or a cool drink."

"Tea would be wonderful." My voice came from a long way off. I was walking in the temple in the cool of the evening with my Lord. It felt right. This was where I belonged. But I was also there, sitting by the lake waiting for my tea. How could I be in two places at once?

Was this what was called a flashback? I'd heard people talk about flashing back to an accident. There was that Gulf war veteran on television, he kept reliving the minutes before he was shot. He said he didn't look back at it, he was there. It was like the clock had turned back, he was living it over and over again. Was that what I did? Flashed back to a previous life? I was certainly there. It was such a strong feeling. Different to the dreams, even though they were incredibly powerful. It couldn't have been my imagination. I loved him so much. It had to be true. It explained everything – those dreams, why it all felt so familiar the moment I landed. Even – no, don't think about *that*.

But how could it be true? How could someone live twice?

How I wished that doubting voice would stop, it was like having someone else in my head with me. I knew it was crazy, but that experience was as real as the chair on which I was sitting. It had to be true. I was there, I stepped through time. I couldn't be the only person to whom it had happened. Other people must have had a similar experience, surely. There had to be an explanation, a way of making sense of it. It wasn't my imagination. I didn't make it up. Surely there must be someone who could explain the how and why of it, but I knew the truth. *I was there. It was that simple.* I'd find out the mechanics when I got back to England. But, at that moment, it was enough. I *knew*.

Peace washed over me. I'd heard about that, peace washing over people, but until it happened I didn't know what it meant. I felt utterly calm.

Tea arrived in a glass with a small packet of dry biscuits and another of those enormous Egyptian smiles. The biscuits tasted like honey cakes as they slid down my throat with the hot tea.

Revived, I looked around. Between the dusty tea stall and the lake a vast palm tree stood silently in the sun and, sitting in its shade, a blue-garbed figure dozed gently alongside postcards set out in the sun. A few books drooped in the heat. My friend took off his hat and said:

"Perhaps I'd better introduce myself. Malcolm Appleyard, at your service. An engineer by profession, but now retired. I passed through Cairo during the Suez crisis and became fascinated with the mythology and the buildings that remain in Egypt. I studied the subject whenever I could and I've promised myself I'll visit all the places mentioned in the myths."

Come on Mecky, I told myself, pull yourself together. Pay attention, show some interest.

"Have you been to many places?" A bit trite, but he seemed pleased I'd asked.

"I've been to Cairo and am working my way up the Nile. I want to honor each of the gods and goddesses and see the major sites where their stories played out. I have such a deep sense of history, I can picture it all clearly."

Glancing at me to see how I took this, he went on:

"Did you know the temple where I found you was dedicated to Sekhmet? She was the destroyer goddess, sent out by her father Ra to punish mankind."

Should I mention how well I'd come to know that? No, better not. This was something I couldn't share, at least not yet, But maybe I could have more confirmation:

"What happened to her? Why did she have that lion's head?"

"That's the form she took. According to the myth, the women eventually drugged her to stop the slaughter. Then she became a healer."

Sitting forward in my chair I asked: "Was she revered, or did the people fear her?"

"There was a great festival in her honor every year. A great orgy some say, with gallons of beer consumed on her behalf. Over that way" – he gestured beyond the sacred lake – "she had a much larger temple where she was known as Mut. It was there women went to birth their babies. Her priestesses were midwives and seers."

"Can I go there?"

"Unfortunately, no, officially it has been closed for years. It is being excavated. You might have caught a glimpse of the back end of it from the coach on the way from the airport?" His eyebrow twitched as he smiled again.

Yes, indeed, but I was afraid to tell this new-found friend the effect it had on me, and how anxious I was to reach it. He might think I was mad – and he could be right! I wanted him to think well of me. But I had to get there. Perhaps Khaled ...

Standing up, my legs were a bit shaky still but my head was clear. Holding out my hand I told him:

"It was nice to meet you, and thank you for rescuing me. I did appreciate the tea and I hope you enjoy your stay."

"I'm sure I will. I've wanted to do this for so long. There is so much to see. Maybe we'll bump into each other again. I'm staying at the Old Winter Palace. The terrace is a marvelous place to have tea and watch the sun set over the Nile. Do call in if you are passing." His handshake was firm, and cool.

"That would be nice. I'll look out for you. Goodbye for now."

How stiff and formal it sounded after the easy manner of the Egyptians.

My attention was caught by tall columns away to my right. We had come almost full circle. To reach the entrance I'd pass back through that vast papyrus swamp. Not so strange now that my feet would know how to find the door hidden in the corner. After all, I'd slipped out that way many times in my other youth as I passed between the two temples. Funny how easily I'd accepted that. No more wondering if it was true. I'd lived there a long time ago and that was all there was to it.

Lingering only for a moment to cover my face against the glare, I passed once more down that long line of sphinxes and out onto the hot paved square. Instantly I was assaulted on all sides:

"Only look."

"Cheap price."

"Hey madam, you want scarabi? Very old. How much you pay?" This last accompanied by furtive scuffling in pockets and a quick flash of something green.

"Imshee," I said firmly. To my surprise, it worked.

A strong smell of horse. And a mass of carriages. Number 72 Khaled had said but it was hard to see with so many possibilities, and so many insistent drivers. Where was Khaled? No sooner thought than a slight figure materialized at my side, eyes dancing and smile gleaming.

"Here you are madam. I told you I wait for you."

On the way back to the hotel, my driver took a different road. Rattling down a dirt track I was too busy holding on to look ahead. Grinning, he stopped by a gray brick wall. Handing me into the care of another policeman, he nodded reassuringly as the ubiquitous blue-robed guardians ushered me through a tall gate, hands held out. One joined us inside, sleeker than the rest. A bit unctuous this one, I wasn't sure I liked him. We passed into a wide courtyard. For a moment I was transfixed. My vision was there, Temple Mut in ruins. Its beauty had fallen but it was in the process of rising again. Proudly my guides showed the remains of walls and statues carefully cobbled together:

"See, madam, take archaeologists many years. Soon Temple Mut whole again."

What a mind-blowing task, so many pieces. How I wished their English was better, I had so many questions. Maybe I could come back with Malcolm Appleyard. He would know.

I was escorted down a steep path to see the Nilometer, which squatted low beneath the high bank. As the sleek guardian furtively groped my bottom, he assured me:

"Here priests measure floodwaters. Most important place. Come see, lady, come."

More pinching came as he tried to push me down dark steps between slimy stone walls to where murky green water, and who knows what else, lurked. It smelt almost as dreadful as he did as he pressed close.

"Imshee" I shouted firmly.

Now I knew why I didn't like him, he was so different to the gentle men who came quickly to my aid. He slipped away, muttering. No baksheesh for him. Moving on, the sacred lake was choked with weeds. Standing for a moment, I was wrapped in memory, seeing again the light of the moon on reed-shrouded water, feeling the touch of the water against my skin.

Here too the archaeologists had been at work. Statue after statue had emerged from the encrusting sand. Battered, bruised, chipped, and broken she may be, but the Lady of the Flame was slowly emerging to reclaim her sacred place. *Sa Sekhem Sahu.* The Goddess had risen. All power to Sekhmet. It was worth the hassle with the baksheesh to be in this sacred space. Home, it was my home.

Sadly I turned to leave, sliding through a gap in the great gates as the guardians closed them with an air of finality. Flinging a handful of coins to the beseeching children who swarmed upon me, I aimed myself at the haven of my carriage. Brushing them off and shouting at the daring few who hung on the back of the caleche, dragging their heels in the dust, Khaled urged his horse to a brisk trot. We returned to the calm of the hotel, arranging to meet the next morning. He had plans for me.

Lunch. I wanted a belated lunch! How amazing to be so hungry. Devouring wonderfully soft chewy bread and spicy humus, I waited for my fish to be grilled. Was this the same bread I saw made on dirt floors in the bazaar? Who cared? It was bliss. The smell of cooking tantalized my nose. My anticipation rose, my nausea gone. I'd forgotten how wonderful food could be.

Lying by the pool, drawing in the warm sunshine of late afternoon, energy pulsated through my body. I was *well.* For the first time in months, I swam. Weak no longer, my legs propelled me through liquid light as the sun set and the world turned pink and purple. Time passed in a rosy glow.

Beyond my balcony, the warm dark night beckoned. Riding the lift was slow, my anticipation high. Still feeling the tingle of energy in my legs, I quickly crossed the lobby and out into the night.

"Taxi? Where you go?"

"You want caleche? Cheap price."

"Banana Island. How 'bout you go Banana Island tomorrow, my friend have boat, we fish, we eat ..."

So many people trying to spend my time for me, but all with big smiles.

"Maybe later?" I smiled back.

Ah, there was the river flowing between its low banks. The water seemed still and deep until I saw the strange green cabbage-like flowers dancing swiftly on the surface of the water. White birds swooped and called, occasionally diving deep to emerge with a glistening fish caught up in a sharp beak. What an incredible smell. Hot and musty, cool and tangy. An undercurrent of something less pleasant. If it was a wine, what would it be? Old socks? No, something much worse. Greg was such a wine snob, that tasting performance we went through to get a drink. No, I told myself, stop right there. The smell from the cooking fires was wonderful, Ramadan must be over for the day. How did they stand it in the heat?

"Madam, you English? Where you live? What your name? How old are you? What you do?" A small voice piped up from somewhere near my knees.

"So many questions, how can I answer you?"

Smiling faces, young and eager with pin bright black eyes. Such beautiful children. That must be their mother watching us from the shadow of a tree.

"My name is Mrs. McKennar and I come from London."

"Bonbons, you have bonbons?" Hands were thrust towards me.

"I'm sorry, no."

"Stilos." The boldest one was making writing motions to accompany his demand.

"No." Tempted to find baksheesh in my bag, I recalled the

swarm of children at Temple Mut. "Goodnight." I said firmly. They ran back to their mother, chattering.

"... Caleche."

"Taxi?"

"Boat, Banana Island ..."

I told myself I must ask Malcolm what "No" was if I saw him again.

Perhaps it would be quieter away from the river.

But another vision was before me. Golden columns glowed, imperious statues beckoned, it was the temple I'd seen that morning. Eagerly I pushed money forward. "One, please."

Walking through magical silence, passing between huge pillars, guarded by seated kings of another age and a stone needle that pierced the night sky, I was in heaven. Quiet figures moved forward from the darkness. Be resolute, I thought, ignore them. This was so close to how it used to be, dark and quiet with golden pools of light. The night sky made a good roof.

Entrancing. That was the word for it. It pulled me in, made me feel I'd stepped back in time. At any moment the shawms would sound, the priests process. Already I could hear the chanting. Now I knew I could reach back into that world surely here it would work as well. I'd better sit down first though.

It was no good, I could picture them but couldn't join them. It seemed time travel wasn't something I could make happen. I might as well walk up to the end. How strange it felt to be stepping on such sacred ground with no preparation.

Those Japanese were there again; it was amazing how they fitted into such small spaces. Maybe they'd perfected the art of moving walls. Their camera flashes ruined the night. But why were they pointing at the sky ...

"Wow. Look at that."

Did they hear me, a silly English woman talking to herself? But that new moon hanging over the crescent on top of the mosque was amazing. Now I knew why Mohammed chose the moon for his symbol. What a fantastic picture that would make. I must get a camera; I was sure the souvenir shop had one of those disposable ones in the window. The mosque was pretty amazing itself, perched on ancient pillars. Up there must have been ground level before the temple was excavated, but once a holy place, forever sacred. I'd return in daylight to see more. Right now, more food would be good – after the photo, of course.

I was so happy. My body felt great. Khaled had plans for me. There was a new day to look forward to. It was wonderful.

"My friends like see something different." Bright eyes grinned at me. "No tourists here."

Khaled was right. All around us mud-brick houses, drainage ditches, and fields of green dozed in the sun. Only the papery stalks of corn were lively, moving to an unseen hand. That water wheel must have been there three thousand years, but surely that child couldn't have been sitting there patiently guarding it all that time.

"You want drink? Carriage driver live here. He invite you his home for tea." His hand pointed to a man standing proudly by the side of a mud-brick home. The once bright paint was peeling, but the doorstep was swept clean.

Another of those huge beaming smiles above the ubiquitous djellabah as a hand gestured me in.

"Thank you, that is kind. It would be nice." Although this time I had brought water the thought of tea was tempting, and I'd love to see inside one of these tiny mud-brick houses. I was sure they'd been there forever.

It was spotless and bare, just beaten earth with sleeping benches around the walls. I'd stepped back in time again. Khaled gestured to the hard wooden bench.

"Sit, madam."

We sat contentedly, without speaking, until our host brought the tea, which was delicious.

"Mint tea," smiled my host. "Egyptian wine."

"You take some England," insisted Khaled. "My friend Mr. Robert take back tea."

"Well then, I will too."

Suddenly, although no word had broken the companionable silence, we all stood, thanking my host again as I waited for the caleche to be brought.

"Where to now?" Khaled asked. "What you want see?"

"I'd like to go back to the hotel and have lunch and after that I'll swim in the pool and sunbathe. There's no sun in England in winter." I laughed as I showed him my pale arms.

"How about tonight you come bazaar? Drink chai?"

The rough wooden benches were hard but everyone was friendly. I didn't know how the man in the spotless white djellabah did it. Brewing tea on a gas burner in a battered tin pot, his hands moved with bewildering speed. Washing glasses, pouring tea, piling in sugar, balancing a coffee pot on a battered blue tray, expertly swirling cups to miss the grounds, and then dodging the donkey carts and the occasional caleche that lurched around the corner and into this quiet street as he handled our drinks with a smile, he was marvelous.

A notice on the wall caught my eye: "The Cab Man's Arms. Best tea in Luxor."

"My friends make it," Khaled laughed. "They come drink tea and Mr. Robert he smoke the shisha."

He pointed to the strange bulbous shape with hot coals on top and boiling smoke in its depths that a young boy had set at his feet. Taking up the snaking mouthpiece, Khaled puffed contentedly. Strange gurgles emanated from the smoky depths, it sounded like gas passing through water. No wonder I'd heard them called hubble-bubbles. Interesting.

"Better than cigarettes." Khaled grinned slyly.

From the smell, it wasn't only tobacco that Mr. Robert enjoyed.

"What you drink? Tea, mint tea?"

It slid down my throat, warm and delicious. And was quickly followed by helba. A strange taste that – brown as the liquid in which it floated. Eventually I tracked it down, fenugreek.

"Good for the stomach," Khaled said patting his slender frame.

As was the strange white drink whose name I never did catch.

Looking round, I thought the fairylight mosque dancing below the smart striped awning was cute, especially as it was next to Santa Claus on his sleigh.

"Khaled, why is Santa Claus up there. You don't celebrate Christmas here do you?"

Khaled grinned: "Moslems no, but Coptic Christians yes. Santa Claus comes for tourists but our children like him too."

Of course, there was that huge one outside the hotel, the one the cat had got stuck in the previous day. Santa had looked so funny without his head, especially as he'd had a pair of sandaled feet sticking out of his top while their owner chased the cat. I did like Egypt, always something new to see. The clack and clatter of dominoes thumped down on the table with great bravura punctuated each moment. They played so fast I couldn't keep up. When they all jeered it seemed as though a fight would break out, but it appeared to be part of the game. Suddenly I realized, there were so many men and yet I was the only woman there.

"Khaled, why are there no women here?" I'd asked. "It is alright for me to be sitting with you?"

"No problem, our women like stay home. But you welcome. I bring many friends. Mrs. Anne, she come to wedding night. Everyone happy."

As a small boy tried to clean my pale suede trainers with black boot polish and an oily rag, Khaled waved him away but a familiar voice said:

"Hey, young fellow, how about doing my shoes?"

Malcolm sat down beside me.

"Are you enjoying yourself?" he asked. "I saw this place earlier today but it was closed for Ramadan. I thought I'd come back later."

"I love it here."

Loud jeers indicated that the onlookers weren't impressed with a move in the domino game. "Except I half expect a fight to break out."

"I've found that most conversations in Egypt sound like an argument," Malcolm replied, laughing.

We were enveloped in sweet white smoke swung from a censer. Our industrious tea-maker had had a spare moment and decided to clean his space. With the other hand he collected the washing-up in a bucket.

When the smoke cleared, a pair of immaculately shined shoes gleamed up at us. My friend handed over an Egyptian pound. To his obvious surprise, change materialized in his hand.

"Too much, only for tourists," said Khaled. "In bazaar you pay Egyptian price."

More tea followed, and the caleche was brought round. Malcolm was persuaded to join us on the ride to the hotel. As we jogged along, Khaled turned his back on the street and talked animatedly to Malcolm.

"How 'bout tomorrow you come my house. Eat Egyptian food?"

Hand absent-mindedly forking his hair, Malcolm turned to me.

"I'm game if you are. I like to see how people live." He twiddled a strand. I nodded with anticipation.

"But Khaled, what about Ramadan?" Malcolm asked, forehead creased.

"My mother not mind. Many friends come my house. She likes cook for them." He turned back to the road just in time for the turn into the hotel. "I wait you here. Twelve o'clock."

Malcolm handed me down from the caleche with old-fashioned charm, at the same time quietly passing Khaled a folded note and a murmured "shokran." I wondered why my husband couldn't have had manners like those? He'd rushed out of cabs and left me to pay. But I told myself, stop it, Mecky, that's over now.

Waking dreamily, I wondered whether it had been wise to agree to go to Khaled's home tomorrow? Several people drooping by the pool had recounted the horrors of "Pharaoh's Revenge." Griping pains, violent sickness, and diarrhea confined them to bed for several days. All were pale and wan. Without exception, all blamed the food. And here I was going to an unknown house. What would the hygiene be like? So far I'd escaped, not even a twinge. Did I really want to chance it? It would be like chemo all over again. I shuddered at the thought. And yet I felt incredibly well. I couldn't believe anything could harm me. There was just time for a stroll in the bazaar before we went.

We were ferried through the Cab Man's Arms and around a corner where children with eyes dark with flies smiled brightly, called out hello, and asked for bonbons. Knowing that Khaled had young brothers and sisters, as well as children of his own, I'd come prepared. But he moved on quickly and turned another corner to a quieter part of town.

Ushered through an ancient wooden doorway into a high-ceilinged room with a lazy fan rotating hot air, we were urged to sit. Around the walls, wide benches were covered with cushions, and a table set for two. The plaster on the thick mud-brick walls showed traces of several colors. How old was this house? It felt *ancient*. On the uneven walls, a black-framed picture of a dignified man wearing a turban sat alongside another of a young boy reading a Koran, with one or two Arabic texts, beautifully penned, facing them.

In the place of honor, an ancient TV set showed an Egyptian soap opera, engrossing and fun to watch while we waited for lunch. No words were necessary, the acting said it all as husband, middle-aged wife, and mistress, or was it new young wife – this was a Moslem country after all – played out a ubiquitous eternal triangle of love and jealousy.

Suddenly the door was thrown open and a procession of dishes emerged, held before shyly smiling faces. Khaled's mother, wife, and sisters presumably – although it was clear we wouldn't be introduced until we had eaten. The table was piled high. Aromatic pigeon stuffed with rice and herbs, peas in a hot rich sauce, fried fish and large chunks of succulent meat, salads, and beans. Plates awash with bread and green sauce, a faintly slimy texture when I experimentally dipped in a finger but the taste was blissful. When not another morsel could be crammed onto the table, we were handed bottles of Coca Cola and urged to eat. The door closed, and we were alone.

"There is enough food here to feed a dozen people. What are we going to do? Moslems do not eat leftovers and we don't want to offend them." Malcolm's face puckered anxiously.

"Well, let's see what we can manage. It looks delicious. Thank goodness I got my appetite back. I must have put on half a stone since I got here, my clothes don't fit. I had to buy this new pair of trousers in the bazaar today, and see how tight this top is." I could hardly breathe without fearing it would split.

We set to, hands tearing at the pigeons. Scooping up food on bread and spooning rice into our mouths, we were like children at a feast. And what a feast. An aroma like some exotic perfume wafted from another time. So many tastes and textures. Hot, sweet, sour, crunchy, soft, stringy. Each mouthful a new revelation. Feeding one another morsels as each new delight unfolded, no one would believe that we had barely met before that day. I was so easy in my new friend's company. It was strange to spend such pleasurable time with a man for whom I had no sexual feelings – would I ever have sexual feelings again, I remember asking myself?

Looking at Malcolm, I laughed aloud.

"What is it?" he asked raising his eyebrow.

"Your hair," I spluttered. "You've greased your hair."

There was a flyblown mirror on the wall; he peered into it.

"It reminds me of when I was a Teddy Boy."

Why this should have been so funny I don't know, but helpless laughter overtook me once more. It felt good to laugh. To feel it bubbling and sloshing around where that hollow space had been. The weight that had sat on my shoulders for months rolled back, I felt *good*.

Just as we could eat no more, Khaled entered with a dignified man, head wrapped in a huge scarf, who smiled benignly and held out his hands.

"My father," he explained. "He want welcome you his house."

"Eat, eat," Mr. Said urged. Politely we managed a few more mouthfuls, patting our stomachs to indicate our delight – and trying to move what we had already eaten a little further down.

"Thank you, but no more," Malcolm said with an air of finality. "It has been wonderful, thank you, but no more. We are replete."

The smiling procession began again. Plates were cleared and we were led to a sink in a dirt-floored courtyard to wash our hands. Tea was brought, and a bubbling shisha, and introductions were made. Khaled's mother was beautiful. The missing front tooth that showed when she smiled gave her an added charm, and, with her elegant, high-nosed profile Khaled's wife looked like a beauty off a tomb painting. There were so many children. It was difficult to tell who belonged to Khaled and who were his brothers and sisters. His aunt was also introduced. She mournfully told us that her husband – the man on the wall – was dead. Although she looked at least sixty, having lost all but two teeth and acquired many wrinkles, she had a small child cradled in one arm so I supposed she couldn't be much older than me.

It was time for presents. I took out pens and pencils, books, sweets, biscuits, chocolate, everything the hotel shop could supply at short notice and a few bits from the bazaar too.

Tomorrow I'd have to leave this land of smiling, generous people. How I'd miss it.

As I made my farewell to Khaled, and handed him his own discreetly folded present, he asked:

"When you come back?"

Had he asked me this a week previously, I'd have burst into tears. As it was:

"Soon," I said firmly. "I will be back soon."

chapter 5

The one who Holds Back Darkness

Afraid to leave my place in case I missed my turn, I stared at the blank wall, thinking back to that previous visit to this hospital, the one that had propelled me to Egypt.

The morning of my strange dream I'd wondered how could I go? There was work to do, doctors to see, and lawyers to instruct; obligations and pressures had weighed me down.

Expectations? No, not any more.

Hopelessness had washed through me, queasy knees fluttering.

What did it matter? There was nothing for me. When my husband Greg had left, he'd taken my future with him. He couldn't seem to separate me from the illness or what was happening to my body. The day I threw up in his precious Jag I thought he'd kill me. His words almost did. He said how much he'd enjoyed having a strong woman at his side but now I was a puking, puling wimp he wasn't having any more of it. And I'd only just bought him that Jag, he'd wheedled it out of me at Christmas, told me it would make things alright between us and I believed him. When I threw up, he'd dropped me off and was gone, made it seem like it was his decision when I'd been telling him to go for months, ever since –

no, don't go there. He hadn't stopped hassling me for a divorce settlement but never asked how I was.

I'd told myself not to think about it. Said: Mecky, get up, it's time to move on. Dressing hurriedly, I'd left the empty flat, forgetting the potions that were supposed to cool my raging blood. No matter, weeks of chemotherapy had left me permanently nauseous and that last pill would have been too much to swallow – even with all the bread to stuff it down. It was too big, too hard, like one of those gobstoppers Aunt Amelia had bought me as a child. I never could get to the end, had to throw them away when no one was looking – and that pill that was supposed to stop the sickness but didn't, that was a waste of time. A horrible choking thing, with a foul aftertaste and the unspeakable effects, it was better not to think about it.

Although it was difficult not to as I'd forgotten to envelope my bald head in its scarf. That scarf had set quite a trend amongst my colleagues, they thought it stylish, or so they said. It was easy for them to show sympathy. When they unveiled nothing changed, whereas I was a non-woman without my mane of russet hair. My brush was like a hairdresser's unswept floor. I'd known the chemo was aggressive, but I hadn't realized it would attack who I was. Never mind, I was still there, even if my head was bald.

It was time to face up to it, so silly avoiding mirrors. I could feel the smoothness of my bare scalp – and visualize it – maybe it was time to look, there in that shop window. Hmmn, not bad, I hadn't known my head was that shape, it gave me a strange dignity, emphasizing my amber eyes – wider without their eyebrow umbrella. My face was thinner though and my neck appeared longer. It was more slender; I seemed to hold my head differently.

My clothes! God, how loose they were. I hadn't realized how much weight I'd lost. I was like a young child again, dressed in those hand-me-downs my cousins passed on. They were too good to throw away, but my cousins were fatter than me – and taller. Mum was always too busy to take the clothes in. Pulling my shoulders back made those clothes look better, ah, yes, there, that haughty look I used to cover up my embarrassment was back. It suited my willowy shape.

I did like my new face, I was glad I hadn't had a wig, despite feeling chilly. It was time to wrap, though. The glittery gold scarf was like some exotic headdress perched atop a queen from an ancient land. Dreaming again, Mecky, time to go. Taxi!

The nurse had briskly taken the last blood and the room blurred.

"There, dear, pop this bit of cotton wool on. You're pale. A glass of water might help? Here, you are. Perhaps you'd like to wait outside, doctor will be here soon." She pointed firmly towards the door.

Head swimming, I'd sipped and stepped outside for the inevitable wait. The sands of time slipped sightlessly through your fingers in there. Didn't those doctors know what it was like to wait? It was bad enough being a private patient, I couldn't imagine what it was like to be treated on the National Health Service, that must consume days at a time.

Coca Cola, I wanted a Coke – I could taste it, craved its cool sweetness. Surely someone could have put a drinks machine in that stark white room with its hard chairs and desperate faces.

Here came the doctor, looking harassed as usual. That flapping coat, white and far too long – perhaps he'd picked up the wrong one? His stethoscope was bobbing as he tried to catch up with a head that poked out in front. He was rather like a stork, but his legs were a bit short for that. Benu bird. Where had I heard that? At the time I couldn't remember what one looked like – apart from him, that was. It was a good name though, I'd call him "Benu Bird."

"Mrs. McKennar," a voice had shouted briskly. "Come along, quickly now."

At last.

Dr Benu Bird sat in a tiny cubicle behind a blond-wood desk on which was a large pad of blotting paper, pristine and untouched. Did anyone actually write anything in here? Stacks of notes suggested that yes, they did, but not with pens that needed blotting. His chair was low, to accommodate those short legs I suppose. His fingers picked up a pen and began twiddling.

"I'm sorry, Mrs. McKennar, Megan, there's nothing more we can do. The type of leukemia that you have is a particularly virulent one. We've thrown all we could at it but there's no sign of improvement. If we don't stop it in its accelerated phase ..."

His voice had passed over my head. What was he on about, what did he mean, surely ... I couldn't ...? His words whirled past:

"... if chemotherapy had worked, ... next step ... bone marrow transplant ... impossible ... something is running amok in your blood and we can't halt it ..."

I couldn't take it in. He couldn't mean what he seemed to be saying, it couldn't be true, I didn't ...

"... a few weeks, months at best." Benu Bird's gray eyes had darted towards the door as he half rose.

In all those months he'd never made eye contact with me, surely he could have just that once. And what was he saying? He'd assured me the chemo would work. How could I only have a few weeks?

"But, surely doctor there must be ..."

"No," he'd said coldly, glancing at his watch and putting my notes firmly to one side. "This last blood test will undoubtedly confirm the prognosis. Come back in two weeks. But, I repeat, there is nothing we can do. You should make suitable arrangements."

Numb and shaking, I'd willed my legs to carry me out. Blindly, trying to outdistance that uncompromising "No." I'd turned from the door, avoiding the thought of suitable arrangements whatever they might be. Outside, a hand had caught my arm:

"Mrs. MacKennart, Megan, don't go ... Is there someone we can call ..."

After all those months, they still couldn't even get my name right, and there was no one to call. Greg had antagonized all my friends years ago with his possessiveness and endless sniping, even my sister Sally was driven away, no I couldn't think about her. My colleagues wouldn't have wanted to know: they'd found me an embarrassment if the truth were told with my falling hair and failed relationship. I told myself: "Don't think about any of it, Mecky, ignore it. That's it, it can't be true, so I won't think about it. I must get out of here ..."

I was running by then, pushing through the unheeding crowd. Cars hooted, lorries menaced, a bus bore down; I'd reached out protestingly, but no one noticed. A taxi passed – I'd hailed it, quickly. It had moved on. Reeling forward, I was pushed through an open gate towards an imposing portal. The British Museum: I could seek refuge there. Thankfully I stepped inside.

Cool, calm, dark air. Shadowy faces stared down in the gloom, awesome gods from another time. Pictures on a wall. There was

Doctor Benu Bird, and an unwrapped head, exactly like mine, I'd have fitted in there. Drifting on, my fingers trailed cold stone.

Suddenly there She was. Proud, poised, kindly now, but unmistakably my nocturnal visitor, the lioness from my dream. Black and faintly shining, she towered over me, leonine head atop a voluptuous female body.

"See," she'd seemed to say. "I am waiting. Come to me." The carved face had regarded me with compassion. "You are mine."

A wave of dizziness had assaulted me. A hand was laid gently on my arm:

"This way, my dear, perhaps a drink will help."

An elderly lady, dressed in an enormous purple hat, had guided me through unseeing crowds into the quiet of the coffee shop. The modern chrome and efficient formica were softened by potted palms. Gratefully sipping the tea my savior had handed me, my strength had returned slowly.

"What is it?" she'd asked quietly. "You are clearly ill."

"Yes, chronic myelogenous leukemia which turned acute."

Her face was kind, I'd felt I could trust her and it had been such a relief to tell someone. "Apparently the first stages are virtually symptomless and I kept putting mine down to flu, so although I've only known about it for just over a year, I've probably had it for four or five years. I've had months of chemo but nothing helped. And now the doctor says there is nothing more they can do."

I could feel my lip wobbling, tears pricked my eyes, but her smile was so sweet. Encouraged, I went on: "I can't believe it's true, it can't be true. I refuse to believe it, I can't give up, just like that. I want to ignore it, live my life. Is that silly?"

"Well dear, you know, there is some evidence that people who ignore their cancer recover better than those who give in." She'd smiled reassuringly.

That's what I'd do, I'd ignore it, pretend it wasn't happening. Perhaps I could tell her.

"There seems to be something I have to do. I know it sounds crazy but I keep being called, in my dreams."

She'd smiled again and took my hand: "Follow your dreams, my dear. Do what is in your heart. That's all anyone can do. Can I call you a cab?"

"No, thank you, you've been most kind but I'd like to walk a little. It might help me to think." I'd shaken her hand and left her sitting there, serenely sipping her tea. Would it work, ignoring it? Well, whatever, it had to be better than worrying about it. I'd always put things aside I couldn't deal with, so why not this.

Walking towards the entrance hall, I'd passed a bookstall. Huge shelves with brightly colored covers standing proud towered above the throng of people clutching a moment of time. Turning aside, I'd looked again on that awesome presence. Checking that it was indeed She who haunted my sleep, and that this wasn't merely a waking dream. Her shining surface had rippled, at any moment she would rise from her plinth. Again she'd whispered:

"Come to me. Now!"

And so I had.

Sitting in that blank hospital room once more with nothing to read, I couldn't bear to look at the faces around me, hope and fear were equally mixed with the resignation of waiting. Waiting, endlessly waiting. Waiting to see Dr Benu Bird, but he wasn't there that day. Neither was my consultant, as usual.

"Can't understand it," said a harassed young doctor who barely knew my name. His clipped tone continued: "Must've been spontaneous remission. Your blood tests 're normal. Make an appointment for a month's time. We'll do another bone marrow test. You c'n go." He opened the door.

But I held back: "Does this mean I am cured?"

"No, leukemia's prone to remission. Never think of y'self as cured. It'll come back. You'll need more drugs. We need to keep checkin', as I said. Goodbye." A hand waved dismissively.

Turning to leave, like a flame my anger rose, I shouted:

"Two hours! Two hours to hear news that could have been given in two minutes on the telephone. A death sentence lifted with no feeling, no compassion. No hope offered, only that you're certain it will return."

He lifted his weary eyes to mine:

"I'm sorry, it's ..." His hand waved disconsolately at the mess of files around him. Dr Benu Bird's neat office at been transformed. Coffee rings stained the once-pristine blotting paper and doodles spoke of a distraught mind.

"And where is my doctor? Surely he could have told me himself."

"Oh, didn't y' know?" His fingers twiddled, a pen fell. "He died, car crash last week. I'm sorry." He glanced at the door uncomfortably.

"He's treated me all this time. Surely the nurse could have told me ..." Stunned, my voice trailed off. Dr Benu Bird dead and in his place was this young, overworked man-child who'd had no time to develop compassion – or maybe he'd squelched it to survive his first week in this desperate place.

"I should have been told!" I retorted.

Again that weary gaze.

"Sorry, no more t' say. Goodbye."

Unable to meet my eyes, he ushered me through the door.

"It's okay," I said gently as I closed the door. "Everything is exactly as it should be. There's been no mistake."

In my heart I knew. I'd walked in the shoes of the goddess, enacted her sacred drama. I'd been healed by the perfect anger of The Lady of the Flame. Rogue cells were excised by the power of her rage. Cells that had been set in flight by Mek'an'ar's last despairing cry. My illness was a resistance to destiny that crossed time. I could not let him go, the Lord of my Heart. It was that ancient tie that had left me incomplete, open to invasion. As a result, the sacred drama began again. But I'd been cured by the love of the god and of the man. Remembering love cooled the raging fire in my veins. Forgiveness turned the bloodlust into new life. Like a benu bird I was resurrected, made whole again. I knew I was cured.

Leaving the hospital, the past was behind me. I had a life to rebuild. A promise to reclaim. But I was curious to know more about how I could have relived the past so graphically. I reminded myself to find a bookshop soon, maybe they'd have something that would explain it. I couldn't be the only person this had happened to, surely?

Standing in the British Museum before Sekhmet, I gave thanks. Touched food to her mouth, poured beer over her head.

" 'Ere, you can't do that in 'ere," an attendant said crossly.

Oh yes I could, my heart sang. I already did! *Sa Sekhem Sahu.* All honor to my Lady.

A frisson of energy shot through me. A shiver ran up my spine. Kundalini was on the move. Turning I met the luminescent eyes of a stranger.

The Great Round began again.

chapter 6.

The gleaming one

An impeccably dressed man, skin the color of latte, green eyes holding mine, gazed down at me. Jet hair swept back from a high forehead over a jutting nose, his eyebrows were forceful and the lips somewhat cruel. He was a magnificent Horus hawk come to life.

"She is quite something, is she not?"

His deep voice vibrated through me, reaching a place no man had touched in ages. I was burning. His English was too perfect, there was a hint of something exotic, a slight accent and a musical cadence to the voice indicated a foreignness that didn't belong to this cold land.

"But I do not understand why you are pouring beer over her head?"

"I was honoring her and giving thanks. Back in the old days she had a beer ration of her own, and she was missing it. Two thousand years is a long time to go without a drink."

He laughed and said, "Two hours has been quite long enough for me. Shall we?"

Gesturing in the direction of the coffee shop, he took my arm. Part of me couldn't believe how natural this felt but the other part was wondering: *Why doesn't he remember? How can he not know?*

As we reached the queue, his manner became formal.

"We have not been introduced. I am Ramon Lavaries. I come from Ibiza." He held out his hand, long slender fingers capped by beautifully manicured nails. Immaculate shirt cuffs showed beneath soft wool tailoring. No, he could not be an Englishman. He was too striking, reminded me of a bird of paradise flower. The angles of his face were haughty and well bred but I sensed that passion moved close beneath his skin. His hand gripped mine firmly. For a moment time shifted. I saw the golden uraeus above his head, the proud eyes filled with love. Hastily I drew in a firm breath:

"Megan McKennar. But most people call me Mecky."

"If you do not mind, I shall call you Megan, it is a beautiful name. Where is it that you come from?"

"I live here in London."

"You have an excellent tan. You did not get that in an English winter." His smile was almost as wide as an Egyptian's, the large teeth as white but they had a sharp edge to them, as though he could bite; no Egyptian would have teeth like that.

"No, I've been in Egypt. It was as hot as an English summer."

About to reveal more, something held me back.

"Was it for that reason you were in the Egyptian gallery?"

"Tea or coffee? Make up your mind or let someone else in. I haven't got all day."

Thank you, you miserable old biddy.

"Tea for two" he said firmly. "And scones and cream."

And as an aside to me:

"I hope it will not be sour. In my country we believe that food should be served with kindness – even in these surroundings." He surveyed the harsh chrome and formica cafeteria rather as though a strange smell had insinuated itself under his nose. What was I doing here with this arrogant man? Why did it feel so right?

Taking up the tray, Ramon led me to a quiet corner screened by a sad potted palm. For a moment I was tempted back to that familiar dusty landscape and the chai stall by the ancient sacred lake. The palms there were healthy enough despite the apparent lack of water. But there was no chance to linger.

"Now, please, tell me about yourself." He sat back and surveyed me quietly from beneath hooded eyes. What could I say? I was sure he could already see every secret of my soul. "Are you married?"

"Well, I was but I've parted from my husband and am waiting for a divorce. It should have gone through by now but I was ill and everything was put on hold. That's why I went to Egypt, I needed time to recover." Before he could ask more, I went on: "How about you?"

"I never had the good fortune to find the woman of my dreams."

Beneath the surface I seemed to hear another conversation.

"I was waiting for you."

"And I for you."

"Where do we go from here?"

Abruptly he stood: "Shall we go?"

Looking down at the cold tea and congealed cream on half-eaten scones, I realized I hadn't tasted a thing. We walked arm in arm, our footsteps getting faster as we reached the porticoed entrance and crossed the gray stone courtyard. By the time we reached the wrought iron gates, we were almost running.

Hailing a taxi, he asked with great courtesy:

"Would you like to come to my hotel for some proper tea? I am staying at the Savoy and they put on an excellent spread."

All I could do was nod.

In the taxi we sat close together, far from relaxed. He held his arms close to himself as though afraid to brush against me. Frissons of energy passed from his thigh to mine. Was he aware of it? From the corner of my eye I saw his lips set hard. His body vibrated urgently and I knew that he felt it too. I wanted to throw myself into his arms. It took all my self-control to wait whilst he paid the taxi and guided me into the hotel. Energy was pulsating up my arm by now, our hands felt like they were locked together by fire. Shouldering his way firmly through the melee before the reception desk, he claimed his key.

With indecent haste we headed for the lifts, melded by a crush of American tourists who were trying to heave a mountain of baggage into far too small a space. I thought that a hotel like this would have porters. Maybe they were too impatient to wait. Ramon certainly was, taking my hand he pulled me to the stairs.

Breathlessly we emerged into a quiet corridor. Abandoning all pretence of decorum, we crashed through a door. As he kicked it shut behind us, he reached for me. Time stood still, and slithered out of gear. His kiss was so familiar. I knew exactly how his body would feel when it was fitted to mine. How his lips would taste. Frantically he tore at his tie and attempted to remove my scarf at the same time – not an easy feat when your lips are glued together as though they will never part. That was the problem with an English winter: we wear too much. Somehow we shed most of our clothes. His hands were everywhere. My body was aflame. As he kissed me insistently, my knees surrendered, I slid to the floor.

And up into the night, stars rushing past. Far out into the Milky Way.

Waves of pleasure racked my body, but my soul was calm in its flight. Once again we were one with the gods. Once again we were united. Pharaoh and his priestess. Honoring She. Redeeming the promise made long ago.

Walking back to my flat, I passed a health food shop. In its window, a poster said: "Past Life Workshop with Anne Cottington. Explore the impact your past has on your present." The paper was dog-eared as though it had been there forever, but the workshop was two days later. Maybe this could help me understand more fully. I searched for paper, never there when I needed it, my checkbook cover would have to do.

The recorded voice had said that they were closed, please ring back tomorrow after ten. I was trying, but each time they were engaged or another call came in. There was too much to sort out – and so much to fend off. My soon-to-be-ex wanted a meeting. As I monitored his call I pondered what brought us together with such catastrophic results. By then I'd learned to let my solicitor deal with such matters. I dropped his demands into her capable hands.

Finally, at 11.30, I called.

"Oh yes," said a bright voice. "I have two places. Would you like them?"

"Yes please, but I'd like to know what's involved. I've never been to anything like this before and I'm a bit scared."

"Why don't I give you the workshop leader's number and you can have a chat with her. Anne's done several of these workshops for the college. They are extremely popular and everyone finds them helpful. You will be in good hands."

An answer-phone replied, but I was sure she was there. I could almost hear her listening.

"This might sound silly, but I am coming to your workshop and ..."

Her voice cut in. "It's okay, nothing you say will sound silly. I'm off to catch the train but I've got a minute or two. How can I help?"

"I wondered what was involved. I'd never heard of a past life workshop until I saw the poster for yours, although I've had one or two strange experiences recently that have convinced me such things exist. I'm wondering whether it's safe."

Silly thing to say after what I've been through, but still ...

"I can reassure you on that point. I've been taking people back to explore their past for thirty years now and no one has had an adverse reaction. Quite the contrary, in fact, many people find that it is extremely beneficial. Problems only occur when people try to do it for themselves and get stuck in something traumatic, or when memories arise spontaneously, as it were. You mentioned strange experiences ...?"

"If you don't mind, I'd like to leave that for now. Could you tell me how you take people back? Is it hypnosis? I've always been rather wary of that."

"No, it's not hypnosis although it does have similarities. I use a form of deep relaxation and guided meditation to take you into the past, but it remains under your control. You can come out of it at any moment."

"Are you qualified in any way?"

I didn't mean it to come out that baldly but she took it well.

"I'm a trained counselor but I don't have any formal qualifications in regression. I was taught by an old lady who had been exploring past lives for fifty years when I met her. Now I've been doing it so long, I train other people."

Her laugh sounded much younger than her voice.

"Do many people do this kind of thing?"

"There's quite a few of us but, unfortunately, there's nothing to stop someone setting themselves up without any training at all, so you're wise to ask. I'll be telling you more on the workshop. I must go now or I'll miss my train."

Talking to her was rather like being with Ramon. It felt familiar. I knew I could trust this woman with my life – or rather my lives.

All I had to do then was to convince Ramon. I'd tell him over dinner. He had a business meeting but was arriving about seven. With a flurry, I flicked a duster haphazardly and set off for the local delicatessen. Tahini, we must have tahini and flat bread, and dates and honey cakes. The food of love.

chapter 7.

mother of images

The taxi dropped us at the end of the road of large, white, stuccoed houses, terraced, imposing, solid, *rich*. Hardly the place I'd expected to find a past life workshop taking place. Up the steps we went, under a portico, an anonymous black door gave nothing away.

Reaching for the bell, Ramon suddenly pulled at my hand, holding me back.

"Megan, are you sure?" He hesitated, tugging at his collar. "What if I do not get anything? I have never done anything like this before. I do not know who this woman is, or even if I can trust her. She might implant something in my mind. Make me believe in it when it might not be true. How can I be certain? After all, two days ago I did not even know what past life memories were and now here I am on a workshop to uncover my own."

Even though I'd thought nothing could shake his urbane assurance, he did look worried. "Don't worry." I replied. "She's been doing this work for a long time, I'm sure you'll like her. When I spoke to her on the phone I instantly trusted her. She's really down to earth. You'll see."

"Why will you not tell me why you wanted me to come?"

There was an edge to his voice. Surely he wasn't going to back out now. But I didn't want to say anything yet.

"You'll see that too. Trust me, Ramon, please." My hand was gently tugging his arm but he wasn't responding.

"Is it something to do with the fact that I felt as though I knew you the moment I set eyes on you, well, before that if I am being truthful. I had dreamed about you for years. I could not believe my eyes when I saw you in front of that statue. I was startled because you had poured beer all over that lion and the attendant shouted, but then I really looked at you. It was like a magnet reached out and grabbed me. It was so physical. I could not wait to touch you. I wanted to tear your clothes off and leap on you. I have never felt that way before. It seemed inappropriate for that austere place, but I simply had to meet you." He turned his eyes away, but he did feel it too. I knew it.

"That attendant was regarding you with so much suspicion, all I could think to do was to take your arm and go to the coffee shop. When you agreed to come back to my hotel I could not believe it. I almost lost control in the taxi and I have never done anything like that in my life."

His eyes were downcast, turned away towards the black painted railings at our side, surely ...

"When we made love that first time, I felt like I knew every nook and cranny of your body, exactly how it would be, how you would feel, what to do to give you the greatest pleasure."

Pleasure I hadn't felt for three and a half thousand years.

"When you put your hand on me, I thought I was on fire. Every nerve was alive. And, suddenly, I was above my body looking down on the two of us on the floor, we never did make it to the bed did we?"

No, and how that carpet had burned.

"I seemed to explode and it went on and on. I have never had an orgasm like that, or so many. And yet, there was still something strange. As though it was not *you* I knew so well. I cannot say how it was, but you were different somehow."

If I'd told him how different he wouldn't have believed me. Reaching out to take his arm, I urged him:

"Come on, let's go in, I'd like to be able to choose my seat, and I think you should sit away from me, Ramon, we can each do our own thing."

At the top of the stairs there was a circle of chairs set on a bare wooden floor. A few people had obviously met before and greeted each other cheerfully. They seemed friendly enough, although one or two people glanced around the room apprehensively. There was a middle-aged woman opposite me who was vaguely familiar. Hair pulled back in a tight bun, she was nondescript, like she was trying to blend into the background and could have been someone's secretary. But she had beautiful eyes, big and brown under strongly arched brows. It was appropriate that Ramon should go and sit by her.

Mostly women there, I hoped Ramon wouldn't feel too out of place. It was a grand room, with beautiful plaster moldings – it must have been the ballroom or something. Funny how they'd cut off the corner with a wooden partition. It spoiled the proportions, and split the circle but I loved the way the sun poured through tall elegant windows, even if it did make it difficult to see. The chairs were hard, I wasn't looking forward to spending two days on one. The portraits opposite were interesting, a severe woman who was rather grandmotherly but the man over the marble fireplace was positively benign. I swear his eyes were twinkling at me. He was vastly amused by what was going on.

At least Anne Cottington was reassuring. I hadn't noticed her slip in. She was very ordinary, nothing weird there, I hoped Ramon would be reassured. Her clothes were smart but comfortable looking, the neutral color blended into the background. Did she wear it on purpose? I wondered how old she was, must have been late fifties. Funny, I'd thought she'd be older, but she seemed young despite her elegantly styled silver hair ...

"Hello everyone. I'm Anne Cottington. Did you know that more than half the people in the world believe that they have lived before and will do so again – and that what happened in your previous lives can have a profound effect on your present?" Her expressive eyebrows raised a fraction above the wide gray eyes: "I've been exploring other lives for years and I still find it fascinating. I'll tell you more about what we're going to do in a moment, but first I'd like you to introduce yourself. Tell me a little about who you are and what you do, and why you've come, what you hope to get out of it...."

It'd never occurred to me that we might have to introduce ourselves, and I never expected to be asked what brought me there. How could I say in front of everyone that I was diagnosed with a cancer in my blood, went to a strange land that was *home,* had a weird experience, and came back cured. Or that I'd met a man I was certain I was closely involved with in that life. And besides, I didn't want Ramon to know yet. I wanted to see what his memories were first. Damn, it was my turn and I'd missed what the others said.

"Can I tell you later? I'd like to see what happens first."

"Okay, but won't you at least tell us your name?" She was smiling reassuringly, it must be alright.

"Yes, of course, that's fine."

But what came out was Mek'an'ar.

"Sorry, I didn't quite catch that."

"Megan, I mean Megan McKennar, but ever since I was little I've thought of myself as Mecky. I couldn't quite say my name and it sort of stuck."

As the others introduced themselves, I was finding it hard to focus. That other land was so close. It was as though the room was dissolving, leaving a smoky haze behind which ... Concentrate, Mecky, I told myself, what's that Anne is saying?

"... as a child I kept having glimpses of other places and times, and seeing different people superimposed on people's faces. I assumed everyone saw them but my parents thought it was my imagination. Then, when my son was born, I had a near-death experience. I was up on the ceiling and could see myself in the hospital bed but I also saw myself dying in childbirth in very different circumstances. I was lying in dirty straw, with a grimy old woman trying to deliver my baby. All around me were a crowd of ragged children. The baby was stuck and I was too tired to go on and so I died. The guide who was with me on the ceiling told me I opted out then and was opting out now. It was my choice. I could get back into my body or I could die, but I'd have to come back one way or the other. I didn't want to have to do it all again, and I found myself back in my body."

"How did you know it was true?" Ramon interrupted: "Could it not have been oxygen deprivation or something like that?"

"It could but I don't think so. There are many well-documented cases now, but at the time I thought that perhaps it was my imagination. Nevertheless, that experience was what brought me into this work, and then years later a man came up to me at a lecture and told me he'd been one of my children but I died and left him. He described exactly that scene – and I hadn't mentioned it at the lecture. When I had that first experience I had no idea what reincarnation was but later ..."

Did approaching death bring on these memories I wondered? Was that what triggered it? Did I have the experience because I was close to death? I told myself to remember to ask her later.

"... a book fell off the library shelf and hit me on the head. It was called *The Case For Reincarnation.* I took it home and read it straight through. It explained how a soul passes from life to life, living in different bodies but having a continuum of experience. The author used to access people's past lives to heal them – she cured her own claustrophobia by going back to a life in Egypt where she was shut up in a sarcophagus."

Egypt again. Why did that place have such an effect on people? I'd better add it to my list of questions.

"I wrote to the author and when we met it was someone I knew well. We'd been together in many lives. We recognized each other instantly on a crowded station."

So we did meet up with people from other lives.

"I'll tell you more about that during the course of the weekend but I'd like to get started. We're going to be using a technique called guided visualization. It helps you to experience life outside the box, as it were. To move beyond ordinary, everyday consciousness into another awareness. I will lead you through a series of images that are specially designed to help you relax and move around in time and space. That will take you into another life ..."

That shouldn't be any problem, I was halfway there already.

"... First of all though we are going to find a guide who will help you during your journey. Guides can be people, or birds or animals. Everyone will experience them differently. Not everyone sees them." Her hands wrapped quotation marks around that *see*. "You might become aware of a touch on your shoulder. Feel yourself wrapped in a cloak, smell a particular perfume, or you might hear a voice."

Like that voice I heard in my dreams?

"Settle yourself comfortably in your chair, put down anything you are holding. I'll talk you into this, give you time to get to know your guide, and then I'll talk you out. The place where we begin the exercise is the starting point for all our explorations and it's important that you follow your own images. Don't think that what I'm saying has to be right. I try to find the best way for the group. Follow your own instincts and pictures. And remember that I can get words wrong; it's not that you are doing anything wrong if you experience it differently. I use the words 'see' and 'picture' but some people will never actually see anything. There are many ways to experience a guide or relive a life. You might hear someone telling you, or feel it in your body ..."

My images were graphic enough, but I'd certainly felt it as well. My body was totally involved.

"... or you might just *know*. Once you learn to trust this *knowing* it can be extremely powerful."

I'd say.

"Some people worry that they are making it all up. If you feel like that, play with it, let it unfold and see where it takes you. Don't judge it too soon."

I remembered that feeling, being so worried it was all imagination. But I soon got over that, had no choice really, it was absolutely real.

"... close your eyes and raise them up to look at the point between and slightly above your eyebrows. This opens the inner eye and helps images to form."

She must mean the spot where I felt all that pressure. Ah, yes, that was better. It was like an inner screen had opened up, then it moved outside and I could step into it.

"Picture yourself in a meadow on a nice, warm, sunny day. There's a gentle breeze blowing to keep you cool and comfortable."

A meadow? Cool? I was surrounded by sand and it was red hot. All the moisture was being sucked out of my skin. Well, she'd said follow your own images ...

"Feel the grass underneath your feet. Smell the flowers and hear the birds singing."

Flowers? Grass? What I smelt was Egypt, warm and pungent. And there was a roaring sound.

"In the distance you'll see a small hill with a building on top. There's a path that leads up to the building. Let your feet follow the path, feel the texture of the ground change as you step on to it, the pull on your legs as you go up the hill."

I was heading down a sand dune, towards the east door of Karnak.

"When you reach the door of the building, put your hand out and open it and step through. Your guide will be waiting to meet you. Take time to get acquainted."

The gatekeeper had seen me coming and the small door was open. My feet hurried to her sanctuary. As I opened the door, there She was, tawny mane rippling above taut breasts. Her chest rose and fell, this was no statue. My Lady herself had come to be my guide. Her voice vibrated within me, her warmth surrounded me as I slid down to rest at her feet. I trusted her utterly.

"It's time to leave now. Thank your guide for being with you and arrange a signal so that you can call on your guide whenever you need to ..."

I didn't want to leave, not now when I'd found Her again, I wanted to stay there forever, but my Lady said she was always with me. I only had to call her name.

"Make your way out of the building and close the door behind you. Your guide may stay in the building, or may accompany you back to the meadow. Let your feet take you down the path and back to your starting place.

"Take your time, breathe a little deeper, feel your feet on the floor, the weight of your body as you sit in the chair, remember your connection to the earth. When you are ready, open your eyes."

How strange everyone looked. Blinking and peering as though they'd been deeply asleep and had woken suddenly. Several were smiling secret smiles, and I must have looked like that too. A man on the other side of the room shook his head slowly as though to shake off the memory, and Ramon was frowning.

"Well, how did everyone get on? Ramon, you look troubled. What happened?"

"I had to make myself follow you. I did not know what a meadow was but I did not think it could be the wide expanse of sand I found myself on. A hawk came and flew in front of me, he led me into a building and there was a shaven-headed priest there. I am Catholic and it did not feel right. He looked at me and said, "Well, I can be whatever you want me to be," and he changed into Christ. It felt blasphemous and I recoiled, and he became a man in jeans and a sweatshirt, then a suit. I felt that he was playing with me – or rather that my imagination was playing tricks on me. When the bird asked if it would do instead, I could not take any more. I opened my eyes." Ramon stared at her as though expecting a challenge, but Anne glanced apologetically at him.

"I'm sorry, I forgot to check that everyone knew what a meadow was but, as I said, it's important to follow your own images. I think your experience was real, you were contacting a guide, he wasn't sure what form to take. That sometimes happens. It sounds as though your imagery was very clear."

Ramon didn't look too convinced. Silently I begged him, please, please, stay, don't leave.

"I will try to keep an open mind. This is new to me and it goes against my religion." He fingered the heavy gold cross he wore beneath his shirt. He'd done that when I first mentioned the workshop but I hadn't thought about his religion, I was too anxious to have my own experiences confirmed by his. It must have put him under enormous pressure; I knew I'd have to apologize, but not in front of all those people.

Anne was nodding: "Yes, it is difficult for Catholics. Even though there is evidence that the Church believed in reincarnation in its early days, it has stamped out the belief since."

"What evidence would that be?" Ramon had his eyes fixed on her intently and he was holding that cross tightly.

"The so-called Gnostic gospels, the ones the Church rejected after the first two hundred years, contain many references, and the idea resurfaced in virtually every 'heresy' that the Church later put down." Anne's hands made emphatic quotation marks. She could probably have said more about heresy but she carried on, I made a note to remember to ask her later.

"Even the four gospels that were left after the purge, the ones that form the New Testament, have some references left in them. For instance, when Jesus heals a man who is blind, the people ask

Jesus whether it was him or his parents who sinned that he was born blind. That presupposes that he lived before, or he could not have sinned before he was born, as it were. We can talk more about this later if you wish."

Ramon nodded. He'd begun to look intrigued, so I guessed he'd decided to stay.

Anne glanced around the group.

"Does anyone else want to say anything about the guide exercise? No, well I think we'll go straight into your first past life session. You will be in two places at once, as it were. Here, aware of the present day, and there in the other life. For some people it will be as though you are tuning in a television. The pictures will be all snowy or like brief flashing images that you can't quite catch. Other people will be able to see, feel, and hear everything happening around you."

Just like I did.

"Remember not to try too hard, there'll be plenty of opportunities throughout the weekend and if you try to force it, it *won't* work. Remember too to pay attention to your body, you might get a strange feeling that will take you into the life, or you might just suddenly know all the details. Everything and anything can happen – and probably will."

She smiled, but one or two people hunched their shoulders forward apprehensively.

"We're going to use the meadow – or wherever you went – for our starting point and walk up to the building, and then go in. I shall count you down some steps. This is not to hypnotize you, it helps you to relax and reach the deeper levels of consciousness where the memories lie ..."

I'd no need of counting, time had collapsed around me, I was back in that land again.

"Now take time to go over what happened, and make notes if you want to. Afterwards, we can discuss it."

Stunned, unable to move, I went back over what I learned. How could I not have realized before? *He,* that alien priest with predatory eyes whose name I never knew, the sight of whom thrust me into the void, had such a voracity for me that he'd sought me out and married me over three thousand years later. Of course, Greg and the priest were one and the same. It made perfect sense.

No wonder I felt when Greg married me that he wanted something from me, something I was unable to give. Back in that other life, he'd wanted the power that sexual congress with the Lady conferred. It was the initiation he'd failed to earn for himself. Believing Pharaoh would die, he'd intended to claim my child – and seize the throne as regent. It would have taken him to the highest position in the land. His ambitions were dark indeed. When my soul left that body I cheated him out of what he thought was rightfully his. He grabbed a knife, ripped open my belly and pulled the child from my womb. But that soul left too. He cursed us both, and followed me across the centuries and charmed me into marriage, and then turned into a monster. The child too was pulled to us by the strength of his longing – and the curse. Greg had never let go of the desire for control over Mek'an'ar's child. He pulled the soul to him, but that soul escaped again ...

Pain sliced my throat, my empty belly cramped. I told myself not to remember, Mecky, stop right there.

It was only when the cancer began to eat my blood that I'd found the power to say no and, finally, he left. Despite feeling devastated, I was glad to be rid of his insistent, what? What was it I sensed in him? A hunger, an excessive desire for sex, a feeling he wanted to possess every particle of me and make it his. So much greed. But there was something more. Greg really thought I owed him something. "I only want what I'm due," he'd say like a sulky little boy. But the why and the how of it escaped him. Now, with hindsight, I saw what he'd sought.

On the way to my lawyer to sign the divorce papers, that bleak medical pronouncement had sent me reeling in another direction. I'd intended to settle money and property on him, anything to get him off my back. I bought into his feeling that I owed him something. After all, he'd adopted my family name and I know he'd hoped my father would leave him the business. He'd hated it when it went to me and was so angry when I'd sold it to meet his debts. But now I knew the real truth. Thank God I was side-tracked and given the opportunity to see. I'd have to tell him all debts were cancelled, if I forgave him it meant I wouldn't have to come back with him again. How did I know that? I was sure it was right. I'd plan the future differently now. He wouldn't get a penny ...

Stop thinking about that, Mecky you idiot, I told myself. Ramon's telling his story, concentrate or you'll miss it.

"Well, at first I could not really see anything. It was all dark and fuzzy. I realized I was hovering above my body. I was wounded, there was a broken spear sticking out of my side. I was being carried on a litter, gently and with great reverence. My troops were pursuing the fleeing enemy and I could vaguely hear cries in the distance. No quarter was being given. They had offended against the living body of Khemet and against the might of Pharaoh. I wondered how I knew all this, was I making it up, but if this was all my imagination it was interesting, I let it unroll."

Shrugging his shoulders he glanced around the room. Enrapt faces looked back and one or two people nodded encouragingly. Ramon began again:

"I was taken into a tent. Surgeons came. They murmured incantations as they worked, and made an offering to the gods before they started. I was glad I was unconscious; it looked really painful. They poured boiled herbs around the wound, to sterilize and anaesthetize it. One of them held the wound open with retractors while the other worked a slim knife down under the spear. I was surprised at how modern the surgical tools looked. Eventually it slid out and the wound filled with blood. They quickly poured a brown powder in and it seemed to clot almost immediately. They added a root and a strong smelling substance – myrrh, I think, as it reminded me of Christmas Masses. It seemed to numb the pain and the wound was dry and clean.

"When the spear was out, there was great perturbation in case it was poisoned. One of my bodyguards offered to lick the spear, but, as I was still alive, even though barely, they presumed it was clean. A physician pulverized malachite in a pestle. Removing the root from the wound, he poured the green powder into a honeycomb, which was bound over the hole. The chief surgeon gave instructions that if the wound began to fester, meat with maggots would be placed over the wound to keep it clean. They would eat the pus and decayed flesh, but otherwise the honey and malachite was to be applied every day for a week and he would be back to take another look. It sounds horrible to me now, but back then, it seemed to be the right thing to do.

"He is in the hands of the gods now," the physician said as he left.

"Time seemed to slip past. There was always a priest with me and they would talk to me and offer up prayers for the safe sojourn of my *ka* in the spirit world; it was obvious they could see me hovering over my body. Eventually they decided it was time to make the long journey home. I would live, although I was still weak. I was transferred to a stately barge on a slowly moving river. I spent most of my day sleeping under a canopy on the deck. It was cool and pleasant. From the banks would come shouts and prayers of thanksgiving but these were inaudible to my physical ears.

"One afternoon I left the barge, or rather was taken away by a luminous being whose face I could barely make out. Leaving the river, we raced over the barren land under the hot bright sun. Stern and proud, my companion never spoke but I knew that something was wrong, a great evil was being perpetrated. This was no dream, no hallucination of a feverish mind. I was traveling, and yet I was also lying on my bed in the care of the priests.

"We stood in the shadowed halls of a far-away temple. I saw my love. I tried to reach out to her, she was so forlorn, and frightened."

Frightened – I had been terrified seeing that alien priest and his predatory eyes in the place of my beloved brother. Did Ramon know who he ...

"I could not understand why she was there, seated in the place of exaltation and wearing the mask of my Lady. Nor why a stranger priest with hard, evil eyes was handing her the sacred cup. Why had she not waited? It could not be that time already surely? How long had I lain in that bed?

" 'No, no.' I had cried out in alarm, 'Do not, it will kill her without me.'

"Then suddenly I was in my body. I do not know how I got there, it had seemed to happen all of a sudden. It ached but when I groaned, someone slipped a few drops of liquid between my teeth and I was sleeping once again. I dreamed of a lioness rushing over the earth and drinking a great pool of blood. Only somehow she got confused with the woman I loved so much but could not marry. When I awoke next time I felt cool and fresh, but still weak. The problem was, my mind seemed blank. I felt I had to do something, urgently, but I'd no idea what.

"They told me there had been a great victory, we had expelled the enemy. Now, we were journeying back to my home but it would take many weeks. I became agitated. I knew there was something, somewhere I had to be. Another sleeping draught was administered and my consciousness slipped away.

"Many times over the next few weeks that elusive feeling returned. It struck me as my litter was carried over sand and a dust storm arose. Where had I breathed this choking air before? Why did it seem so urgent? As we gently slipped upstream propelled by a strong wind against an equally fierce current, I realized we were on the barge of Pharaoh journeying up the great river, and knew that I had an appointment. But where, and with whom?

"Even though myself, as I sit here now, fights against the idea, I know I was Pharaoh – although they called me something else. A name I cannot now remember."

Ibi, my beloved Suten, Ibi, my brother. So Ramon did remember –

"One day I recognized a temple on an island at the edge of the river. Temple Luxor, we were coming home to Thebes. As the barge neared Aphet-sut and turned down the wide canal to the landing stage in front of the temple, I knew this was where my appointment was.

"By now I could stand unsupported, but my knees went suddenly weak as I realized that I was too late. The river had been high, but it was now very low. I should have been here before inundation.

"Memory flooded back. I was needed for the great festival. My beloved Mek'an'ar was to make the journey for the goddess once more. She had to renew the blood of Khemet. And I remembered my journey with the luminous being, seeing my beloved and that stranger priest before her. I was not there to guard her. Did the priests force it? Who took my place, and what happened? In anguish, I rushed forward ...

"And then you called us back, Anne. I did not want to come but I realized I could not bear to know what happened either. When I opened my eyes, I was here in this room and the first thing I saw was Megan. But for a moment she looked like Mek'an'ar in her lion headdress. My heart almost leaped out of my body, I was indeed surprised. Now I know why she was familiar when we met, in front of Sekhmet of all places. It could be my imagination but I do not think that is the case, I am sure we have been together before. Did I get back to you in time, Megan, or did something awful happen?"

For a moment I couldn't answer.

"Well, Megan, is this why you couldn't tell us why you were here?" Anne's voice was sympathetic.

"Yes, and no. I knew all this and I wanted to see if it was confirmed, but there is much more."

Before I could go on, the secretary-like woman across the

room, the one with the beautiful eyes who been vaguely familiar, Alison her name was, leant forward and said:

"I don't like to interrupt but could I tell you what happened to me? I think it might be relevant and I want to tell it before Megan tells her story in case you think I am making it up."

I nodded, knowing what was to come.

"I was standing by a lake. It was beautiful in the clear starlight. All around were other women in pleated linen robes and plaited wigs. Silently we took off the wigs and laid them aside, and let the robes fall. We stepped into the water, chanting as the full moon rose. I saw the walls of a temple, and statues of a lion-headed goddess. I knew I was in Egypt.

"I became aware of how unclean I felt. I'd had sex with a man and his semen and my blood were running down my leg. The sex had left me feeling unfulfilled and somehow not right. The man was older and a bit smelly as though he'd been eating something strong like onions. I can still smell it."

Wrinkling her nose she continued:

"I knew that the goddess wanted her essence to pass to all men on this special night and that I was a vehicle for this. But I was only young and it was my first time. There was something about this man that made me profoundly uneasy.

"This wasn't what made me unclean. I violated a temple precept. When he grunted and rolled off me, I waited a moment and followed him. He moved furtively. We'd been outside the north gate – he'd dragged me there quickly – although everyone else went off in other directions. He made his way to a shadowy temple that was close to the wall. A sacred place, forbidden to all but the highest initiates on that special night.

"I saw him slip noiselessly up the steps at the front and onto the roof. I waited until he came down. He was muttering to himself. 'Next time it will be me. I've seen the future and he won't be there. Next time, next time. I swear.'

"As he disappeared, I couldn't contain my curiosity any longer. Holding my breath in fear and trepidation, I climbed the steps. I saw light coming out of a hole in the roof opposite. Silently, crouching down, I made my way to the hole and looked in. Stifling a cry, I started back. There, below me, was the Lady of the Flame, the living goddess, Sekhmet. I saw her tawny mane. Indeed, I had dared, I could have reached my hand down and touched it. At her feet, I saw entwined feet. Human this time. Instantly I knew this was my high priestess and Pharaoh himself, communing with the goddess. They were ..."

A red tide rose slowly up her neck and engulfed her face.

"I'm sorry, Megan, I didn't mean to ..."

She looked down at her lap, hands toying with a tissue she had pulled from her pocket. Glancing at Anne through lowered lashes she went on:

"At that moment, Pharaoh cried out. The temple lurched. Fearing that it was an earthquake, I hurried from the roof. But in my heart I knew that it was the moment of creation.

"I'd violated the sacred moment with my presence. Afraid, I scurried back across the quiet temple and made my way silently down the causeway to Aphet-sut. When the procession began, I joined the other priestesses and made my way to the sacred lake. Perhaps the water could take away my unclean act.

"As I immersed myself in the water I looked across at Mek'an'ar, wondering why she wasn't the Great God's Wife as other High Priestesses had been. Why was she not married to

Pharaoh? What was it in her past that fitted her for such high office but not for marriage to the Pharaoh? When I arose out of the water, she was looking at me, compassion in her gaze. I clearly heard in my mind: 'Do not be troubled. You cannot yet know such things. And do not worry that you have violated the goddess. She forgives you. It is the man, the priest who was at fault. There will be much to reconcile there before that deed is cleansed.'

"As I came back to awareness of being in this room, and in my present body, I felt that enormous forgiveness all around me."

And then I could tell all I'd experienced over the long preceding month. The relief of sharing my slide into the Egyptian life with people who believed me was so wonderful, I cried softly as I talked. Someone handed me a tissue but I waved it away. The tears were cleansing, such a great healing. They were drops of that sacred lake which was my home.

Over a cup of tea in the low-ceilinged kitchen with its mismatched chairs and a ring-marked dining table embarrassed to find itself in the servants' part of the house, I talked with the woman and the man, Pharaoh and the young priestess. This was no wild feat of an overheated imagination run riot. Three people shared in such detail a memory from another time, it must be truth.

"How are you getting on?" asked Anne, pulling up a chair.

"We have much to share," I told her. "It makes so much sense and explains a lot. I suppose you hear this all the time."

"Well, yes," she replied. "I know it sounds far-fetched and difficult to believe but groups are drawn back together, usually because there is unfinished business but that's not always so. Groups travel together through the centuries and people do share experiences. Sometimes they slot into place like yours has, everyone contributing something to remembering a previous life. It can explain a great deal."

From the way she glanced at Ramon she was expecting an argument but he held onto that crucifix of his and kept quiet. He seemed thoughtful though, eyes looking inward.

"I've heard soul groups mentioned here at the college," Alison said, "but I'm not sure how this fits into reincarnation."

"There are groups of souls that travel together loosely over many incarnations. Sometimes they all meet up again, at other times only a few will be in touch during a specific lifetime. It all depends on what they intended to do and how carefully the planning has been done in the between life state."

"What pulls them back together?" I needed to know.

"Intentions and unfinished business often pull souls back together – and old promises. They act as magnets, compelling two or more souls to meet. It often manifests as a strong sexual attraction, which can cause problems if people act on it too impulsively and then find it was an old memory rather than an intention."

Shifting uneasily on my chair, I wondered if Anne had guessed? Somehow I didn't think she'd judge me if she had. To cover my momentary confusion, I asked:

"Are all these memories true? Do memories ever overlap? What happens if several people have the same memory? Who would you believe?"

"A group will sometimes have the same memory as another group has already had. This links into the memories held by a place rather than what happened to that group there. But sometimes several people 'remember' being the same person."

"Can you give us an example?" Ramon interrupted harshly.

"Judas was common a few years ago and you wouldn't choose to be him now would you?" She was smiling but Ramon was still troubled.

"No, I would not. But does not all this throw doubt on past life memories?"

He was fingering that cross again, was he doubting his experience?

"Not at all, there's plenty of evidence to support having lived before, but it does show that you need to differentiate between a true reliving and something that may tap into collective experience, or be an illusion, what I call a 'fantasy in fancy dress.' Ego can play a part in some regressions – and that's difficult for people to accept because the emotion and the gut feeling of it can be strong. But it doesn't really matter. All these things are true at some level. You wouldn't remember unless your soul experience resonated with those things and it was in essence your story."

Ramon's expression was still intense but he'd stopped holding that cross: "So, if you remembered yourself as Judas, do you mean you could be working out a betrayal theme from another life not as Judas?" Funny, I hadn't noticed that v-shaped line his forehead made when he was puzzled. It was quite cute, made him look less stern in a boyish sort of way. Fitting into the ballroom upstairs perfectly, he'd looked out of place ever since we'd come down here to the basement, like an exotic bird caged in a grotty backyard shed.

"Yes," Anne nodded emphatically: "That's right. Although the people who were 'Judas' actually thought they were saving their best friend's life rather than betraying him."

"Is it that people are always famous?" That foreign rhythm was very noticeable in his voice.

"No, quite the reverse, most people go back to being servants or peasants who made no impact on the world around them and wouldn't be recorded by history. In fact, if you recall being someone from history you should examine what is happening to you carefully. People do unconsciously regurgitate things they heard or read as a child, or go back to being someone that they have admired in the past. Although, of course, someone had to be those souls."

"Quite a few people on this workshop seemed to go back to traumatic events." Alison's voice was quiet but she too looked worried.

"That's quite usual. When you think about it, it's the extremes we remember in our present life. The very happy times, or the deeply sad, the shocks and the traumas. These are the things that make most impact – and which may need healing as the effects carry forward."

Ramon jumped in again: "Where does the notion of time fit into all of this? I felt as though I had lived through many months and yet it was, how long, twenty minutes?"

I'd lived a whole year in a few moments, but I didn't mention it.

"I've found that time as we know it doesn't exist outside this physical plane. We need it here to make sense of our experiences but universal time is something entirely different. It's like being in the center of a wheel, as it were, you can access anywhere on the wheel, past, present, or future, and while you do so time has no meaning. You can experience it in everyday life too: apparent time is different to how we measure time. If you get totally absorbed in something, time passes quickly, but get bored and it drags. Yet exactly the same amount of actual time has elapsed. Does that answer your question, Ramon?" Her eyes pleaded with him to understand.

"I think so. When I came out of the regression everything seemed to be in slow motion. Is that usual?" That v-shape was still between his eyes.

"Oh yes, when people are in regression they often speak extremely slowly, especially when they've passed through their past life death, or are close to it. I think the space where they are is vibrating faster but it's a difficult thing to explain in terms of our science. Quantum physics can provide an answer but it is leading edge stuff and I'm not sure I fully understand it. Quantum also explains how we can be in two places at once, but you'd need to talk to a physicist about that, it's beyond me." She shook her head regretfully.

Ramon leaned forward again. "It is possible to explore past lives further? Do you give private sessions?"

Why hadn't that occurred to me? There was so much more I wanted to understand. It felt like a small part of a jigsaw completed, and yet there were other pieces I hadn't seen yet. I needed to get to the bottom of it.

"Well, it depends where you live. I used to do private sessions here at the college, but now I only do them in Cornwall. I concentrate more on writing these days. But I can recommend someone in London if you like. His name is Ronald Rollingston. He's exceptionally good. Ronald's a hypnotherapist by training, with years of experience, but he found past lives came up for his clients again and again so he decided to specialize in past life therapy."

"Is there a difference between hypnosis, hypnotherapy, and past life therapy?" Alison asked, her face screwed up as though she was using her muscles to concentrate.

"Yes. If someone experiences a past life under hypnosis they re-run it like a video, although it can be extremely graphic with powerful sensations – rather like Megan's flashback. The difference is they may not remember it when they come out of hypnosis and experiencing the life again makes little impact on their present life. In hypnotherapy, or past life therapy, the root cause of a present life problem is being sought. The therapist will assist the client to let the experience go and find a new way to be in the present."

"Rather as you did when you told us to shut the door and leave the past behind and to ask our guides for healing if it was necessary?" Alison was happier now.

"Yes. In one-to-one therapy I can suggest the reframing or healing work that is needed as we go along, but in a workshop that's not possible, so I give some general suggestions people can apply to their own situation."

"If we decide to work with Ronald will he use the same techniques as you do Anne, or will he insist on hypnosis?" Ramon broke in again. "And what will happen if he accesses something he cannot deal with? Some of this material seems to be exceedingly traumatic."

"That's why it's not a good idea to do it on your own. Unless it comes up suddenly as it did for Megan, it's sensible to have someone guiding the process. Ronald is very experienced. His hypnotherapy training was first class and he also trained with me in past life healing."

"Would you consult him yourself?" Ramon was very insistent.

"He's the person I go to if I need to explore my own past lives, I can't give any higher recommendation than that. We often work together. You could start with a few sessions with him in London and come down to Cornwall later if you needed my help."

And that, we decided, was what we'd do.

chapter 8.

inspirer of males

"Open this bloody door. Do you hear me? Open it. Come on, Mecky. I know he's in there. If you don't open it I'll break it down." Each word was punctuated by a blow on the door.

"Who is that? If that banging does not stop the whole neighborhood will be awake." Ramon's voice was thick with sleep but he was already pulling on his clothes.

"My soon-to-be-ex husband, I'm afraid. God knows what he's doing here. It must be nearly dawn. My solicitor has told him to stay away but he doesn't listen. Wait here and I'll see if I can persuade him to go."

Ramon put out his hand:

"Do not open the door, Megan. He sounds like a madman. You should not let him in." He tried to pull me away from the door but I shouted:

"Greg, it's Mecky, can you hear me?"

"Of course I can bloody hear you. Open this door." Each word was emphasised by a loud bang.

"Please stop that noise. I'm not going to talk to you at this time of the morning. We'll meet in my solicitor's office later."

"Too bloody right we will. We'll see what she has to say about you having a man in there. I saw the two of you as you got out of that taxi. He's been in there hours. Disgusting! Now you'll have to give me the money. I deserve it, married to you all those years. Anyway I need it. I want to set up a business ..."

"Yes, Greg, you told me. But we can't talk about it now. Please go away." Wearily I shook my aching head. Why did he have to be so difficult? Why couldn't he just let me go?

"I'm not going anywhere 'till you promise to give me what's rightfully mine."

Strange how detached I felt from him. Knowing what lay behind this gave me such strength – and peace. My stomach would have been in knots before, but it was calm.

"I can't promise anything in the middle of the night."

The door rattled and creaked under his renewed onslaught but held steady. It was comforting to know the reinforced door I'd put on after the burglary would do everything the salesman claimed. What a pity I still hadn't painted the dingy hall. Ramon reappeared beside me.

"Megan, let me call the police. They will deal with this."

"No, he'll go. Greg, please leave now. I'll see you at 10.30 in Miss Webster's office."

Silence.

"Megan, it was unwise of you to open yourself to this but it doesn't change anything. There's no such thing as a divorce on the grounds of adultery now and the property you brought to the marriage – and what you later inherited, or rather what's left of it – will remain yours. It was sensible not to break the terms of your trust fund and put things into your husband's name."

Miss Webster shook her tightly braided hair. She was nothing like I'd imagined a solicitor to be. Almost six feet tall, thin and long boned, warm-black skin, and so elegant she could have been a model. Her mother was a Masai woman from a warrior tribe, she'd told me. No wonder Greg didn't frighten her. Thank goodness I'd found her, a lucky stab in the phone book when the family solicitor refused to act for me.

"He tried hard enough to make me do that but I think my father must have known when he set the trust up that Greg would have designs on it. He never did like Greg and the feeling was mutual. Greg was glad enough to live off the money, and to have the house bought for us, if it meant he didn't have to work for a living."

How awful it had been even in the very early days, how embarrassed I had felt whenever Dad came round and Greg tried to pump him for more and more money for his silly ideas.

"His first two businesses failing used up all the savings I'd had, and most of the money from the sale of Dad's business. But, of course, he knows I had stock options from the company and that they went into my pension fund. I don't have to give him that, do I?"

Especially now.

Raised voices beyond the mahogany door communicated Greg's arrival.

"Come in, Mr. McKennar, and sit down. If this harassment doesn't stop we will have no option but to go to court to seek an injunction."

That was a very firm tone; Greg's bully and bluster tactics wouldn't work against her. That sulky small boy look appeared on his face again. How could I ever have thought him handsome? Miss Webster tried to forestall the inevitable.

"If you take advice from your own solicitor I'm sure he would advise you to let things drop."

"What, after what she's done?" He was pushing his face forward in that pugnacious way he used to frighten people, but, at the same time, he was leering at me. Did he know, how could he ...

"I don't know what you mean." She sat back, frostily.

Greg's face became redder and he smirked, lip curling back from yellowed teeth. He wasn't going to bring that up, was he? Not here, not now. Surely ...

"She aborted my baby."

Miss Webster started, her professional cool dropped away as she turned shocked eyes to mine.

"An abortion? Megan, you didn't tell me ..."

"It wasn't like that. When I started the chemo I didn't know I was pregnant. All those years and I'd never conceived. I thought it was part of the illness. Of course I lost the baby. If I'd known I'd never have had treatment. He, Greg I mean, came to see me after it happened. Saw spontaneous abortion written on my notes and stormed out. Refused to believe I hadn't done it deliberately."

Hot liquid scalded my eyes. I didn't want to cry in front of him, but I couldn't help it. I'd wanted a baby so much. Even though I hadn't known I was pregnant, I had grieved for that baby. Still did. How could he be so cruel? He hadn't even wanted a child.

"Mr. McKennar, this changes nothing. Your wife will still be granted a divorce on the grounds of irretrievable breakdown of the marriage. And you, sir, will get nothing more from her."

The look of distaste on her face would have withered any other man. Greg was still protesting as he was escorted to the door.

"Melanie, could you be a love and bring in some tea? Here you are, dear." She handed me an enormous box of tissues and, reaching into her huge desk, produced an equally large tin of biscuits. Picking up scattered papers and hitting them sharply on the desk to rattle them into order, she said:

"I'll ring his solicitor later and report what's happened. If Greg doesn't stop we have grounds for an injunction. The sooner this divorce goes through the better."

Outside, Greg was waiting.

"Give me what is mine. You were going to before that slime-ball came on the scene. I suppose you want to give it to him now. He must be after your money; no one would want you now. Look at you. I made you into a stylish woman and look what you did to yourself. I made you, I have rights." His angry fists beat the air.

"No, Greg not any more."

"If you hadn't aborted that kid I'd have had it all, they would have had to give me control when you die. I'd have been its guardian. It was mine. And you took it away. It would have given me the money. It's mine!"

How could he talk about our baby that way? Grief exploded in my womb. I yelled: "No, Greg, never. I know why you think I owe you something. In another life you tried to make me do something that would give you ultimate power but I evaded you. You even planned to take my baby. You've been trying to make me give you what you feel you're owed ever since we married. But it won't work. If anything, you owe me for what you did to me back then, and in this life, but I forgive you that. I don't want another life with you."

Oh dear, I hadn't meant to mention other lives, especially not to him.

"Have you gone soft in the head, Mecky? Another life indeed.

112

Who's been telling you all that nonsense? I know there are idiots out there who believe in reincarnation but I never thought you'd be one of them. Load of rubbish. How can you possibly believe it?"

He was astounded. It was worth telling him to see his face.

"I'm not prepared to discuss it any more. The divorce is going through and that's it. Taxi!"

Sa Sekhem Sahu. The goddess was with me.

But, waking in the night paralyzed, unable to move a muscle, I didn't feel this was so. An enormous weight pressed down on my chest, something was in the room with me, a brooding being, its breathing hissed loud in the silence. This wasn't a person, it was a *presence* and its intent was malign. Struggling to open my eyes, I remembered those feelings from childhood nights of terror. And, when I was finally released, the horror of turning inch by slow inch to face that patch of impenetrable darkness. It eventually faded away but always left an unspoken message lingering in my mind. "You cannot escape, I will be back."

No part of my body moved in response to my urgent commands. The weight got heavier and I was drenched in clammy sweat. Why couldn't Ramon have been there, he could have reached me, brought me back.

Think, Mecky, think, I urged myself. What did you do as a child? Oh yes, my little finger. Concentrated on that, just a tiny movement, nothing huge. Yes! There it was, a twitch and I was back in control of my muscles but the presence was still there, although the weight was lifting. It smelt like old trainers, may the goddess protect me. Mek'an'ar must have known a banishing ritual, why couldn't I remember, it was so frustrating. I wondered what time it was, it must be nearing dawn, yes, there, the first rays touched the window.

And it was gone.

No more sleep for me, I might as well make some coffee.

Looking out at the unkempt garden in the ghostly light of dawn, I recalled the curse that renegade priest cast after me as I fell into the deep. Somehow I knew this latest attack had something to do with Greg. Come to think of it, the childhood terrors may well have been down to him, they only stopped after we were married. I'd had one or two incidents since he left, but I'd put that down to my illness.

My garden really did need attention. It had been so pretty when I first arrived, sitting in the sun on the tiny patio had been such a solace to me and I'd enjoyed weeding and tidying. But as my energy flagged, I simply sagged in the sun and slept.

Was Grey lying awake in the night cursing me once again? It wouldn't have surprised me. I must talk to Anne about it. I thought, I'd believed, remembering would release that ancient curse, but had it? Was there still a remnant clinging to my soul to reappear in the night? From the shudders in my body, it could well be so.

chapter 9.

Mother of the Gods

Prostrate. Head in the dirt, I wait. Eyes peeping upwards beneath lowered lashes. Waiting to catch a glimpse of Her, the Great Mother. Tiye, Mut incarnate. Remembering her awesome power. Her majesty. My absolute humility as once before I'd lain prostrate before her, I'd not lifted my head as she stood before me, singling me out.

"Shen-en-k'art, beloved of Mut, be true to me."

"Oh, I will," my heart had answered.

My whole being is dedicated to this Lady. The Great God's Wife – and the Goddess inviolate.

Tiye was to have been the guide who took me beyond my initiation into the Deeper Mysteries. The mentor for my sacred powers.

How did this calamity befall us? A scant half-decan later, the old king dead, the temple that was to have been my lifelong home is to close. Its priestesses will be cast out. The Great Mother toppled from her throne. The pantheon of gods is fallen. Set aside in favor of The One.

Auburn hair shining in the sun, a luxuriant flame haloed around her head, the Great Queen Tiye herself comes to tell the assembled priestesses the names of those who will be spared. Her proud eyes hold the glint of a tear.

"My dear ones, I cannot take you all. Some of you must return to your families."

Families? I have no family. Am I to be abandoned to the brothels? "Great Mother preserve me," I cry in the depths of my pain. Forgetting that to call on the Mother is forbidden.

As soon as the mourning period was ended, the Suten had sent out an edict. Only Aten, the hidden and invisible One, is to guide the land and the lives of the people. From henceforth, Suten would be known as Akhenaten. Beloved by the Aten, Son of the Sun. But how can I call on Aten, that remote and unforgiving being? How can I set aside the Great Lady Mut? Since childhood I have been in her care. Her temple the only home I know. I was three when the priests of Amon plucked me from the arms of my dead mother and spirited me away to Waste. The great and winged lady who watched over me from birth nodded, smiling.

"Go with them child, they will bring you to the Mother."

Her shimmering presence faded but came to me from time to time in the dark of the night ...

When the tears of loneliness and fear touched my cheeks.

The priests were kind, but dry and old. They honored my visions and smiled benignly when I recounted the color of the lights clustered around the heads of those we passed. If I glimpsed black or murky green, we went another way. Red would cause us to fade out of sight. After all, it was my power of sight that had caused them to seek me out. To find me before Weneset, the Eater of Souls, came. They foresaw the dark times that would fall upon the shining ones. They wanted to gather up the goddesses' children whilst there was still time. Time to train us, to bring us to perfect vision and clarity. Time for us to master the magic of Sekhmet, the sekhem power. Time for us to join the hustle and bustle of her home, the Great Temple Mut.

Set high on a priest's shoulder, I come at last to Aphet-sut. Light shines out. Rainbow colors sparkle and dance. Laughing delightedly I reach out and am gathered into the arms of the Great Wife. The Queen Tiye.

All around are silent, awed to see her haughty face break into a smile.

"Welcome back, Shen-en-k'art," she whispers into my ear. "You are just in time. Your initiation will be completed before the temple falls. The goddess wills that you will not remember who you were until much time has passed. A new order will rise, and fall, before your wisdom can come to fruition. You will forget me. You will look on me with awe and unknowingness. But your heart will know that we are sisters beneath the skin. Children of the same small village, humble in origin but great of purpose. And one day, you too will pass on the powers of our Lady to your successor."

Handing me to one of the nursemaids, she smiles and thanks the priests who brought me.

"Blessed be."

Her benediction is to be all I hold of her for several years.

I am eight before I see that weaving rainbow of colors again. But this time, by now well trained in the temple etiquette, I fall to the floor and prostrate myself before her.

And the Great Wife walks past without a sideways glance.

To have acknowledged me, would, by that time, have brought me into terrible danger. But, child that I am, I cannot know this for certain, and my heart dies a little.

That night, my winged and shining lady comes to me to soothe and gentle me.

"This is how it must be. One day you will understand. Meanwhile study diligently and keep the trust in your heart."

Many times in the years that follow I prostrate myself before the Lady Tiye.

And many times, in the secret recesses of the temple, she guides me through the initiations as my soul remembers. She sits with me one long night whilst I do battle and regain my *akhar*, the essence and power of my being. Without this, I cannot control the magic. With no magic, there would be no power. With no power, there can be no magic. This is my ultimate test.

As I range far and wide upon the shores of Amenti in search of my *akhar*, I know that the Great Mother is with me. My blood is the blood of Sekhmet, The Lady of The Place Beyond Time, called to aid me. Together we face the demons of the twelfth sphere.

Here my soul had been cast at my previous death.

Inviolable and surrounded by flames, my *akhar* is a column of golden light. It has not been destroyed!

But it is well guarded.

I speak the words of power. The secret resonances that control even this heinous place.

Not a trace of fear in my voice. The courage in my heart is that of a lion – my Lady Sekhmet.

My will is honed by twelve years of temple training. It cuts through the fire.

Opening the Way.

I flow towards my *akhar*. Embrace it. Embody it.

And find myself back in Aphet-sut with the Queen.

"Well done, my child. Now drink this."

She hands me a cup of herbs.

"Sleep child, sleep, and know that I am with you."

But when I awake, I am alone. The Queen's husband is dead. And the land of Khemet is cast adrift.

When next I see her, she tells me that I, and a small group of priestesses, young and unrecognizable as belonging to the Mut, will accompany her to the new Court at Akhet-Aten.

All around us the statues are tumbling. The huge gates thrown open wide. The soldiers of the young Suten Akhenaten are defiling the Great Temple of the Mother and not all of us escape unharmed.

Shepherded by the Queen, we leave the temple by a side gate and come at last to the palace. Donning servants' gowns, we pack for the long journey to our new home.

"Leave that scene now and come back to the present moment, moving forward in time." Ronald's voice was insistent. With his swept-back hair and glasses perched on the end of his nose he would be more at home in a university surely. But he'd been a good facilitator for me, made the process of remembering easy. I supposed I'd have to return to my present body. It sat quietly there in the chair beside his desk. Waiting for me.

Coming out of the regression, tears poured down my face.

"What do you remember most?" Ronald's voice was gentle.

"An absolute sense of awe and majesty as I looked upon the face of that haughty, but well loved, Egyptian Queen long ago. The reverence I still feel for her, although the sense of worshipping a divinity made manifest and incarnated within a human being is alien to me in my present life. A childhood knee injury prevents my kneeling before any god. It's unthinkable that I'd prostrate myself full length on the ground in front of another woman. And yet I did and felt more *right* than I've ever known. More at peace than I'd have thought possible."

A remnant of the peace is with me now, curling gently around my child.

"Did you recognize anyone?" Ronald's eyes were bright, his head cocked on one side, eyebrows lifting. The way he leant forward intently made me wonder how much he knew.

Misunderstanding was easier than telling the truth.

"This isn't the first time I've seen Tiye's majestic face. I saw it recently on a postcard, sent by a friend from Anne's workshop, with a cryptic note: 'Anyone you know?'

"The dark face, carved out of wood, seemed alive, the eyes were electric. It called to me across the centuries. It was so familiar I wondered if it was me. Had I seen this face reflected in the mirror of time? Or in a polished mirror of bronze? That's why I came to see you."

That and something I wasn't yet prepared to share with him.

"To find myself face down in the dust of Egypt at a time of turmoil and change, a time with which I felt great affinity, wasn't a total surprise. The first time I looked on the face of Akhenaten, the so-called Heretic Pharaoh, in the British Museum, I felt such loving respect, such *knowing*. He was my Lord."

He was someone I knew intimately and loved in the depths of night. So why in my regression did I feel that he was tearing my world apart? Why did I fear him, and his priests of Aten, so deeply?

And where was Ramon in all this? I needed to explore my links with him – and to know why he left me abruptly, saying only that there was urgent business to attend to at home. But exactly where that home was, he didn't say. Nor did he leave me a number. Half of me had been torn away, I could hardly breathe for the pain. I missed him so much.

And I was with child again.

My only clue was that Ramon saw Ronald just before he left. I knew I must come back, soon. The answer was back there, in that place that was *here* as much as *there*.

I sought solace in the British Museum.

Each time I went there, I saw so much that was familiar. I could almost reach out and touch the answers. I'd thought I'd be able to regress without Ronald's help, even though Anne had warned us against regressing ourselves, but it hadn't worked. As Ramon was seeing Ronald at the time, I'd thought he might guide me towards something Ramon remembered rather than what I needed to know. But after Ramon left I needed answers ...

My head was reeling. I recognized the pressure in the middle of my forehead, the roaring in my ears. Could I open my third eye like Anne showed us?

Palm frond brush in hand, I was sweeping a floor, a beautiful tiled floor of lush green papyrus and brilliant blue lotus flowers. Above it, a frieze of kingfishers and doves skipped lightly over the water.

It was so easy to step in and out of time.

That same beautiful floor was beneath my feet now. A bit faded, it was true, but undoubtedly identical flowers. A small plaque on the wall announced: "Floor from Tel el Armana, the Palace of Akhenaten."

Groping my way to a nearby seat, trying to calm my thudding heart, I breathed deeply as they'd taught me in chemo.

Getting centered again. Closing my eyes, leaning against a pillar, I drifted away.

The river breeze carried the perfumes of the night. I was on a barge, moving slowly downstream. One of many such. Tucked in among a vast cargo and looking back with longing at the shadow of the Great Temple rearing against the night sky. In the dark of the moon it was hard to see anything. But there, surely that was the corner of a pylon. Guardian of my beloved home, Aphet-sut.

Tears stung my eyes. My heart was wrenched, jolted as it strove to return. Part of me would remain there, awaiting my return.

Almost a full inundation season had passed since the Great Queen Mother had taken me to the Malkata palace. There I cleaned and packed, and wove and prepared, and packed some more. Keeping myself hidden, head down veiling my light. Make me dim was the prayer on my lips. I'd no wish to attract attention.

Suten had issued an edict. The work on his new temple at Aphet-sut completed, a few priests would remain to praise and serve the One God. The renamed Suten, Akhenaten and his court, his soldiers, spies and builder-craftsmen, and all the hangers-on needed to complete the vast work, several thousand people, would head downstream to his new capital, The Horizon of the Aten, set in the harsh and unforgiving desert exactly half way between the old Memphian capital of Lower Egypt and the newer but still ancient site of Waset.

It was rumored that Suten had secret reasons for choosing this new site but the Suten was rumored to have clandestine reasons for everything from changing to the worship of the One God to choosing to marry the mistress Nephertiti, "the Beautiful One," around whom even more rumors flowed.

I ignored the rumors. Confined to Queen Tiye's private apartments, I never saw this ruler who'd turned my world on its head, and I retreated into the background on the rare occasions his lady wife came to call. Here on the river, my mistress had her own barge that traveled far from the royal couple.

Now, as we moved down the Nile under cover of darkness, it seemed we had slipped into another world entirely. Why did we leave so surreptitiously? Why did Suten not leave with the rising of the symbol of his One God? What did he fear? Was it true that the old priests plotted against him? Was he fleeing for his life? All seemed calm, would we be pursued?

It seemed not. The river turned toward the east. Beyond the bend, hoopoes stood like guardians on the bank, preening their white feathers in honor of our arrival, calling softly to each other:

"They are come, they are here."

We docked within a harsh red landscape. The pitiless sun sought out every corner of our being, sucking out the moisture in seconds.

Picking up my bundle, I followed the other girls off the boat. The Nubian soldiers who watched over Akhenhaten, although some said it was more like imprisonment, lined the dusty way. Keeping my head bowed, I saw my feet turn red. I dared not look into their eyes.

Putting my bundle down, I risked a glance around me. Pegged out in the dusty sand was a vast square. In the middle, Queen Tiye oversaw the erection of a tent not unlike the traveling pavilions in which the Sutens of former times went to war. Only a handful of us knew that the Great Queen had liberated these very tents from the storehouses where they had lain for many years. Newly embellished, fresh hangings giving some scant privacy, within these ancient tents we would have our home until her dwelling was completed.

Having shot arrows to the four directions from his great golden bow, Orphet, the Suten declared:

"I will never again leave these sacred walls, here I will stay under the gaze of my father the Aten," and proclaimed: "Finishing the temple will be the first task for the artisans and craftsmen. The half-completed palaces can wait."

The white alabaster temple blazed from sunrise to sunset, and took on a ghostly hue by the light of the exiled Hathor. It was open to the sky.

"There is no need for shade," Suten said. "My Father, the Great God, whose light is reflected in the sun's rays, is everywhere. And nowhere is more fitting than in this place where those merciless rays seek out every secret and hidden thing."

The priests might disagree. The old gods appreciated the shadowed cool of the temple, and so do they. But the Great God's wife, Nefertiti, Exquisite Beauty of the Sun-Disc, in her pleated gown of fine linen tied beneath her breasts and her new, Nubian-styled short wig on her head, stood unhesitatingly in the noonday sun to make the daily offering. If such a great lady could do so uncomplainingly, even when large with child, how could the poor priests do anything but likewise?

There were those that whispered that the Queen was with child when she married her Lord. That the great god visited her in the night and impregnated her, telling her that the child would be a special one. That kind of rumor often ran around the court. Other stories told about her eldest child, certainly not the issue of her husband. This child accompanied her on her first visit to the court. The moment when the young king set eyes on his bride for the first time and fell, they say, instantly in love – although already we heard it said that Suten and his Queen grew up together and loved each other as children.

Up to that moment there had been few women, other than his mother, in his life. His preferred companions were the young boys with whom he played as a youth, but on whom he turned his back when his god spoke. Few accompanied him on this journey except his beloved brother Smenkhare, the golden one, and cynics said that he was leaving temptation behind. Certainly as his pregnant wife stood out under the noonday sun, he was solicitous and loving, to her and to her elder child whom he had adopted.

Fortunately Queen Tiye, now relegated to the role of Queen Mother, had little to do on ceremonial occasions and her assigned quarters were well away from the main thoroughfare. Having been the High Priestess of the Temple Mut, it seemed unsurprising that her son, with whom she'd been close but who had withdrawn his face since embracing the one god, should allow her to recede into the background.

Which was why, some three years later, I had still not seen the new monarch close to, although his lady wife from time to time conferred with her mother-in-law to whom she prettily deferred.

Coming to with a start, I realized someone was speaking to me.

"The museum's closing now. You'll have to leave. You'll find a taxi outside."

Not quite able to focus, I stumbled to my feet. A kindly hand held me upright and guided me along the long corridor, down the steps, and across the vast open courtyard. Time wavered for a moment, but this floor was dirty gray and shining with rain. Hailing a taxi, the attendant asked:

"Where do you want to go?"

A good question.

"Vauxhall," I murmured to the driver's indifferent face. "I'll show you when we get there."

Hoping against hope the blankness would recede.

chapter 10.

flaming one

"Just relax," Ronald's soothing voices reassured me. "Go back to that moment. You are standing on the pavement sweeping. Look around you. You can talk to me without losing the picture, now, what do you see?"

"Half-built walls to head height only. Plastered and painted. Outside, a palm-fronded colonnade covering the newly planted borders. The garden shaded with figs and sycamores, their flowers scented with the breath of Hathor; the living quarters open to the sky but covered in canvas sails strung from posts. Queen Tiye has defied the edict of her god-son. She needs shade, she says, at her advanced age. Not that there is any sign of aging on that beautiful face. She has simply grown more regal, more handsome as time has molded her face to its bones. Her rich auburn hair is as vital as ever, thick and luxuriant it forms that shining halo around her head and falls in curls to well below her shoulders in defiance of the new fashion for the short Nubian wig. It is hot here, despite the cool colors of the Nile spread out beneath my feet as I sweep that tiled floor. I sprinkle water to settle the ever-present dust.

A tug on my skirt.

A child, slender and serious.

"Do you know me?"

Yes, yes, my heart sings.

But: "No," my puzzled brain replies, "I don't think so."

"I am the princess Merit'aten," she says with an impish smile. Her china-blue eyes beguile me. "Leave that and keep me company, please. My mother has been here for such a long time and my nurse has taken the young ones for a sleep. I am terribly lonely." Her slight shoulders lift in an exaggerated sigh. "And thirsty. Come." Catching my hand she tugs me out of the door.

The garden is bright, enchanting. Queen Tiye, old village woman that she is, knows the value of living plants and has her garden tended carefully. At the far end, a pool glistens. The Lady Merit'aten slips off her jeweled sandals and dips her feet into the water. A frog plops off a lily pad, startling her for a moment. It investigates her toes and retires to the bottom of the pool. She laughs delightedly.

"Hekat at least has not forgotten me."

Seeing a garden boy, I quietly call for cool juices and sweetmeats to be brought. My new friend chatters inconsequentially. It feels as though we have known each other forever.

Behind the chatter, another conversation flows. Unheard by anyone but we two. Our inner ears are open.

"Do you recall, my child, how I nurtured you when you first came to the temple? My sister-in-law Tiye asked me to keep a special eye on you. As sister-in-law to the old King, my place was assured. Knowing you were destined for something special, I made sure you were taught all that you would need. I wanted to be there for your initiation but someone wanted me out of the way.

When I died prematurely, I hurried to come back to be with you. I was sired by my father, the Lady Nefertiti's great love. But he was only a soldier in the palace guard and, frightened by what her father might do, she told everyone that a god had joined with her and told her that she was to be Queen of Egypt. She was so beautiful that everyone believed her and her father arranged for her to be seen by the old Suten and his son. He was beguiled by her beauty and she kept her true nature veiled. No one but me knows that, from time to time, that soldier slips into the palace even here. Their love is strong, they cannot deny it.

And there are many times now that her husband stays away from her bed. That younger half brother of his, Smenkhare, whose beauty almost outrivals that of my mother, takes up more and more of his time. Proclaiming him co-regent was an unwise step in my opinion. Ever since my young sister Ankhes-en-paaten was born I think my father has suspected my mother's infidelity, but he hardly seems to care any more. And now she's with child again. She told the same story as she did about my birth. Said that the Aten, the one god, had come to her in the night to impregnate her so that he could incarnate on the earth. Why do you think it is only men who can be the incarnation of the god? When I was born a girl, she still maintained I was the child of the god, but not the god himself."

"I do not know," I told her. "I hardly understand myself what is happening. I have only dim memories of who I was in the past. Queen Tiye says I will remember when the time comes and until then it is safer for me not to know."

"Well, I can tell you some of the story, if you think it would help."

"Oh yes, please do. I get bewildered and confused."

"Well, when the Great Suten went to find his Great Queen, Tiye, it was in response to a vision. The god told him that he would find her in a humble village. And that her father should be elevated to great things. What the god omitted to say was that her father was a worshipper of Yahweh, who claimed to be the one god. Queen Tiye had been brought up to worship him. But, as Suten's wife, she had to be initiated into the temple. For some years she was torn between the god of her people and the gods of her husband. Mut spoke to her and called her to be one of her own. But before that happened, she had told her son the stories that her father told her. The harsh and unforgiving Aten is none other than the god of the Israelites."

"But where do I come into this story?"

"I haven't forgotten about you. Your mother was a seer of old, a priestess who had fallen in love with Suten – and he with her. When she was with child, she was smuggled out and taken to Queen Tiye's old home. The Queen knew that the child who would be born would have special powers that would be needed when the old order had to be restored. She realized that your mother was in great danger, and so were you. She sent out the priests to fetch you back into her care and disguised your birth to keep you safe."

"I am the old Suten's daughter?"

"Yes, and my niece – or rather you were. Now I think we have a more complicated connection. But it doesn't matter. We will teach each other, share what we know. I have not been initiated this time around. My father won't allow it and my mother doesn't have the knowledge. Queen Tiye says it is unsafe. But you could take me through the stages, couldn't you? We could sit here in the shade, cooling our feet. Or better still, you could come to be with me at the palace. I am old enough to need a companion."

"No, no, child, I cannot do that. Queen Tiye insists no one must see me. She keeps me here, hidden from sight."

But the impetuous child dashes away. Running to her mother, she tugs her hand.

"Come and see my new friend. I want her to come to the palace with us."

Behind her, appalled, stands Queen Tiye. What has this child done? Has she really put us all in such danger? Keeping my head down and my light veiled, I allow myself to be inspected by Queen Nefertiti. With her alabaster skin and lapis blue eyes, she is truly beautiful – a beauty her child has inherited. She exudes a strong smell of tuberose and musk, it's heady and sensual, but the Queen eyes me with haughty disdain.

"She is comely enough. Is she educated?"

"Barely," replies the older woman motioning to me with her eyes. Turning, I try to leave. What have I done? Will this be the end of us all?

"Never mind all that," cries Merit'aten. "I want her to be with me."

"Very well, child" replies her mother, and turning to me she says "Pack your belongings. Hurry, you have only a short time."

There is no time to take leave of Queen Tiye, who stands helpless at my plight. Inwardly I hear her command: *'Keep your light dim, this time will pass. And don't let my son see you. He may guess.'*

But her warning is in vain. As we approach the palace Suten is there. A great black shape outlined in flames of light, I hide my eyes. It is his time to see the children. Running to him, Merit'aten, who seems to have forgotten our inner conversation, says excitedly.

"Come and see my new friend, father."

A smile of extraordinary sweetness lights up the room. Eyes filled with brilliant, shattered light look down at me. And that is how it begins."

"Before you become too involved in that, I think it is time you came back to the present moment. We can look at this new phase in our next session. Bring your attention back into the room, become aware of your body again. Feel its weight against the chair ... Move around, sit up, put your feet firmly on the floor." Ronald's voice was insistent as he called me forward in time. Part of me was relieved, but the other part couldn't wait to get back. We were getting close to the key, I could almost remember, almost touch it. But it was fading, it would have to wait. I hadn't realized how easy it would be to move in and out of time. Anne was right, Ronald was skilled, he made it so easy for me, just like watching a movie, only I was the star and I felt the feelings so strongly because they were *mine*. And yet, I was detached, me here and now was watching me there and then. I was reliving and yet experiencing all at the same time. It was a bit confusing but Ronald didn't seem thrown; I supposed he was used to all this time traveling. Well, we'd have to see what the next session brought.

chapter 11.

Destroyer by plagues

Appalled, shaking, I stared at the washbasin. Blood, so much blood. My shaky knees could barely hold me up, sweat and chills swept over me in waves, my mouth was dry. Putting my forehead against the cool of the mirror, I turned on the tap. The streaks of blood paled, swirled, and flowed away. Why couldn't I wash this curse from my blood as easily.

That was how it had started before: gums streaming blood. I'd been putting my tiredness and nausea down to the child I carried, but had that fatal weakness returned? It couldn't have. I was *cured*. I knew I was. It couldn't have come back.

There'd been those night sweats, but I put those down to pregnancy, too. Gingerly I checked my body with my hands. The glands in my neck were swollen. Dare I look in the mirror? That bruise on my thigh, that was when I brushed against the table. But that dark stain in the middle of my back, like spilled Coca Cola, how could I explain that, and across the tops and backs of my arms ... that tiny rash of red. No!

Trembling I phoned the hospital:

"An appointment as soon as possible ... Yes ... please ..."

Back in that stark room, blood taken, cotton wool pad in my elbow, the waiting began. They'd put a coffee machine in since I was last there but it spat out my money. At least I'd remembered to bring a magazine this time, but it was no good, I couldn't concentrate. I had to know, how could it come back? Here came Dr Benu Bird's replacement, maybe now I could get some answers.

"Mrs. MacKennar, I warned you it'd return any time. We'll wait for the blood tests, of course, but it looks conclusive to me. You're enterin' the myeloid blast crisis. There's no more we c'n do. Deterioration'll be swift. Come back in two weeks." His clipped tones dismissed me.

"What about my child? I'm pregnant." My hands clutched my belly protectively. His eyes darted around the room, looking anywhere but there.

"You're unlikely to go to term. I'll know more when we've the test results. But I'm sure there's nothing more to do." He ushered me out of the door.

This time, no one tried to stop me leaving.

Standing before my Lady, I was still shaking. I leant my head against the cool black stone. How could this have happened? I was so sure ... Did Ramon leaving stir it all up again? If only I could see him ... talk to him. And what about our child?

That familiar jolt, the slipping of time, and the voice of My Lady:

"Come to me child. Hurry. There is more to learn."

chapter 12.

Lady of Intoxications

Should I have ignored that phone, no, there was always a chance it was Ramon. I listened to the answer machine, I could always pick up.

"Megan, it's Anne Cottington. I've just been asked to lead a group going down the Nile. There are vacancies in the group and I thought of you. It's last minute, I'm afraid. But Alison is coming and one or two other people you know–"

"Anne, it's good to hear from you. Yes, please I'd like to come." Perhaps I could find the answer out there.

"I don't suppose Ramon ... I tried to get in touch with him but he's not at the hotel." Her voice was hesitant, did she know, had she guessed?

"No, I think he went home."

Better not to tell her. Instead I asked: "When are you leaving?"

"Day after tomorrow. We're meeting at Heathrow at 4am. I'm sorry it's so early dear but it'll give us time to get settled in when we arrive there. Do you have a pen, I'll give you the travel agent's number."

"Megan. What are you doing here? You're the last person I expected to see." A hand forked through spiked hair.

Malcolm. Such a reassuring presence. Now I knew I'd be okay. If anything happened I could rely on Malcolm – and Alison. It was good to see her again. She was less like a secretary in her smart linen trousers and bright silk top. It was no surprise she was standing next to Malcolm. This was my family.

"It is good to make contact with you. I mislaid the number you gave me, left the book I scribbled it in on the plane, I think." Malcolm forked his hair again in that familiar gesture.

"I can't believe you're on a past life exploration workshop, Malcolm."

"Surprised me, I can tell you. But as I went on to other temples, it felt as though I'd been there before. I kept getting glimpses of what it had been like, smelt the incense, heard the priests chanting. I even found myself before a stela in Abydos chanting to the High Priest K'am Uast to keep him safe in the other world. When I researched it, I found there had actually been such a person and his false door – the entrance his spirit could use to get to the afterlife – was in the temple at Abydos. Shook me up for a while, I can tell you. I tried to put it out of my mind but then I saw this trip advertised and decided it was time to find out more. When the tour leader dropped out I thought that would be the end but I gather Anne stepped in at the last minute. She looks capable." He nodded towards Anne, and smiled warmly at Alison.

"Yes, she is. I've done work with her. I'll tell you both about it on the plane."

Swooping in to land, it was all so utterly familiar. Stepping into the dry, dusty air, with brilliant sunshine all around, Ra was lighting his celestial dome. That smell. There was nothing else quite like it, I was home. Now the answer would come. It was my turn to lead the way to where the visa man waited in his corner.

The boat was too big, too impersonal. I'd thought it would be small and intimate, that we'd be together as a group. But it towered over the others tied to the bank, the ones we'd crossed through to get here looked cozy, why ever were we on this monstrosity? How would I ever find my way round? My cabin was so far from the others, oh, why, I asked myself, did I come? That tiny porthole, all I could see was the river lapping at the window, it was so claustrophobic. I supposed I should unpack but I was tired, the journey must have taken more out of me than I thought, the wretched illness and the baby –

My self-pity was interrupted by a knock on the door.

"Malcolm, thank goodness. Come in."

"Don't bother to unpack, Megan. Anne has organized new cabins for us. Apparently there are only a handful of people on the boat so we've all got upper deck cabins with balconies and a comfortable lounge for the exclusive use of the group. Although there'll be a few other people on the excursions, it will be like having our own private cruise."

He grinned like a small boy invited to a birthday party.

"I'm so glad, to tell you the truth I was feeling horribly depressed down here in the bowels of the ship."

"You'll feel much better when you get up into the air. Come on." With that, he picked up my case and set off down the corridor and up the rather grand staircase.

"Here is the lounge."

A comfortable room with padded chairs clustered around small tables, and sun streaming in through large windows, the floor spread with bright Egyptian rugs. It looked comfortable enough, and the air conditioning made it cool.

"We'll be having afternoon tea in here and then Anne will tell us what to expect. After that we are off to the Sound and Light at Karnak. Did you go last time?"

"No, I meant to. Khaled said I should but I never made it."

Taking my arm, he walked me down an endless corridor. At least it seemed I'd be on the same floor.

"Not far now, the dining room's one floor down by the way. I forgot to show you but I'll take you down later. The Sound and Light is quite impressive in a theatrical sort of way, gives a real feel of the place – I'm sure the ancient Egyptians would have approved although they would have been surprised to find it actually taking place in the inner sanctum of the temple."

"But I seem to remember there were festivals all the time?"

"Yes, but plebs like us would have been confined to the outer courts. We must try to find Khaled, if only to say hello. See, here is your cabin, between mine and Anne's. Anne noticed you were looking a bit peaky and thought you would like to have people you know close by. Alison's just opposite by the way. "

He nodded to the anonymous brown door across the corridor.

"Have a quick lie down and I'll see you at four thirty." Smiling, he shut the door.

What a relief it was to be there, such a nice cabin, fresh and clean. The simple painted furniture made the room timeless in a funny sort of way. The balcony doors were thrown open to the afternoon breeze, letting in the sunlight – and carrying that unforgettable riverbank smell. How did I describe it to Ramon? Oh yes, the ghost of moldy cabbage with a hint of sewage and cocoa. There was a comfortable chair, with a view of the Peak of the West on the other side of the river. I'd sit there and admire the scene, never mind unpacking.

"... Between the excursions, we're going to be doing regressions as a group and I'll be available for extra one-to-one help if anyone feels the need. As there are only a few of us on the tour, we can do our meditations and maybe even an initiation or two in the temples. I've had a word with the guide, Josef, and he's used to taking groups like ours round. He'll show us the power spots and he's promised to tell us about the mythology and the rituals rather than the usual stuff he spouts for tourists."

"Isn't Josef an unusual name for an Egyptian, Anne?" Malcolm asked.

"Josef is a Coptic Christian; they're directly descended from the ancient Egyptians and their liturgical language is the same, so Josef could be said to have inside information on the Egyptian mysteries, although his English is not always clear, but you'll get the gist and I'll be able to help out, I've been here so often I know it by heart. I think Josef's rather looking forward to it."

All of a sudden, so was I.

Crossing the last gangplank in the ruby light of sunset, the air wavered and the hotel buildings collapsed, revealing low mud-walled dwellings – and the sheen of water all around. The old town of Waset, or should I call it Thebes, on its island mound. There, surely that was the causeway that led to Karnak. The ram-headed sphinxes glowed red as Ra slid beneath the horizon and Nuit spread her mantle for the night. It would be easy to step through to that other time. But could I return? If it wasn't for Ramon I wouldn't want to, I'd be quite happy to end my days back there in that other time, bringing my child up to serve the mysteries.

"Are you alright, Megan, you look a bit pale? Here, take my arm."

Courteous as ever, Malcolm helped me up the steep slope to the road.

"Hey, madam! Mr. Malcolm! Over here. You go Sound and Light?" Head swathed against the night, Khaled's dusky skin was barely visible under Nuit's mantle. All flashing eyes and white teeth, his smile was broad as he jumped down to greet us.

"Khaled. Hello. Yes, we are going to Karnak but we are here with a group ..." Malcolm gestured behind us.

"No problem." Josef materialized at our side. "As we are small group, we travel in style. Khaled and friends take us. Climb aboard. Only two to caleche, please, save horses."

It was good to be back in that comfortable leather seat, much nicer than a coach. Khaled had gone to greet Anne. From the way she'd thrown her arms around him they'd already met. Yes, he was bringing her over to join us.

"Anne, it seems we have a mutual friend." Malcolm beamed as Anne took her place up front and Khaled handed her the reins. She'd obviously done this before as she competently started the horse moving and turned out into the traffic. Calmly ignoring the angry hooting of a coterie of taxis, Khaled turned his back on the melee. He was busy imparting all his news to Anne but he wanted to include us.

"Another baby horse ... a baby daughter ... a new house ..."

"Wake up Megan, we have arrived." Malcolm's voice was gentle.

"Khaled, I'm sorry, how rude of me, I've been so tired ..."

"No problem madam, my wife like that when she have baby."

"Baby?" Malcolm was horrified. "Are you really pregnant, Megan? I wouldn't have thought a woman should travel here in that condition."

"Yes, I am, nearly four months and, I might as well be truthful, my illness has returned but I just had to come. The leukemia went into remission last time I was here. Anne, I'm sorry, I should have told you."

Anne was un-phased: "Don't worry, my dear. There's a very good doctor on the boat and Terri's an ex-nurse turned homoeopath. I'm sure we can cope. You can tell us about the illness later – if you want to, of course. But for now let's go and enjoy the Sound and Light."

Dark and shadowy walls rose into night, tops lost in darkness, a few torches pierced the gloom with pools of golden light. All around us, the rustle of palms. The way those statues of the gods were lit made them look alive. At any moment, one could get up and walk over to see what all the fuss was about. May they smile down on us with kindness.

Malcolm was right, it was just like it used to be. I could almost believe I was back there. I could hear the priests chanting, smell the incense, it was so strong – oh, that was Terri lighting a joss stick. Nice smell. The guardians seemed to agree, they were clamoring for one for themselves. Terri was such a generous soul she handed over all she had. Her ample bosom appealed to the Egyptians, she wouldn't get out of there without having her bum groped at least once.

At least our group contented themselves with incense. A loud-mouthed American who had been on the plane was shepherding her flock through the Hypostyle Hall and they were attired in full regalia. They were like something out of *Aida*, no wonder the guardians seemed to think they were going to slip off in the night and do something unspeakable. They'd got them penned in a corner. She kept offering the guardians money, but, for once, no one was taking it.

Over there was where Mek'an'ar had taken her journey with the goddess. Was that where that loud American wanted to go I wondered? It would be a potent place for ritual. Anne was planning to take us there. It was too dark to see My Lady's chapel, maybe I'd get a chance tomorrow ...

The seat was cold, it was a good thing Anne had suggested we take wraps and cushions with us. It was a good thing too that that American had taken her group down to the other end. I got such jangling vibes from them, what were they up to? The temple was particularly beautiful lit up at night, the changing colors wove a wonderful tapestry – it was almost like when the wall paint was fresh – and the music was dramatic.

"Welcome, travelers to Ancient Egypt. You are at the House of the Father ..."

"Asleep again, Megan?" Malcolm's face appeared out of the dim light.

"No, not at all, just remembering ... and trying to find answers."

"I've had some memories of my own." He was looking rather smug. "I now know who I was and there is plenty of evidence for what I remember. I cannot wait to tell the group."

Was that a frown that passed over Anne's face? Surely not, she was usually so equable. I'd have thought she'd be glad he was remembering, but she wasn't encouraging him, nor those other people who were clamoring around.

"Wait until tomorrow. We can share experiences then, when everyone can join in. We'll have plenty of time while we sail up to Edfu."

Sail? Edfu?

"Aren't we coming back to Karnak? I was looking forward to ..."

"Yes, of course, Megan, but after our trip up the river. We'll have several days here."

A quick cup of chai at the Cabman's Arms, a stop off for the bottled water Khaled assured us was much cheaper in the bazaar, and then he delivered us back to the ship.

I never did unpack. It was so hot I thought I wouldn't need nightclothes.

Big mistake. I hadn't given a thought to mosquitoes, they'd obviously been munching all night. I needed to get something for them, but not then, 6am was far too early, Ra's fingers were slowly creeping over the horizon. I still felt tired and a bit nauseous, so I'd give Esna a miss and wait for Edfu before I started temple gazing. I phoned Malcolm and let him know. Thank goodness breakfast was at a more civilized hour.

chapter 13.

Lady of the Many Faces

"Well, everyone, many of you said last night that you'd had memories surfacing at the Sound and Light. What I suggest is, we wait to discuss those until we've done the first group regression. You may well have more to add, or get a different slant on things."

Anne's glance around the circle gathered before her was brisk; she clearly wasn't giving anyone time to disagree. Reaching for a glass of water she picked up a book. How relaxed she looked, so competent and motherly. I was soothed simply by being with her.

"Before we start I want to read something to you. I found it years ago. It purports to be by the Nazarene – Jesus in other words. I think it explains how spontaneous past life memories surface: *'The Angel of Forgetfulness sometimes forgets to remove from our memories the records of the former world, and then our senses are haunted by fragmentary recollections of another life. They drift like torn clouds above the hills and valleys of the mind, and weave themselves into the incidents of our current existence.'*

"Our aim today is to catch those fragments and turn them into clear memory. I know most of you have heard this before but for the benefit of the one or two of you who don't know what to expect, I'll run through it and it will remind those of you who have worked this way before if you've forgotten ..."

As if I could forget; it was as clear to me then as it was when it happened. I hadn't forgotten a single moment. All I needed to know was why the illness had returned?

I must have been trying too hard, couldn't see anything, except a dark mist ... I wondered how Malcolm was getting on:

"Last night, when I heard the name Hatshepshut and the narrator told the story of her obelisk at the Sound and Light, I remembered how I'd felt when I saw the statue of Tutmoses the Third in Luxor Museum. It's a wonderful piece of sculpture, so noble. His face was familiar to me. The finely chiseled nose – I'd seen it somewhere before. And Hatshepshut: I knew her too. When I was here a few months ago and visited her temple, I became really angry. She'd usurped the power of the Pharaoh and I felt she was right to portray herself as the cow goddess, Hathor."

Malcolm glared around the room, sitting up straighter in his chair and gripping the arms:

"I knew instinctively that she'd taken advantage after her husband had died to snaffle control from a stepson who was still too young to fight her."

His hair was sticking out wildly as his fingers alternatively smoothed and ruffled. He'd looked like that that day at Karnak, when he rescued me. Never thought he'd be here doing this. Better pay attention, Mecky, you might miss something important:

"All this rubbish that is spouted about her standing up for women's rights. It wasn't true. She had a strong man behind her, a lover who pulled her strings. The bloody woman had the impudence to have the story of her, alleged, divine birth plastered all over her mortuary temple to bolster up her claim to the throne."

How unlike Malcolm. I'd never heard him be rude about anyone before. He certainly felt strongly about her. "I realized last night that I'd been that young Pharaoh, who was helpless when his stepmother started to wear a false beard and men's clothing, and had herself proclaimed Pharaoh instead of Regent. She kept me a virtual prisoner for twenty years. Eventually she sent me into the army and, although I was acknowledged as joint Pharaoh, she took all the decisions. She refused to stand down when I reached my majority.

"Just now, I relived the time when I regained control after her death. It made me feel really powerful, I can tell you, when that woman was finally put in her place and her memory wiped out. I recognized several people. Alison, you were my nursemaid, a kind of surrogate mother as you had cared for me from birth and comforted me when my real mother died. Hatshepshut overlooked you when she sent the people who cared about me away. No wonder I felt I knew you as soon as I saw you."

Alison nodded vigorously, she'd obviously seen something similar.

"You, Anne, I'm sorry to say this, you were Hatshepshut and you, Megan, were Senenmut, the architect-priest who was her lover and who helped her control the country. You were tutor to her daughter – although you acted more like a father. I think maybe she was your child."

Me? Anne's lover? I knew her but not in that way. Senenmut? I couldn't get any feel for it. I was reading about the female Pharaoh, a book I'd picked up at the airport, but nothing seemed familiar – mind you, I did admire her for standing up to all those men and taking her rightful place as her father's daughter. And what about changing sex? Had I been a man? Surely not, I didn't feel like I had been. I must ask Anne: "Anne, is it possible to change sex like that?"

"Yes, Megan, it is. In my experience, we have as many incarnations in male bodies as we do in female, although some people will feel happier in one body and others in another gender. In the between-life state people tend to revert to whichever sex feels comfortable – although the soul is genderless, of course. Malcolm, would you like to tell us more?"

"That is all there is to say. It was absolutely real to me, I'm sure I was Tutmoses." Arms folded across his chest, he glared defiantly around the room.

Anne's face was deadpan. She hadn't commented on what Malcolm saw but she knew her own past lives. Could she have been Hatshepshut? Before anything more could be said, Beatrice rose majestically to her feet:

"Actually, Malcolm, I was Hatshepshut. I could feel the false beard tickling my face, the stiff headdress around my head, the wig, and everything. I was a powerful and able woman and I saved the country when my brother-husband died and his son was too young to rule."

Beatrice stood ramrod straight; she was bristling as she challenged Malcolm. She certainly looked regal enough. Up went her head again:

"Yes, I had a man, a clever one who gave me enormous support but he certainly didn't pull my strings. The child was his. We were secretly married and one day we would have told the world but he died – killed by jealous courtiers. Soon afterwards, I was killed by my enemies and they dared to erase my cartouche from my great building works. With the loss of my name from the stories of my great acts, I was soon forgotten. My lover was a high priest and we made a spiritual marriage; I'd know him again anywhere. Megan certainly does not fit the bill. I know who he is, but he is quite famous and I am not going to say anything more."

She was blushing. Who could he be?

"Stephen, you were one of the men who killed him. You were jealous of his influence over me and you wanted me for yourself. My ex-husband was also involved in my death. Hardly surprising, considering the way he has treated me in this life."

Her tight lips twitched and I hoped we were not going to hear about that again. Stephen didn't look like a murderer. He was much younger than Beatrice, and a bit shorter, but nice looking. Seemed quite sensitive and rather quiet; I wasn't sure what their relationship was. She'd joked earlier about him being her toy boy but they were not sharing a cabin, she was in with Joan. Beatrice paid for his drinks and he followed her around willingly enough. He'd said when he'd introduced himself that he hadn't had any experience of past lives and didn't think he believed in them, but Beatrice had insisted he came along on the trip. He certainly didn't look convinced now.

"Well, Bea, actually, you know, I ...er ... don't think ... I'm not sure I ..."

It was a pity he was so submissive, she needed someone to stand up to her overbearing ways.

"Of course it was you! It explains why you pursued me so avidly in this present life." Her look was triumphant. "And you, Joan, you were there too. Only a servant, of course, but devoted to me. You'd been my nanny and never married so you could stay with me. You worshipped me."

Her friend was quietly skeptical. She didn't have much to say for herself when Beatrice was around but we'd had a good chat over breakfast. She'd got a sharp eye for what made people tick and her observations were funny without being cruel. It would be interesting to see how she'd handle Beatrice's Hatshepsut idea.

"As it happens, I didn't see anything like that, Bea. I was a wife and mother who enjoyed a peaceful life in Roman Egypt."

Beatrice was affronted. "You'll see, the memory will come back. I know that I'm right. And there were more of you involved ..." Those gimlet eyes were daring anyone to contradict her.

Several heads were nodding excitedly but Miranda jumped in.

"Can I tell you what I saw? I think, you know, that it could be true, although it seemed like something out of a novel. I certainly changed my gender."

Anne nodded: "By all means dear, go ahead."

"It is quite a sexy story. I found myself in a small village, which must have been close to Luxor because I could see that pyramid-shaped mountain hanging in the heat ..."

As her hands sketched a pyramid in the air, Miranda had everyone hanging on her words. She'd got a good voice, low and husky, and certainly knew how to tell a story – and how to exploit a dramatic pause.

"My name is Hormose, a lute player and singer. I am young and all I ever think about is music – rather like my present life, you know – I much prefer musicals to dramatic roles. My best friend is called Amenhotep. His elder brother is an important man at the Court and I beg him to get me a place there.

"Senenmut – that's his brother's name, brings me before Pharaoh for an audition. After I make my obeisance, flat on the floor, I sneak a look at the king. It is hard not to giggle. Pharaoh is clearly a woman although he – or do I mean she – wears a false beard and a man's pleated tunic with a big jeweled collar, and a linen headdress with a uraeus on the front."

Rather like that picture on the cover of my book, except there's no false beard. Did Miranda spot the book when I was reading it on the plane? She'd made a point of chatting to everyone and getting to know the group, nice girl.

"I could see that under the tunic her breasts were bound to make them look flat but they stuck up over the top. It was really funny. She tried to make her voice deep but it was too high to be a real man.

"Hormose is a good-looking young man, dark skinned but with shapely lips and wavy hair, and I sing well. When Pharaoh has heard several songs, she asks me if I dance. I do some gymnastic-type movements and her eyes follow me everywhere. It is extremely embarrassing, I feel like she is undressing me. She tells me to report to the Court music master.

"The music master is a blind harpist, positively ancient and so decrepit, hardly any hair left, only one tooth, and a scaly skin, but he's kind. He has a class all ages from little ones to my own age. Although he has no eyes, he doesn't miss a thing and if one of the dancers misses a step, he knows. After hearing me play, he sets me in charge of a group of young lutenists – real scallywags but fun to teach. Apart from my time with them, I have little work during the day. The best time is when we play at the temple – we have to be specially initiated in order to accompany Pharaoh onto the holy soil. Occasionally we have to practice for feasts or public festivals but I manage to swim in the river most afternoons."

It was hard to believe Miranda had been a young man but her

story had a certain ring to it. I couldn't put my finger on quite why, but it sounded true.

"Pharaoh often sends for me to play to her in the evenings, especially if she's alone. Much of the time, however, my friend's brother is with her. They are clearly intimate – they lie on the bed almost naked. It doesn't seem to worry them that I see this – and it is quite obvious that she's a woman. Quite often, he'll be caressing her and she'll look at me from under her eyelashes as she moves so that his hand is on her breast. I think she's deliberately teasing me."

Miranda's luscious young body had begun to move like a man. I knew she was an actress but this was something more. This was memory.

"One time, a young boy came in. She spoke sharply to him and sent him out of the room. Later I learned that this was her stepson. She was supposed to be Regent until he was old enough, but she'd clearly taken over as Pharaoh.

"Then Senenmut went on a long trip. By this time, Amenhotep is also at the palace, being trained as an architect. One day, Pharaoh comes upon us larking around in the garden. We have been swimming and have wet loincloths on. She orders me to join her in her private courtyard. I tell her I will have to fetch my lute but she says I won't need it – and casually adds that I might as well bring my friend along as well. He is even better looking than I am, and much taller. His mother was a captive from another land and he is striking looking, long golden-red hair and green eyes. The wet loincloth is transparent and moulds itself around his prominent genitals. Hatshepshut can't take her eyes off the bulge."

Suddenly Miranda was herself again, laughing at another woman's lust for that naked boy. Shaking her shoulders she continued:

"Pharaoh makes us wrestle in the nude and she oils us herself. I notice how her hand lingers when she reaches my private parts – and on Amenhotep too. He has quite an erection when we begin the bout but I'm too scared to respond to her attentions. My friend had been a champion wrestler when we were younger and he soon has me on the floor.

"By the time we've had three more bouts, everyone is breathing heavily. Pharaoh has the servants bring food and drink. Obviously word gets round because a rather pompous official arrives and announces that Pharaoh has people waiting for an audience. She looks cross but asks for a special crown and robe to be brought, puts on her false beard, and leaves. We are shooed out of the room and told to go about our business.

"Over the next few weeks, Pharaoh often sends for us. Sometimes I play while Amenhotep dances, other times we wrestle. The officious official always finds an excuse to break things up – actually Beatrice, he looked a lot like you."

That didn't go down too well. Beatrice drew herself up in her chair again. That woman's look could freeze hell.

"This is exactly the kind of over-the-top story I'd have expected from a professional actress." Her muttered aside to Joan was audible right across the room.

Anne's hand signal quieted her for the moment though.

"Late one night, we are summoned to Pharaoh's bedchamber. The excuse is insomnia but we can see she is strongly aroused. After pacing around for a while, she throws herself on her big, cushioned bed. She tells Amenhotep that his brother will return the next day and pats the bed invitingly. He joins her while I play the lute. He is stroking her all over her body – which arches and shudders. He is sexually experienced, all the women like him. He says his skill comes from handling a lute, his fingers are very sensitive and he can read their bodies. Then she starts to fondle him. It is extremely erotic, and I'm feeling very randy, but I'm not quite sure what to do when she beckons me to join them. I have never made love to a woman, and this is Pharaoh, the living god."

And she was just an embarrassed boy. How alive Miranda made it, I could almost step into the picture with her.

"Suddenly the officious official rushes in with some guards and shouts, 'Kill the intruders.' Next thing I know, I'm looking down at my body which has a dagger sticking out of it, and they are stabbing Amenhotep with lances. Our bodies are bundled up and thrown into another room. When Senenmut arrives back the next day, he is told his brother and I had been mistaken for intruders. He is heartbroken and has us taken to his own tomb where we are interred together after the proper mummification rituals are completed."

Before Anne could say anything, Beatrice cut in quickly, her tightly pursed lips making it difficult for her to speak with her usual booming projection.

"Well, I certainly wasn't an officious official and I didn't have you killed. I was Hatshepshut, and several of those present were my servants." She was in a towering rage, out of her chair and pacing around like a caged lion.

Anne leant forward: "Please sit down again, Beatrice. I know your experience probably seemed very real to you and to Malcolm, but I'm sorry to have to tell you that almost every group who've gone down the Nile and 'remembered' a life in Egypt came up with the Hatshepshut story. This has happened a bit earlier in the trip than with most groups. It usually surfaces around day three."

Smiling, Anne picked up a piece of paper.

"I think this about sums it up. It's by, I believe, a guy called Jay Gatz. He wrote it about a town in America, but it could just as easily be Egypt.

"The past is everywhere,
If you listen,
For that is not the wind you hear,
It is the whispering ghost of yesteryear."

Turning to put the paper on the table, she continued: "Hatshepshut is a common enough 'memory' even for people who've never been to Egypt – the singer Tina Turner thought she was Hatshepshut and came here looking for confirmation, and there have been many other claimants."

"So what's going on then Anne?" Joan asked quietly; she's obviously used to Beatrice's rages.

"This is what I call a 'fantasy in fancy dress.' They can be extremely vivid and it can be difficult to tell the difference between personal memory and plugging into a story that belongs to a particular place or person – a kind of virtual reality program, as it were, that's been left behind by events that anyone can step into for a while."

"Why Hatshepshut, Anne?" Mary jiggled as though she was bursting to say something more but Anne went on.

"Hatshepshut made a strong impact on the land – probably because, after she died, someone made a determined effort to erase her memory and she was lost to history for so long. I think it's unlikely that our group were major players in her drama."

"What about me? It felt absolutely real, you know? Exactly like the regressions I've done before. Could what I saw have been true?" Lower lip thrust over the upper, Miranda was bewildered. I knew exactly how the poor girl must be feeling.

"Well, Miranda, you came up with a story that is not in the history books and which sounds to me like it could well have been a true remembering, although even so, it may not have been your own memory. You could have been picking up on the Hatshepshut theme and plugged into a real story from that time. Then again, of course, you could have been there. They were minor characters so it's more likely than if you'd remembered being Hatshepshut for instance. It's impossible to tell for sure, so let's see what else emerges this week, but you had better do some healing and reframing on that death, just in case. Remember to take the dagger out and heal the place where it was before you do any more exploration."

Miranda nodded thoughtfully and rubbed her shoulder.

"It certainly felt like me. And, you know, that dagger going in was incredibly real – I've got a scar there in my present life. I've never wrestled, or played the lute in my life, but now I know exactly what it feels like – and I could feel the weight of my penis against my leg, and against my belly when it got hard – and I've certainly never experienced that in this life."

The thought of Miranda's voluptuous body having a penis made everyone smile, releasing some of the tension, but Malcolm wriggled uncomfortably, almost squirming in his chair. This was all new to him and he was bound to have doubts, especially as he seemed certain he'd found out who he was. He wasn't going to let it go.

"What else can distort memory, Anne? Is it possible to regurgitate a book, for instance?"

"Yes, Malcolm, there've been quite a few instances of that. People, or groups, also unconsciously go back to things that they've seen on television or a film. Shortly after *Braveheart* came out there was a group of people in the North of England who believed they were William Wallace and his compatriots. But they all 'remembered' something that had been put in to make the film dramatic but which hadn't actually happened. Fact and fiction got mixed up."

"Why did people believe it?" Malcolm no longer seemed so angry, he was more intrigued than anything.

"The leader of the group was a charismatic, and plausible, man and when he said it was so, people were flattered to think they'd been with him – it made them feel important, as though they had a place in history. People can respond to these suggestions partly because of ego and wishful thinking, and partly because the theme resonates with something inside themselves – in essence it is their story in disguise, as it were."

Sunlight suddenly flooded through the window. The boat was moving quickly upriver now and we'd suddenly swung around. Shading my eyes with my hand, I moved to pull the blinds. Yes, the river was making quite a sharp bend here. Beyond the window, a ubiquitous mud-walled town slept in sun.

"Why would I think I was a man over whom such a strong woman had control?" Malcolm's lips were pursed and Anne was gentle with him:

"Well, Malcolm, I remember you telling me that when you first came to Egypt with the army all those years ago you went home determined to be an archaeologist but your mother insisted that you work as a civil engineer in the family business. Do you think there's any kind of resonance there?"

Her question was met with silence. Malcolm shuffled even more, head turned away, twiddling that piece of hair round and round his finger. Perhaps I could divert attention from him.

"Anne, I've been meaning to ask you. Why is it Egypt features in so many regressions and past life memories?"

"That's a good point, Megan. No one seems surprised to have had several incarnations in Christian times – spread over the last two thousand years. Egyptian civilization actually lasted for a lot longer than that – at least three and a half thousand years in dynastic times and who knows how long before that, and even though it was a small country it was highly populated and an important staging post for people's spiritual development. The temples offered special training in healing and mystical vision, as well as practical magic, so it doesn't surprise me that, if developing these kind of gifts was on your agenda, you would have incarnated two or three times in Egypt and perhaps more. As we've all found, the country still has a special fascination."

She picked up her bag and half rose:

"But now, it's time for lunch."

Behind me, Beatrice was talking loudly to Joan: "I know who I was. Just wait until tonight. They'll have to take notice of me. I'll show Miranda I wasn't a trumped-up palace official. When I ..."

Ah well, no doubt Anne could handle her.

"Megan, do you know how I remember the female Pharaoh's name?" Terri whispered in my ear.

"Do tell me." From the grin on her homely face, this would be good.

"It's easy. Hot Chicken Soup."

It felt like Beatrice was throwing daggers at our backs – I guess she didn't like our laughing out loud but it felt so good to laugh. I needed a bit of light relief. Perhaps that was what past life therapy was: hot chicken soup for the soul.

In the afternoon regression, there was still nothing but that gray mist. Had I lost the ability to travel back in time, just when my need was greatest? I must talk to Anne about it over tea. Meanwhile, I dozed quietly whilst the others dreamed their dreams. The motion of the boat was soporific and the repetitious sand beyond the windows soothed my eyes. I'd sightsee later; for now, I slept.

"It could be that you are trying too hard, of course. I know how anxious you are to find answers to your illness. But there could be another reason. Sometimes people find themselves stuck in the outer deep, it's a kind of non-place. Not quite in the other world but not here either."

Her hands moved this way and that as she tried to draw this place that was neither here nor there. Beyond the rail, endless sand unfurled, rather like the outer deep. It was pleasant up here on deck, after a time that air-conditioned atmosphere in the lounge seemed stale. It was good to smell the river again.

"How would I have got there?"

"Souls could be banished to this void after they died to prevent them interfering with plans they wouldn't have supported. Did you know the ancient Egyptians believed the dead could interact with the living?" She'd put down her cup and had her teacher face on; this should be good.

"No, not really."

"A letter was found attached to a statue of a woman. It was from her husband asking his dead wife to desist from interfering in his life. Apparently he believed she'd bewitched him and caused a deep depression from which he couldn't escape."

Grinning, Anne picked up her cake and bit into it.

"What could he have done about it, got her exorcised?"

"More or less. In cases like that spells would be said, offerings made, and rituals carried out to appease the *ka*. But what I'm talking about is rather more serious than that. Someone, usually a priest, actually carried out a ritual to banish the *akhar*, or soul essence, to the outer deep –"

"Oh yes, that happened to Mek'an'ar after her death. The priest who wanted her power banished her – and he cursed her and the child. It didn't stop me incarnating again though, and I'd have thought that without my soul that wouldn't be possible."

"Well, Megan, the soul is a complex thing. Not at all the single entity we in the West have traditionally seen it as. The ancient Egyptians recognized at least five different facets to it and I think there are probably more than that. The *akhar* carried spiritual power from life to life. One of the stages of initiation involved journeying to retrieve the *akhar*." Her gray eyes were intent.

"Yes, I remember doing that when I was Shen-whatever-it-was, that life I saw with Ronald. Queen Tiye sent her to find her *akhar*. It was the last thing they achieved before the temple fell. Do you think there's more to it? "

"Well, it's certainly possible, I think we should do a one-to-one session so that you can undertake that journey for Mek'an'ar and yourself. You probably need to break the curse too."

That thought sent a shudder through me.

"I meant to talk to you about that. I think the night terrors and sleep paralysis I had as a child, which went on into adulthood, have something to do with Greg and the curse. I had an attack of sleep paralysis when he found out about Ramon and I told him I was definitely going to divorce him without a settlement. Although the attack wasn't by a person, I still felt it was Greg's energy. Could that be true?"

And the past was so close. That village on the far bank looked just like old Waset, Thebes in its heyday. Nothing had changed here in several thousand years.

"More than likely. He wouldn't be doing it consciously, of course, especially when you were both young, but things like that have a nasty habit of hanging around on the etheric level and being activated whenever someone gets angry, and from what you've told me, Greg is very angry indeed, and feeling cheated. That would be more than enough to set a curse in motion again."

"Is there anything I can do?"

"You'd better buy an Eye of Horus amulet like this."

From her blouse she drew out a bold, stylized gold, red, and blue eye like I'd seen on so many stalls full of tourist tat. Could that really help me? It seemed unlikely but Anne was the expert. Tucking the charm back into her blouse, Anne went on:

"That'll protect you. You'll be able to get one when we go to the temple tomorrow."

"And what about breaking the curse, can we do that there?"

"It would be more appropriate to do this work when we return to Karnak. In the meantime, you could explore other lives, perhaps not as closely related to Egypt. Now, let's have some more tea, and more of those delicious cakes."

Her smiling wave brought a waiter hurrying to her side. I did like that boat.

"Will you look at that." Miranda had her hand to her mouth trying to stifle her giggles. "I've never seen anything quite like it."

Neither had I. I'd quickly bought a djellabah and necklace from the gift shop when I'd found this 'Come as you were' party had been organized. Beatrice must have shopped at a theatrical costumiers before she left home.

"She looks like something out of *Aida*. I raided the charades box at home, you know, and couldn't come up with anything half as splendid." Miranda wiggled her hips, twitching her belly expertly like a very sexy dancing girl, but she was right, she couldn't match Beatrice for impact.

"What's going on here, ladies?" Malcolm was imposing in his blue robe, a striped headdress taming his wayward hair: "Oh my, words fail me. She looks like a golden wedding cake."

So she did. Her full-length golden robe, liberally iced with gold braid, was girdled with yet more gold, a huge golden menat collar sat above her shelf of a bosom. But it was her headdress that took my breath away. A tall golden crown with a serpent rising out from the front. It made Beatrice look seven feet tall.

No wonder she'd had so much luggage: that lot needed a suitcase all its own, especially as she'd decked Stephen out in an outfit that was almost as theatrical. He kept pulling his short kilt down but it had got a long way to go before it met his knees. It was clearly made for a much shorter man, though it showed off his legs well. Did the ancient Egyptians really wear boxer shorts I wondered? Beatrice had even persuaded Joan to don a servant's gown, or what, I'm sure, was Beatrice's idea of one. Dowdy in the extreme.

"Well, everyone, what do you think? I told you I was Hatshepshut." Beatrice did a stately twirl and smirked, well pleased with the impact she was making.

A couple who'd joined the boat before us sat on a low divan in a far corner of the bar. He was reclining back with a shisha and from the smell Mr. Robert's wacky baccy had found its way on board. His eyes bulged and her mouth was hanging open. Germans I thought, although they'd kept themselves apart from us so I wasn't sure. Clearly neither had seen anything like this before. Come to that, neither had I.

"Clothes do not make the man, or rather the Pharaoh." Malcolm's voice boomed across the sudden silence.

"Come on everyone, let's have a parade and the others can guess who we are. Josef, you can be the judge of the most appropriate costume." Miranda glided to the front, figure shown off to great advantage in her skimpy, diaphanous top and long, baggy see-through trousers, her coal-black eyes peeping coquettishly round a face veil. On her head, a jeweled circlet sat with raised cobra hood. "Now who do you think I was?"

"Pharaoh's favorite tart?" Stephen grinned, and then recoiled as Hot Chicken Soup rounded on him:

"Don't be so bloody ridiculous."

Miranda waved a rubber snake in her face.

"*You* could not possibly have been Cleopatra." Beatrice's lip curled.

Such scorn, she certainly resonated with the arrogant Pharaoh archetype. Now, Mecky, don't be so judgmental, I had to tell myself.

Hastily I looked around the bar. The bar boys were busily polishing glasses but I could hear the murmured commentary and catch the low laughter. As one turned to the optics at the back of the bar, his laughing face was reflected in the shining mirror behind them. Seeing me, he winked and shrugged. He must have seen this a thousand times before.

"Only kidding," said Miranda cheerfully. "It was all I could find and I thought I must have been in a harem somewhere or other, always fancied myself as a belly dancer, you know." She gave a few expert gyrations. "Never thought I'd turn out to be a toy boy instead."

Ouch. Beatrice wasn't rising to the bait:

"Well, we all know who I was. Alison, what about you?"

Alison's plain gray robe and headscarf could be anything, her beautiful brown eyes were lowered, and her cheeks pink.

"Any ideas anyone?" Hot Chicken Soup had clearly taken over as ringmaster to this past life circus, perhaps no one would notice if I slipped away.

"Megan, where do you think you are going? We haven't yet got to you. Who do you think Alison was?"

"A priestess of Mut?"

Alison shook her head. "Not this time, sorry."

"Well, you'd better tell us." Beatrice clearly wasn't happy for her to have too much attention.

"Well, like Malcolm said, I was a nursemaid to the young Pharaoh and I stayed on as one of the servants when he grew too old to need me as a surrogate mother, but I always loved him as though he was my own son. I don't care what you think, I know Malcolm's right. He was Tutmoses." She was fighting back tears and Mary put an arm around her, shielding her from Beatrice.

Well, that was a surprise. I hadn't thought Alison had it in her to stand up to Beatrice, nor to Anne for that matter. Where was Anne anyway?

"Malcolm, have you seen Anne?"

"Not since supper. She said she was tired after the early start and was going to have a lie down before the party. She's probably fallen asleep. Shall I go and see?" He turned towards the door.

"No, I'll do it, I could use some air." And a chance to escape.

No reply from Anne, what should I do? Leave her to sleep? She'd been working really hard and could be taking the opportunity to rest. I might as well slip into my cabin for a snooze myself.

Was that vomiting I could hear? The walls were thin, there was no privacy. It must be Anne, I'd better check she was okay. Perhaps I'd give her a few minutes and phone.

There was still no reply. Was her cabin door locked? Damn. The boys would be round to turn the beds down soon, they'd have a key, I'd ask them.

"I've never succumbed on previous visits. A herbalist gave me some Chinese pills before I left, in case, but I can't find them, could you look ... there in that sponge bag, little brown ones."

Anne's face was deathly pale and her normally immaculate hair ratty and greasily gray. If she felt anywhere near as bad as she looked, she must feel truly dreadful. Now where were those pills? Ah, there, those must be the ones. Where was that recycled Nile Water we had to drink on board – were they sure all the bugs had been sterilized out of it? Could that have something to do with Anne's bugs? Surely they could have sold us mineral water instead.

"I need to take them all." She grimaced, holding her stomach.

"Really, the whole lot? Okay, hold on and I'll help you. There, how's that?"

Anne's smile was wan but she'd kept those pills down.

"Do you want me to find the doctor?"

"Heavens, no. He'd dose me with some dreadful antibiotic cocktail, you heard what he said at the welcome meeting. I was assured these will do the trick. I'll be alright in the morning."

And she was, but there were only five of us at breakfast.

"I'd better take some of my magic potions round," Terri said, getting up. "After my experiences last time, I made sure I brought plenty along. Are you sure you four are alright? Megan? You can have some of this Arsenicum if you like, it's really good for sickness and mild food poisoning – and it's quite safe to take homoeopathics when you're pregnant, you know, Megan."

"Does it do much for nausea, I'm still suffering it most of the day?"

Queasily I rubbed my stomach. It felt like I'd drunk fizzy lemonade too quickly and a huge burp could escape at any moment. Only it might not be a burp. Best not to think about that.

"It should. Here, I'll give you some and we'll see how you go. Take one now, dissolve it under your tongue, and another in about half an hour. If it doesn't have any effect, let me know before we go to the temple and I'll give you something else to try."

The tiny pills were marvelous, the effect almost instantaneous. I hoped they would work as well for Pharaoh's Revenge.

"Everyone, come and look at this. It must be Edfu." Beatrice beckoned imperiously from the door.

As we reached the deck, the view was stunning. In the near

distance, a white town spread along the riverbank and rose above the rooftops, dominating even the minaret of the mosque. Behind, a dark stone temple loomed like the sails of a ship floating on a sea of houses.

I went to fetch my hat and my camera, wondering who would join us on the trip.

chapter 14.

Ruler of serpents and of dragons

A clutch of caleches awaited us on the bank. Swiftly we were borne through the quiet streets and into the bustle of the tourist stalls at the temple entrance. Josef strode forward between two huge stone pylons.

"Here would have been gates." He gestured to the deeply incised walls harboring deep shadows where Pharaoh was defeating his enemies. Or, as Josef had told us the previous day, the divine self was overcoming the lower nature.

As we stepped into a courtyard, the light was blinding. Heat bounced off the flagstones at our feet. No wonder Josef had suggested we should arrive here early.

Stone hawks almost the size of a man guarded the entranceway to the temple buildings. Their chiseled profiles were Ramon's face set in stone.

"Here Lord Horus." Josef said. "This his temple. Here we hear his story."

Coming to a stop before a section of wall, he announced: "You standing before one of greatest libraries in ancient world."

Hieroglyphs stood out sharply against the early morning light but there were no books out there. What could he be talking about? It was difficult enough to understand his broken English, which always seemed to get worse when he got excited – and he was positively fizzing now. He didn't seem to understand the use of verbs, but then neither did most of the Egyptians I'd talked to. The huge walls towered all around, it felt quite intimidating. Not at all like the libraries I was used to. But Josef was continuing:

"Everything put on temple walls for those with eyes to see, to read and understand. Here, outside main temple where crowds gathered at festivals and feast days, and where sacred dramas enacted. Reliefs on courtyard walls spoke to people, like picture books today. Inside, language on walls directed to initiates and priests. Remember, always inner and outer meaning to stories. Translation of picture book in front you, here."

He pointed to a section of the wall and handed round tattered sheets that looked like a script.

"Miranda, you Isis and Stephen, young Horus. Who like be reader?" He nodded encouragingly.

Beatrice stepped forward. Pharaoh's scourge wouldn't have dared attack her. She'd got her amateur dramatics face on, and she towered over Josef as she waved imperiously for a script. No doubt she thought she'd done this before. Watch it, Mecky, you're being bitchy again, I told myself. That woman brought out the worst in me. Drawing herself up to her full height she squared her shoulders, took a breath that shot her stomach out another foot and began:

"Horus, Great God and Lord of the Sky
Falcon Lord, with dappled feathers, who comes forth from the horizon.
A hero of great strength who sails into battle

With his mother Isis protecting him."

Not bad, a bit declamatory but dramatic, but could Stephen match it?

"I cause your majesty to prevail against him that is rebellious
towards you.
On the day of the fight, I put valor and strength into your arms
And the might of my hands into your hands."

Surprisingly strong, his voice rolled around the courtyard. He was a good actor and played up to Beatrice well.

"Isis the great, mother of the god, the Scorpion who nurses the
Falcon of Gold."

Miranda should do Isis rather well.

"I fortify your heart, Horus my son, I strengthen your arm,
Pierce the great hippopotamus, your father's foe."

Her script wobbled as she spoke and her voice didn't have its usual resonance. She'd sat down very abruptly when we arrived in the courtyard and she clearly wasn't going to get up now. Pharaoh's Revenge certainly lived up to its name.

"Long live the Good God, the son of the Victorious Horus.
An excellent offspring. A bold man from the marshes.
Valiant in the chase. The archetypal Man.
Horus the warrior, the anchor.

Lord of Valor, Son of Ra. May he live for ever, the blessed Horus, beloved of Ptah."

Wow, Beatrice had really got into the spirit of that last bit. Perhaps I'd misjudged her. For a moment I could see her in costume.

"That's all very well, Josef, but what does it mean?" Mary's face was pale and peevish. I hoped she wasn't coming down with Pharaoh's Revenge again.

"This allegory. Horus Set myth conflict between good and evil. On one level god help Pharaoh overcome enemies. Hippopotamus Set."

Anne broke in:

"Set represents great cycles of time, and incarnation into matter."

Josef nodded and Anne continued:

"This is the story of all the births, deaths, and rebirths that occur in each life and in the larger whole."

But Josef took over again:

"Set protector god who stand in prow solar barque when Ra travels into Duat to battle serpent Apopep. He keep forces of chaos at bay so creation, earth, hold steady."

I was getting the picture. But were all the guides like this? From the ones I'd heard at Luxor, some were better than others. Josef certainly knew his stuff, but he'd have benefited from some English lessons.

"Wasn't he the one who cut Osiris to pieces?" Miranda had obviously heard the story before.

"Yes, is right. Isis gather pieces together and join by spell. She hover over body and conceive Horus. Set sworn enemy of Osiris but defeat by Horus, magical son born after Osiris death. Horus resurrection and rebirth."

"What's the inner story then Josef?"

How could anyone resist her wan smile? Josef seemed about to speak but Anne stepped in:

"Set represents the material, earthy energies of the incarnated self."

"What about Horus?" Miranda seemed to have forgotten her shakiness. Did this have special meaning for her?

"Horus represents spirit. He is the divine part of a human being that is not trapped in matter. When he plunges his harpoon into Set, he kills the outworn portions of personality so that the spiritual self can emerge. But, in his role as magical protector, he guards against evil taking over. The Horus myth is a symbol of rebirth, is that not so Josef?"

Josef nodded happily.

"Speaking of rebirth," Anne glanced pointedly at her watch, "Josef's arranged for us to go down into the crypts. We can do an ancient rebirth ritual there. We're going to leave our bodies and journey through the underworld. As we pass through the gates we'll leave pieces of ourselves behind that we've outgrown and which no longer serve us until at last we come stripped and naked to the core of ourselves. Finally, we'll be reborn."

"Anne, do we have to do this? I'm not feeling too good." Mary was sweaty and anxious, her pale face such a contrast to her usual high color. Another middle aged, man-less woman, strange how this trip had attracted so many.

"No, it's entirely up to you. The crypt is a powerful place – but exceedingly claustrophobic, and this is a graphic experience so anyone who doesn't feel ready for this, or who is easily spooked, should stay above ground. You can either continue to look around the temple or go back to the boat – the caleches are waiting for you. Most of us have already done the purging and purifying that would normally precede this ritual thanks to the scourge of Pharaoh. So, if you're ready, those of you who want to do the ritual, follow Josef." She waved us forward.

I wasn't sure I was ready. The temple was so gloomy, there was no light coming down from the heavy stone roof. I knew it was blazing sunlight outside, but in there it was hard to see. It felt creepy. I hadn't liked the look of the entrance in the floor, a small black hole, and it had sounded really doomful when the guardian pulled up the stone slab, definitely a horror movie set. To distract myself, I wondered how many people had walked over the entrance without realizing what was below? But it didn't work. Those stairs were terribly narrow and the bottom was pitch black, claustrophobia was crawling up my spine already. Josef said there were several crypts that we could explore but we'd have to bend low. It didn't sound like my sort of thing.

Still, as I'd gone that far I might as well give it a go, but I made sure I was last in case I wanted to bail out. Yes, as I'd thought, the stairs were narrow, I couldn't see my feet in the dark but the steps felt worn and chipped, it was easy to slip. How did Beatrice fit down there, she was a big lady? Nothing seemed to intimidate her though. Head raised high, she'd led the way. Once I got to the bottom I decided, right, that was far enough, I'd stay right there.

I hadn't realized Josef would close the entrance slab, though. Pitch-black didn't describe it. It was blackness congealed. If I put my hand out the air resisted, I couldn't push against it. It wasn't an absence of light, there was something eating the light. And it was so cold, my backbone was shivering. How could initiates have spent twenty-four hours there in the dark, alone? There were ten people close by but the few seconds since the torch went out had given me the heebie-jeebies. I couldn't breathe, black air was pressing on me, the walls were closing in. I could hear the stones grinding together as they moved closer and sense the skittering of scorpions, smell the musk of sharp-toothed rodents, and the decay of the tomb.

Silently I urged Anne to hurry or I'd have to leave. There were demons and unspeakable things of the night crowding in, horned beings and serpents crawling near. I knew there was a huge black hooded cobra waiting to strike, and a strange triple-headed beast swallowing the light. I bet those old priests conjured them up and forgot to banish them again. They'd attack at any moment, they didn't know how many thousands of years had passed.

Get a grip, Mecky, I told myself, you know how to fight them. It's all a matter of mind. Of course, I'd done this before. It was an illusion. If I stood firm, I could send them back where they belonged. My Lady would protect me.

"Be gone foul beasts and creatures of the depths of night. Return to him that sent you. Be gone great snake that waits to strike, resist me not. Return to your lair. Be gone triple headed demons of Set, return to the far reaches of the desert to him who made you. Be gone in the name of light.

Walls stand firm, hold your place. Protect those who come in light. Protect us."

I didn't know where that had come from, but I could get comfortable now. Might as well lie back, the bottom step made a

173

handy stone pillow – and it was really warm. Suffocatingly hot in fact but it was best not to dwell on that.

"Allow your *ka*, the etheric self to stand up, to leave the physical body behind. Before setting off, hear the invocation: *My cavern is opened, the spirits fall within the darkness. The Eye of Horus makes me holy. Wepwawet has caressed me, O Imperishable Stars, hide me among you. May the immortal ones protect me.*"

I could see again, a bit shadowy rather like looking through night glasses, but clear enough. A misty halo surrounded each person, some blending together, others were more sharply defined.

"You appear before the Interrogator who asks, Who are you who comes?

You reply: I am an initiate.

Is your motive pure?

It is pure.

Is your mind clear?

It is clear.

Is your heart open?

It is open.

Are you whole?

I am whole.

Are you equipped?

I am equipped.

Are you ready to become Adept?

I am ready.

Are you ready to be reborn?

So be it.

Go forth.

As you approach the first gate, strip off your clothes and leave them before the gate, putting off the outward appearance that you showed to the world."

Mmm, must have left mine behind with my body, I could see right through myself.

"Hold your head high, take your courage in both hands and step past the guardians of the gate."

That wasn't so bad. Three animal-headed beings. Serpent-head hissed a bit but the hare and the dog were quiet. I thought they'd be much more fierce than that.

"As you approach the second gate lay before it your inner appearance, the picture you have of yourself."

The lion-headed being was rather fierce but a look cowered him. The man and the dog stood well back. What was next?

"As you approach the third gate, lay before it your personality."

I was beginning to feel a bit bare by now. Hardly noticed the jackal-headed being until he took a swipe at me. Once again, the dog and the serpent stood back; it seemed like, although there was always three, only one had a go at a time.

"As you approach the fourth gate, step out of your ego, the constricting small-self."

That felt good. The man, the hawk, and the lion-headed beings nodded in approval.

"As you approach the fifth gate, leave your past behind you, let your programming fall away, your patterns dissolve."

That was better, much lighter, I could see them spiraling away into the darkness, shattering into interstellar dust.

"As you approach the sixth gate lay before it your hopes and wishes for the future."

That was a hard one, what about my child – and my health, and seeing Ramon again. That hawk was looking intently at me.

The serpent was ready to strike. Only the man-being nodded encouraging. Better do as she said.

"At the seventh gate, lay before it your family, your parents, your partner, your children."

How could I leave Ramon behind? Such anguish. And my child. To see my baby lying there, it was breaking my heart. What if those jackal-headed beings ate him? No, this was too much, I couldn't do it. I'd already let my sister go, and I had no one else in the world. But trying to snatch my baby up again, my hands passed through his body. I had to leave him. Come on, onward and upward, I told myself, though the path moved steeply down.

"As you approach the eighth gate, bring to mind all the names you have been known by. Lay them before the gate. Step through with no name."

It was strange to have no name, no identity. Now I really felt stripped, as though I no longer existed. That dragon-like creature soon had them consumed with its breath.

"As you reach the ninth gate, lay before it your etheric self. Fly forth in your *ba*, the soul bird."

That was brilliant, flying free ... I could travel more quickly now, anxious to get out, surely I must be nearly there.

"And at the tenth gate, leave your *akhar*, your soul essence.

Strange, but I didn't seem to have that with me.

"At the eleventh gate lay your I, your sense of individuality, of self."

My I, what would be left? What would I be if I wasn't an I? Oh ... what was that?

In a chamber of flames, Sekhmet, The Terrible One, The Lady of the Bloodbath stood watching, her stance implacable, with the totally absorbed, unhurried stare of a lion surveying her prey. Her eyes reflected the flickering flames. This was her in destroyer mode. And yet she looked almost playful.

No, no, no ... surely not that ...

Turning, she ripped me to pieces, pulling off arms and legs, separating the torso, tossing the head aside, tearing out the heart, eating lungs and stomach, unwinding intestines, taking my life ... Flames shot around her, she was the Wrath of Ra. No, my Lady, no ... Small, sharp toothed rodents slobbered over my entrails, triple-headed beasts crunched my bones. I was consumed by flame.

I descended into night, looked on my dismemberment, saw my death. There was nothing left, I was extinguished.

The great heartbeat of time paused –

Terror fissioned into understanding. Pure spirit, all that Is. Such peace, blissful, bathed in light. In all things, of all things, no separation now. Light eternal. Spirit unceasing.

No time passes in eternity.

"And then step through the final gate, into the twelfth level of the Duat to meet Anubis."

A black, jackal head, with fearsome fangs, holding a feather, the feather of Maat.

My heart was being weighed against the feather of Maat, Divine Justice. It balanced perfectly. The Devourer of Souls slunk away; there was no task for him today.

"Enter into the presence of the Lord Osiris. Lay an offering before him. Petition for a good rebirth."

A great green god, sprouting corn from every orifice.

I didn't want rebirth. I wanted to stay there forever.

But no, I was being molded, shaped like clay. I was on Ptah's wheel and he was breathing me back to life. Quickly, I checked the spleen and the blood. It looked good, and the child? A shining being, one of the bright ones.

"Go forth with blessings, my child," the Lord Osiris sent me on my way. Power poured into me. The portal burst open, I was reborn into sunlight.

"To me belongs everything, and the whole of it has been given to me. I went in as a falcon. I came out as a phoenix; the Morning Star has made a path for me, and I enter in peace in to the beautiful East. I have been in the Garden of Osiris, and a path is made for me so that I may go in and worship Osiris the Lord of life."

Amen to that.

The torch was blinding.

"Megan, could you lead the way back up the stairs. If you shout, Josef will have the guardians open the slab."

Fumbling blindly, I rushed up the stairs, night vision gone now I was back in my ordinary body. Anne's torch didn't reach that far. As I shouted to Josef, for a moment nothing happened and there was the awful weight of that stone slab pressing down on me. What if he couldn't hear me? Deep breaths, don't panic now I told myself. The slab grated and a halo of light appeared, and expanded rapidly. Josef's head was outlined against it. Before the guardian could turn to help me, I was out, taking deep breaths of fresh, cool air. God, that felt better. I was reborn.

I couldn't believe how I took these weird things for granted now. A few months ago I'd have freaked out at that. Even if it was a product of an overactive imagination, it felt right, I knew it'd had an effect on my illness, like a car being stripped down and completely rebuilt. I was much stronger and couldn't wait to get back and have another blood test. I was sure I was in remission again even if I couldn't say cured. But I would be, I just needed to find the key. Josef had told me Sekhmet's action was always appropriate, she destroyed only what needed to be let go. She never did things randomly, she moved in accordance with *ma'at*, universal harmony. By tearing apart my old self she'd helped me to be reborn, to move out of my past. It must help my healing process, surely?

"That was an experience best digested alone to avoid dissipating the effect. I suggest you don't discuss it with anyone until tomorrow – unless you have something you need to talk to me about, in which case let me know and we'll arrange a time."

Anne shepherded us towards the sunlight, was she as anxious to get out of there as I was?

"Tonight is a free night, there's a folk show on the boat after supper that you might like to attend, or you could spend the time quietly reviewing what happened. Now, if everyone's here, we'd better run the gauntlet of the bazaar buzzards and get back to the ship."

"What are the bazaar buzzards? Another strange ritual from ancient times?" Malcolm had one eyebrow raised.

"No, that's what my husband calls the boys who come rushing up to sell you things – says they look like buzzards circling round waiting to go for the kill. But you're right, getting past them is like an initiation ritual. You can't call yourself an experienced Egyptian traveler until you can pass by without being persuaded to buy. Come on or we'll miss tea."

I knew where I'd be tonight – in my bed. I didn't think I'd forget that experience in a hurry.

Close by the caleche was a small dark shop in which I saw the gleam of gold. A handsome man beckoned to me:

"Lady, come, I have Eye of Horus to protect you."

Should I go? Anne said one would be helpful and he wasn't like those buzzards we'd just passed. He had a quiet dignity.

"Come on Megan, this is just the place." Anne breezed past me, greeting the shopkeeper with deference:

"Sabah-il-kheyr, Mohammed. Shalom." Putting her hands together as if in prayer, she bowed her head as he returned her greeting.

"Mohammed is an old friend. He won't cheat you; sit here." Anne patted the bench invitingly. As we adjusted the worn cushions, mint tea materialized before us.

Row upon row of amulets were laid out, gleaming gold and precious stones, beautiful enamels in turquoise, orange, red, and lapis blue. Most were the stylized Eye of Horus, but there in the corner, that one looked like my Lady's ankh:

"Here, this one for you."

Taking the ankh set with a beautiful turquoise at its center, Mohammed held it in his hands for a few moments. Head bowed, he muttered under his breath. Was it a prayer or an incantation? It didn't matter. I knew it would protect me. After a few moments, he fastened it around my neck on a slender chain.

"Never take off." He wagged his finger at me. "It protect you always."

The amulet was warm and golden as it lay against my skin. Power radiated from it. The amulet of my Lady was there to protect me.

chapter 15.

Lady of the scarlet-colored garment

"Good morning, Megan, did you sleep well?"

Mary was looking much perkier that morning as she joined me in the dining room. Her green outfit suited her. I couldn't say I'd really looked at her before yesterday when she'd seemed so ill. The only thing I'd noticed was how flushed she often was. Red, shiny face and neck; she glowed. I couldn't have said what color her hair was, not surprising perhaps with that faded blonde. A good hairdresser could do wonders with that. She kept herself to herself, not an easy person to get to know, and I'd been a bit self-absorbed myself that trip. Still, she seemed to be making an effort to be friendly.

"Yes, I did, thank you Mary, I thought perhaps I'd have nightmares after that crypt but it was extremely positive for me. How about you?"

The flash of a white bird on the river enticed my eyes. When I turned my head back Mary was sitting forward in her chair, hands fidgeting restlessly with some bread.

"It was positive for me too, Megan, although initially, as you know, I wasn't going to do it, I felt so ill. When so many of the group decided they would join in, I thought I'd better give it a try. Glad I did, it carried on when we got back on board."

She looked as though she'd burst if she didn't tell me more, I'd better ask.:

"What happened?"

"After we'd been stripped bare and gone before Osiris, when the portal opened I realized I'd come out of the underworld with a big, pregnant belly. It felt a bit strange I can tell you – particularly as I've been going through a bad menopause. You might have noticed my hot flushes, Megan."

I certainly had, that red glow walked everywhere with her but I'd put it down to blood pressure or something like that. Hot flushes were not part of my world and if they were like this, I'd rather like it to stay that way.

"It feels like I'm on fire most of the time. I skipped supper and went to bed because I was feeling rather weird. As soon as I lay on my bed the birth pangs began. It was quite frightening, I didn't know whether to call someone or not. But I decided I'd go with it and see what happened – so I called on my guide. Do you remember when we did that guide meditation with Anne at the College, Megan?" Her hands were hopping all over the table gathering up the breadcrumbs she had made.

"Yes, of course, that was powerful too, wasn't it?"

"It was very strong for me. I had Hekat, the frog-headed goddess, although I didn't know who she was until Anne told me afterwards. She's the sacred midwife so I thought she was the perfect person to help me this time. With her aid I was able to birth my 'baby' and I realized it was me; I'd given birth to my self. I was tremendously excited."

"Have you told Anne yet?"

"No, I'm hoping to have a word before we start this morning." She looked round hopefully but Anne was nowhere in sight. Most of the white-clothed tables were empty, we were either early or very late. Glancing at my watch, I saw that it was almost time for our session to begin. Picking up my coffee cup, I half rose:

"I'm sure she'll think it's significant. You look totally different."

Her face had a light dusting of tan from the Egyptian sun. The sweat and the glow were gone. It was hard to picture that red, puffing face I'd seen only yesterday. Anne certainly worked some miracles with these rituals of hers.

"I feel different. I knew I had to come on this cruise but I never thought it would be for something like this. Oh, there's Anne now, excuse me Megan while I ..."

"Right everyone, we've got a lot to do today. This morning's not strictly to do with past lives but it is to do with freeing yourself from the past – whenever that might have been – and then reconnecting parts of the self. We're going to do some tie-cutting first and then make the sacred marriage. When we've finished, Mary has kindly promised to share the fruits of yesterday with us."

Mary was positively beaming so Anne must have had something good to say about her experience.

"We'll also have time to share your experiences from the crypt – sounds like something out of a horror movie, doesn't it? From what I've heard, one or two of you would agree."

Emphatic heads nodded round the room but they were all smiling so it must have turned out okay for everyone.

"We'll come back to that. We're going to start with tie-cutting.

For those of you who haven't done this before, let me say that this is a process that is intended to free you from the effects of the past, from any conditions, debts, expectations and demands, 'oughts,' 'shoulds,' and karma that have accrued in your relationships. It is not intended to cut off any unconditional love that exists between you and the person with whom you are cutting the ties."

"What sort of person would that be?" Malcolm had his "let's get this right" face on, and his hand was forking frantically through his hair. Now what, or who, did he have in his past that needed to be let go?

"You can do this process with anyone – parents, children, partners or even something like cigarettes if you want to give up smoking. It has a powerful effect on any kind of relationship – and it can work what seem to be miracles. I've seen children who've left home and been cut off from their parents for years contact the family the day after the mother has done a tie-cutting with them, and addicts who've gone into recovery when either they or their partner have done a cutting."

"I'd have thought tie cutting would make things worse." Beatrice was frowning and I seemed to recall she'd said she hadn't heard from her son in a long time. "Doesn't it create a bigger gap that has to be resolved later?"

"On the contrary, it sets you free to be yourselves as you were each meant to be, and that seems to free something up in the relationship, even though the other person has no – conscious – idea that the work has been done. The forgiveness part of the exercise is extremely effective, as you will see."

Will this work with Ramon? Could I really let him go? Easier to look at the bank drifting by, so timeless those mud-brick houses.

"Pay attention Megan, this is important."
Yes my Lady.

"Does it work with people who have died?" Alison asked eagerly.

"Yes, it is an excellent way of letting go of a parent who has died, for instance. Or of a past partner. But you can do it with anyone. I'm going to do the exercise three times, talking you through it as we go. I'll give you time to do the work before we move onto the next stage."

"How many people can we do?" Beatrice has taken up the idea with her usual exuberance.

"It's usual to put only one person at a time in the circle, but sometimes you find more than one person goes in – that can teach you a great deal about underlying common dynamics of relationships"

"Anne, can I do this with someone I want to stay in relationship with? Someone I've only met recently? I wouldn't want him to, you know, think I've withdrawn my interest." Miranda twinkled pinkly.

"Yes, of course, it can only improve that relationship. It won't have the weight of the past behind it. "

"You're sure? I'd hate to ruin what seems to be a promising relationship." She was grinning. Was she teasing Anne? She was young enough to be her daughter and they had known each other a long time.

"Yes, I'm positive. I always cut the ties with my husband when we do this exercise, and we've been together for over thirty years – and very happily so. Now, if there are no more questions, we'll begin."

How handsome Ramon had looked that day we met. So like

the Horus hawk. Surely I didn't have to let him go, surely my Lady
didn't mean me to ... my hand cupped my belly, cradling my baby
gently. Round and round my belly my hand moved. Was I
comforting myself or my child? Would anything take away the
emptiness where my love should be? Even this baby could not fill
that space. Surely this child of ours is not meant to ... Pain rose up
into my throat, like a tight hard ball. Squeezing my eyes shut I
forced down the tears. Come on, Mecky, listen to Anne. She knows
what you must do.

"Sit comfortably and let your breathing establish a steady
rhythm. Picture yourself in your meadow and explore the
meadow until you find the right place to do the work."

I was back in the desert. Why did I always end up there?

"Draw a circle around yourself to mark out your space."

That was easy in the sand.

"And another in front of you for the other person. Now put the
person you want to cut the ties with into the circle."

Right Greg, I said to myself, this was where I cut my ties with
you. Anne had mentioned a cylinder of light so I put that in place
first to keep him out of my space. It was a good job I did because
he was fuming and kept trying to move his circle towards mine. A
big peg would take care of that. The big stone that suddenly rolled
in was perfect.

"And tell them why you're doing this work, it's not to cut off
any unconditional love between you but it is to remove any
expectations, oughts, and shoulds that are in the relationship –
and, especially, to let go of any karma."

Greg didn't like that, he didn't want to let go of his precious
expectations. He wasn't going to have any choice though; this was
my imagery and I wanted to be free.

"Now, see how the ties manifest between you."

I didn't like the look of them at all; it was like being enfolded in a big, black, sticky octopus. Good job the cylinder of light kept most of it away.

"And cut the ties from yourself first and then the other person, and pile them up outside the circle."

As fast as I cut them off the thing grew another arm and stuck back on. I wondered if Sekhmet could help me.

Thought so, that blast of fire certainly did the trick, the thing shriveled up instantly. Nothing to pile up, the ash had blown away. Oh yes, I must remember the healing light.

Anne had said to check for hidden ties. There was a long cord going into my vagina and it had a hook on the end. I couldn't pull it out and Sekhmet's fire wasn't going to help here. She put that ankh of hers in and gently twisted, it felt strange and I was worried for my baby but she seemed to know what she was doing and it was okay, it was out. I put healing light in before removing the other end from Greg. Perhaps it was best to leave that part to Sekhmet. I didn't want to reach over into his circle. Sekhmet obviously didn't have any scruples, I thought she was going to castrate him with a big pair of scissors, but she cleared the tie.

"Check that you have cleared all the ties and that you have healed and sealed each place with light."

It looked pretty clear to me.

"Where possible, let unconditional love and forgiveness flow between you."

That was a hard one, but I tried to send Greg forgiveness. There was no forgiveness from him and certainly no unconditional love. But Sekhmet was wrapping me in her love, it felt good.

"Now move the other person right back, out of your space entirely. Let them go to where they belong, into their own space."

That felt better. You can't resist a lion in a hurry. She had him out of there in a trice.

"Now bring your attention to the ties. Have a big blazing bonfire and throw them on. Feel your transformed and purified creative energy flowing back into yourself. Let it re-energize your whole body."

There was only that cord and Sekhmet breathed on that. You don't need a bonfire when you've got the Lady of Flame on your side. But it felt good to get that energy back, Greg was so draining.

"Now repeat the process with the next person. Make sure your circle is still intact, draw another circle in front of it, and place the person in the circle.

Was there anyone else? Could I possibly ... Surely I didn't have to ...?

But I did. Sekhmet chivvied Ramon into the circle. I didn't want to cut the ties with him. How could I be sure I'd see him again? My heart had already broken, I couldn't take any more.

I remembered how it had been that first day. How he had vibrated whilst he sat beside me in the taxi, and how we'd run along that hotel corridor and burst into the room. How fast our clothes had come off and how we'd started on the sofa but soon ended up in the floor in our impatience to be part of one another. I don't recall any part of that room, don't think I looked at it once. My body remembered how he felt though, how it was like being complete for the very first time, now it ached for him. How could I let him go?

Still, Anne said tie-cutting sometimes worked miracles. Perhaps if I could do this it would clear the way for him to come back. Um, that sounded conditional and I didn't think Anne would approve of that. I'd better do it for its own sake. Would Ramon hear me? He was looking a bit bewildered. Mind you, I would if I'd been chased by a lion and stuck in a circle of light.

"And tell them why you are doing this work."

Come on, Mecky, you can do this. Deep breath, there, that's better, now.

"Ramon, I have to tell you I'm doing this to clear the past and to allow us each to be as we are meant to be, no strings attached, no promises pulling us together. If it's right that I never see you again, so be it. But if I am meant to see you again, that's fine too."

He's nodding so it must be okay.

"Now see how the ties manifest themselves."

This was going to be hard. That big cord between our hearts looked strong and the one that went between the top of our heads was all golden, and there were all these little fine hairs everywhere. They formed a silken net that bound us both together. I didn't know what I was going to do about that. Perhaps I could start on this rod between our foreheads, it looked a bit like a lightning conductor. Yes, it came out easily, put it to one side for now. Then the throat one, that's okay. Better leave the heart for now and move onto the solar plexus, good. These below the waist might be tricky, no, that's okay, they slipped out easily enough. What should I do about that tie between my child and Ramon? Better leave that and ask Anne later.

I needed some help from my Lady with those hairy bits, so I asked her to breathe on the net – gently though, I didn't want to get consumed in the flames. That was better. Now what about those two ties that were left?

"Leave them be for now."

189

What? Was she sure? Anne had said ... Well okay, yes, I would leave them for now. I could always check that with Anne later too. That looked good, lots of healing light around.

"Now let unconditional love and forgiveness flow between you."

It was like a big pink fluffy candy-floss river engulfing me, a river of bliss. Ramon I did love you, so much, and I forgave you too.

"Move the person back out of your space."

"No, Sekhmet, please, let him stay a little longer ... Please let me be surrounded by this for a few more minutes ..."

I couldn't bear seeing him fade away like that, couldn't stop those silly tears. Ramon ... It was no good, I'd have to go out ...

"Megan, please sit down, you need to finish this. Pick up the ties and throw them into the flames ... watch them being consumed."

Sekhmet, help me please, I begged, I couldn't seem to find them. There, that was better. Those rods were a bit heavy to throw, perhaps I could roll them. That did it, they were melting now.

"Draw as near to the fire as you can and absorb its energy. This is your transformed and purified creative energy coming back to you."

Mmm, that felt good. I could feel it pouring into my womb and filling up all those other empty places where the rods had been. Not sure whether I should have kept these other ties though, I'd better ask Anne. All that metal had formed an ankh in the ashes, that ancient symbol of life that looked so like a robed woman. Sekhmet was scooping it out with her own ankh and blowing on it. Was it really for me?

"And now make your final circle ..."

Not just now, I thought. I'd sit that one out and hold my ankh.

There'd been a lot of tears, there was hardly a dry eye in the place, even Malcolm had pink lids. But it felt good, particularly to be free of the ties with Greg. How could I have spent so many years tied to that man? What was it Anne had said? Oh yes – that emotionally abused women – strange to think of myself as that but it must be true – were so browbeaten by having their husbands constantly telling them that it was their behavior that was unreasonable and their expectations that were unrealistic that they began to believe it themselves, and then it was too late, they blamed themselves for everything wrong in the marriage. I certainly did. Greg eroded my sense of self, my individuality, my creative spark. And still he demanded more. Well, it was time to let that go now and find myself. I couldn't wait until we got to Karnack and I reclaimed my power.

"Before we go and have our coffee, does anyone need to say anything about that process, anything urgent?" Anne's bright face peered expectantly in my direction.

It seemed a good time to check on those ties:

"Well, one thing, Anne. There was a link from my baby to his father, and I also had two ties with his father that my guide told me not to break, one was a strong heart connection and the other was a golden light between the tops of our heads. Was it okay to leave those, all the others were cleared?"

"Well, if your guide said it was alright it's best to leave them for now, but keep checking. And as for your baby, you can't cut the ties for anyone else, you have to leave it to them to do when they are ready."

"But what about if they are too young or they don't know

about this?" Joan said with a catch in her voice. "I did it for one of my children with someone else."

"As a rule, it's not a good idea to do this on anyone else's behalf without permission. You could be violating their free will and interfering in their karma. But as you've done it, you'd better ask that it's for your child's highest good." Her smile was reassuring and Joan's shoulders sagged with relief.

"I'm sure it is: she was flashed at by a neighbor on her way home from school when she was thirteen and it really has blighted her life. It made her afraid to go out alone, took away her confidence. She went to a local university because she was so uncertain of herself. I hoped this would make a difference as she's been given an opportunity to go to Canada to do some research work."

"I suggest you tell her about the work you did when you get home, Joan, and, if possible, talk her through it herself. It would set her free. And now," she said firmly, "it's time for coffee."

I loved it out there on deck, watching the world go by. So different to what we'd been doing and yet not that different in a way. The scene hadn't changed in thousands of years. Everything seemed to happen on the banks – it was like looking into their world from another dimension. Exactly how it felt in regression, being part of it but still a part of me looking on.

There was such a feast of color and noise. The cooking and washing, the women in their bright clothes chattering and laughing, and the small children like brilliant birds bobbing about, shouting and waving. All spotlessly clean although some of those mud houses looked primitive. I didn't think I'd like to have my clothes washed in that murky green Nile water. Those strange spiked towers – pigeon houses, Josef had said. How long had they been there, I wondered. I saw several in one of my regressions. The fishermen were casting their nets as though frozen in time. Nothing had changed. The waterwheels, what did Josef call them, oh yes, shadoofs, they'd been in use since biblical times. Such an ancient land.

Which brought me back to what I'd been avoiding. The tie-cutting. Why were those ties with Ramon so strong and why did Sekhmet tell me to leave them? Was it because we were soul-mates – souls that split into two, eons ago? Malcolm had told me that the Greek philosopher, Plato, had a story about this. How, way back in time, humans were two-headed beings with four arms and four legs. They became arrogant and angered the gods who split them into two and Malcolm said, with a surprising amount of feeling, "ever the twain shall wander, each seeking the other half." Could that be the answer? Were Ramon and I soul-mates? Were we split in half long ago?

"Megan, did you manage to cut the ties with Greg? I take it that wasn't him you left the ties in place with?" Anne's voice sharpened as she sat beside me.

"Goodness no, that was Ramon. I tried to let him go but it was hard not knowing why he left. Greg was quite easy once Sekhmet came in to help me. He didn't like the process but it felt good to me."

"Well, don't forget to keep checking on the ties with Ramon, and remember to do a revoking of vows with Greg when your divorce is finalized." Her hand touched my shoulder as though to emphasize the point.

"Yes, I will. Anne, can I ask you about soul-mates? I have wondered whether Ramon and I ...?"

"Ah, the old Plato theory Malcolm was expounding. Did he mention some of the beings were hermaphrodites and others one sex only so that when they were split there were as many men seeking their other male half – or women their female – as there were heterosexual couples?"

I didn't remember that. I don't know many gay men, or women for that matter. I hadn't given any thought to their previous lives or where a desire for the same sex came from. How interesting.

"No he didn't, how fascinating. That could explain homosexuality couldn't it?"

"Well it could, if you take Plato literally. Personally I think it's an allegory for how we get cut off from parts of our self – or from memories of lives as the other sex. Some men are exceedingly macho and need to seek their 'feminine' side, whilst others are overly soft and sensitive and might need to find their more assertive 'male' side – women too. It certainly teaches us to think outside the box. The soul group theory, though, seems to me to more satisfactorily explain the way relationships work."

Anne reached out for the sugar and then her hand tapped the spoon against the cup as though to emphasize the point. Didn't she believe in soul-mates?

"But surely, within a group two souls do get joined together, sometimes for eternity – like Ramon and I seem to be."

"Yes, that's true. Some relationships do seem to echo down across the years, although whether they are meant to stay together for all of eternity is a moot point."

"Are you sure, Anne, couldn't it be that there are couples like that ..."

"Again, it's my personal view, based on all my years spent

exploring karmic relationships, that some couples are meant to travel together through time for a while, but it's often necessary for them to part in order that they round themselves out, fill in the gaps as it were. The problem comes when one person has let go but the other still hangs on."

Putting down her cup and glancing at her watch, she said briskly: "Much as I'd love to stay here in the sun chatting, we need to get back. I'd like to do the sacred marriage exercise before lunch."

"The sacred marriage used to be made in the temple. Initiates were carefully prepared and only one marriage was allowed – and people were encouraged to seek out their previous partner from other lives. The Egyptians used astrology to check that the pair were compatible at all levels. If one partner fell behind in their studies, the other had to wait until they caught up. They were joined on the physical, mental, emotional, and spiritual levels of being."

"Is there any evidence for this Anne?" Malcolm was forking his hair again, surely this didn't worry him?

"There is a papyrus that gives nine of the twelve stages of joining – the rest was torn away. Many of these sacred marriages remain in place today and they can cause havoc if the partners are no longer intended to be together or if they've married someone else in the meantime – many affairs start because of the pull of a sacred marriage from the past."

Like the pull I had with Ramon? Was that what bound me to him, why I couldn't cut those ties? I knew Mek'an'ar had made the sacred marriage with her Pharaoh and there was that promise he'd made before he went off to the war. But Anne seemed to think some couples were meant to part ... How I wished I could sort this out.

"The sacred marriage we are making today is different. It is the marriage of our own inner masculine and feminine energies. This is sacred marriage with yourself, not anyone else. It's the way you become a whole being, intact within yourself. Once your inner masculine and feminine energies are united, you can be your whole, undivided self, as it were. If you find anyone you know coming into your imaging, you need to be strong and ask for them to be replaced by your own inner figure. Don't allow yourself to go back into a previous sacred marriage."

She was looking rather pointedly in my direction. I'd better nod to show I was listening. Okay, Anne, I hear you.

"As you close your eyes you'll see that, in the near distance, there is a temple with a path that leads to its entrance. Walk over to this temple. As you approach, the great doors swing open to admit you."

I was heading towards the Sekhmet temple, was this why Anne warned me?

"You will be greeted by temple attendants and taken to a purification room. Here you will disrobe and step into the ritual bath that has been prepared for you."

I was bathing in the sacred lake at the Mut, a bit of a detour from the Sekhmet temple, so perhaps it would be alright. Maybe my mind was putting together familiar images to create the scene. If that's so, perhaps I can change it. But no, I could only see what I could see. The images unfolded in their way or not at all.

"There's a clean robe laid out ready for you. Put this on and a temple attendant will show you the way out."

My robe was the color of lapis, that beautiful royal blue of the bright night sky. Quickly I slipped it on.

"In the next room, you'll find an offering table. Put whatever you find in your hand onto the altar as an offering."

It was that cross that Ramon always wore around his neck. Why had I got to put that there? It looked a little strange on Sekhmet's lap alongside her ankh.

"Now, the temple attendants will come to lead you to the chamber where the sacred marriage will take place. This needs no priest, it is blessed by the gods and consummated between you and your lover. As the doors to this sumptuous inner chamber open, you will find your lover waiting for you on the bed."

Oh no, it was Ramon lying on the bed before My Lady, and I'd only just cut the ties with him. Anne said I couldn't do this with anyone I knew.

"Ramon, please leave. Much as I love you I cannot do this. My Lady, help me."

"But child, you were joined before me for all time."

"I know, but I didn't realize how long that would be, or that we wouldn't be together when we met again. I can't remain tied to him in a sacred marriage forever. Please My Lady, I beg of you, help me to find a way out of this."

"Very well, but you must realize the consequences. Should you meet again in this present life, he will have no memory of the ancient sacred tie between you, you will have lost your connection and it will be up to you both whether or not you renew it."

I'd meet that when it came. For now: "Please, I implore you set me free and allow me my own inner joining."

A door opened and Sekhmet make a sign over us both, that arc of light that had joined our heads dissolved, but the heart tie was still there, stretched thin but still strong. Maybe that didn't relate to our sacred marriage. Ramon left, not looking back. Was he hurt that I broke the ancient marriage tie? Surely he understood ...

That was a handsome man – it was a man wasn't it? It was rather disconcerting, like looking in the mirror first thing in the morning before you've braced yourself for the shock. He was so like me. Taller, but his eyes and hair were tawny like mine. Was this my bridegroom? Seemed to be, how tender he was, how gentle. His fingertip quietly traced my lips. His hands cupped my face gazing deep into my eyes. It was like looking into a mirror of myself. Gently, he kissed first one eyelid, and then the next; now one check and then the other, then slid his mouth down to meet my own. His kiss was sweet, it was making me tingle all over, my bottom chakra was on fire just from that one kiss.

His lovemaking was different to anything I'd ever known. Exactly what I would have asked for myself. Sensuous and slow. Giving everything, wanting nothing for himself. Patiently stroking my hands, then my feet, moving languorously to the backs of my knees, the inner thighs and up to my buttocks. Working slowly along my spine. Waves of pleasure were coursing leisurely through my body. Unhurriedly his tongue caressed my erect nipples, his hands brushed lightly over my breasts. Softly he infused himself between my thighs, blending, melting, mmm ... it was truly blissful. A long, slow orgasm, peak building upon peak, breath on breath, a rolling wave and I was staying in my body, no flying off to the stars this time. His form pulsated and his rhythm quickened. As his essence spasmed into mine, we merged, became one flesh, one being.

A quiet moment of infinity passing through, a shift of perception. Utter stillness, total union, expansion beyond knowing.

"It is time to leave the inner chamber but before you do, see if it is possible for your lover to become one with you."

It was already done.

"Now make your way out of the temple, back through the great doors and into the meadow where you started your journey. Take your time and when you are ready, open your eyes."

What effect would that have? It felt amazing. How had everyone else got on – most of them had a contented, post-orgasmic glow that suggested a successful completion. Was Anne going to ask for details, surely not, but it could be interesting ... No, it didn't look like it, she was gathering her things together as she spoke:

"After that exercise, relationships will be different for you. Instead of restlessly seeking something that was missing in yourself 'out there,' in another person, as it were trying to get them to make you feel complete, you'll be bringing your whole self into the relationship. This brings about much greater intimacy, a true relating. You'll notice the difference very quickly.

"Well, now, as it's time for lunch we'll leave that there. It's a good thing to let that settle in without too much discussion. There'll be an opportunity to bring it before the main group later if you want to."

It was great out on deck, what a feast we had. All those Egyptian dishes. It made a nice change to eat out there, I don't know why we hadn't before. The breeze was really pleasant. We could see through the windows in the dining room but it was different somehow, viewing things from on deck instead of down by the waterline. The food tasted wonderful, all my favorite things, and those salads, so cool and crunchy, just what I needed. It was so good to have my appetite back.

Was that pool warm enough for a quick swim before the afternoon session? It wouldn't hurt to try it. The cold bit into my hand, it was freezing. It would need to be midsummer before I went in there. Perhaps I'd siesta on a sun bed for a few minutes, it was quite tiring doing all that inner work.

"We've still a couple of hours until we reach Kom Ombo so we'll take the opportunity to do some more past life exploration. You can either ask to be shown the most useful life for you to know about at this time – it could be one where you learned something or where you got something right, there are lives like that, you know, or you could ask for whatever is appropriate to appear."

This would be a good time to follow Anne's advice, I'd simply ask for a life that threw light on my illness rather than trying to get anything more on the Egyptian lives.

"... in front of you you'll see a door, open it and go in ..."

Phew, the place stank. I couldn't see clearly but I thought there was another door over beyond. It was even worse, absolutely reeked, indescribable, my stomach was heaving ... I wished I hadn't eaten all that lunch ...

"Well Megan, did you see anything this time?"

"I was a young slave-girl who worked in the dye pits. It was dreadfully smelly work. We used pots of urine – collected from all around the city – and strong chemicals as well as plants. Men brought rocks from the desert and they'd be broken up and heated over braziers with some sticky black stuff. It made our eyes sting and we coughed and coughed. Then it was thrown into the pit. There was much boiling and bubbling, lots of smoke – and the most awful smell, which made us cough even more.

"My hands and arms were raw because of the stuff we used to wash the skins and the wool – I don't know what it was, but it stripped the fat off the skins like magic. We had to plunge them into the pits – after a time my hands were permanently blue-green, all broken sores, but I had to keep on working. I had no appetite, everything tasted of the dreadful smell, we lived and slept in a tiny room at the side of the pits so we never got away from it. Sometimes I was too tired to stand, and I fell into the pit.

"All of us had the same kind of problems and we helped each other but eventually people sickened and died, then they brought in a new lot of slaves. The men who supervised the work kept away from the braziers and the pits. I think they knew it was poisonous and I suspect I died of a kind of cancer, I couldn't see exactly how this connected to my present illness but I'm sure it does. I kept asking but nothing more came about my illness."

"It sounds like you have another piece of the puzzle but maybe it won't make sense until the last piece slots into place. Remembering can be like that – you get snippets that eventually link up to make a whole, but it can take time – that's why I suggested you kept notes on this trip."

I didn't have such a thing as time, but I couldn't say that out loud. Nor could I say that I'd learned why Mek'an'ar couldn't marry her Pharaoh. The story would make a good film script. I needed to go over it in my mind to be sure, so I wrote it down; it certainly felt like truth.

I am a small child sitting quietly by a lotus pond. The blue lotus blossoms are shining luminous in moonlight. I stare at them for a long time, it seems they speak to me but I do not understand the words. My mother, Suten's Great Wife, has just died. My father has gone to conduct the mourning rites for her and her stillborn child. He has taken my half-brother, Ibi, with him. It seems like everyone has forgotten me.

As I sit there, a woman creeps slyly up to me. With her raven black, uncombed curls snaking around her head and her dark visage she looks like a creature of night. She is my father's most recent wife. She was sent to him to create an alliance with a former enemy from the far south. The servants whisper that she was a priestess of a snake goddess in her homeland and that she is well versed in magic and sorcery. Some say that my mother's death might be due to her malign influence. My father is under her spell. Since she came to the palace, I never see him.

"What do you want?" I ask fearfully.

"Only to comfort you, child," she smiles.

Why do I not believe her?

She strokes my head. "Peace child, your mother is with the gods in Amenti."

A sharp tug. Did she take my hair? Turning quickly I look at her hand but it is concealed beneath the scanty tunic that does nothing to hide her erotic figure.

Quickly I run to my old nurse. She will know what to do. She rushes me into the little temple in a corner of the palace where we keep the household gods, and utters an incantation to protect me against evil spells. Around my neck she slips an amulet of My Lady.

"Here, child, this will keep you safe. Wear it always, don't lose it."

Some years later, it is still around my neck and my hand goes to it as my father stands before me.

"Mek'an'ar, you are old enough to join the temple and begin your training as a priestess of Mut. Your brother will learn the rites with you as he will one day take my place. Yours will be a sacred marriage, you must be joined on all levels."

When we enter the temple together, my brother and I are instructed in our duties, he lives at the main temple, I at her Lady's. Every day we sit with the other novices and learn the sacred teachings. But each month, when the moon grows dim, we are brought together by our teachers in the secret temple. We have been dedicated to My Lady and must spend these nights with her on another plane. We are told that, when we are old enough, we will be joined on the sacred and the sexual levels. But this time seems far in the future.

When that future is reached and I have been installed as High Priestess, my nurse, who is herself an initiated priestess, brings me news from the palace when she attends the monthly rites. My stepmother, Magrat, is wielding great power. She has been trying to birth a son but produced only daughters. She has made my father promise that their eldest daughter will marry my brother and that she will be his only wife. Such a thing has never been heard before.

"I have been promised to my brother from birth," I say angrily, "this cannot be."

Sutens always have many minor wives and concubines. But, says my nurse quietly, my father's minor wives and concubines have been dying of unnatural causes, and, although there is no proof, everyone suspects Magrat has bewitched them. Several appear to have died from snake venom and it is known that Magrat has the gift of snake charming; she can milk the venom from a living cobra.

"You must not cross her," my nurse whispers. "I am not sure that my magic, nor even that of our Lady Mut, will be strong enough to protect you."

My brother comes to me in the night, he too has heard the rumors. "I love only you," Ibi tells me. "We have been promised from birth. I will hold to it. We will marry."

But he has no power. The marriage is made between him and Magrat's daughter. Magrat cannot take from me my place as High Priestess of the temple of The Lady Mut, nor can she insist that the midsummer rites be put aside. When the time comes for the first rite of joining, my nurse whispers to me that Magrat is sick. One of her cobras turned on her. She is not expected to live. I dare not ask who had a hand in this.

When my brother and I perform the ceremony of Going Forth With My Lady and the rites of joining are complete, I beg him to marry me. Surely our father will now allow this. But my brother has had a vision in which the shade of Magrat told him that, if he takes another wife in defiance of his father's promise, his line will be cursed. As his wife has just given birth to a son, my brother is unwilling to take the risk. Even after our father dies and he becomes Pharaoh he still feels bound. He has many concubines, whom he never visits, but takes no other wife. Ours is a mystic marriage, but it must remain one in flesh and spirit only, we cannot make the vows in front of the people.

When I look again at the renegade priest who thrust me into the void and tore my child from my belly, I see he is one of Magrat's entourage. It seems that her hand reached beyond the tomb to ensure that only her descendants took the throne. Was he acting on her behalf or was ..."

"I know that it is true, I tell, you, it's what I saw." Beatrice was shouting at Malcolm as my attention was jolted back into the present moment. I'd missed what led up to it but she'd got her lips pursed again. She was looking to Joan for support. She always seems to be with her these days. Funny, I hadn't seen Stephen with the group since the "come as you were" party, except for meals, and he hadn't come down to the crypt at Edfu. Past life exploration didn't seem to be for him, he'd probably prefer to sun himself on deck.

"All I am saying, Beatrice, is that you have already heard Anne's opinion on the Hatshepshut story. I've had to accept I wasn't Tutmoses, can you not accept that you are unlikely to have been Hatshepshut, instead of insisting on this fantasy?"

Why couldn't the two of them let it go? Anne had already told them it was the whispering ghost of yesteryear. I loved that phrase, so evocative of how it felt in regression. Like drifting through time listening to the whispers of your soul.

"No I can't. I know what I saw. I was standing before my temple greeting the expedition from the land of Punt. They'd bought me incense trees, cinnamon bark, kohl, and spices; several varieties of animals including giraffes and baboons, and a plethora of small, native people to plant the trees and tend them. It was an amazing sight. They were paying homage to me as a Great Queen. I know it's right, I've been to her temple and seen ..."

Malcolm pounced: "Oh, you've never mentioned that before."

"No, because I knew you'd think I was using that prior knowledge to create a past life for myself. But I'm not, I've read extensively on the Queen and everything I've seen has been recorded."

Once again, Bea drew herself up to her full height. She sucked in a deep breath but before she could speak ...

"Was that before or after you supposedly 'saw' it?" Malcolm's hands formed ironic quotation marks.

"I..." Beatrice was speechless for once. Had Malcolm really silenced her for good? It seemed hard to believe but I did hope so.

Voices were clamoring. Some people in the group must feel very left out in all this although Anne does try to be fair, but Josef's head appeared round the door.

"I hear talking. We arrive Kom Ombo and there no other boats. It good idea to visit temple now. Is unique, only one on Nile dedicated two gods. Atmosphere tranquil – when tour boats allow." He withdrew before anyone could say anything.

"Right, unless anyone has anything urgent, we can discuss this afternoon's experiences later. From what I remember of Kom Ombo, it's highly photogenic, bring plenty of film. It gets really magnificent as the sun sets."

Anne was right, those majestic walls did look magnificent starkly outlined against the bright blue of the sky, and the temple was beautifully sited on the bend of the river, like a serene old lady gathering her skirts around herself. If we got one of those psychedelic Nile sunsets, it would be an amazing sight. The fact that it was ruined seemed to make it more impressive: you could see how huge the building blocks were. It was interesting how the temple was so close to the river, most of the others had been set back from the river, away from the green, cultivated strip. Josef was waving us towards the back wall. Did he have something special to show us?

"Here physicians' tools and those of midwife. This medical text book set in stone." Josef pointed to the knives, saws, and drills pictured on the wall. "The Roman Emperor Trajan makes offering to Imhotep, great healer who became god for services to medicine."

The shisha-smoking man from the boat, not one of our group,

stepped forward. In rather precise English underlined by his guttural accent he said: "I have been reading a different version to that. Those instruments are too clumsy for surgery. The book I have suggested that they were actually the tools of the masons being offered up during the building work."

"Could be possible." Josef shrugged dismissively and went on: "But further along scenes of birth and I believe these medical instruments. Ancient Egyptians have great knowledge of healing, do brain surgery. "

Nerissa peered at the wall: "Not with that saw, I hope. It's massive, Josef, perhaps it was for sawing stone?"

With her iridescent black hair in long, tight spirals and her striking looks Nerissa too could have stepped out of ancient Egypt. Josef seemed rather taken with her and he'd been very patient about answering her incessant questions. He'd found her sunglasses several times when she'd apparently lost them but she seemed to have left them behind again today. And he'd hovered around her after he'd chosen her costume as the best at the "come as you were" party. Mind you, it was even more striking than Miranda's outfit. That fine pleated linen was almost transparent and the white highlighted her olive skin. It didn't leave anything to the imagination but it suited her slim figure. She said she'd got the outfit on an earlier visit to Egypt. She and Terri had been several times before, and they'd done a lot of work with Anne.

"Take a look in there, it's disgusting." Mary laughed and pointed to a small room, which seemed innocuous enough despite its barred entrance. "A heap of mummified crocodiles."

So there were, but you could hardly see them in the dusty gloom.

"Well," laughed Anne, "this was the Sobek temple. Crocodiles were worshipped here for a thousand years. They were tamed and kept in the temple grounds. Some were given earrings and necklaces to wear. When they died, they were mummified and revered. Crocodiles were powerful symbols of death, and you can't have resurrection or rebirth without death."

It seemed that rebirth was everywhere in Egypt. Would I be reborn? It seemed a strong possibility, but I'd have preferred not to have to die first. Didn't Josef say Horus symbolized the small births, deaths, and rebirths in an individual life? I liked that idea. In this present life I'd already had an incarnation as an impoverished child who became a rich man's daughter, emerged into another incarnation as Greg's wife, but that came to an end, as did my brief brush with motherhood; I'd faced death with the leukemia and come through – so far at any rate. Then I met Ramon and who knows where that would go, it seemed to have ended but had it? There was that death-and-rebirth with Sekhmet in the crypts at Edfu. It seemed to symbolize all those tearings apart of my life that I experienced. But each time I picked myself up, got reborn as it were. Now I was imbued with new life. What was next?

After supper we gathered again in our lounge; it was beginning to feel like home. Someone had put a few hibiscus flowers in a glass next to Anne's table and their bright colors lifted the room, as did the colorful Egyptian rug at her feet. The chairs in there were a bit itchy with their stiff velvet covers, but soft enough, better than the first ones we'd perched on.

"Well, everyone, I hope you found Kom Ombo interesting – and restful after all the work we've been doing. I think that sunset was a special gift from the old gods of Egypt to the photographers amongst us. Wasn't it spectacular? Ra certainly put on his best show. Impossibly colorful. That shocking-pink was amazing. But, now, I think we have some loose ends to tie up, especially between Malcolm and Beatrice, and I know many of you have something you want to share with the group."

Hands were waving, but Anne went on.

"First of all, though, I'd like to say that all of this could be true – or none of it. In my view, it really doesn't matter. What matters is how you handle it, what it tells you, where it takes you on your spiritual journey – and how it affects your everyday life."

Idly I glanced at the shore. The banks were taller and nearer than they had been. Deep chestnut earth had been undercut in places by the river's force. Children chattered and waved, it almost felt as though I could reach over and touch them. Some of them were holding up lengths of garish cloth – how the Egyptians loved fluorescent colors. Small boys tried to make a sale. Budding bazaar buzzards in training.

"If you want to believe you were Hatshepshut, Beatrice, that's fine by me. But please, look at what it tells you about yourself. Apply what you know about her life to your own. It is possible that your reading has influenced you, but you only resonate with what is, essentially, your story. If you're honest with yourself, you can learn a great deal from this experience."

Beatrice shrugged petulantly. Her mouth tightened but, for once, she said nothing. Wounded dignity was the phrase that came to mind, or a right royal sulk.

"And Malcolm, the same applies to you. I know you've given up the idea now, but what would you have learned if you had been Tutmoses? After all, he ruled for thirty-eight years after the demise of Hatshepshut and was an extremely able leader. It can be a useful exercise to play 'what if' with a story like that – or with something you instinctively reject as 'not mine.' You learn so much more about yourself that way."

Malcolm nodded, and at least he seemed to be willing to listen to Anne. After all she'd been at this for years.

"Anne, could I tell you what I saw? I think it definitely comes into the 'feeling not mine" category and yet my stomach is still queasy with the suspicion that it does have something to do with me." Alison's face pinked. Whatever did she see?

"Yes, please, dear, do share it with us."

"As you know, I saw myself as the nursemaid to Tutmoses – whom, I have to admit, I still think of as Malcolm."

She stared defiantly at Anne, who simply smiled.

"This afternoon's picture was a very different kind of life. I was a prostitute. I wasn't quite sure which country I was in. It was hot and dusty but it didn't really feel like Egypt. Somewhere further along North Africa perhaps or the Near East. There were a lot of soldiers around, it was a garrison town. I was a young girl when it started. I was quite pretty, sexy I suppose I should say, and proud of the power I had over the local boys. They followed me everywhere."

Her shrugged shoulder was dismissive but her eyes and downcast smile were pleased.

"I loved singing and dancing – a kind of belly dancing with lots of gyrations. It made me feel sensual and womanly. My parents were anxious to marry me off. I started to make eyes at the soldiers. I seemed to think that they could offer me a much more exciting life than any of the local men could – I'd have been married off to someone much older than myself, probably with children from another wife, and I didn't want that.

"One day, I went walking and I saw this incredibly handsome man – I can feel myself blushing when I think about it. He was a good few years older than me. He started to, as I thought, court me. He brought me gifts, took me out to see some musical performances and plays – all with the agreement of my parents who thought he would be a good catch. He was an officer and he had a house outside the town. It was a beautiful place, cool shady gardens and lots of fountains. He told my parents that he was giving a banquet for his fellow officers and that he would like me to be the hostess.

"When I went to the banquet, I was surprised to see that there were many woman there. Not my class, I suppose I'd call them tarts. They were scantily dressed and hanging around the men. Some were doing things that embarrassed me. When I voiced my fears to my companion, he laughed and said they were there to keep the men happy, it was the custom.

"As the feast went on, he plied me with wine. I wasn't used to drinking and I soon began to laugh loudly and flirt even more boldly than usual. Some musicians were brought in and one or two of the women danced. I told my officer that they were nowhere near as good as I was – and before I knew it, I was out there dancing before all the men. Now in my culture, this wasn't done. Women danced amongst themselves, as did the men. They didn't dance for the opposite sex. I felt ashamed and took more drink to cover my confusion."

Alison hesitated, fiddling with a handkerchief in her lap and winding it around her fingers, pulling it through over and over again. Anne nodded at her to continue.

"The next thing I was aware of was lying on a bed with my officer. He was stroking me and telling me how wonderfully I danced but that I'd exhausted myself and he'd brought me here to rest. When I tried to get up, he laughed and asked where I thought

I was going. He started kissing me, I have to admit I got quite carried away. I really enjoyed it. By no stretch of the imagination could it be described as a rape, I was all for it. It really surprised me how sexual I felt."

Her eyes were lowered. Had she had any sexual experience in this life? Not the kind of thing to ask in a group, but perhaps I could talk to her later.

"But, next morning, I was ashamed. I assumed he would marry me, but he said I could live in his house and entertain him and his friends. I didn't feel I could go home, I was dishonored. I stayed with him as his concubine. He taught me all about the arts of love and I became extremely skilful. It wasn't a bad life, I had a certain amount of independence and I loved all the partying. I saved up the gifts he gave me – and when I danced for his friends they always gave me money. Fortunately I kept my looks and we lived together for many years. Eventually he died but he'd given me the house and I was able to continue to live in style. In fact, I enjoyed the lifestyle, the parties and so on, so much that I continued them and had my own girls, whom I trained. I suppose you could call me a brothel keeper."

Alison's chin pulled back, a grimace of distaste distorted her usually serene face. It was difficult to picture this quiet spinster as a harlot, or a madam.

"What do you think, Anne? I hate the thought that that was me, but somehow I suspect it was."

"Well, dear, you know we can experience different ends of the spectrum in our various lives, especially where sexuality or religion are concerned. In your present life I suspect you've been quite reserved – you told me you were at a girls' boarding school and went on to be the bursar at a girls' school ..."

Alison nodded.

"After your parents died you went to the College of Psychic Studies to try to contact them and that brought you into spiritual matters ..."

Another nod.

"That means that wild, sexy side of yourself was never explored."

Was that doubt or regret on Alison's face?

"No, I remember I fancied taking up belly dancing once but my mother was horrified so I never did. And I never met young men or had boyfriends. Too quiet for them, I suppose, and too content to be at home with Mum and Dad." Her smile was regretful.

"This life you've just seen has opened up a whole new side of you, a gutsy, sexy woman. I'm not suggesting you should become a brothel keeper, but you could try belly dancing. It's an excellent way to keep fit after all, and it's increasingly popular."

Alison was looking thoughtful. Those big eyes of hers were her best feature, especially when she had that dreamy look in them. It softened her somewhat severe appearance.

"I'll give you a few lessons if you'd like to learn. Perhaps you'd all like to have a go. We can try it tonight in the bar," Miranda said eagerly. "You know, I've been learning back in England, and some of the boys on the boat are excellent dancers, they've been teaching Stephen and me a few moves."

That was why she'd been smiling. To my surprise Alison took up the offer and I thought I'd go along to see the fun. But for the time being, I was sure no one would mind if I napped while the others discuss their experiences. Pregnant mums had to keep their strength up.

As we headed towards the bar, Malcolm whispered to me.

"Fancy Alison being the Cynthia Payne of her day. A brothel keeper, I'm beginning to see her in a whole new light."

I hoped so. I'd like to see these two dear friends of mine together, they'd be perfect for each other even though there was a big age gap. Megan McKennar, you're turning into a matchmaker, I told myself. Watch it, don't meddle in other people's lives, you know the penalty for that. No, I wouldn't meddle, but I could always hope.

The belly dancing was fun. I'd never thought my pregnant body could gyrate like that but Miranda said it would help the birth – toned up the vaginal muscles apparently. She said she took it up to improve her sex life: it intensified orgasm. I wasn't sure whether her huge wink meant she'd found it successful or if she was pulling my leg.

Stephen was an excellent dancer. Thrusting his hips forward with a suggestive twitch, he'd moved towards the man in front of him. He'd certainly come out of his shell, and looked really sexy moving his hips like that. It showed off his cute bum, although I thought it was more like he was flaunting himself for the other men, especially the one who was matching him move for move. I supposed it was the guy who'd been teaching Miranda. But then, didn't someone say the men danced for each other in Egypt, not for women?

The Egyptian guys were having fun, the djembas and flutes had come out and they were wailing a suitably sensuous song. I wondered if they were employed on the strength of their entertainment skills rather than their ability to wait table? They certainly had to be versatile on those cruises.

I needed a drink, belly dancing was more strenuous than I'd thought; I'd better rest and watch the others.

"How are you doing, Megan, my legs can't take too much of this."

Anne dropped heavily onto the cushioned seat beside me. The ice in her drink sloshed and dripped and she wiped her finger reflectively down the glass and then raised it to her lips, licking it gently. "Shouldn't really have ice, bad for the stomach, but I needed it after that."

"I'm fine, I'm beginning to feel really good but I'm looking forward to Karnak, I haven't forgotten I need to regain my *akhar* and to break that curse. I'm sure that will make a difference."

"It certainly should. Your child is a special one and we have to get you fit for his birth." She smiled knowingly.

"His, Anne? Do you know something I don't?"

"Not really, I feel sure it's a boy. But we shall see."

"Phew, that's hot work, I seem to have lost my old skill but I think I'll take it up when I get home. Miranda's offered to introduce me to her teacher. Perhaps you could come along, Megan?"

Alison settled on the divan opposite Anne. Her hair was down and it rippled over her shoulders. It made such a difference, she should wear it that way more often. It didn't look ridiculous in the way so many middle-aged women did when they let their hair down, but then, nothing could ruffle her quiet dignity.

"I'm glad I found you two alone like this. I'd really like to have a word about that life I saw."

Anne and I sat forward in unison.

"What is it?"

"Well, I didn't like to say in the group, but I had the strongest feeling that the officer was Malcolm. I wasn't sure how he'd react to the idea of having a concubine even if it was in another life."

Anne opened her mouth to speak but I got there first: "Why don't you discuss it with him, he's on his way over. He looks hot. You could take him out onto deck for some air. Here, have some of Anne's ice." I quickly scooped it into a napkin and handed it to her.

Megan McKennar, I thought you weren't going to interfere, but I was only giving a helping hand.

chapter 16.

shining of countenance

What's that? Something's woken me. It feels like rocks piled on my chest but whatever it is, it is breathing very, very slowly. I can't move under the weight but I can open my eyes. Ah, the big daddy of all crocodiles. They don't grow that big unless they are the pampered pet of a Sobek priest at the temple. Yes, I thought so. Turquoise earrings and a rather attractive gold necklace.

Why did you get stuck half way across my bed? You're a bit big to be snuggling up next to me – and far too ugly even if you are a sacred beast. Come on, move. As my hand pushes ineffectually at a shoulder, the great head turns to look into my eyes.

"Do not be afraid of death. It is the gateway to life."

Well, well, philosophical wisdom from a crocodile. Mecky, you really are losing it. Overheated imagination? That sounds about right. Go back to sleep.

Next time I awoke it was well into morning. Was my nocturnal visitor a dream, a suggestion left over from yesterday; surely it could not have been real? How blasé I'd felt, pushing it off with my hand. What a risk to take, especially with an emblem of death.

All those teeth, better not to think about that, let's see what the day would hold.

We were at Aswan, Aswan the Beautiful as Khaled called it. His mother's family were from there. He was right, that view was fantastic. This was what brought me to Egypt, that view in a travel brochure. It felt so long ago now. When we'd docked it was too dark to see those towering, shimmering copper sand dunes, or the lush vegetation on that island in the middle of the river around which the white sails swooped and danced. The famous cataract must be further up. We'd see it that afternoon when we went to Philae. I was glad I hadn't bothered to get up early for the Aga Khan's tomb, I'd had enough of death.

Magical, that was the only word for it. As the launch moved away from the barren, black shore with its flock of tut buzzards, under a flawless blue sky, a siren temple beckoned. I couldn't believe Philae had been moved from its old site, it looked as though it had been there forever as we crossed the still water. The rosy temple on its rocky island was perfectly reflected in the shimmering lake. Two temples, one above, one below. One for Isis, one for Osiris. The Duat rose close to the surface here.

"This place of pilgrimage, and partying. There pleasure kiosk of goddess Hathor, set apart at lake edge. You see pictures of gods playing musical instruments, and vast quantities of beer they drink. Egyptians like party," Josef grinned.

Across the water drifted the suggestion of music: flute, zither, and djemba accompanied the high voices, dimly sensed shapes whirled and swirled in the dance, sistrums twirling. This had been a lively and frenetic place. Potent beer scented the air. It was different from the serene air of the main temple, like a tart snuggled up to a bishop. Perhaps Alison would find more memories there. I could see her as a dancing girl in a temple very like this one.

Coming in to land, Anne reminded us: "This is the Holy Island of Isis. Ask the goddess's permission to enter."

Stepping out of the launch, I could sense this was sacred ground. It felt like coming home, don't tell me I was here too, I thought. This was where Sekhmet ended her killing spree but this temple was built much later than that. Anne said it was one of her favorite places in all Egypt, and I could see why.

Nerissa and the others rushed off with Josef to look at Imhotep's medical sanctuary but I was quite happy with the moon goddess in her many guises bedecking the tall columns in that quiet corner of the wide courtyard. Her face was so serene as she gazed out across the lake. I too could look out to Biggah Island, resting place of Osiris, it was immensely peaceful ...

What the ...

The willowy blonde American woman who was at the Sound and Light in Luxor was prancing about giving orders to her flock – why did I call them that? Could it be the way they bleated about after her? I mustn't be bitchy but it was a bit groveling, anyone would think she was royal. She was too showy for me; I liked the quiet spiritual authority of Anne – or the immense power of The Old Queen Tiye.

There they went. Dancing round the courtyard. Sistrums, drums, chanting, the whole works. Anyone watching would be fooled into thinking it authentic, but she should have gone to Hathor's kiosk, it would have been more appropriate there. Those costumes made Beatrice seem tame, even more gold than she wore, and the headdresses: Anubis, the Cobra goddess – couldn't remember her name, Ma'at, Hathor, I assumed that Sun Disk was Ra and the Moon Isis, and they'd even got my Lady and a great green Osiris. Where was Horus? How could they see with those things on?

A group of Japanese tourists seemed to think it was a show put on by the temple. They'd brought seats from the Sound and Light show over and were clapping enthusiastically. I didn't think I'd seen Japanese that animated before.

It looked like Jane's group was about to present a sacred drama. Didn't she know this was never meant for unbeliever's eyes? She was narrating the myth of Isis and Osiris while her group acted it out. Oh dear, she shouldn't have stood on the trunk Set needed to trap Osiris, that was an unceremonious removal by one of the followers – and didn't his hands linger for a little longer than was proper? Were they going to throw the box in the lake? No, they simply put it to one side while they enacted the search. If this was pantomime I could have shouted, "It's behind you."

Then some of the group gathered round the trunk, waving about and rustling – Isis couldn't have missed a clue like that. Which garden did those leaves come out of, I wondered. They were probably staying at The Old Cataract Hotel. I bet they would need plenty of baksheesh to get the gardeners there to part with their manicured shrubs.

How sad that the guardians announced closing time and Osiris was still in his box. Maybe the gods stepped in. The group were being herded out. She was waving baksheesh around again and one of the guardians pocketed it, but he was still waving them away.

I'd better go and join our boat. Anne said we'd have to appear to leave and afterwards we would come back and have an hour to ourselves before the Sound and Light show begins.

But we were being tailed by the loud American. I wasn't sure the Egyptians really understood the concept of one group having the place to themselves, not when there was money involved. Thought as much, they were disembarking again and heading off for the Nileometer on the far side of the courtyard, lugging their trunk with them, it must double as a costume box. Anne was leading us in the other direction.

"I thought we'd do some quiet meditation here in the Isis sanctuary. This temple has many stories to tell, especially the Isis and Osiris myth. That is a great love story, and another allegorical tale of death and rebirth, with a bit of adultery and treachery thrown in for good measure, and the birth of the magical child who becomes the hero. Lots of magic and mystery for you there."

And this seemed a suitable place to experience it. Was the roof replaced in the rebuilding, I wondered, or had it survived intact? Its shadowy corners seemed peopled with the old goddess and the priestesses who served her. There, behind that pillar, surely that was the moon goddess herself looking on.

"Josef told you the basic story on the boat so I'm not going to say anything this time. You've done enough work with me by now to be able to find your own way in – and out, although I'll warn you when it's time to finish your meditation and make sure everyone's back with us ready for the Sound and Light show. Find a comfortable spot, close your eyes and away you go."

Before me, a shining being, veiled in silver light beneath a crescent moon. Hand held out to me.

"I am the Lady Isis, Queen of Night, one of five children born to Geb and Nuit in the days that Thoth stole for her. My beautiful twin sister Nephthys is married to our brother Set. I to his twin, the handsome Osiris. They rule the Red Lands, we the Black, but our houses are united in kinship and in love.

"My brother-husband and I have brought many gifts to our land. He the knowledge of agriculture, writing, and astronomy. I the crafts of spinning and weaving, the mysteries of medicine and magic. My husband taught men how to grow the vine and make wine. Together we raised our people from the darkness of ignorance into the light of civilization, we taught them law and government, religion and morals. Our achievements are many but there is a sadness upon me: I have not conceived a child. My sister Nephthys too is barren. In vain she lies with her husband in the night.

"Then, while I am in the far north teaching my women the mysteries of inner vision, my brother-husband gives a party to celebrate the Sed Festival.

"In my mind's eye I see my sister sitting forlorn in the moonlight. My lord Osiris, deep in drink, mistakes her for me. She, desperate to have a child, lies with him under the stars that line our mother Nuit's belly, and conceives Anubis: the jackal-headed god. Returning from the Delta, putting aside the hurt in my heart, I give shelter to my beloved sister. She fears that, if she returns to her husband, he will tear out her womb and devour the child. His temper is wild and passionate, like the lands he rules. But when she births her child, my sister exposes him to be eaten by wild dogs and returns like a dutiful wife to her husband. I rescue the child, Anubis, he becomes my constant companion, guardian of my days and nights.

"Before I return again to the Delta, the Lord Set gives a banquet to which he invites my brother-husband. Whilst servants scatter rose petals around the room and the guests sing, wine is passed around. My Lord Osiris has one weakness. For him, one drink is never enough, a million cannot satisfy his thirst. In vain with my all-seeing eye do I try to warn him. "Watch out my Lord, Set has evil intent for you. Put aside intoxication. Take care."

"I see the evil one, the red-haired Lord Set, order his servants to bring forth a great, bejeweled chest. Throwing back the lid, with words sweet as honey he promises it to anyone around whom it fits perfectly. Many try but all are too lacking in stature. At length my befuddled husband struggles to his feet and falls into the chest. Instantly the servants of Set slam the lid shut and tie it around with leather bindings. It is nailed shut and sealed with lead so that my Lord cannot breathe. The entire party accompanies the casket to the Nile, into which it is cast.

"Desperately I seek the casket, searching the length of the great river but to no avail. Anubis is sent to search the Duat, this child of my sister and brother-husband has free passage in and out of the underworld. Desolate and inconsolable, my sister joins me. She can no longer bear to be by her husband-brother's side. She knows his jealousy has brought about this great tribulation on our family. We search for my Lord's body for seven long years, roaming far and wide. So great is my grief, I cannot stay in the Black Land. My Lord could be far from here. I leave my sister and travel to the furthest reaches of our empire. At last I hear that he has been washed ashore on the land of Byblos.

"Taking ship, I travel to the court of King Malkander and Queen Astarte. In the center of their palace, there is a great wooden pillar. With my inner eye I see the casket containing my Lord Osiris held at the heart of the pillar. The casket had been washed to the shores of this land into the arms of a Tamarind tree. With great tenderness the tree enfolded my Lord. The tree, which grew to an enormous girth, was cut down to make the central pillar for the palace. Wailing piteously I tear my clothes and pull out my hair. Seeing my great grief, and thinking me but a servant, the King and Queen take pity on me and give me a position as nursemaid to their children.

"One night, when I am grieving for my Lord and have let the magical protection that disguises me fall, the King's beloved eldest son comes sleepily into my room. Seeing my full might, he falls dead to the floor. Reviving him with my magic, I plunge him into the fire to make him immortal. For many long nights I utter the incantations and immerse him in the fire. On the final night, just as the light of divinity touches him, an anguished wailing interrupts my ritual, his mother has seen us. The spell is broken. He will be mortal forever more.

"Revealing myself in all my glory, the Queen falls to her knees before me. Her husband presents me with the precious pillar. Catching up an axe, I cleave the tree from the casket and cut the leather thongs. Lifting the lid, I gaze upon my sleeping Lord. Strewing precious spices and scented flowers around his body, I take ship and transport the casket deep into the swamps of the Delta.

"Using my incantations and magical powers, I transmogrify and take the form of a kite. Hovering over my Lord's body, I flap my wings to awaken him. He stirs as though from a long dream, hand rubbing his eyes in bewilderment. He is neither alive nor dead, being held in suspension. I go to gather herbs for the sorcery I will need to restore him fully to life.

"But the Lord Set, on a hunting expedition in the marshes, has found my hiding place. When I leave the Lord Osiris unattended, he steals the body of my husband and severs him into fourteen pieces which he scatters the length and breadth of the Black Land.

"Searching diligently, my sister and I recover thirteen pieces. Wherever we find a part of the god, we leave a temple to honor him. But the fourteenth piece, his great member, eludes us. A fisherman tells me he saw it eaten by a crocodile, the creature of my brother Set. Another tells me it was eaten by a fish, my own symbol of rebirth. Not knowing whom to believe, I take my Lord to my spinning mill in the Delta. Here I re-member his body and fashion a wooden phallus to replace that which was lost. Hovering over it, I imbue his dead body with life long enough to conceive a magical child.

"My brother-enemy Set, who has taken over rulership of the land, seeks me out and imprisons me in my spinning mill. Before my child is born, I cast a spell of invisibility over myself and slip past his guards. Hiding in the reeds I birth my child squatting upon the birthing blocks. Labor is long and hard, I share the travails of woman. Two of my sister goddesses appear and smear my forehead with blood, immediately my body splits and I bring forth Horus, who rises like a falcon on the wind.

"He goes forth to fight his uncle, devourer of the Black Land. The battle for the succession is protracted and destructive, it rages from one end of the land to the other. My son loses an eye, but not the battle. The gods grow tired of the contest and convene a debate to decide on whose side they will intervene. The fairer sex are banned, so, disguising my beauty in a wall-eyed old hag, I use my famed sorcery to trick my way into the meeting. Sensing injustice, the gods give strength to the arm of Horus.

"With the gods on his side, my son skillfully spears his uncle and victory is his. Accepting Set's war-like nature, the Great God, Amon-Ra, places him at the prow of his solar barque. He becomes the God of Storms, who shall raise his voice in the sky and men will be afraid of him, intimidating humankind for his master and protecting Ra from his enemies.

"The land of Khemet rejoices at my son's victory. But I retire to my island home, Philae, the most serene temple. The body of my husband is placed on Biggah Island and, each year, I visit with him and rekindle the flame of our love. Fertility for the land is assured. Meanwhile, my Lord resides in the Duat, he is the Great Green Judge of the Dead. Everyone must come before him to have their heart weighed in truth and justice.

"So you see, I am Woman. I have known love and loss, betrayal and forgiveness. I have birthed my son and buried my husband. You, my child, have earned the girdle of Isis. By your suffering we are become one. Take it, wear it. It will bring you clear sight and spiritual authority. In time, when you truly understand all you have been through and have re-membered yourself, it will bring you healing."

"Now, it's time to return your awareness ..."

Perfect timing as always, Anne.

As Ra fell behind the horizon and the world turned rosy purple, a rising wind howled like the ululations of priests and the baying of sacrificial animals hung in the air. Shivering, I reached for my wrap. This temple still held secrets. There would be some way to go before I fully understood all that had happened in that last, long year. Meanwhile I could give myself over to the Sound and Light performance.

"You will have seen the other group who were at Philae?" Anne eyed us quizzically, the corner of her mouth twitching slightly. "Well, their leader, Jane Abrams, spoke to me before we left Philae last night. Apparently they are putting on a performance at the Old Cataract Hotel tonight and we are invited. I know it's your last day here in Aswan, but if anyone is interested ..."

"What are they doing?"

Trust Miranda to be interested in a performance.

"The Lament of Isis and Nephthys. Apparently Jane has worked out that this is the twenty-fifth day of the fourth summer month, the traditional time for its performance. I'd take issue with that, I think it's much more likely to be later in the year, nearer midsummer, but it would be interesting to hear such an ancient poem performed."

"Oh do let's go." Miranda bubbled. "It would fit in well with the Isis and Osiris theme. You didn't have anything planned for tonight, did you, Anne?"

"Only a meal at a good local restaurant. But we'll be in plenty of time, the performance doesn't start until ten. The hotel is just up the road from the restaurant. Those of you who don't want to see the show can easily walk back to the boat through the bazaar, or down the corniche if you prefer."

What am I doing here, I asked myself? I had a wonderful meal, felt really rested and exceptionally well. So why was I about to watch a performance I'd had no intention of catching? Ah well, better make the most of it. It should be a good laugh if nothing else. Pay attention, the lights are going out ... Here they come. The costumes were superb, they could have stepped straight off the walls at Philae ...

"Glorify his soul. Stabilize his dead body.

Praise his spirit. Give breath to his nostrils and to his parched throat.

Give gladness unto the heart of Isis and to that of Nephthys;
Place Horus upon the throne of his father;
Give life, stability, and power to Osiris within the Duat,
Born of the great forsaken one, she who is called Truthful –
Glorious are her acts, according to the words of the gods.
Behold now, Isis speaks –

"Come to your temple, come to your temple, oh Lord
Come to the temple, for your enemies are gone.
Behold the excellent sistrum-bearer – come to your temple.
Oh I, your sister, love you – do not depart from me.
Behold, oh Lord, the beautiful one.
Come to your temple immediately – Behold my heart which grieves for you;
Behold me seeking you – I am searching for you to behold you.
Lo, I am prevented from beholding you –
I am prevented from beholding you, oh Lord.
It is blessed to behold you – come to the one who loves you.
Come to the one who loves you, oh you who art beautiful, Osiris, deceased.
Come to your sister – come to your wife –
Come to your wife, oh you who makes the heart to rest.
I, your sister, born of your mother, go about to each of your temples.
Yet you come not forth to me.
Gods, and men before the face of the gods, are weeping for you at the same time, when they behold me.
Lo, I invoke you with wailing that reaches high as heaven –

Yet, you hear not my voice. Lo, I, your sister
I love you more than all the earth – And you love not another as
you love your sister
Surely you love not another as you do your sister.

"Behold now Nephthys speaks
Behold the excellent sistrum-bearer. Come to your temple.
Cause your heart to rejoice, for your enemies are gone.
All your sister-goddesses are at your side and behind your couch.
Calling upon you with weeping – yet you are prostrate upon
your bed.
Hearken unto the beautiful words uttered by us and by every
noble one among us.
Subdue your every sorrow which is in the hearts of us your
sisters,
Oh strong one among the gods – strong among men who behold
you.
We come before you, oh prince, our lord.
Live before us, desiring to behold you.
Turn not away your face before us.
Sweeten our hearts when we behold you, oh prince.
Beautify our hearts when we behold you.
I, Nephthys your sister, I love you.
Your foes are subdued, there is not one remaining.
Lo, I am with you. I shall protect your limbs forever, eternally.

"Behold now, Isis speaks –
Depart not from us who behold you.
There proceeds from you the strong Orion in heaven at evening
in the resting of every day.

Lo, it is I, at the approach of the Sothis period, who does watch for him.

Nor will I leave off watching for him, for that which proceeds from you is revered.

Come you to us from your chamber, in the day when your soul gives forth emanations –

The day when offerings upon offerings are made to your spirit, which causes the gods and men likewise to live.

Your soul possesses the earth, and your likenesses the underworld.

Lo, it is prepared for and contains your hidden shrine.

Your wife is ready to protect you, and your son Horus also, as prince of the lands.

"Behold now, Nephthys speaks –

Behold the excellent sistrum-bearer. Come to your temple Osiris deceased

Come to your beloved enclosure. Come to the place your soul loves and the souls of your fathers likewise.

Your son, your child Horus born of your sister-goddesses is before your face.

It is I who does illuminate and protect you every day –

I will not depart from you forever.

Oh come for your name is protector.

Behold your mother, Nuit, lovely child.

Depart not from her. Come to her breasts, abundance is therein.

Your sister, too, is beautiful, depart not from her,

Come to your temple Osiris.

You will rest beside your mother eternally.

She preserves your limbs and procures terror among your enemies, for she protects you forever.

Behold the excellent sistrum-bearer. Come to your temple.

Come, behold your son Horus as prince of gods and men.

He takes possession of the cities and the nomes by the magnitude of his terrors.

Heaven and earth are filled with fear of him,

And the barbarians are submissive under his terrors. Your children are among gods and men.

And the eastern and western horizons are among the attributes of your producing.

Your two sisters are at your side, purifying your soul.

And your son Horus honors your attributes. There come forth funeral and other offerings – beer, bulls and geese – for you.

Every day your son Horus glorifies your spirit,

And he avenges your name by offerings for your soul placed at your secret shrine.

As for the gods, their arms bear libation vases for the purifying of your spirit.

Come to your child, oh prince, our lord, nor depart you from us. Lo, he comes."

I hoped the others couldn't see the tears. My raging hormones must be to blame for my weepiness. I wasn't usually that sentimental. Jane had been superb, she seemed to lose that grating American accent. The other woman was excellent too, I didn't catch her name but Anne said she was a professional actress and Miranda seemed to know her so I assumed she was a professional actress too. It hadn't seemed over the top at all, despite the elaborate costumes. I was surprised how moved I was.

I was there, at Philae, with someone I loved and respected, a teacher of the mysteries. So often we walked in the cool of the evening, so often we enacted the sacred dramas, climbed the secret staircases of initiation. Her loss was deeper even than that of Ramon. He was the Lord of my Heart, she was Mistress of my Soul, guide on my journey. Would I ever see her again, it felt like she was gone from me like Osiris was from Isis. Gone from my life, like Isis I was bereft.

Don't think about it, Mecky, move on.

There was a remarkable smell, spicy and exotic. Anne said this was the medical souk, which sold herbs and spices. Shuttered and silent now, I could imagine it humming like Luxor bazaar. There'd be time in the morning to shop before we got the plane. I didn't need djellabahs and the like so I wouldn't bother, I was anxious to get to Karnak.

chapter 17.

guide and protectress from the perils of the underworld

"Hey, my friends? You enjoy Aswan?" Khaled beamed at us.

The Cabman's Arms hung suspended in time. The same domino players laughed and shouted, the young shoe-shine boy still squatted hopefully at our feet, and the shisha smokers lolled on the battered blue benches talking quietly between gurgling inhalations. Only the fairy lights had gone, replaced by a smart, brightly colored awning strung across the street.

I'd needed a stroll after the wait at the airport. It was time for some helba and, perhaps, a quick game of dominoes before bed. Terri had promised to teach me; apparently she was quite a whiz at it. I was glad to see Alison and Malcolm walking together behind us, they seemed to have a lot to say to each other. I wondered what was in the mysterious brown paper bag Malcolm was handing to Khaled.

I felt so happy sitting there sipping helba, but I couldn't get my brain around dominoes that night. I was glad Anne had got tomorrow all set up. After the museum, it was a free day for the group so we could go to Karnak; it felt right that she'd asked

Alison and Malcolm to come along. I needed them there, though I didn't know why. Mmm, I was tired, perhaps Khaled would get the horse out, I'd rather like to be taken back to the hotel in style.

It was like coming home. I'd grown to love that angular building, stark pink walls belying the warmth of its opulent, chattering interior. The foyer was crowded as usual, with the bar crowd spilling out onto the seats. The live music was a bit overpowering though, so I thought I'd go straight to bed, but it didn't look like that would work – Joan was heading our way.

"Anne, you'll never guess what happened?"

"What is it?"

"I rang my daughter and she's taking that research post in Canada. That tie-cutting did make a difference." The look she gave Anne was defiant.

"That's good news, I'm glad it worked out for her." Anne seemed genuinely pleased. "In the morning, we can walk down to the museum. It will be pleasant on the corniche before the sun gets too hot. I'll see you here in the foyer at eight thirty."

Taking the slow stairway to heaven, heading back to my old room, I couldn't help wondering whether this visit would work the same kind of miracle for me as the previous trip had. If only I could see Ramon, know what he was thinking, why he'd left like that. Perhaps then I could truly cut the ties with him. Our sacred marriage may have been dissolved but we still had that strong heart connection. So much had happened since I was last in that room, but I'd a nagging suspicion that there was more to find out.

As I looked down on the lights way below, the air shimmered and My Lady appeared outside the window.

"*Look to the bigger picture Megan. If you were down there, you'd see the individual cars, hear their hooting, dodge from their path, maybe catch a ride in one. Up here, you get a different perspective, all you see is that shining ribbon of light. Look at your lives like that. Then you will know."*

Anne had said it would be cool walking down to the museum but the pavement was burning my feet already through my thin sandals and the trees were few and far between. The museum was a strange building: a long, corrugated, concrete slab sitting there staring blankly out at the Nile. Still, it rather suited those statues standing guard outside, reminded me in a way of Hatshepshut's temple.

At least it was cool inside, those marble floors were great. I slipped off my shoes and walked barefoot.

Oh, look. My Lord. Akhenaten. That huge head was exactly like him. What a superb carving. So alive, it could step forward at any moment – if it had a body. That secret smile he always wore was playing around his mouth, so full of delight, as though he was listening to a joke no one else heard. Only his visionary eyes were wrong, their strange shattered light didn't show in the stone. The sculptor had captured that dreamy, mystical quality of his. Such a distinctive face, so much more than a mere human. Only a god could look like that. But there was a tormented soul behind there somewhere, I knew there was.

"Megan, come along, don't linger. You can see that stuff anytime, I want to show you the Tutmoses statue I told you about." Malcolm grasped my arm and rushed me past some wonderful pieces. I'd have to come back for a proper look. "Here, what do you think? Does he look like me?" His impish smile beamed out as he presented his profile for my inspection.

The statue was smaller than I expected, but wonderfully carved, each line finely incised. This was the work of a master sculptor. Like Akhenaten, Tutmoses too looked as though he would swing into motion at any moment; what skills those ancient craftsmen had. Such a handsome man, his eyes were wonderful, you could see his noble soul gazing out, but he lacked that otherworldly quality that made my Lord unique.

"It has to be one of the best things I've seen, Malcolm. It's a wonderful carving, and, yes, he does have the look of you. It must be the nose. Quick, stand there and I'll take a photo of you both. That's it, squat down to the same level so I can get both your profiles side by side. That's good. Has Beatrice seen it yet?"

"No, she went rushing off to show Joan and Alison what she claims is a statue of Hatshepshut, and I haven't seen her since. Now, if you want to get back to Akhenaten, I suggest you go upstairs. There's a whole wall of his temple up there." He pointed to a ramp leading upward to a hidden gallery.

So there was, but what I was more interested in were the statues and stelae that showed the family. From what I recalled, only my Lord had an elongated head, and that wasn't as big as this one. Nefertiti and the children were quite normal, even though the artists had shown them with stylized profiles that mirrored Akhenaten. Neferititi was beautiful though, there was no getting away from that. Absolutely stunning, it was a pity she'd been so distorted on these stelae, they didn't really capture her properly; that broken head over there, from the early Armana period, was much closer to how she was. I wanted to see if I recognized anyone else. Yes, there, that was Merit'aten standing beside her father. I wondered if I could find Smenkhare ...

A hand on my arm made me jump:

"Megan, dear, I've been looking everywhere for you. It's time we went to meet Khaled, he'll be waiting to take us to Karnak." Anne hurried me towards the staircase like one of those secretary birds chivvying a wayward ibis.

"Okay, Anne, I wouldn't miss that for the world, but I'd like to come back later to study these in more detail, if there's time."

"The museum is only open in the mornings. If you got up early, you'd have time to visit before we leave for the airport."

"It's not like Khaled to be late. Should we go down to the house, do you think? He said he would be here."

Anne had been fussing with her watch for the last twenty minutes.

"I'm sure he'll be here soon." Malcolm seemed unperturbed. "We can do a bit of window shopping while we wait. Have you seen that statue of Sekhmet? It's a nineteenth-century fake but it is absolutely exquisite. I tried to buy it last time I was here but the guy wasn't selling – said it was made by his great, great, great grandfather. I suppose it has an antique value of its own now."

The shop looked as though it too was an antique. Dust was piled high along the windows and over the precious objects; I even spied a cobweb or two although I'd seen few spiders in Egypt. Dirty brown shutters were opened back against the wooden walls, but surely they hadn't been painted since great, great, great granddaddy's time.

"It's beautiful – oh, look. Here's Khaled. Good job that horse knows its way. Whatever's wrong with him, he looks awful, slumped down like that."

Malcolm smiled ruefully.

"That's my fault, I'm afraid. He told me last time I was here that cab drivers have a special dispensation to drink beer. I gathered he likes beer so I bought him a selection of Real Ales – that was what was in that mysterious brown paper package last night. He looks like he's been on the Theakston's Old Peculier – did you know that was named after an ecclesiastical official, by the way?"

Trust Malcolm to know something like that.

"You shouldn't have done that. As a good Muslim he shouldn't be drinking beer at all and that real ale is much stronger than the stuff they brew here." Anne's voice had never been sharp like that before, but poor Khaled did look terrible, he couldn't seem to open his eyes properly.

"Khaled, do you want to go home, we can easily get a cab down to Karnak." Alison clearly wanted to smooth things over but Khaled drew himself up and said stiffly:

"Friend coming other horse. We go Karnak."

These Egyptians were touchy; strong pride lay under the smiling faces. And, sure enough, Ahmed came into view in the other caleche. Sagging in his seat his gray complexion matched the faded and stained djellabah that hung askew on one shoulder revealing a ragged t-shirt beneath.

"Heavens," said Anne, "he's in an even worse state than Khaled. Thank goodness it's an easy drive."

Anne took me and Malcolm was keen to chauffeur Alison. There definitely seemed to be a friendship developing there, I know he was quite a bit older than her but ... he'd never mentioned the idea that he was her protector. What did he think of that? I didn't like to ask him, seemed a bit personal, and I wouldn't want to spoil what was happening between them.

"Shall we go over and pay our respects to Sekhmet?" Anne was already striding purposefully across the shining white courtyard, heading for that familiar path.

"Yes, please. I'd rather hoped we might be able to do the work there."

"It rather depends on how many people are about, you know what the guardians are like, they won't pass up the chance of baksheesh and I don't want you pulled back at an inopportune moment. Perhaps Khaled being late did us a favor. The coaches seem to have gone and it's pretty quiet now. If we can't work in her temple I know another spot tucked away at the back where we won't be disturbed. I'm sure it was a room used for dream incubation – it always brings up images for me, and it has the advantage that there're never any guardians there."

Alison hurried forward to walk beside Anne.

"Anne, was dream incubation part of the temple training? I've always had vivid dreams and since I started my healing training at the college I've had several where I seemed to be healing someone – I've also found myself telling someone the meaning of their dreams and it almost always has something to do with changing their life in some way. Was that the kind of thing that went on?"

"Well, that was part of temple training but dream incubation meant asking for a dream to help you understand or heal something. Priestesses, and priests too, were trained to sit with the dreamer and accompany them in their dreams as a kind of guide. Afterwards they talked to them about the experience. Dream therapy, we'd probably call it."

Alison nodded: "That's happened to me sometimes, I've found myself in someone else's dream – "

"Oh no, that's never happened before. There's always someone to unlock the door." Anne glanced all around but the way to

Sekhmet remained barred. The guardians were nowhere to be seen. "Sorry I cut you off, Alison, but I was surprised, I've never seen this place deserted before."

"That's alright, Anne, we can talk about dreams later. This is Megan's healing time, we should focus on her, isn't that right Malcolm?"

He nodded.

"Perhaps we could do the work first and come back later. It must be past lunchtime now, I expect they're sneaking a siesta, what do you think Anne?"

Malcolm was wearing that hat again. A piece of his hair had escaped and was standing up like a cobra. There were times when I could have sworn he was a Pharaoh, but if that perfectly carved statue of Tutmoses in the museum was anything to go by, Tutmoses was a meticulous chap, unlike Malcolm, in appearance at least. Malcolm must have been one of the others.

"Perhaps we could have a cup of tea and something to eat before we start work."

Trust Anne to be thinking of her stomach; she certainly liked her food, but this would be a good idea, as long as there was something else other than tea. A Coke would be nice and I could do with a sandwich – those biscuits I'd taken along weren't very filling. Looking at our two friends, I wondered whether perhaps Anne and I should sit at a separate table, but that would look rather obvious ... Come on, Mecky, stop interfering, I had to tell myself again. I didn't know what had got into me and I knew I had to let things take their own course.

"This is the place, I'm sure we won't be disturbed." Anne glanced around the quiet courtyard. Nothing moved in the intense heat.

We hadn't seen a soul as we'd clambered around those broken walls. No wonder no one came this way, it was such a jumble. It was difficult to see what part of the temple this could have been with all those blocks lying about but Anne seemed to think it was a garden courtyard with the dream healing rooms all around. She said it was tucked away at the back because of the peace and quiet.

Strange how that chamber had remained intact. It felt good, nice and cool – and safe. Not smelly like some of the other chambers the tourists seemed to think doubled as loos. The stone floor was hard though, it was a good job Khaled had found us mats and cushions. I needed to lie down.

"Malcolm, could you stand guard at the door, please, to ensure we're not disturbed. You'll be the Guardian of the West in case Megan needs extra strength." Anne nodded towards the square of light.

"Of course, I'll do anything to help Megan, you know that. But I'm not sure I can be of much magical use. I've never done anything like this before." His hand forked his hair, disarraying the punk halo outlined against the light.

"Are you sure of that?" Anne quizzed him. " I believe you were initiated long ago and you'll remember when the time comes. I have every confidence in you, and in Alison too. I want you to sit near Megan's feet, please, Alison. You'll anchor her *ka* to the earth and protect her physical body while she's gone. All you need is your own quiet strength, and a strong intent to aid her."

"Ever since I first saw you, Megan, I've felt that we had some purpose in meeting, other than simply remembering that life we shared. I'll be honored to help in this." Alison curtsied to the ground at my feet.

Anne's face had taken on that quiet authority I knew so well. It was as though she put on a mantle of power as she placed her ritual tools on a scarf laid in the dirt in front of her.

"Right, if everyone is settled, we'll begin.

"We call on the Lady Sekhmet to aid us in our endeavors, to protect us against our enemies, and to bring courage into our hearts as we seek to aid Megan in vanquishing her enemies."

Anne gently shook a sistrum; it was used to calm My Lady but I suspected I might need her in destroyer mode before this was finished.

"We make this offering of beer in your honor as each of us drink from the sacred cup."

She poured a libation of beer into the paper cup, and drank deeply herself.

I hadn't realized I'd be drinking but it was okay, Anne propped my head up and I managed a sip. Then she offered it to Alison, and to Malcolm. There was a powerful smell as she poured the rest over the small stone altar lying overturned in a corner. All honor to My Lady. Sekhmet be with me. Sa Sekhem Sahu.

"As we light this candle and offer this incense, bring light into our hearts and open our inner eyes that we may see."

Anne walked round the chamber, purifying it and us with light and sacred smoke.

With pounding pressure, my third eye burst open. The walls were luminous, and wonderful bright rainbow colors swirled around. Malcolm's outline had a red tinge, Anne violet, and Alison pink. I'd be able to recognize them from that if I met them in the outer deep.

"Now, Megan, it's time to begin your journey. Close your eyes and stand up in your *ka*. Travel with the Lady Sekhmet at your side. She will take you to the outer deep so that there you may find your *akhar*."

The rushing wind, time moving past, whirling space and stars unlimited, and then, a sudden stillness. Ahead of me, my shining self. Quickly I reached out and touched it – what was this? A barrier, hard and strong. I couldn't see it, but it tingled when I touched it and sprang back if I tried to press through. I must break through to reach my *akhar*. Who had set this in place?

Ah, there, I saw that renegade priest at his altar. He had the body of my child and was trying to breathe life into him, but to no avail. He turned to my own body, placing a small amulet within the outer wrapping.

"Cursed be this woman for all time. May her body cease to exist, may her heart cease to exist, may her *ka* cease to exist. I command her soul to fly to the outer deep and remain there. Mighty is the command I set upon her that she shall not return until I claim her. Her soul is within my grasp, her power is mine, her strength flows into me."

No, no, this couldn't be. Why had no one performed the rituals to save me, to guide me to Amenti, why had I been given to this renegade priest to do with what he would? No, I could not have this.

"*My Lady, help me, send your flames to consume him, turn back his curses, return to me my power. I am your High Priestess, Mek'an'ar, I command that the gods strike down this impertinent priest. My initiation is greater than his, I have journeyed with My Lady, I have seen the secrets beyond telling. I am Mek'an'ar, save me.*

"*The demons of the night cannot hurt me, the beasts of Set cannot touch me, nothing he sends against me has power, he cannot hold my* akhar. *I demand it, I claim it back in the name of My Lady and by the power of my word. Sa Sekhem Sahu.*"

I grasped the amulet and threw it into the hands of my Lady. She had the power to remove threats against me, vengeance belonged to her alone.

The barrier was thinning, there was a way through. My Lady touched it with her ankh and a gateway opened. Quickly, I regained the *akhar*, rejoined it with my *ka*. Then I stood once more in the full power of my soul, with the knowledge of the power of all my lives, all my initiations.

"All curses be gone from me. Renegade priest, you have done your worst and you have not harmed me. Be gone!"

But what was this? The Lady Magrat rose tall above me, wreathed about with snakes and serpents of darkness. Her snakes struck at me, her hands clawed my skin, she sought my soul because I bore Suten's child. Imprisoning me in her serpent's flickering gaze, she mesmerized my will with their swaying hoods.

"My Lady, help me. Show me the way to break free. Guardian of the West, come to my aid, strike dead the Lady Magrat and her venomous beasts."

He was tall, armed in red. Huge, shining kiri in his hand. He struck once. Reptilian heads rolled and he struck again. He reached her heart, the black blood flowed. The snakes toppled and fell, lifeless without her power. The curse was gone. My soul was free. I reclaimed my power.

My child! He was still imprisoned. I needed to claim his soul. The renegade priest and the Lady Magrat had disposed of his body in the desert, jackals ate it. He had no burial, no place for me to mourn him. His father did not know him. I had to reclaim his soul.

I took his body to a tomb, placed it inside for his father the Great Suten to watch over for all time. My child was freed from the curse. His *akhar* returned from the outer deep. It was with me, it moved into the child in my womb. The baby quickened and stirred. The soul had seeded itself. He would be born. *Sa Sekhem Sahu*. The shining one would be birthed.

But my illness? Where lay the source of that? The curses were released. Could my body heal?

"In time, child, in time. There is more to do, be strong. You will succeed. Go with the blessing of Sekhmet."

Falling into light.

Coming to, lying quietly on the ground with my friends around me, everyone seemed relaxed, though I'd thought I might have given them a fright.

"Are you back with us, Megan? Here, have some water." Anne helped me sit up and held the cup to my lips. "I stayed with you for as long as I could but you went beyond my reach. When you came back, you brought your *akhar*, I saw it clearly. I thought I'd let you rest awhile. Did you break the curse?"

"Yes, there were two. One from Greg and the other from Magrat, Mek'an'ar's stepmother, she was determined I wouldn't marry my Pharaoh."

"And what about your illness, will that heal?" Alison asked.

"It seems so but apparently there is more to do before it goes completely. Malcolm, I have to thank you, you were magnificent fighting Magrat and her serpents."

Malcolm shuddered: "Can't remember that, thank God, I hate snakes."

"Well, you waded in against them with your dagger without a second thought. Perhaps you'll feel differently about them now. You were quite splendid, invincible."

He smiled, pleased and faintly pink: "As long as you feel it did some good." His hand strayed to his hair, smoothing it under that ridiculous hat. Despite the hat, though, he had his dignity. Such a lovely man, my heart went out to him:

"Yes, I'm sure of it. Can we go and see Sekhmet now? I want to thank her."

We made our way in silence. The guardians had returned to duty.

As the ancient doors creaked open the dying sun was reflected through the hole above her great black basalt head. For a moment she was bathed in blood, but Anne's torch shone out its cleansing light. Thank you, My Lady, I murmured as I raised the cup to her smiling lips.

Quickly, while Malcolm was keeping the guardians talking – arguing the price no doubt, I poured the beer over her head and feet.

Anne touched my hand to My Lady's forehead and then to my own; she moved it to throat, heart, and solar plexus. My body was alight. Sa Sekhem Sahu. May the power of the goddess be upon us and remain with us.

"Anne, the guardian says the temple is closing. We must hurry."

"Be right out." Anne touched the Great Lady's ankh and murmured her own thanks.

Color was draining from the world, the last dregs of pink lit up the fading aquamarine sky, fiery fingers flamed and died. Quickly we walked to the entrance and slipped through the gap in the great gates to where Khaled was waiting. Smile back in place, it seemed he'd recovered.

"Where to? You want go eat?

"Why not, shall we go to the Marhaba and celebrate? My treat?" Malcolm's face had become younger, more virile. "I often ate there when I was here before. The food's great and I like the atmosphere. It's usually quiet this early on so we should have no trouble getting a table."

"Sounds wonderful to me. Thank you." I could've eaten anywhere, was ravenous in fact, but this sounded fun. "Is it alright with you two?"

Alison and Anne nodded happily.

"Always glad to eat, and I like that place too." Anne took the reins again but Malcolm sat beside Alison in Ahmed's caleche. Perhaps I could doze as we drove back. Getting my *akhar* back had been hard work and I didn't want to talk about it yet.

"Thank you, Khaled. We can walk back to the hotel from here. I will see you tomorrow night for chai." Malcolm handed over a discreet bundle and ushered us down a dark alley.

"Sorry, this back entrance is a bit grotty, but if we go through the bazaar we'll be hassled to buy something. It'll be fine when we get upstairs."

And so it was. An immaculate pink marble entrance hall opened onto a wide, blue-paneled room. The slatted windows and lazy ceiling fans must make it cool during the day. We were cocooned against darkness and yet the night outside was full of color and light – and the ubiquitous shouts of the drivers seeking another fare. Always the offers: "calache" – heralded by the cracking of a whip, "taxi" – the honk of a horn, "boat" – " 'wanna go Banana Island?" Did it ever stop?

A white-coated waiter bustled forward, hand outstretched.

"Hello sir, I see you again. How are you?"

"I am well, shokran – these guys never forget a face – could we have a table at the front?"

"Of course, you come this way, madams, please." A smiling face ushered us forward and deftly pulled out chairs.

"What a wonderful view, I love the way the river sparkles under the lights. What's that lit up over there?" Alison was making sure she was seated next to Malcolm as she pointed across the river to a temple façade hanging like a golden necklace around the barely-seen bulk of the dark-engulfed mountain.

"Deir el Bahari – Hatshepshut's temple. You'll see it tomorrow. I think it is the most impressive temple in Egypt – even if I no longer believe I was Tutmoses." Malcolm's grin was slightly embarrassed.

Alison touched his arm. "I still think what I saw was true. I'm sure I ..."

Her words were drowned out by the attentive waiter calling for our drinks order and offering menus.

"Do you have om ali?" Anne asked.

"Yes madam, but this is pudding ..." He shook his head in patient resignation at the foibles of yet another tourist.

"Yes, I know, but it's my favorite and I want to make sure I leave room for it. I'll have some fish, please, and tahini to start, with some mint tea."

"Yes madam. And you sir ...?"

"Please bring me some of that dreadful beer you sell and some mineral water. What about you, ladies?" Malcolm beamed enquiringly.

"I'll have what Anne's having, sounds good to me but with Coca Cola please."

"Same for me but with mineral water."

"What you eat sir?"

"Pigeon please, and babaghanoogg – do you remember, Megan, we had pigeon at Khaled's house?"

"Oh yes, it was delicious. Was babaghanoogg the eggplant stuff we had on the boat? Yes? Some for me too, please." I was so hungry, it was wonderful to have my appetite back.

"I bring you bread and you share food." A dazzling smile and our waiter was away, calling excitedly to the old man who sat at the door.

"Alison, you were saying?" Malcolm gazed at her intently.

"It doesn't matter. You know what I saw. Maybe I'll feel differently tomorrow when we've been to her temple. What about him, did Tutmoses have a temple, Malcolm?" Her voice had a sharp edge.

"Nothing like Deir el Bahari. Though his tomb is quite spectacular. You have to climb up a huge metal ladder and plunge deep into the cliff. It has the 'Book of What Is In The Duat' around the walls, like an unrolled papyrus scroll. Fascinating. Tutmoses has shrines at Karnak and Luxor temples – I could show you after we've eaten, if you'd like. I think Temple Luxor is open until quite late tonight, is it not, Anne?"

"I'm not sure, but as it's only across the road, you can easily check. The temple is absolutely magical at night, well worth seeing inside, Alison." Anne fidgeted with her napkin. I knew she didn't want to upset Alison. Perhaps I could ...

"Last time I was here there was an amazing crescent moon hanging above the mosque. Quite extraordinary, I intended to take a picture but had run out of film." I remembered that moon so well, the moon of new beginnings.

"Well, there's a full moon tonight, it should be stunning." Anne smiled as Alison turned excitedly to Malcolm:

"Good job I've brought my camera. Malcolm, we must go."

"Of course, we will." Bless him, he was patting her hand. Was it avuncular? I hoped not.

Dishes were appearing on the table as if by magic; surely we hadn't ordered all that? But it was delicious and I was starving. I loved the textures of Egyptian food, the bread was so chewy and it slid down wonderfully with the tahini. A hint of chilli, exactly how I liked it. And that babaghanoogg tasted like it sounded, only backwards. Sort of oozed down and then caught you by surprise with a chunky bit you had to chew thoroughly. Strange to have a few soggy chips with the fish but I supposed some of the tourists liked them.

"Well, I must say, that feels better." Malcolm patted his stomach. At least he'd managed not to grease his hair, that had been so funny, I must tell Alison about it sometime. "Now, what about pudding? Anne, we know what you want. Megan, how about you?"

"I'd like something fairly plain please."

"They do an excellent white pudding here, never did find out what it was made from but it's delicious and easy to digest."

"That sounds exactly what I need."

"Alison, how about you? Do you fancy the sweetness of om ali?"

"Yes please. I was on a diet when I came here, always am, but I've forgotten all about it and I don't seem to have put on any weight. I think Egypt suits me."

It suited us all.

"Where is that waiter? He stopped hovering once that party of Japanese came in. I know, I have the perfect thing. This should do the trick." Malcolm's mischievous eyes twinkled. What was he up to?

"Oh Thou who dwellest in the furthest reaches of the Rest Au Rant, hearken unto me! Many hours have I spent over the feast thou served me. I thirsteth for the sacred drink known as Koka Kola and the sweet confections prepared by thy priests. Turn thy face from the tourists from the East and cast thy countenance upon me. Hasten unto me and I will reward thee mightily.

"That is spell 269 from The Book of Going Forth by Day and Coming Out at Night, the Spell for Summoning the Waiter. Seems to have done the trick, here he comes."

That man never ceased to amaze me.

"Well, that was delicious. Thank you so much, Malcolm. I'm tired and a gentle stroll back to the hotel will suit me nicely. What about you, Megan?" Anne held out my bag invitingly.

"Yes, I'll walk back with you. I enjoy Luxor temple at night, but I don't think I'll go in. I haven't got my camera with me but I can nip into the hotel and come back and get the picture from the gate if the moon's in the right place."

"Goodnight you two, enjoy the rest of the evening." She smiled back at them as we made our way towards the marble entrance and down the smelly stairs. "I thought we should leave them together, they seem to be getting on well and I know they're both lonely so a bit of matchmaking won't go amiss." She flashed that mischievous smile of hers.

"Exactly what I thought, but I didn't want to interfere."

"Let's call it a helping hand, shall we, dear? Do you want a caleche, we can pick one up over there if you're tired." She gestured towards the horses patiently waiting in line whilst their drivers chattered in the dark night.

"No, let's walk. I love the feeling of being enfolded in the

Egyptian night and we can admire the temple as we go. I find it impossible to believe there was a town on top of it for all those years. Imagine Napoleon walking up there where the mosque is and realizing all that was under his feet."

I glanced over at the mosque perched atop the temple walls. Khaled had promised to take me in for a visit, I must remind him of that. Although it looked so high from this side, on the other it was at ground level; how those old floods must have whirled and swirled around this temple. In the floodlit dark it almost looked like a stately riverboat sailing down the Nile.

"I like the way the layers of history in the ground mirror our past lives. They lie buried till something brings them to our notice, then we have to dig down to reveal what's been there all along, as it were. I find it such a satisfying process." Her hands carved layers in the air.

"Anne, there's one thing I've been meaning to ask, I know it's your night off and you've helped me so much today already ..."

"Don't worry about that, dear; on these trips I'm never really off duty and anyway I find it fascinating, wouldn't still be doing it if I didn't. What is it?"

"Well, it was after Philae. I had an experience of being with a beloved teacher and I felt totally bereft afterward. I wondered whether we meet everyone again?"

"Not always, although we do seem to meet quite a lot of our past contacts as you've discovered. I was fortunate enough to meet my teacher again. Christine and I were at Philae towards the end of the Egyptian religion – it held out there for many years after the rest of Egypt became Christian. We'd been together in many other places too, of course, but when I went to Philae not long after her death she came to walk with me one evening while I waited for the Sound and Light performance. I'd been missing her terribly so it was a wonderful experience. She gave me a profound teaching before she left and I never saw her again, but I don't miss her now. I know we'll meet up again in another life – or in the between life, possibly, to plan next time."

Is that what would happen with Ramon? Dared I ask ...or hope.

"Oh look, Megan, look at the moon. It's so beautiful hanging low in the sky behind the temple columns like that. Do you know that line of poetry: The full moon hangs pregnant with the old? Look, you can almost see the bulge." She gestured to the golden glow almost as bright as sunlight. Not at all the colorless light we had at home. Perhaps it was all those spotlights picking out the temple, light meeting light.

"So you can, I must go and get my camera. By the time I get back it'll have risen up out of its imprisoning bars to hang above the temple. I prefer it free and unfettered, a sign of things coming to fruition. Maybe it's a good omen for my baby's birth."

"I'll sit on the wall and pay homage to Isis and Hathor – and to the Moon god, did you know the Egyptians were the only ones ... but hurry or you'll miss a spectacular picture. I can tell you about the Moon god later." She waved me away.

"That's the end of the film, so that'll have to be it. Look I bought these white flowers from the hotel garden, I didn't think anyone would mind. I thought it would be a good offering for the moon goddesses – and your god, who was he?"

"Khonsu, the son of Mut and Amon-Ra at Thebes."

Sekhmet's son. Didn't know she had one. Well, well, well, you kept that quiet, my Lady.

"He's sometimes portrayed as a sun-god and sometimes as a moon-god. He seems to partake of both natures."

Like that night's full moon. Perhaps that was why it was so golden. Honoring my Lady's son.

"That little triple shrine on the right as you go into the temple is dedicated to their divine family – and it was built by Tutmoses III. That's where Alison and Malcolm are heading – they came along just after you left to get your camera by the way."

"In that case we'd better make this offering and go, I checked the closing time and it'll be any moment now. We don't want them to think we're waiting for them."

"It's about time I was in bed anyway, we've got a busy day tomorrow and I think we might have some fireworks when we reach Deir el Bahari. Beatrice is still convinced she was Hatshepshut and Jane Abrams lays claim to the same title. She passed by too while you were gone, and she and her group will be there tomorrow. Apparently they're spending the day at the temple carrying out rituals, so we can't avoid seeing them." Anne shook her head with a hint of despair.

"That could get quite heated. They're both strong women."

"I know, but these things are as they are. I know it sounds a cliché, and I'm not fatalistic as you know, but I do believe that in matters like this, what will be, will be."

That sounded like a good philosophy to adopt. Perhaps I wouldn't worry about seeing Ramon again if I thought that way – mind you, I hadn't spent every spare minute thinking about him like I usually did, perhaps something had shifted. Maybe that tie-cutting worked after all.

"I'll see you in the morning, dear. Don't forget to bring plenty of water and a hat. It gets incredibly hot by midday at Deir el

Bahari, even at this time of year, and it's an exposed site with little shade – imposing, though. I'd have preferred to be there earlier in the morning but it gets crowded and Josef thought it would be better to see the tombs first. I'm sure you'll find it interesting even if we don't have any histrionics from Beatrice and Jane. Goodnight Megan."

Anne turned towards the garden and I headed for my slow stairway to heaven.

chapter 18.

unrivalled and invincible one

It was so nice to sit down after all those tombs, I was glad the coach was air-conditioned, I'd breathed in enough hot stale air for one day, I wondered how many other tourists' lungs it had passed through before mine? At least a century's worth, it must amount to thousands of people. Malcolm was right again, though, Tutmoses' tomb was worth the climb, much more impressive than Tutankhamen's. The stick people drawings that decorated it were surprisingly powerful; at first glance they were rather naïve but their simplicity was deceptive. Josef seemed to feel the intention was to portray the teaching in its essence but his English wasn't always clear and I couldn't quite get to what the core teaching was. There was still a lot to understand, ancient Egyptian thought was so sophisticated.

Seeing the whole story of the Duat laid out like that was fascinating. I saw quite a few of my old friends from the Edfu crypt; it was nice to know it wasn't all my imagination, the Duat really was peopled with strange three-headed beings and animal-headed men.

It'd felt really eerie puffing our way out up that steep slope, I had to laugh when Anne complained that they didn't think about old grannies when they built these places and Malcolm said that old grannies weren't meant to climb out again – that was the whole point. His old fashioned manner concealed a quick wit.

I opened my lunch box. The cold boiled eggs smelled a bit but I was hungry and they'd go well in the rolls with the cheese. They were a bit dry and chewy but I'd still got a can of Coke from the Rest House somewhere and hoped it hadn't gone warm. No, it was perfect.

"We approaching Deir el Bahari. According ancient Egyptians, this mortuary temple most splendid of all. Follow me when we off coach and I take you straight to temple. Bazaar sellers persistent, ignore them. If you want shop, do it on way back."

If Josef said they were pushy it must be bad. He didn't usually notice. Oh no, Beatrice was getting out her costume. She wasn't putting it on surely? Heavens, she'd be hot in that, what would everyone make of her? She even carried her crown. I'd noticed Stephen had been sitting with Miranda. Things definitely seemed to have cooled between him and Beatrice. He was looking a bit hot and bothered, very red faced when he got back on the bus after the tombs, though it was hot in that valley. He hadn't come up to Tutmoses' tomb with us. Where had he been? Never mind, at least Beatrice would catch the attention of the buzzards.

"I know another of those spells," Malcolm was whispering over my shoulder.

"Oh thee who lurketh at the entrance to the Tombs of the Kings with thy crooked smile and wheedling demeanor. Oh thou who waitest at the temples of the Gods, I desireth not thy phoney statue of Horus, neither do I covet thy fake scarabi that thou carvest in the night, neither do I wish for thy resin Osiris from the far off land of Ty-won. Begone from me for I have no baksheesh to give thee.

Behold I have spent all my money on ten measures of beer and a pickle salad. My stomach turneth over and my bowels rebel within me. Where is the toilet? I am Unwell! I am Unwell!"

It certainly seemed to work, no one bothered us. I hoped that the last bit wouldn't come true for him.

Long and low, the creamy sandstone building was more like a contemporary office block than a temple. So different to anything else we'd seen. Malcolm said it had inspired many modern architects. I wasn't surprised. Elegant with its long colonnades set with square pillars and great ramps up to the terraces, it sat well in its surroundings. It was magnificent enough not to be overpowered by the great rock wall towering over it. The pyramidal Peak of the West that crowned the mountain range was always impressive, I wondered if this was natural or whether the ancients had molded it? It certainly had majesty, no wonder it was sacred.

It was incredibly hot; the amphitheatre cradled the heat. The air shimmered dustily and burned my lungs like a first cigarette. It was a good job Anne had warned me about water and a hat. I'd better catch up with Josef, it looked like he was starting his talk already. But, no, it was Beatrice speaking, what on earth was she on about now?

"When I ruled, all around us there was a great courtyard and a splendid garden. There were exquisite statues and abundant flowers beds with pools of water linked by rills flowing gently down the slope, and a grove of trees for shade. This ramp was shaded with awnings to keep off the sun. I had avenues of sphinxes built, leading down to the river. It was the most beautiful place on earth. If you follow me, I'll show you the story of my expedition to Punt."

Didn't look like Josef was going to get a word in. I wondered how true what she was saying was? Did she really remember, or had she read a good guidebook?

"Here, you can see me being commanded by Amon to undertake the expedition to the Holy Land of Punt so that incense could be obtained to glorify his name." She gestured grandly at the wall. "He came to me in a vision, you know, to give me his instructions. Here are the five ships setting off and here is the scene when they landed in Africa – see, these beehive-shaped huts built out over the water, you can also see the native people with their dogs and their cattle."

I must admit, the story was interesting and Beatrice told it well. One of the women was the twin of Nerissa with her spiral curls.

"This is the king with his lady wife, surrounded by all their subjects."

She was grotesque, she must have had something like elephantiasis from the look of those huge legs and that enormous bum, and she had at least four chins.

"The inscription says that they brought 'all goodly fragrant woods of God's land, heaps of myrrh resin, fresh myrrh trees, ebony and ivory and the green gold of Emu, together with cinnamon wood, incense, kohl, baboons, monkeys, dogs, and the skins of the southern panther with natives and their children to honor Pharaoh.' It shows how important I was."

Pity about that smirk, I was getting really caught up in her story until she brought herself into it.

"Here I am accepting the homage of the natives."

Did the female Pharaoh really go along, surely she didn't? The frieze suggested they had come to her.

"And now, we can go and see the story of my divine birth. It says that I was Deity you know, the Beginning of Existence."

Heavens, she was putting her crown on. Beatrice really believed that nonsense. But why did I feel she'd got it wrong? I was sure I was Mek'an'ar, and Shen-en-k'art, and anyone else might think those stories were far-fetched. Or that I was too credulous, but I knew it was true. I supposed it was because Beatrice was so over the top about it – and because it clearly made her feel superior judging from the way she swept along in front.

But I bet she didn't expect to meet Jane Abrams and Co. in full regalia. The clash of the female Pharaohs. I thought I'd better sit down for this; I'd got a feeling we could be there awhile.

"And who do ya think y'all are? The Queen o' Sheba?"

First round to Jane. I wondered why she was exaggerating her accent like that? Was it what passed for American irony? It certainly caught Beatrice on a sore spot, she was bristling again, full of regal dignity, not like Jane, who'd draped herself languidly against a pillar. Up went Beatrice to her full height, close to seven feet with that crown on, that must win her a few points in the Interregnal Stakes, but Jane didn't look overawed.

"I am her Majesty Queen Hatshepshut, Pharaoh of all Egypt, builder of this temple and erecter of the Great Obelisk at Karnak. My name is glorified throughout Egypt." If she'd puffed herself up anymore, she'd have exploded.

"If yar Hat Shep Shoot, I'm h' baboon's ass. Let m' tell ya lady, I'm only one can claim that title. That's ma likeness on the wall. I'm Hat Shep Shoot. This is ma divine birth."

A sweeping hand gesture took in the wall behind her, it was a pity it was blocked by her followers or I'd have taken a closer look. They clearly believed she was who she said she was. I was getting bored with this fight over Hot Chicken Soup. A few of the group were slipping away with Josef, so I joined them.

Jane's words drifted behind us.

"Whatever floats ya boat, honey ..."

This was more like it. What an exquisite chapel. The slender columns with the horned cow-faces on them were splendid.

"This Hatshepshut as goddess Hathor, you see cow ears below headdress. Each pillar unique, showing different face to goddess, reflects phases of moon. Over there Queen suckling from goddess in form of divine cow."

She was beautiful, I must get a photograph or two here.

"And there, at back chapel only known image Senenmut, outside tomb." Josef pointed to a barred entrance.

"His tomb? Is that it?" Malcolm's face was intense and he was forking his hair like mad.

Josef shook his head.

"Where is he buried?"

"Below, down mountain. He have tomb excavate under temple and passage goes under mountain towards Valley of Kings – is my belief joins with tomb Hatshepshut. His tomb full esoteric symbols."

"Can we see it?" Malcolm was almost beside himself with excitement.

"No, tomb being excavate and is closed. Mrs. Anne, she tell you 'bout it, we go down when she and husband here some years ago." He gestured to Anne who had quietly joined us.

"It was quite an experience, I can tell you. First of all we had to pay baksheesh to the guardians, who went to bribe the policeman while we had a cup of tea in their hut. After a long wait, an inconspicuous little wooden door was opened and the guardian grabbed two bare wires and twisted. Lots of crackling, then dim lights came on all the way down – and it was a long, long way. Very narrow stairs, not like the Pharaohs' tombs."

Anne shuddered. It sounded like quite a trip.

"We reached a sort of half landing with strange reliefs on the ceiling, and went down another flight by the light of a dim torch. I was sure the battery was going to run out before we got to the bottom.

"When we got to the next level, the guardian showed us where the steps had been filled in and not yet excavated – like a child's mud slide. My husband had been smoking hash with Khaled and he kept saying wow, the ceiling's in motion. He said it was the celestial portal and he could move through it into another world. I half expected him to disappear but, I must admit, I couldn't see much." She shrugged, but her eyes shone. That husband of hers sounded quite a character.

"Josef worked out we were under the Peak of the West – that's a couple of thousand feet of rock at least. It was incredible realizing that we were under the weight of that mountain – it made the climb out go a lot faster, I can tell you, six hundred steps is quite a distance but it didn't take me long. My husband and our guide couldn't keep up – and I had the torch."

Anne flashed her wicked grin and Malcolm burst out with:

"I'd like to try to see it. Could you point the way for me, Anne, I'll make my own way back. Do you want to come, Alison?"

"Not really, those tombs in the Valley of the Kings made me claustrophobic. I don't think I could stand Senenmut's tomb from the sound of it, interesting though it would be. I'll see you back at the hotel."

She was blushing again, did she realize we were all rooting for her?

On the way back to the coach, I told myself, remember, Mecky, eyes straight ahead. Don't let the buzzards get you, but I thought some of that stuff was quite tasteful, perhaps ... no. Don't give in. Once you hesitated, they'd pounce. I remember that spell of Malcolm's, such a surprising man.

Beatrice returned looking cowed. Jane Abrams must have triumphed. She had the weight of her group behind her. They implicitly believed she was the female Pharaoh but no one in our group believed Beatrice. Did she still think she was Hot Chicken Soup? How could she? Now, don't be unkind, Mecky. As soon as I was back in England I intended to be back with Akhenaten again. What would Beatrice say to that?

It was so restful sitting there in the opulent bar, it was like the inside of a Bedouin tent with all those oriental hangings and Persian rugs. How fascinating people watching could be. There was every shape, size, and color, and so many languages. Other people's conversations were much more fun when you couldn't understand a word and could make it up. That young guy over there was propositioning that German girl, trying to persuade her he was the gods' gift to women. Selling himself like a souvenir but she didn't look impressed. Then he was off to try his luck somewhere else. Couldn't blame him, Egyptian girls were well chaperoned and the tourists so easy.

A blonde guy was trying to offload the genuine antique he picked up on his trip, now he'd found it was a fake. But he was assuring that American that it was the real thing, a snip at only one thousand Egyptian pounds. He needed Malcolm's spell against the souvenir sellers. I wondered how Malcolm had got on? I'd hoped to see him here. Did he get into that tomb? What if he didn't get out? I didn't suppose he'd been smoking hash and feel ready to step through the portal into another dimension, although he'd probably have enjoyed it if he did.

"Hi, Megan, mind if we join you?"

Miranda fell gracefully onto the plumply cushioned seat beside me but Stephen held back. He'd the kind of look on his face Greg used to get when he'd done something he didn't want me to know about. But, of course, I always found out in the end. Better not to think about Greg. Miranda was clearly going to tell me even if Stephen didn't:

"We wanted to talk to you because you've had, you know, so many past life experiences." She glanced at Stephen who was looking around as though he'd got no part in this.

"Well, if you think I can help, but Anne's the expert."

"Yes, but Stephen didn't really want to bring this up with her."

No, I could see that. I wasn't sure he wanted to bring it up with me; oh well, better prompt him:

"What is it?" What could he possibly have seen that he couldn't tell Anne? He'd only attended one or two sessions, I didn't think he'd had a glimpse of a past life. But Miranda was carrying on:

"You know that life I saw, the one where I was the musician?" She smirked. How could I forget the image of Miranda with an erect penis?

"Well, I think that Stephen was my friend, the one I was killed with. What do you think?"

"It's possible, I suppose. I've certainly met people I was with before. What do you think, Stephen?" He'd moved closer, perhaps he was ready to talk:

"Well, as you know, I don't really believe in past lives and I'm not sure about this. But it feels like it could be possible, and it could explain a few things. Miranda's become a good friend to me on this trip and I felt immensely attracted to her when I met her – she seemed familiar somehow. Nothing sexual, you understand."

He looked away to the side, a nerve in his cheek twitching. Why was he blushing? And why wouldn't it be sexual? Miranda was an incredibly attractive young woman, she oozed sexuality.

"You see, I'm gay. I know Beatrice tried to tell everyone I was with her but she brought Joan and I along because she wanted company – acolytes would be a more appropriate word. I didn't realize how bossy she'd be, but I've tried to keep the peace." He grimaced ruefully.

"What's your connection with her?"

"We're in a local amateur dramatics group together, and teach at the same small village school. Beatrice used to be good company, had a great sense of fun, until her husband left her for another woman. His leaving seemed to sour her, although several people have hinted that the marriage hadn't been good for some years. He waited 'till their children left home and quickly followed. She's a very lonely woman you know."

He sounded sorry for her.

"Why do women do that? Put up with a far from perfect marriage, stay together for the sake of the children, and act like martyrs afterwards. And then to pretend you were having a relationship with her." Miranda sounded quite angry. Didn't she say something about her mother having been divorced recently?

"I think some people prefer to live a lie because they can't face the truth. Bea is being offered early retirement, she finds it difficult to adapt to new ideas and the children find her too authoritarian. Things have changed greatly in teaching since she trained. She's just approaching her fiftieth birthday and must feel her life's falling to pieces, so she's desperate to hold everything together."

He lifted his glass but, finding it empty, placed it carefully on the table once again, half rose, and then subsided back into his chair shrugging quietly.

"Unfortunately, she comes across as a despot." Miranda couldn't resist the jab.

"I know. I'm sure this is what lies behind her belief that she's Hatshepshut. It makes her feel like a woman who matters, someone who's in control. The female pharaoh supports this domineering facade she's constructed for herself perfectly. I feel sorry for her."

He was a sweet, sensitive man.

"Is she aware you're gay?"

Stephen gay, well that could explain a few things. He looks so straight though, I'd never have guessed. And why should you guess, Mecky, I told myself sternly, what has it got to do with you?

"I've kept my sexual orientation secret. It's difficult living in such a small place, it would be different if I was in a city. People in villages like mine don't understand and they don't tolerate difference, especially if you're a teacher. They worry about their children you know, mix us up with pedophiles. I haven't had a boyfriend for years. But I don't think Bea wants to face the truth about me either. She used to make comments that made me suspect she'd guessed, but not any more. When her husband left she made a beeline for me and flaunted our so-called relationship at him – he's still part of the drama group. For me, she was good cover."

He was so downcast. What could I say?

"So what's this got to do with past lives?"

"I've had one or two encounters whilst I was here in Egypt. There was a boy on the boat who made advances to me. He seemed to instinctively recognize that I fancied him like mad. We'd meet in my cabin while you were doing your sessions with Anne. Then, when I was in Aswan bazaar, I went into a shop and this guy put his hand on my cock – sorry, Megan, I didn't mean to ..."

"Don't worry, I'm not that easily shocked. Go on, what's this leading up to?"

"When we got to the Valley of the Kings I wanted to stay away from Bea – we'd had words earlier; she didn't like the fact I refused to wear that awful costume at Deir el Bahari. So I went to look for Seti's tomb – Josef had told me it was amazing but badly damaged so the public weren't allowed in but that, if it was quiet, a bit of baksheesh would get me in."

Ah yes, baksheesh, the opener of all doors.

"And did it?"

"Yes. A couple of the guardians took me in. It was an incredible place. It had quite an atmosphere. It made me feel strange, really creepy. Like I was walking through a dream or one of those myths Josef told us. I can't explain, seeing all those blue figures in the gloom had such an effect. It felt horribly claustrophobic towards the end, great chunks of the ceiling had fallen down and I began to imagine them coming down on my head. So I paid the baksheesh while the guys were locking the door and rushed up the steps to get out."

No wonder he been so flustered on the coach, it must have been horribly claustrophobic in there. I remember how I'd felt in the Edfu crypt, and again in the tombs. Tons of rock pressing down, made me shudder just to think about it ...

"If it was anything like Tutmoses' tomb, I'm not surprised you felt like that."

"Tell Megan what happened next." Miranda had obviously heard the story and wanted him to get on with it.

"There was this young guy waiting at the top. He was gorgeous, so handsome, like something out of the tomb paintings I'd just been looking at – or, if I'm honest, straight out of the fantasies I've been having. He was mesmerizing. He beckoned to me and took me down into the entrance to another tomb. Someone shouted to him but he said something and waved them away. He made it clear what he wanted and I was only too happy to go along with it. I thought I might wake up and find I was dreaming."

His eyes were down and he was blushing again.

"The funny thing was, although I was enjoying it, part of me wasn't there with him. I was watching myself wrestling with Miranda, only she wasn't Miranda, she was a young man I was in love with. I was quite a hit with the ladies and everyone thought I was such a stud, but really I longed for my friend. I used women as a smokescreen – much as I've been doing with Bea, I suppose. When the Queen had me in bed with her, I was hoping he would join in so I could touch him in that way. Only the guards came in and killed us." His shoulders sagged dejectedly.

"That death Miranda saw?"

"Yes, that's right. I don't know if that influenced me or not but it seemed so real when I was watching it. Like looking in on an actual event with me in it."

"I know how that feels, like you're standing outside yourself watching another you and it's all so familiar, it must be true?"

"Yes, that's it. And the funny thing is, when I'd died, I looked at my friend and thought, I really wanted you. Why did I waste my opportunities, it would have been so easy, no one would have thought anything of it, yet I held back. Too afraid of rejection I suppose. Deep down, where it mattered, women didn't interest me then, or now. When I'm with Miranda, I don't feel at all sexual. Yet somehow that experience confirms me in my sexuality. Do you think we carry our sexual orientation on through different lives?" He brightened at the thought.

"It sounds possible, but I think it's the unsatisfied desires that carry over – and the unfinished business. It certainly seems to be that way for me. Perhaps if you had made a move, had a relationship with your friend back then you might feel differently now. But I'm not sure."

"I think this is the real me. I don't want to hide it any more. I need love and affection, a steady relationship, I'm not going to go looking for casual encounters. I want something more than that."

"That's what we all want, Stephen." I couldn't help it, my eyes filled up again. Damn those hormones. Ramon ...

"Don't be upset, Megan. I'm sure it will work out for you, and it has really helped me to tell you my story. I knew you'd understand – and I'll tell you something else. There's a guy at the drama society, a bit younger than me. He never has girlfriends either and sometimes he looks at me, as though he's challenging me to make a move on him, stands up close, not quite flirting but, there's something ... When I get back, I'm going to talk to him about it. I don't want to die again without fulfilling myself."

"You do that, Stephen. I think that it's worth a try." Miranda placed her hand over his.

"Yes, don't miss out on a chance for love. I know it's a cliché but everyone needs someone. Remember Plato's soul-mates; there are just as many men looking for their male soul-mate. I hope you find yours."

"I'll drink to that. What would you like, another Coke?"

As he moved towards the bar, he was taller, more sure of himself.

"He's not hiding any more, is he?" Miranda smiled. "Looks more of a man."

Exactly.

chapter 19.

Ruler of the Desert

"Hello, Megan, it's good to see you again. Come in. How was Egypt?" Ronald gestured me in and took my coat.

It seemed like only five minutes since I was last in his austere consulting room but a great deal had happened since then. Would I be able to go back into the past so easily this time?

"Well, I found out why my disease came back and Anne did some work to help me with that, but there are still many gaps. It was difficult to get a coherent picture. So much was happening on the boat, and there was a lot of stuff going on in the group."

Shaking my head at the memory, I put down my bag.

"Do you want to tell me what you found out?" He held his hand out for my coat and hung it beside the door. Head cocked on one side, he was like an ibis peering at me with enquiring eyes.

"Do you mind if I go straight into the regression and I'll tell you about Egypt later? This feels urgent."

"That's fine by me. Don't forget you can talk to me without it interrupting the flow, and if you need a break you can move further back from it as though you're looking at a film. Do you want to see what comes up or do you need me to be specific? Is there somewhere you want to start?" He sat forward intently, eyes focused on mine.

"Be specific please, Ronald. I want to go back to the moment when I met Akhenaten; I think that holds the key. I can't get that smile of his out of my mind."

"Now then, Megan, make yourself comfortable and we'll get started ..."

"I can see that dazzling smile again and the eyes full of shattered light. It's hard to describe them, they look like a crystal that has lots of planes and flaws that break up the light and make it glitter deep within. But it's his smile that is so powerful, it seems to fill the whole room with light. So luminous, I can't explain. Everything pales beside it. It's as though a god is standing there; I fall down in front of him, kissing the dust before his feet. Honoring Suten and god. It's as though he's wearing an aura of love, I can feel it radiating out towards me. I want to stay in it forever.

The lady Nefertiti pushes Merit'aten towards him.

"Go on child, say goodnight to your father. It's getting late and even Suten's daughter has to sleep."

With a mulish look to her face, she stands her ground.

"I want Father to tell me one of his stories about the Great God. How he revealed his secret to Father."

"You're much too old for bedtime stories. It won't be long now before your betrothal to Smenkhare is announced."

"I don't want to be betrothed! He is much too old! And he looks like a woman!" A foot stamps to emphasize each word, blue eyes fixed winsomely on her father.

He's lifting me up, telling me to get to my feet, not to be so formal. His daughter's friend is welcome in his house. I can feel his long, bony fingers on my arm. They're so thin they look like spider's legs on my bare skin. He's tall, he towers above me. He's got a powerful smell, rather sweet and cloying. Everyone in Egypt uses perfume, but this is different, it's as though it is his own smell, not something added artificially.

Distance has always hidden how strange this Suten looks. His elongated face has bulbous, slanting eyes full of that strange, shattered light, His thick, sensual lips have a secret smile playing about them like he's smiling at a joke only he can hear, above a prominent jaw and sharp chin. His skull, carried on a long slender neck, looks distorted, misshapen, and his headdress exaggerates the shape rather than hiding it. His light-filled blue eyes are those of a mystic, a dreamer, he gazes into different worlds. I fear he can see straight through me.

Akhenaten looks fondly at the child. His voice is high and light, surprising in such a tall man but it fits his feminine appearance.

"We can talk about that another day, it's really only a few years' difference – you won't notice it at all when you are grown, and he is a Prince of the Blood, part of the *per aa*, our great family. For now, run along with – what's your name, young lady?"

"Shen my Lord." My head is lowered; I remember the Great Queen's instructions.

All he's wearing is the golden menat collar of the Aten sun-disk with its sun's rays pushing out between his slender shoulders and pendulous breasts, and a pleated linen kilt threaded with gold hanging below a bulging belly that looks like it belongs on a woman. He has enormous hips and thighs atop spindly legs and sandaled feet. To tell the truth, he looks effeminate. If he wasn't king, it would be comical. He must be a god, no mortal looks like this.

"Shen. Little Shen. Take the lady Merit'aten to her bedchamber and help her prepare for bed. I'll be along in a few moments, child, and I'll tell you a story, but first, I need to talk to your mother."

As Merit'aten pulls me by the hand, I look back. Two heads are close together, Suten and his Queen in affectionate embrace. His hand rests on her pregnant stomach. Can I really believe Merit'aten when she says the child is not his? He looks like a loving husband, and where does Smenkhare fit in? I've heard the gossip about him and Suten, but he's supposed to be betrothed to Merit'aten. How complicated everything is."

"Move forward to the next important event." Ronald was aware of time passing even if I wasn't.

"I'm in a bedchamber. It can't be Merit'aten's, it's much too grand. There's a huge platform bed with a golden lion's head at the top and lion's paws at the side, strewn with gold cushions and curtained around with gossamer golden net and a big golden sun disk on the wall above it. Such a lot of gold. The furniture is all covered in it, it shines in the lamplight. I'm sitting on a stool in the corner. Akhenaten comes in and I rise and go to help him undress. I've been having an affair with him for sometime. He came to my chamber just after that first meeting and asked some searching questions but I managed to avoid telling him who I was. Said I was a peasant girl to whom Queen Tiye had been kind because she knew my father. That seemed to satisfy him.

A few weeks later he came to see Merit'aten, and complained of a headache. I massaged his neck for him. After that, he'd send for me and I'd massage him. One day he started to caress me. I was worried that someone would see us and tell Queen Nefertiti but he said we would be safe, he'd given orders that no one should enter. Nefertiti has moved to the Northern Palace with the younger children but she still visits Merit'aten."

"What about Shen-en-k'art? What happens to you?" Ronald was pushing me where I didn't want to go but I thought it would be okay.

"When the time came for Merit'aten to be betrothed to Smenkhare she moved into the part of the palace he shared with Akhenaten, although she still had her own rooms. I went too. More and more often Akhenaten calls for me to visit him. He seems to be overcome by bouts of melancholy. Eventually he starts to make love to me. I've had no sexual experience at all and I don't realize that he isn't fully making love – it isn't penetrative sex, merely rubbing himself against me and he doesn't ejaculate but I find it exciting. Sometimes when I go to him there isn't any sex; I massage his thin shoulders and his bony neck where his huge skull flares out, and leave again."

"Megan, what happens in that room, the one with the big bed?" Ronald was insistent, he wasn't going to let me wriggle way.

"It's Suten's. It's where we make love."

"But what happens there? What is the important event?"

I didn't want to go there, didn't want to know, Ronald mustn't make me look.

"Pull back a little Megan," Ronald coaxed, "let yourself observe it from a distance, look at it as though it's a film. Breathe gently, it's alright, you can do this. Take it slowly, let yourself see."

"I'm lying on the great golden bed with Suten, he's rubbing

himself against me like he always does. The curtains are pulled back to let in the evening breeze. Oh no! Smenkhare's just walked in. He's all golden, with the slightly extended skull that marks out this family and a somewhat effeminate body with noticeable breasts, but he's not grossly distorted like his elder brother. Nor has he got that special inner light Akhenaten has. To my eyes, his elder brother is much more charismatic."

But I recognized him instantly, it was Ramon. How could I not have recognized him before? I knew I've only seen Smenkhare at a distance but surely I should have known. I couldn't tell Ronald. He knew Smenkhare was having a homosexual affair with Akhenaten. Did Ramon see this? Was this why he left me?

"Come on, Megan, let yourself see what happens next. Draw back as though you were observing it from that stool in the corner of the room." I had to follow Ronald's voice, even if I didn't want to see.

"Smenkhare's laughing. He's teasing his brother because he kept me a secret, says he should have realized something was going on. But he says he can see that Suten is keeping the best of himself for his brother in blood. I'm trying to get off the bed, to reach my clothes but Smenkhare's taken his kilt off and he's on the bed behind me. He reaches over and strokes Akhenaten. Akhenaten has been quite limp but as soon as his brother touches him he goes hard. Smenkhare starts rubbing him. I can feel something big and hard pressing into my back. I wriggle around because it's uncomfortable. Smenkhare says that, as I'm inviting him, he might as well show me what a real man feels like, he's not half-woman like his brother. He says Akhenaten has only ever wanted him, it's been that way since they were children and shared a bed. That's why he allowed Nefertiti to have her soldier to father his children.

Smenkhare shoves himself between my legs. It hurts so much, I'm crying and begging him to stop but he pushes me against Akhenaten. I struggle but it seems to excite him more. His hand is moving on his brother, keeping time with driving himself into me. They groan and convulse, and suddenly I feel all slippery and wet. Something hot is trickling down my stomach and from between my legs. Smenkhare leaps from behind me and onto his brother. I'm pinned underneath. The two of them are groaning and grunting as he pumps up and down. In my innocence I think Smenkhare must be hurting Akhenaten. I hit him, try to push him off but he swats at me with his hand. He must have knocked me out, or perhaps I fainted, because next thing I know he's gone and Akhenaten is washing me gently with a cloth and whispering tenderly to me.

"This must be our secret, little Shen. No one must know. My brother is impetuous, but, you see, I love him more than anything except my god. He's the only person who has ever really understood what I need. One night when we were children, I woke up and he was rubbing himself between my legs. I got so excited, it had never happened to me before. After that, I could never properly satisfy a woman. I preferred to make love to boys. When I married Queen Nefertiti she came to me with a child. She was beautiful and I truly loved her. I thought it would be possible to make love to her and put aside my past. But it didn't happen. She told me of her great love for her soldier. We agreed to continue our marriage and I'd pretend the children she conceived were mine. For a time I lived without physical love – this was when I turned to the Aten. He understood me like no other god, and he loved me as I was.

"Then Smenkhare returned from the army and it was like a lost part of myself had come back, we have been together ever since. The nights I called you to my bed were when he was away on Suten's business and I needed consolation. Now, you must promise me that you will never tell anyone on pain of your immortal soul what happened tonight." He kisses and caresses me. "Promise me little one. Promise your Lord." I feel overwhelmed with love for him – and gratitude. I promise him my undying love and silence forever. We fall asleep with his arms around me."

"Megan, leave that scene now." Ronald's voice broke through my reverie. I didn't want to let Smenkhare go, but I knew I must. What was that Ronald was saying. Oh yes, the vow, it had locked me in that life, better do what he said.

"Before you come completely back, revoke that vow. Promise only to keep the secret for as long as it is appropriate to do so and then to let it go. You are no longer bound by it."

It was a struggle but I managed to release myself, Ronald was right, I did need to do that.

"Now come back to the present moment, leaving the past behind but bringing the knowledge with you."

"No, I need to know what happened next." I couldn't leave it, I simply had to know.

"Yes, I know, but you can do that another time. That is enough for now. You've had a traumatic experience. That was a big thing to face. We'll need to do some healing work on it. Come back now. Open your eyes. I need to know you are fully back with me. That's it. Sit quietly and I'll get you a cup of tea."

So that was why Ramon left so hurriedly. He must have remembered the rape and couldn't face me. The homosexual stuff would have been hard enough for a good Catholic, the rape impossible. I wished I could confirm with Ronald that it was what Ramon saw but I didn't want to tell him Ramon was Smenkhare in case he didn't know. If only I could speak to Ramon.

"Here you are, do you take milk and sugar?"

How banal after such a drama, and I forgot to tell him I couldn't drink tea now that I was pregnant.

Oh yes, I must tell him about my eyes:

"Ronald, I realized something just now. It answers something that has been puzzling me. I must have had poor eyesight in that life. Anything at a distance was all fuzzy – which was why I didn't know what Akhenaten looked like until I saw him close up, and I could have seen Smenkhare before and not known him."

"From the number of references to eye ointments in the herbals, it looks as though there were many people who suffered from ophthalmic diseases and, of course, there were no spectacles in those days, although they did have lenses." He grinned and touched his own wire rimmed specs. "I'd have been blind as a bat."

"And there's another thing. He wasn't referred to as Pharaoh. Everyone called him Suten. I don't understand that."

"That was the correct form of address. It means king or ruler. Pharaoh came much later with the Greeks. They corrupted *per aa*, which means Great House, or royal family, into Pharaoh."

Trust Ronald to know, I was sure he'd done a crash course. But I hadn't studied it, hardly had time to read anything and I didn't want to influence myself. I certainly hadn't learnt the language – and, come to think of it, I didn't even seem to be able to speak it when I was reliving the past.

"Ronald, apart from a few words, I don't speak ancient Egyptian in these memories. Why's that?"

"That is common. Language has to pass through your present-life brain and, as neither of us speak Egyptian now, neither of us would understand what you were talking about if you did. It might be interesting from a research point of view, but it wouldn't be useful in therapy. But, Megan, we need to talk about the rape, you cannot go on avoiding it."

His eyes met mine, propelling me back to that moment.

"How did you know? You kept pushing me towards it, and you wouldn't let me get away."

"I could see from your breathing and the way your eyes were moving that there was something traumatic happening. You were restless, kept thrashing about, your body was remembering but your mind kept veering away. I had to bring you back on track. You will feel much better now you've remembered."

Would I? If this was what drove Ramon away it would never feel better. But I couldn't say that.

"Why do you think I still loved Akhenaten after he'd allowed something like that to take place? I'd have thought I'd have turned against him."

"Well, you were taken from your home at an early age and it doesn't sound as though there was much of an outlet for loving in your young life, so when you had the chance you poured it all out on Akhenaten. He was kind to you, and you clearly regarded him as a special person, a god incarnate. You probably rationalized that he hadn't initiated the sex, and thought it was all Smenkhare's fault. You could well have believed that Smenkhare was abusing him and felt sorry for him."

"But why would Akhenaten be that close to someone who abused him? He seemed to love his brother so much."

"Well, incest was obligatory in the Egyptian royal family, of course. They married within the close family to keep the blood pure. This happened to be between two family members of the same sex and it clearly started when they were young. Children frequently love their abusers, especially in incest cases. The abuser is likely to be one of their primary carers and, in the case of homosexual abuse, that includes a brother or an uncle. They confuse abuse with love because it's all they've ever known."

It sounded like Ronald knew what he was talking about but I wasn't so sure. He'd been a hypnotherapist a long time, was he trained in such matters?

"Are you sure about that, it sounds so unlikely to me?"

"I've worked with a lot of cases where the child was told they were much loved and were special, and they believed it. It hurt them more to acknowledge, as an adult, that someone they loved had abused them than the abuse did at the time."

His bottom lip came out to cover his top one, I'd noticed that mannerism before when we got into deep stuff and he'd look away into the distance, like he was reading something from another place. Perhaps it was just the way he was when he was concentrating, after all, I couldn't see his face when I was in regression. He might look like that all the time.

"Abuse runs in families, doesn't it? I'm sure I heard abusers were most likely abused as a child."

"Yes, abuse is a family pattern. Many battered women were abused as children. They stay with their husbands because, so they say, they still love them. But abuse isn't necessarily physical, you know, from what you've told me about Greg, I'd call him an abusive man." He nodded in emphasis.

"But I had a happy childhood, my father wasn't abusive. He didn't want to see anyone take advantage of me, especially as regards money. If anything he was over-protective. That's what caused the problems with Greg."

Ronald smiled reassuringly: "Are you sure, Megan? Could it have been that he saw through Greg? He wouldn't have known the past life causes, but he could probably read that hunger you've talked of and tried to protect you."

"Yes, I think he did. He was such a gentle man, he hated it when Greg made demands."

"It's not surprising that in that other life you still loved your gentle Pharaoh. If you were going to hate anyone, it's more likely to have been Smenkhare, after all he instigated the rape."

And yet I still loved him with all my heart almost four thousand years later. Why? Did his also being Mek'an'ar's beloved Pharaoh cancel out the rape? Historically, that came after Akhenaten's time, although I didn't suppose there would be any record of it now. So much of Egypt had been lost. Maybe I could talk to Anne about it.

"Why isn't what I've seen in the history books and why are there gaps in my knowledge of what happened and of the people concerned? I lived quietly, trying to keep out of sight, but I heard rumors. People at the time must have known what was going on."

"Not necessarily, unless they were directly involved. We're used to seeing everything on television these days, virtually as it happens, but back then word wouldn't have got around for months. By that time it would have been grossly distorted. It's like Chinese whispers, by the time it's passed through a few mouths and got caught up in the propaganda machine, it's far from the truth. If you weren't actually present, you most probably wouldn't know what was true."

"Was I making up what I did seem to know? It's all so different from what I've read about Akhenaten. How could the Great Lord and Bringer of Light and Truth have had a homosexual affair with his brother?"

"It's human nature, and you have to remember that what we think we know has been edited by time and bias, the new Pharaohs Aye and Horemheb tried to suppress all memory of Akhenaten and King Tut. History is always distorted. What we have left is fragmentary evidence, rumor, speculation, and what those in power wanted us to know." His nose wrinkled up in frustration.

"Aren't there records?"

"Very little, because papyrus rotted so archaeologists have to rely on the pottery shards and bits of stone that were used rather like we'd use scrap paper today. There's a lot of official letters from Amarna, but they don't shed much light on the private lives of the royal family. New stuff is being discovered all the time, of course, so more might be discovered. Egyptologists have as many theories as there are Egyptologists, they can't seem to agree on anything, especially about this period."

Ronald laughed and went on:

"They haven't even reached an accord on whether Smenkhare and Tutankhamen were Akhenaten's sons or his brothers, as your memories would seem to suggest – and some of them believe Smenkhare might have been Nefertiti ruling as Pharaoh, it's so complex."

Ronald had his professorial look on again. Was I about to get a lecture on ancient history? I wouldn't put it past him to have researched this after Ramon's experience – assuming Ramon had the same memories. He must have done, surely. If only I could talk to Ramon, know what it was that sent him away from me. It kept coming back to that question. How would he have reacted to a homoerotic three-in-a-bed scene? I was sure he would have felt guilty and embarrassed, he was Catholic after all, they got fed guilt with their mother's milk. Did Smenkhare know I got pregnant?

"... It's the same old story, going round and round. Lots of gossip and speculation but little formally recorded. Contrast it with our royal family. At the beginning of the twentieth century, kings had mistresses – they always have had. We now know that one had a morganatic wife but it never made the papers at the time."

I seemed to remember something on TV about that, but I hadn't taken much notice; too busy with my chemo.

"Up until recently, royalty's privacy has been fiercely guarded. They were treated like gods, just like the Pharaohs. Even after ten years of marriage and with Diana in the news constantly, we didn't know about Charles and Camilla. Until suddenly, it hit the headlines a year or two later ..."

Of course, but at least he had a woman for a lover. What would the public have said had Charles confessed to being gay?

"Since then we've had the parentage of a royal prince discussed in the tabloids. According to a society gossip writer a few years ago, Prince Philip has a constant companion, an attractive woman half his age, but it only merited two column inches and nothing more has been written – probably had a D notice slapped on to protect his privacy although I gather there's a book out about it in America. He's still regarded as untouchable.

But think what a writer will do with that in forty years time, let alone four thousand."

Four thousand years. I'd forgotten how long ago it was, to me it was yesterday. Ronald was glancing at his watch and I realized it was getting late. We'd gone way over our usual time.

"Do you have time to see me again tomorrow, Ronald? I'd really like to find out what happened next, I don't think the rape is the reason for my illness."

"Yes, of course. Would the evening suit you, about six?"

"That'll be fine. I'll be back from belly dancing by then. I'm having private lessons with Miranda's teacher. She's a wonderful Greek woman who was born in Egypt, and who studied dance there. She runs special antenatal classes. Around six would be fine, I'll see you then."

Ronald nodded but his face was troubled:

"Megan, we should do some reframing on that experience."

"Do you think I could do it when I have the full story? It doesn't feel quite time and I'm alright, really I am, except for being tired. Could you call me a cab?"

chapter 20.

terrible one

My hand halted on the tarnished knocker. Did I really want to do this? Could I take any more knowing? I'd slept so badly last night, kept dreaming of the young and golden Smenkhare pounding away on top of Akhenaten, only his body was transparent and made of light. Every time Smenkhare pushed into Akhenaten's body, bits of light shot off in all directions. Eventually they were both all light and they turned into creation. Weird. I'd had to stay in bed all day to get the strength together for this evening. It was a pity about missing my class. Still, I might as well get on with it.

"Someone is pulling me from the bed, shaking me and shouting. "Who is this?" I'm trying to open my eyes and find my clothes but Akhenaten's lying on my tunic and it's covered in blood. I can feel something crusted on my thighs and belly. It shames me for another woman to see me like this. She is so angry, she shakes and shakes my arm. Tears are spurting from her large, dark eyes. She's shouting at Akhenaten. "Who is this? Why is she in your bed when you reject me! I'm your lawful wife and I should be there, not some strumpet of a girl." I don't understand, it's not Nefertiti, I've never seen this one before.

Akhenaten draws the sheet over me and says quietly. "Go, Kiya, go. Leave us, please." She stomps out of the room muttering to herself. I'm very frightened. Suten tells me to dress and go to my room, but I slip out to the old Queen's palace. Queen Tiye finds me sobbing in the garden by the lily pond. If only I had not met the child Merit'aten there that day. When I tell the Queen a carefully edited version of what happened, she responds.

"Oh yes, poor Kiya. She is my son's second wife but he has never taken any notice of her. She has a child she says is his, from their honeymoon, but I've never been sure. She lives with Nefertiti in the North Palace, I didn't realize she still went to the Southern. She's got a sharp tongue and some powerful friends who don't always agree with what my son is doing. We need to watch out for that one."

Suddenly, as though realizing the state I am in, she takes me to her private bathing pool and places me in the water. It stings and I whimper but she says.

"Stay there child, the warm water will help you and I'll send Luit to you with salves and clean clothes."

By the time I am dressed, the Queen has received an order from her son. She, and all her retinue, are to return to Waset immediately to take up residence with Suten's sister, the Princess Sitamon, at the Malkata palace. Even I am aware that, as well as being daughter to the old Suten and Queen Tiye, Sitamon had been a wife to her father at the end of his reign. These two women are old allies. We will be safe there.

In the haste to pack there is no time to talk, and no privacy on the barges that make their slow way upstream. As the river turns west, my glance is drawn back to the last glimpse of Akhet-Aten shimmering white on the dusty plain. The city blushes like a young maiden on her wedding night as the sun slips beneath the horizon. This sun is not the great god Ra on his journey to fight the forces of darkness, this is the stern Aten who has turned his face away for the night. The enemies of Khemet may ravish this night, there will be no protection. A shudder passes through me, a premonition of things to come. Tears rolling down my face, I leave my king, the shining one. The keeper of my heart. "I will come back," I whisper into the gathering gloom, "I promise, I will love you for ever."

It is several weeks before we arrive: in the heat of midsummer the strong wind that normally blows upstream is stilled, and the rowers must struggle against the current to move the heavy royal barges. Their rowing is ragged, dry throats cannot chant the rhythms that keep time, hands slick with sweat cannot beat time on the djembas. Oftentimes the barges are pulled with ropes by teams of men. Queen Tiye's guard has been co-opted to the task. It is so hot they cannot pull for more than an hour or two. Men collapse constantly and the Queen commands that we move only at night.

In the darkness it is difficult to see obstacles. One night the boat collides with a pack of river horses who are making their way rapidly downstream. From afar these strange creatures with their bulbous eyes perched on top of their heads and big padded cheeks look gentle, but their squat bodies and short legs are powerful, they can kill a man, trampling him under the water or snapping him in two with their great jaws. The boat master orders the oars shipped, luckily no one is in the water when we meet them. The ropes from the shore hold the barge against the current until the animals have passed. We are lucky not to be capsized, had they fallen into a rage they would have attacked the boat, but they seem anxious to move downstream.

On the barge there is not a breath of air and we lie listlessly in the veiled pavilion on the deck. I am glad of a time to rest, to heal, but I miss my Suten dreadfully, there is a place beneath my ribs that feels bruised and empty, as though something precious has been taken from me. With half closed eyes I gaze out on the villages strung like jewels along the riverbanks. Washerwomen laundering their bright clothes, children playing in the reeds, fishermen and wildfowlers casting their nets. They seem to have no fear of crocodiles or river horses – to be taken by the waters ensures a safe journey to Amenti.

Then all is barren, sand closes in all around. The oxen in the fields are left far behind. Even the ubiquitous stork fears to make his nest so far from habitation.

The old priests come before the Queen. They are agitated. They have seen the midsummer star rise twice, Sothis, herald of The Time of Ahket: inundation. Sothis clings to the nipple of Nuit in the dawn sky. It is brighter than any other star. Hastily the barges are steered into the shelter of a steep bank and tied with slack ropes to stakes driven deep into the earth. This is a desolate stretch of river. The distant hills, vibrating in the heat, are too far away. We cannot disembark. No one knows how high the flood will rise. Had we reached Waset, the news would have been sent down from Aswan. As it is, we can only wait. The rowers stand by with long poles. Everything has been tied down so that nothing can be washed away.

It is here! Hapi is rising. A roaring wall of water twice the height of a man breaks crashing and foaming over the barges. Tipped this way and that, we are showered with flotsam and dead creatures. Rushing and pounding, the turbulent water swirls around us, the barges rising and twirling up out of the flood like river fish dancing on a line. Will the mooring lines hold? Surely nothing can survive this. There, a vortex sucks a dead ox down into its depths. An offering for the river god. The harvest will be good this year, but I fear we will not live to see it. Hapi protect me. I hide my head beneath my arm, burrowing into a corner of the deck.

The mooring ropes plunge straight down. Almost twenty cubits, higher than living memory. A little more and the barges will be pulled beneath the waters forever.

It's quiet now, the roaring has ceased. As I look out, water stretches as far as my eye can see. A shining lake, reflecting the face of the god golden upon the flood, rimmed with purple. It must have been like this at creation when the sacred mound rose out of the waters.

The captain of the guard takes an inventory. Only two people lost but all the stores are wet and soggy, water has breached the casks of beer, and many oars have been broken. From the look of things, many houses upriver are without doors or shutters. The flood has torn everything away.

There is much to do while we wait for the floodwaters to recede and our food stocks to be replenished by the hunters. To eat the dead beasts that float past is forbidden and they must travel far to reach dry ground. Meanwhile, we are desperate. Some brave souls swim after game that has been stranded on the debris moving swiftly down the river; others paddle to the logs washed into great mounds where the water is shallow. Fishermen cast their nets into the teeming waters, bringing the slippery, silvery fish to the surface. Even the old priests put aside their taboo on eating river fish, too hungry to wait for the hunters' return.

I am grateful when we reach the palace. The journey has been cursed with much sickness among the crew and many of the retinue are ill with river fever. It is fortunate that the palace was built on the higher land away from the river, although the waters lapped even here. Queen Tiye orders a ritual purification and fasting. We are dosed with the bitter herbs that expel worms, but my stomach expels the foul brew before it can reach them.

I retreat for several days to a quiet corner of the Queen's suite, leaving food untouched outside the door. My stomach rejects even water, only paw paw fruit soothes it. I crave its cool juices and beg a maid to bring more.

The maid reports my sickness to Queen Tiye. The Queen removes me to a far corner of the palace, to the room I occupied at the time of the Great Upheaval. She warns everyone that I have a contagion. Once in my old room, she asks anxiously.

"Are you with child?"

Hanging my head, I cannot look at her.

"I do not know. My menses have always been sparse and have not shown themselves for the past three months but that could be the difficult river journey, surely?"

Queen Tiye carefully examines my belly and my breasts. Tracing a line from my navel down into my pubic hair, she shakes her head. Looking at my swollen nipples with the veins standing out, she raises her eyes to the goddess.

"Lady Mut protect us."

Muttering incantations under her breath, the Great Lady places barley and wheat grains in a pot and orders me to make water upon them each morning for seven days. When the time is up, the newly visible sprouts cause consternation.

"More barley than wheat, a boy. My child, this cannot be. My son's enemies grow ever stronger. If you bear his son there will be great danger. If the Lady Kiya hears of this we will all be killed.

Her son is sickly but he is Akhenaten's only male heir and she is determined he will succeed his alleged father."

My heart contracts. I cannot cause harm to my lord and I cannot tell her that this is not my lord's child but his brother's ... but my baby ... how ... My hand goes protectively to my belly. The Queen nods gently but her eyes are steely. I know I must not carry this child.

Calling Luit, her most trusted wise-woman, she orders her to bring niaia and besbes from the herb garden and the ished fruit with a fresh onion. These are ground to a paste with salt and bound with senetjer-resin. Gently the wise woman introduces them into my *kat*. My belly is poulticed with more onion, salt, and senetjer, this time pounded with sut-hemet and white emmer. The whole bound around with bandages soaked in pine oil and djesret beer.

As they work, the Queen patiently explains the effect of each ingredient. Strange how she continues her teaching even in these painful circumstances. She must believe I will need the knowledge one day. Could that day come? Will I take what she says is my rightful place at the Mut temple again? If only I could believe it.

And then we wait. After two days, I am given date juice with salt, herbs, and oil. My stomach heaves. My body rebels. I am racked with cramps for several days but to no avail. The child is fast within my womb.

"Well child, it looks as though the gods have other plans. We will have to be patient. You must stay here, keep out of sight."

Barely five months later I am woken in the night. Pains wrack my belly, water is in my bed. Surely it must be something I have eaten, but no, I can feel my baby's head emerging from my *kat*. If

I birth this child alone maybe I can keep him hidden. I must not scream, must not cry for aid, but I can ask the goddesses of my youth. Surely they will aid me, hide me from the merciless gaze of the sun-disc. They must have saved my child when the lady Tiye tried to abort him. What do I have to lose by petitioning them?

"My lady Mut, help me. Taweret protect me. Isis assist me, Nephthys hold me in your safe hands. Hekat hasten this birth."

Lacking a birthing stool, I squat on the bed. The child slithers out. Tiny and wizened, he does not cry. He is so still, surely this is not a child for whom there is no *ba* to imbue life. Without that spark of life force, his body cannot breathe. His *ka* was so strong, he could not be aborted, but where is his *ba*? Bes be with him, guard his spirit that it will not wander. Call his *ba* home to join the strong *ka* that Ptah spun for him on his potter's wheel.

Trembling, I bite through the cord and rub him in the sheet. His frail blue body shudders and he whimpers. He is alive! Quickly I put him to my breast, scarcely noticing the placenta slipping out behind him. His tiny mouth barely sucks, his little hands wave feebly in protest as nothing issues forth. I push my hand down my breast, willing the milk to flow. Soon he sleeps. Laying him down, I gather up his precious placenta and cord. He is royal. I must make his bundle to be carried before him. As I try to stand, blood pours down my legs. My head spins and I fall back on the bed.

When I wake, my child is gone."

Sobs shake my body and my belly feels numb.

"Megan, do you wish to continue or do you need to take a rest?" Ronald's voice sounded anxious.

I was okay, just wished he wouldn't interrupt me at such an

important moment, I must talk to him about that later. I knew I could go on seeing but he was being intrusive. Still, Anne did say he knew what he was doing, he probably felt it was for the best.

"I must find out about my child."

"Very well, is there anyone you can ask?"

"No. I'm quite alone."

"Let yourself move forward in time until someone arrives."

"Luit's here. She's come in quietly and glances at me. It's clear she doesn't expect to see me awake. She helps me to drink another of her foul concoctions and then motions me to lie down again. Luit can't speak, someone cut her tongue out when she was a young woman, no one knows why but of course there are rumors about a royal abortion. She signals that she will fetch the Queen.

When the Great Wife comes I beg her to tell me where my child is. Tiye smiles reassuringly.

"He is being cared for. You have been very ill with a fever from the bleeding. I'm afraid you will never bear another child but, child, you were not meant to." Her voice is stern. Have I transgressed against ma'at, the orderly and ordained flow of life?

"But my child, what about him, surely he needs my milk?"

"You couldn't feed him yourself, everyone would know you had birthed a child. This way, you will be able to take your place in my retinue again and no one will guess."

My child. I want him with me, but I know better than to voice this desire.

"Who has care of him?"

"It is probably better that you do not know."

"You have to tell me. Please, I beg of you."

"He is in the Princess Sitamon's apartments. One of her women birthed a stillborn child. Luit was called in to help as it was a difficult birth. She fetched your little one. He was put to the woman's breast while she was drowsy after the birth. I do not know if she is aware of the substitution, but if she is, Min'et will tell no one. Her husband was a priest of Amon before the Great Upheaval. Apparently he used to sneak into Karnak to perform the midsummer rites.

"Smenkhare, who is charged by my son to see that only the Aten is worshipped throughout the two lands, heard rumors that the rite would take place. He and his soldiers were waiting. The woman's husband was slain. If she had not been pregnant, she too might have been present at the rite and she would be dead now. As long as she is suckling the child, she cannot be put to question, Smenkhare cannot touch her. And Sitamon will find a way to protect her after that."

"Surely it is dangerous for the princess to give her shelter?"

"No child, Smenkhare would not dare to touch his elder sister. She is much loved by the people and is careful to be seen to worship the Aten no matter what her private thoughts may be. Your child is in the safest place possible. Now sleep, you have much healing to do."

"Megan, before you come out of that let yourself heal fully, feel the effects of all the abortive potions you were given during that life fade away, washed out and neutralized by healing light, and allow any antidotes you may need to be administered." Ronald had clearly decided that was enough for today.

A cup was handed to me by Luit. It sparkled with light and tasted rather like elderflower champagne. It coursed through my blood, bubbling with health.

"Allow any lingering effects of the chemotherapy you had in this life be healed also. Let your uterus heal so that your baby will be in a safe, nurturing place and can go safely to full term."

I was floating, bathed in light – Akhenaten's light and love. This beloved Pharaoh was reaching out and healing me across time. Asking that I forgive him and his brother. Of course I did. How could I be bitter against the Lords of my Heart?

"And, Megan, you had better revoke that vow you made to love Akhenaten forever. Make it for that life only – if that is appropriate."

No, no. I could not revoke my vow. My lord had just healed me and I'd forgiven him. I couldn't let go the love ... at least, not yet. But I didn't tell Ronald. It might have been better if I had.

"Well, Megan, is that it? Have you found your answers?" Bright eyes peered intently into mine.

" 'Fraid not, although it's pretty clear what made it difficult to conceive or bear a child in this present life – that abortion attempt on top of Mek'an'ar's experience must have thoroughly messed me up. But it didn't throw any more light on my illness or other questions I have. I still need to know how that life turned out. I know what happened after I was dead, but not what led up to that. Did my child grow to manhood? What I saw with Anne would indicate that wasn't the case. And what happened to Akhenaten?" I could hear my voice rising, come on, calm yourself, deep breaths now, I told myself.

"If you can answer that, you will have done something the Egyptologists have failed to do in two hundred years." Ronald's laugh was more like a bark. Was he amused or critical?

"Do they know about Kiya? Did Akhenaten really have another wife in addition to Nefertiti?"

"Yes, he did, she's mentioned in some inscriptions they've found but she hasn't caught the public's heart like Nefertiti did – that beautiful statue of Nefertiti captures everyone's imagination. Shall we schedule another session?" He reached for his diary.

"Yes please, soon."

chapter 21.

overcomer of all enemies

The red light was insistent. Thought I'd turned the machine off
again after I spoke to Ronald; I must have forgotten. I couldn't
face speaking to anyone while I was so confused, not even Ramon.

Especially not Ramon.

What if it was Ramon? Stop beating so fast, heart. He would
ring when I wasn't here, hope he left a message. But what would
I say to him? So many questions and I was exhausted, leave it till
tomorrow. No, it was demanding attention, I'd better listen.

"Megan, Megan, where are you? If you are there, pick up
please, it's Serena Webster. I've been trying to reach you for days,
you haven't answered any of my letters. Your divorce hearing is
tomorrow. You must appear in Court at 11am. If you want to
prevent Greg from receiving a settlement, be in my office at nine.
You have my home number, please call me to confirm you've got
this message."

Not Ramon after all then. Could I call her? It was late, the cab
had taken an age. She sounded rather worried, perhaps I'd better
... damn, her machine ...

"See you in the morning, Miss Webster."

Waking suddenly in the night, I couldn't move, it must be Greg again. I thought we'd broken this in Egypt. He must have been trying it to prevent the divorce. Why did I take my ankh off, Mohammed told me to wear it always.

Right, come, Mecky, you knew how to handle this. Deep breath, up and out, my etheric body could move even if my physical one couldn't. Over to Greg's house, whew that was fast. Looked at him lying there innocently in his bed. But what was hovering over him wasn't so innocent. The shade of that renegade priest again, although he didn't look to have so much power since we'd had that battle.

"In the name of all that is good, I strip you of your powers. I command you back to the other-world that is your home. You are banished. Return to earth no more, oh shade of a former life. Remain at peace in Amenti."

It was effective, but I sometimes wondered whether I'd gone mad and these things were merely the hallucinations of a deranged mind.

"I'm sorry, I was in Egypt and then I was so busy and I felt so tired, I never looked at the post, kept meaning to. I forgot all about the divorce."

And the hospital appointments that had no doubt piled up. Even though they didn't expect me to go to term, they still expected me to attend their clinics.

"Never mind, I think I know what Pharaoh's Revenge is like. We have it all over Africa under different names."

What? Oh, she must have thought I'd had that dreadful Egyptian tummy bug. Well, probably better to let her think that than to know the truth. It might complicate matters.

"Now, we must run over your deposition because the Court is bound to ask questions and, as it's some time since you gave it, you'll probably have forgotten a few things."

But I'd remembered an awful lot more.

"Have you heard from Greg?" The rustling papers sounded loud in the sudden silence as she rummaged through the thick file.

"No, not as far as I know. I've been leaving the answer phone off and ignoring the phone, and, as you know, I haven't opened the post."

So silly, not answering the phone. What about Ramon? How could he contact me if I didn't leave the phone on? What was the matter with me, I'd felt so heavy and leaden since I got back and yet I was sure the cancer was going, and I'd been so well before we left Luxor. What was it?

"Right, well, maybe Greg won't turn up. His solicitor advised him to make it an uncontested case but he was so insistent I'll be surprised if he lets it go without a fight."

"Mrs. McKennar, you say your marriage irretrievably broke down when your husband left during your, extremely serious, illness?"

"Yes ..." I realized I'd forgotten to ask Miss Webster what to call him. "... your lordship."

"Mrs. McKennar, you don't need to call me your lordship. Simply answer my questions."

"Yes, er, sir." My knees were knocking, and my head felt swimmy again; I hoped I wasn't going to be sick. Not there, it would be too awful. Thank God Greg wasn't there. He'd have known exactly how to twist things to his advantage.

"You look pale, would you like to sit down and have a glass of water?"

I nodded gingerly, any sudden movement could precipitate ...Perhaps I should take one of those homoeopathic pills ... Ah, that was better, they worked incredibly fast.

The door at the back of the court crashed open. I didn't need to turn round to know who it was. Breathe, remember, Mecky, deep breaths. Greg's solicitor was already hurrying forward but it was too late, Greg was striding up to the front shouting. What a noise, but it gave me time to recover. Pull yourself together, girl, I told myself, you need to think clearly now.

"Mr. McKennar, there is no necessity for this hearing to wait for you if you are late. You should have taken adequate precautions to see that you arrived on time. Everyone else did. Now sit down sir or I'll have you escorted out." His voice was sharp and his look distasteful, but Greg crashed on.

"You can't do that. It's my right to be here ..." So pugnacious, come to think of it he was a pug with his face all screwed up like that. But dogs didn't have such red faces. It matched the registrar's, who clearly wasn't used to being argued with like that.

"Sit down, sir. Now. Your wife brought this petition and I wish to hear her speak."

I didn't think Greg was helping his case, maybe it would be alright after all. Deep breath ...

"Mrs. McKennar, you were about to tell me about your family trust. I understand it was set up by your father for your benefit and that this was the only money in the marriage apart from what you yourself earned through your occupation? When did ..."

"That trust was for both of us, not just her. I changed my name to theirs to please him, like a son I was. He meant me to have the money, meant for it to finance my ideas."

Greg hammered his fist on the table, his face so red it must surely burst.

"Mr. McKennar, one more interruption and you will be removed from the court. Now sit down." As usual a look that would quell anyone else bounced off Greg.

"I want what's mine. And anyway, she's mad, thinks she lived before, some reincarnation nonsense. Barking, that's what she is, shouldn't have control of money." He glared at me balefully.

"Bailiff, please escort Mr. McKennar out of the court and do not allow him to return. Mrs. McKennar, your petition for divorce is granted. No financial settlement will be made to your ex-husband and no maintenance will be granted. Costs are awarded for the petitioner. Mr. Birkett, you will notify your client immediately that if he harasses his ex-wife, he will be brought before the court on a charge of contempt."

Costs for the petitioner, did that mean I had to pay?

Miss Webster was whispering.

"Greg has to pay the costs of the divorce. Don't worry. That's it, Megan. You are free."

Free, was I really? If so, why did I feel so dreadful?

"Come, on you'll be better in the fresh air."

I opened my eyes to unfamiliar white walls, a painting of flowers, and a window looking out onto a blank wall.

"Where am I? What am I doing here?"

"In the hospital, dear, you fainted and your solicitor called an ambulance when she couldn't bring you round. What with your condition and all, we thought you'd be better off in here. This is the private maternity wing. Your solicitor said you would want that, and she said she'll be back to see you later. Now don't move that arm, doctor thought you needed fluids and now we've moved onto blood." One hand briskly tucked in the sheet and plumped my pillow whilst her other hand fiddled with a drip.

"I want to see him, now. Please."

"She's dealing with an emergency. I'm sure she'll be along to see you shortly. Stay there and I'll bring you a nice cup of tea." Twitching the rather stylish duvet cover smooth, she moved towards the door.

Why did everybody offer me tea? I couldn't be the only pregnant woman who threw up at the smell of it. There should be some of that ginger tea in my handbag, maybe she would make me a cup of that. Another tip from Terri, it worked like a dream.

"Megan, how are you feeling? You didn't tell me you were pregnant, I thought it was the illness. I take it this is not Greg's child?" Miss Webster laid a huge bunch of lilies on the bed. Lilies reminded me of death in Egypt, better not think about that.

"No, you're right, it's not. Miss Webster, I can't thank you enough for what you did for me in getting the divorce, and for getting me settled in here. I'd have hated a big ward and I've got my private medical cover."

"I think it's about time you called me Serena. I take it this child is by the other man that Greg spoke about." She raised an eyebrow quizzically.

"Yes, but he's gone away ..." Silly to cry, but I couldn't seem to stop.

"There, there." Miss Webster, Serena, took my hand, found tissues and mopped my eyes dry. Anyone would have thought I was a child. But it was comforting and she didn't seem to be shocked.

"Now, I know it probably doesn't feel like a good time to

discuss this, but we have to be practical. If you don't make proper arrangements, Greg could claim the child. By rights we should have told the court today but it's not too late to arrange a court-appointed guardian in case the unthinkable happens."

I definitely didn't want to think about the unthinkable. Instead I focused my attention on the pattern the light falling through the slatted blinds made on the wall behind her. Like bars on a window, better not go there either.

"That will ensure that your child will be looked after if the worst does happen and that he, or she, will get the benefit of your money, and Greg won't get either the child or the money."

"Whatever you think best. Sorry I ..."

My jaw ached from yawning, I was too tired to argue, couldn't seem to keep my eyes open.

"Sleep now Megan and I'll be back to see you tomorrow."

Tomorrow? I intended to be out of there that day.

But when I awoke it was dark outside. An immaculately dressed Indian man and a middle-aged woman in a white coat with a baggy cardigan thrown over it were conferring in the corner of my room.

"Ah, we're awake are we?"

That nurse was still on duty then. What was her name? Oh yes, Merryweather. It was strange how only her head appeared round the door. Was that the royal we? Mustn't be bitchy, but the way they talked drove me mad.

"I am awake and I'd like to speak to my doctor. I'm afraid last time we met I didn't have long enough to find out his name."

"Dr Rahim's here, he's your cancer specialist, and Dr Catermoule, your antenatal consultant."

Didn't know I had one, but I might as well find out what she thought. With her hair flopping from a scraggy bun and glasses perched on the end of her nose, she seemed approachable enough.

"Dr Catermoule, excuse me, can you tell me how my baby is?"

"Please call me Fran. If you'd kept your appointments I could be certain, but as far as I can tell without an ultrasound, baby is fine. It's you we are concerned with, an elderly primigravida is a tough enough proposition without cancer intervening."

She didn't pull her punches and she wasn't wearing a ring. Had she ever been pregnant?

"An elderly primigravida? What does that mean?"

"Sorry, that's our jargon for a mother who is rather, shall we say, older than most of our first-time mums. Primigravida means 'first pregnancy.'" She smiled wearily.

First time? She obviously didn't know, hadn't anyone found my notes? Glancing out of the window onto that blank wall I struggled to find the words:

"It's not ... I mean, I was ..."

Dr Rahim shuffled the notes.

"Well, actually, Dr Catermoule, err, this is not Mrs. MacKennat's first pregnancy ..."

"McKennar, McKennar. Can't anyone in this place get my name right?"

"Steady, Megan, I'm sorry." Dr Catermoule, Fran, put her hand on my shoulder. "Your notes have only just come down from records. I haven't had time to study them yet. Have you had another child?"

"Sort of, I was pregnant, but the chemo ... I lost ..." I couldn't help it, those tears were back.

"Is that why you're not being treated this time?" She was clearly puzzled and I didn't know what to say.

"Well, not exactly. The doctor said there was no point. He didn't even think I'd live to have my baby." My voice wailed as rising sobs turned into hiccups. My baby turned restlessly and I winced as a stray kick caught me under the ribs. Could he feel my pain?

"Steady on, Megan, remember the baby. There's always hope. Even if we have to deliver early, I promise you I'll do everything I can to save your baby and to give you the best of care – and Dr Rahim here is the finest there is. If anyone can perform miracles with your cancer it'll be him."

Her gaze held mine. That tender smile, those soft brown eyes, I knew her – Luit, dear Luit, back in my life again to help me once more. Thanks be to the goddess.

"I'm sorry, Megan, you can't leave. When you came in yesterday you were somewhat dehydrated. The drip we had you on should have helped with that but we need to monitor you. Have you been eating properly?"

Fran pushed back her scraggly hair again, her shoulders sagged wearily. How many hours did this incredible woman work?

"Well, I did in Egypt but since I got back I haven't had much of an appetite, I do try to eat healthily for the baby's sake. I've had lots of fruit and vegetables."

Fran shook her head: "That's not enough for a pregnant woman in your condition. I want to get more blood into you to counteract the effects of the cancer. Your baby needs healthy blood cells. With your rare blood group I've had to put out a call for donors; we've used the existing stock. The new blood should be here later today. You'll have to be in hospital for several weeks, and I know Dr Rahim wants to explore the possibility of a new treatment with you." Now the sleeves were being pushed up again. Her face was reassuring though.

"I'm not going to have anything that will affect my baby."

"Don't worry, dear, Dr Rahim won't do anything to jeopardize that. He has some revolutionary ideas, they caused quite a stir when he first came here, but the results have been remarkable. Fortunately, with you being in the private wing it's not a problem to treat you somewhat unorthodoxly, but he uses his treatments in the NHS part of the hospital."

"Why haven't I seen him before?"

Fran opened her hands and raised her shoulders:

"It's the luck of the draw really, although your GP probably referred you to a specific consultant as you were a private patient, and you'd be sent to his outpatient clinic when you were first diagnosed. Once you're in the system, that's it, you stay with the same consultant throughout your treatment. Dr Rahim joined us after your treatment began." Her lips curled up, was that a secret smile?

"Why was I able to see him yesterday?"

"You were lucky he was on duty when you came in. Because I saw you in ER and brought you here to Maternity, I was able to ask him to take a look at you. If you'd gone to one of the cancer wards, your consultant would have been informed, but you'd probably have seen a junior doctor. Even as a private patient, you tend to get the juniors. I'm not supposed to say this, but the consultant you were under is stuffy, he sticks to conservative treatment even in cases like yours, and he hardly ever sees patients in the clinics. Rahim is different, he is not afraid to take a risk."

There was a twinkle in her eye that I remembered well.

Sa Sekhem Sahu who brought Luit back to me, and Dr Rahim.

"Now, Megan, we need to discuss your treatment." His face was grave. "I want to be straight with you, there are dangers as I am sure Dr Catermoule has told you, but these are for you rather than your child. As long as we can get to a point where the child is viable he – and we know it is a he from the ultrasound we did earlier today – will be fine."

Strange how like Ramon Dr Rahim sounded. I supposed language had a different rhythm in his country too. And, a boy, why did nobody tell me? Anne was right.

"Excessive bleeding will be our main concern at the delivery, but I have an extremely effective Chinese herb that will take care of that, and as soon as you have been safely delivered we will be giving you a new drug that has been very successful with your type of leukemia." He was fiddling with the blood pressure cuff, and didn't meet my eyes, but he spoke confidently enough.

"But what about now, it feels like I've still got a long way to go."

My arm throbbed as the cuff pulled tight.

"Yes, that is true, we need to get you over this next month. But I have been using acupuncture here in the hospital to great effect. It will help to stabilize you and increase the immune response of your body to give you a better chance of fighting the cancer."

Releasing the cuff he gently pulled it away from my arm.

"But will it hurt my baby?"

"No, I can assure you that it will not. Dr Catermoule and I have used it before – it can also provide pain relief during the delivery – although we may decide to do a caesarean section. You are fortunate, I have been able to secure a Chinese doctor who trained in a special technique. He is an experienced man. You will have to learn some exercises to improve your chi – that is your vital energy – and circulate your blood more efficiently. Dr Shen-Tao will be along to see you later. Once these blood transfusions are over, you will be able to go home and come in as an outpatient to his clinic." He was starting to leave, I wondered if ...

"Dr Rahim, can I ask you ...?"

How could I put this, would he approve?

"What is it that you wish to say, Megan?" His black eye peered into mine, he reminded me of Ronald and the secretary bird.

"I met a homoeopath on the boat in Egypt and she was talking about using homoeopathy to help in my cancer. I wondered if you would mind if I saw her?"

"Not at all. I think that in your situation you must be exploring every possibility. I shall be most interested to see the results. In India we use a great deal of homeopathy, we have a long tradition of natural medicine. Why not ask her to visit you here, when I shall have the pleasure of meeting her and I can brief her on your condition."

In an English hospital? I was in a private room but I never expected that. I must ring Terri quickly.

"Megan. I'm glad you phoned. I've been trying to reach you but you didn't answer your phone and no one seemed to know where you were." Terri sounded so glad to hear from me, her voice was reassuring, even over the phone.

"I'm in hospital. That's why I'm phoning. Can you come in and meet my consultant?"

"Your consultant? Yes, it'll be a pleasure. I've been doing some research and I think I might have come up with something. Would this afternoon be okay, Megan?"

"You see, Megan, after that past life experience where you worked in the dye pits ..." Terri paused, wriggled uncertainly, and then, as though making up her mind finally, asked: "Has Megan told you about her past life exploration, Dr Rahim?"

"No, she has kept it a secret. In my culture we take past lives for granted, please, tell me what you found." He smiled encouragingly at her.

"Well, she said she got ill from some rocks and black sticky stuff that were burnt in a brazier and then thrown into the dye pits. I did some research on traditional dyeing practices and apparently they used naphtha and benzene in the processing. Benzene is strongly carcinogenic and I understand it is often responsible for leukemia."

Dr Rahim nodded, looking thoughtful.

"But how could contact with benzene in a past life have an affect on the present?"

"It leaves an energetic imprint, a soul memory as it were. When we look at Megan's present life history, benzene features strongly. I think it could be one of the root causes. Do you remember, Megan, you told me that story about being a student and living in the flat above a dry-cleaner's? Well, dry cleaning fluid is a potent source of benzene emissions, especially when it isn't properly vented, and Megan told me the flat reeked of it, Dr Rahim, and it takes up to twenty years for the full effect to manifest. Cars are another source and, of course, you've always lived in cities with heavy traffic, Megan."

I nodded, remembering how my father had always promised we would move to the country when the factory was well established, but of course we never did. He was a city man through and through, spending what little spare time he had in bookshops and concerts.

"Didn't you say you worked in your father's plastics factory as part of your design course? That is another major contributor to benzene overload."

I nodded again:

"I worked for Dad for several years, especially as a teenager when the factory was just getting going and he didn't want to pay the men overtime. Then I went back to help full time with design and sales when I left college. It was only after his death I sold the business and became a design consultant for other people."

"I suspect that you have a benzene miasm from that previous life which made you particularly susceptible to the toxicity effects in your present life. From what you said, Megan, you could well have died of a cancer in that other life too. If we treat the miasm, it will be a good start. "

"How would you treat her miasm?" Dr Rahim had been listening intently, was he taking her seriously? If only he …

"High potency snake venom and drainage remedies to push out the miasm and any toxic residues as a first stage. After that, we can look again."

It sounded like a treatment straight out of ancient Egypt. Good job I trusted Terri, her remedies had worked well on the boat. Dr Rahim seemed to have confidence in her too when he said he was looking forward to seeing the results. I was lucky to have found him – Terri too.

"Megan, now Dr Rahim's gone, there's one more thing I think you should do as soon as possible. You remember Anne taught us that separation ritual on the boat? Well, now your divorce has come through it would be a good time for you to repeat it with Greg, especially as you had a church wedding. I know you did the tie-cutting on the boat, but revoking your vows is appropriate now."

"Thanks, Terri, I'd intended to do it when I left the court but all this happened and - "

"Would you like me to guide you through it? It might make it easier for you as you are feeling a bit woozy still. I wouldn't like you to fall asleep in the middle. I could come in tomorrow?"

Struggling up on my pillows I asked:

"Do you think we could do it now? They know you're treating me, we shouldn't be disturbed."

"Of course. It'll be a pleasure. Make yourself comfortable and we can begin. Here, let me help"

Terri deftly moved a few pillows, lowered the backrest, and smoothed my sheet.

"Where would you like to start?"

She reminded me of Anne as she settled herself back in her chair.

"Guided visualizations always start in the desert for me but perhaps we could turn it into a beach – the sand is great for making circles."

"Okay, Megan, close your eyes and picture yourself on a beach. Find yourself a nice flat space. Make your circle at arm's length all around you in the sand. Now make another circle in front of yours, but not touching it. Put Greg in the circle."

"He's not happy, he's trying to shout at me so I've popped one of those old fashioned glass bell jars that Anne used over the top of him. He looks really comical, arms waving about, getting all red in the face."

"Good idea. Check that no more ties have attached themselves since you did the tie-cutting."

"No, I'm clear."

"Excellent. Now tell Greg firmly that you give back to him all that is rightfully his and take back all that is rightfully yours – you may need to make an opening in the top of the bell jar, Megan."

"He's jumping up and down and telling me the money is rightfully his. Oh dear, this is so funny. His solicitor has bicycled in and handed him the decree nisi. Greg's turning puce as he reads it but his solicitor says that's it. There's no going back on the court's decision."

Terri's rich chuckle rolled round the room.

"Good, now what does he hold of yours?"

"Only my promise to love, honor, and obey him this time. There doesn't seem to be anything from the past."

"Right we'll rescind that in a moment. What do you hold of his?"

"I don't think I ... Goodness, I have his heart in my hand. I remember now, when he proposed he got down on one knee and went all flowery, said he'd love me for ever and here was his heart to prove it – gave me a red heart cut from an old Valentine card, and it wasn't even one I'd sent him. I'd forgotten all about that."

"Good, give that back to him with his heart. Say to him clearly and firmly that you hereby revoke all vows and promises that are no longer appropriate, whether made in this or any other lifetime, and that you set him free."

"He doesn't like that, he's getting really cross. Says what God has joined man cannot put asunder. Oh, the vicar who took our wedding service has come in. He's told Greg he made a terrible mistake in marrying us and that he is releasing me from the vow

I made – says God was having a day off and it wasn't made in his sight. Greg has stomped off and the vicar's giving me a blessing and asking for my ring back in order that he can deconsecrate it. Now the tide's come in and washed Greg's circle away. If I don't hurry I'll get my feet wet, it's going to wash my circle away too."

"Well done, Megan. Let your forgiveness go with Greg. When you're ready you can open your eyes ... How does that feel?"

"Great! I do love the way images take over and do their own thing. It makes me feel I can't be making it up, I'd never have thought of getting the vicar back for a spiritual divorce, and the way the tide washed away the circles was brilliant."

"It is brilliant, isn't it? I've learnt so much from Anne over the years. I always use that rescinding the vows visualization with my patients who've been divorced or bereaved. It makes such a difference to them. Sets them free to move into a whole new life. Now, Megan, how about a big hug to celebrate?"

Such a big-hearted woman. It felt good to be wrapped in her generous arms.

"Anyone for tea? Oh, sorry to interrupt ... I'll just ..." She seemed surprised to see us hugging like that. Can't think why, it was the maternity ward and women do do that after all.

"Not at all, yes, you can give Terri the tea, and perhaps you'll make some ginger tea for me please?"

"Of course, dearie, anything to oblige." Her smiling face retreated.

The joys of private medicine.

chapter 22.

mistress and lady of the tomb

"Hello, Megan, long time no see."

As I opened the door Ronald bounded in, head dripping.

"Ronald, it's good to see you. Thanks for coming. I never seem to have enough time with all these trips to the hospital and my belly dancing classes – I wanted to keep that up in case I can have a normal labor."

He waved his wet coat around like a dog shaking itself after rain. Turning, he saw a chair and hooked it over.

"Will it – that's okay. How are you feeling?"

"Much better, the Chinese exercises I've been prescribed boost my energy and Dr Rahim thinks I'm holding my own against the cancer. It seems to be in remission again."

"That's excellent news. I'll do some hypno-healing with you after the regression. We can boost your immune system."

"That would be good. I'm anxious to find out what happened to Shen-en-k'art's baby, I'm sure the key to my illness is back there. Do you mind if I lie on my bed, it's more comfortable now I've got the bulge; little blighter kicks like mad but Dr Catermoule says it's a healthy sign."

I patted my bulge indulgently. I'd learned to love the occasional sharp pain but I'd be glad when the discomfort ceased.

"How long to go?"

"Only a month to the earliest date for the caesar but they want to wait as long as possible so it could be longer – it depends on how I am. I'm still hoping for a natural birth."

"Right, let's get started."

"No, no, no. It can't be. He was well. How could he ..."

Dry, heaving sobs racked my body, my shoulders convulsed, gulping air. I was aware of Ronald sitting forward quickly, but I motioned to him to keep quiet. I needed to see this.

"I rush forward, flinging open the doors. His small body lies stiff upon the bed. He looks perfect, unmarked except for the blackness of his skin. My beautiful child.

"The poison must have been insidious, no one realized until it was too late. When I awoke this morning, he was dead." His mother too is dry-eyed but she looks like she's been drugged. She reaches out her hand:

"Shen-en-k'art, I know what you did for me. I know the sacrifice you made. But I thought no one else knew, I thought he was safe here with me." A single tear slowly trickles down her cheek. "How could they have found out?"

How indeed? We live quietly. The Great Queen is old, only her indomitable will keeps her alive. She has not been seen in public for four years, and many people believe she is dead already. We thought the outside world had forgotten us. The Princess Sitamon is still much loved by the people; we trusted that we were safe under her protection. Why now? What is happening in the world that makes it necessary to kill my child? How did the tendrils of Set ensnare him? For I know it is so.

"Mistress, the priests of Anubis are here to bear his body to the mummification temple. You must let them take him now."

They are wearing the jackal-headed mask of a mortuary priest. If the priests are those of Anubis, the Aten can hold no power in Waset. Does Suten know? Surely Smenkhare will have told him ...

Min'et grasps my hand. I can hear her thought. Be strong. Heads bowed, we wait until the bier with its pitifully small burden has left. No mourners wail for him, it wouldn't do to draw further attention to this small soul.

"Min'et, you said the poison must have been insidious. How do you know it was poison?"

"When the Lady Sitamon's physicians saw how his skin had changed color, they said at first it must be a serpent bite but no trace was found. Then they declared it must be poison."

My back is crawling. There is something more here. My inner eye shows a coal-black heart, deadly magic, a curse inflicted from afar. A mighty serpent slipping through the night. Nefertiti's soldier, he has great ambition that one, and great occult power.

"The child was accursed."

"But he will never gain Amenti. We must tell the priests ..."

"I doubt if any priest here has the power to neutralize this venom, and we do not know whom we can trust. We must go to the Great Lady, she can tell us what to do."

But when we reach the Old Queen's room, she too is dead.

"She left you a message, Shen-en-k'art. 'Hold to your faith, remember your training.' And she made me promise to give you this."

A package, carefully wrapped. Opening it in the privacy of my room, a huge golden ankh and chain slide out. Turning it over, the Lady Mut. The symbol of the High Priestess of her temple. As I hold it, I feel the power flowing into me, hear my Lady speaking. "My child, your time will come. Until then, I will keep the soul of your child safe. When the time comes, you will bury him in the tomb of a Suten, protected by powerful spells. The curse will be dissolved."

Suddenly I am speeding, rushing through night.

I carry the mummy of my child in its outer case. There are guards beside a doorway, small and mean, beneath the Peak of the West. As though invisible, I slip between them and down a short corridor. Turning right, at the end there is an enormous golden shrine. Hundreds of items have been thrown in beside it with neither reverence nor care. I am chanting the prayer for the dead:

"Osiris shall not be weary, he shall not putrefy, he shall not decay nor swell. May it be done to this child in like manner, for he is Osiris. Let him fly like the Lord Horus straight to the realms of Amenti. Let the magic of the Great God and of the royal blood of Suten unite to protect him. For he is risen."

And touching the great ankh that I wear to his head, I place my child beneath a large statue of My Lady laying haphazardly against the far wall, praying that she will keep him safe and lift the curse. Tomorrow the tomb will be sealed. He will rest here with his uncle throughout eternity."

"Who is his uncle?"

Ronald's voice startled me out of the scene. I was so deeply immersed I had forgotten he was sitting beside me. It's funny, I never did talk to him about interrupting me. Still I knew by then I could slip back in without any problem.

"Tutankhaten, or rather Tutankhamen as he was known by that time."

"What had happened to Akhenaten?" Ronald was on the edge of his seat, electricity crackling off him, he was taking this very seriously.

"I don't know, I didn't see ... it's confusing. I think I shot forward several years. I was older, more dignified and powerful. I'd put a spell of invisibility on myself and it obviously worked because the guards didn't notice me passing. But I didn't have time to explore what I knew ..."

"Yes, I'm sorry, that was my fault, I jumped in. I got more caught up in the story than I should have done, and I was seeing King Tut's tomb and had to know if I was right."

He was biting his lip. I hadn't meant to be so sharp with him.

"That's alright. Do you think we can continue, I'm anxious to know what happens?"

"Of course, let's go back to the first part just after the death of the child."

"Akhenaten demands that the Old Queen be returned to Akhet-Aten for burial in the new family tomb. Two of Nefertiti's young daughters are already buried there. Smenkhare and Tutankhaten come to Waset for the funeral procession but Akhenaten does not leave his beloved home to escort his mother.

The Princess Sitamon has told me that I can remain in her household but, on the day before the procession is due to leave, Smenkhare seeks me out. Without acknowledging me in any way, he tells me that Suten had been on the point of sending for his mother. He had heard whispers that one in her retinue, a young servant girl, had been pregnant with Suten's child when she left

Akhet-Aten some years previously. He was calling his mother to account.

"As my mother cannot answer for herself, you must come with us. My brother can ask you for himself."

I am placed in the baggage barge, under guard although I am not supposed to realize this. Ahead of us floats the great royal barge, the coffin draped in purple, blue, and gold, dressed in lilies. Priests chant continuously beside it. Djembas beat time. The thick smell of incense and lilies drifts back to us like a ghost over water.

There is little chance I will try to escape. I have nowhere to go and I am in any case paralyzed by grief. The double loss of the woman who had been like a mother to me and of my child has dimmed my light. There are times when I feel I will tiptoe into the other world to join them. I have no appetite but Smenkhare has issued orders and broth is spooned into my mouth. The Princess Sitamon has sent Min'et to accompany me and the two of us spend much time huddled together at the stern, watching the river pass by. All the life of Khemet is on its banks but we see it as though reflected in a glass. We have no part in it. I was fearful that Min'et would be arrested but time has moved on and her husband's "crime" has been forgotten.

After we land, it is some time before Suten turns his attention to me. I assume he is attending to the burial of his mother but no word reaches us. I have been lodged in my old room in Queen Tiye's palace. It is ramshackle now, paint flaking off, the gardens unkempt, and the fishpond barren. Soon it will return to the earth. But Min'et and I are comfortable enough. I wait in agony for my audience with my beloved Lord.

In the cool of the night he sends for me.

"Little Shen, it is long since I have seen you."

His face is soft and gentle. His fingers stroke my face. "They tell me you were with child when my mother took you away. Is this true?"

Keeping my eyes downcast, I say quietly, "There is no child, my lord."

"Are you sure?"

"Yes, my lord, I am sure."

Eyes remote, looking into the far distance, he dismisses me.

Why did he send for me? Was it because he has only daughters and seeks an heir as Min'et suggests? She does not know that even these children are not the fruit of his loins. He has two brothers in blood to inherit the Double Crown, and what about the Lady Kiya? She had a child ... All I know is that the person I love so much has removed himself from me. He is beyond my reach. But I cannot cry, I am beyond grief, drained dry."

I was stuck, unmoving, for a long, long time. The silence stretched out. This time I could have done with some help but Ronald remained quiet. Surely he couldn't have fallen asleep? Maybe he was just letting me rest awhile, it was peaceful ...

His voice quietly reached my attention.

"Allow yourself to move forward in time; leave that immense grief behind, let it go, feel it roll off you, move forward and tell me what happens to Shen."

"Some weeks later, Suten sends for me again. He has one of his blinding headaches and wants me to massage him. I think it must be migraine for he speaks of flashing lights although he tells me this is the Aten speaking to him. As I work on his bony shoulders, he places his hand over mine. "It would have been nice to have a boy of my own," he says, wistfully "One to whom I could hand on my vision of The One God. I fear when I am gone my brothers will revert to the worship of Amon. Smenkhare has gone from me, I have few friends now."

A tear descends towards each pendulous ear. I trace one with my finger and lick salt from its tip. Suten, God Incarnate, a member of the *per aa* spilling salt from his eyes like one of his subjects. My heart goes out to this strange man-god. "Do not leave me, little Shen, who will comfort my heart if you are gone?"

And now it is blank.'

"Okay Megan, let yourself return to awareness of this room, feel the bed you are lying on, be aware of your body. We'll take a short break and afterwards we can do the hypno-healing. Do you feel you are getting closer to the answer?"

Stretching myself, I moved carefully, sudden movements precipitated a flurry of kicks, and heartburn, and I didn't need that right now.

"I'm more confused than ever, to be truthful, but paradoxically I feel like I'm getting there. Why does he want to keep me close when he's rejected me? He clearly doesn't want any sexual contact."

"It sounds like he was confused. It must have been sad for him to know he had no heir – if he really did have the kind of endocrine disease some people suggest, he'd probably have been sterile but he wouldn't have known that, of course. Maybe the thought of you having a child gave him hope."

Ronald looked at my bulge. As clearly as though he had spoken I could hear him wondering how this new child of mine would fare without a father.

"Akhenaten was obviously deluding himself that it would have been his; perhaps he'd conveniently forgotten that night with Smenkhare. The mind plays strange tricks and I don't think he was a very stable character. Visionaries rarely are."

"Maybe that's it. He doesn't look like a man who's grounded in the real world. He spends too much time in the other world with his god. Standing out in that hot sun for hours can't be good for him either. He is a moody, introspective man. All that blinding light and certainty he'd had when he was young has been extinguished. He seems so lonely without Smenkhare."

My mind went back to that sad, remote face. The visionary whose light had gone out when his golden, shining brother left him. I knew exactly how he'd felt.

"Any idea what had happened between them?"

"Not at the moment."

"Well maybe we'll find out more in the next session. For now, I think we'd better do your healing and then I'll let you rest. Do you want me to come back in a day or two?"

"Please."

"Anne, it's Megan. I'm sorry to bother you but I have a question I can't ask Ronald."

"Megan, dear, it's good to hear your voice. How are you?"

"Very well, all things considered. The birth is getting closer and I feel strong. I can't help hoping that this time I've beaten it."

"What can I do for you?"

"Well, it's difficult. I've had more information on that Tel-el-Armana life I told you about on the boat."

"The one where you were being trained to be High Priestess but the overthrow of Amon intervened and you were a servant with Queen Tiye?"

"Yes, that's the one. Ramon has appeared in it."

"I see, that's not surprising, you two are closely linked."

"Mmm, but he wasn't very nice to me in that life. He was Akhenaten's brother, Smenkhare, who became co-Regent. They were having a homosexual affair and I think that's why Ramon disappeared after his regression."

"Sounds possible, Ramon is a religious man. He would have found that hard to deal with."

"It gets worse. Smenkhare raped me and Pharaoh when he found us together. I had his baby but the child was killed soon afterwards. I can't understand it. Why would Ramon do that?"

Suddenly I realized I had knotted the phone's cord tight around my hand. Hastily disentangling it, I almost missed her next words.

"Sometimes someone who loves us very much puts us through a hard experience. From the perspective of earth it's impossible to understand why, but it's as though, at a soul level, they want it to be from a loving source. People are surprised when they go back into the spirit world and find it was all set up before they incarnated."

"I can't believe I'd have set something like that up. Is it always pre-arranged?"

"No, if the planning wasn't done well you could get caught up in something that was never meant to be, as it were. What happened to you afterwards?"

"Well, I seem to have become the High Priestess. I haven't filled in the gaps yet between Queen Tiye dying and my going back to the temple to be installed, but by the time Tutankhamen was dead, I was back at the Mut."

"And this life came before the one where you were a High

Priestess doing the Sekhmet ritual with your Pharaoh?"

"That's right."

"It sounds like Ramon tried to balance out the previous 'bad' experience, although I remember you saying that you couldn't marry your Pharaoh in that life – did you ever find out why?"

"Only that I saw back to the early part of that life and a woman called Magrat married my father, the then Pharaoh. She somehow killed my mother and insisted that my stepbrother and I – that was Ramon – should not marry but instead he had to marry her daughter. She was bitten by one of her own snakes and died but Ramon wouldn't marry me because of a vision in which she promised to end his line if he did. It was one of her entourage who killed me – the priest who was Greg, my ex-husband. It all seems so involved and a bit far-fetched, I sometimes wonder if I'm making all this up."

"I don't think so, dear, the Egyptian papyruses are full of stories like that. I'm sure in this present life Ramon has a deep love for you but ..."

Did she know more than she was telling me?

"... you could be repeating that pattern of loving an unattainable or unavailable man, as it were."

If she did, she wasn't letting on.

"Anne, have you heard from Ramon, have you any idea where he is? I really need to talk to him, He still doesn't know about the baby." It was a good job she couldn't see those tears.

"Megan, don't upset yourself. Think of the baby."

I should have known I couldn't fool her.

"I'm sure he has a good reason for staying away, something more than mere embarrassment at a past life memory he's not even sure he fully believes. It will be alright, you'll see."

"What should I do?" I didn't mean to sound pitiful.

"Concentrate for now on having this baby and on staying well. Are you seeing Ronald again?"

"Yes, tomorrow."

"Try to fit in the missing pieces. I feel sure there is something more to your illness, something you haven't come across yet."

"Well, I know Shen-en-k'art was royal, that's why her child was killed. Someone wanted to make sure he never made it to the throne, nor her either."

I hadn't realized till then they might have been after me too. I wasn't sure who the someone was. It wouldn't have been Smenkhare, surely. He didn't seem to bear me any malice.

"It must have been a turbulent time after Akhenaten was no longer Pharaoh. Smenkhare, Tutankhamen, Ay, and Horemheb ruled in fairly quick succession."

Such a procession of names, I couldn't keep up, and although I knew most of them ...

"Horemheb? I don't recall him although I seem to remember Ronald mentioned the name."

"He was a general who took over after Ay; he had a long reign and began the Ramasses-Seti dynasty. He didn't have any royal blood and you know how much emphasis they placed on that."

"Nefertiti's soldier?"

"Sorry, I didn't catch that."

"There was a soldier, he was living with Nefertiti and fathered her children. I felt he had something to do with the curse that killed my child. But I never heard the name Horemheb."

"All these Egyptians had several names so that's not surprising, and names do slip from our far memory. You've remembered far more than most people; often they don't know their own name. If I remember rightly, Horemheb married Nefertiti's sister to try to legitimize his position, but such a lot was wiped from the records. Maybe your regression will tell you."

"I'll try to pursue that. Thanks Anne."

"Keep in touch and don't forget, if there's anything I can do ..."

"Of course, bye for now."

The call left me with a great deal to think about. Anne had talked about soul groups at that first workshop and how they supported each other through many lives. I'd forgotten that. I'd assumed soul-mates made each other blissfully happy but she did say that sometimes they helped each other to learn some hard lessons. I couldn't think what I was learning from this but I was willing to find out. She'd sidestepped that question about hearing from Ramon. Had he been in touch with her? She said something about him not really believing in the past life regression, perhaps he'd discussed things with her. I wished I could speak to him.

Gnawing on my knuckles, I went to make some chamomile tea, perhaps that would help me sleep.

roamer of Deserts

"Right, Megan, are you ready to find out what happened to Akhenaten?"

"Well, I hope I can. It feels close to the surface, so it should be easy to access and I'm intrigued but I'm also rather tired, all this going backwards and forwards to the hospital is exhausting."

"Would you rather wait a day or two?" Ronald frowned.

Was I still as pale as I'd been when I looked in the mirror that morning? I couldn't be bothered with make-up, it took too much effort.

"No, it looks like I'll be going into hospital next week or the week after, they want to monitor me more closely. I'd really like to do as much as possible today and maybe another session with you this week and try to wrap it up before the weekend, otherwise it could be some time before there's another opportunity. For my baby's sake, I need to do this now."

"It's the time of inundation again. Incredibly hot, nothing moves in the heat of the midday sun – except Suten. He's standing, bare headed and bare footed, out in the middle of the Aten temple. It's blindingly white out there, I have to shade my eyes to see him.

Having made a low obeisance, he has risen and thrown his head back, looking up at the sky. His face is ecstatic, otherworldly, as though he's communing with his god.

I can see this because I'm close by, watching from the corner of the temple, crouching under one of the sails the priests strung to form colonnades of shade. Akhenaten has sent for me, but he's totally unaware of my presence. I don't think anything could get through to him. His priests are nowhere to be seen.

I have to crouch here all day, my mouth is dry. I brought water with me though it's long gone; now I dare not move or the Aten will strike me down with his rays. In this place, he has overpowered all the other gods, my Lady included. There is nothing here but the Sun-God and his earthly representative, the Pharaoh Akhenaten, beloved of the Aten, life, health and prosperity be his.

Eventually, once the sun has set and the earth cooled, I move towards my Lord. He stands like a statue, his eyes filmed over, burned out from staring into the sun, the shattered light in their depths is dulled now.

"Shen, little Shen, is that you?" Croaking, like one of the bullfrogs that call at Waset in the night.

"Yes my Lord, here, let me help you." I put out my hand, which he ignores. His face is still turned to the sky but then his hand gropes out to mine and quickly I take him out of the temple into the night, away from the sight of his god burning into his eyes.

"Shen, I cannot see anything except the Aten burned into my mind. But my god has called me, I am to go into the desert with my people. He will guide us."

Into the desert? At midsummer? Surely he will perish.

"But my Lord, what about your country, its inhabitants need

you, they cannot all go surely, and there's your brother, me ...your children."

"Little Shen, nothing matters but my god. But you could come with me..."

What do I say? Can I refuse this god-man who holds my heart? But I know I cannot go. I know my Lady calls me, her great ankh is hidden beneath my robe, it grows heavy against my skin.

"My Lord, let me lead you to your palace." Gently I tug his hand but his great bulk resists.

"No, no, little Shen. I must go to the Window of Appearances. I must tell my people."

His people. For some time now people have been slipping away from Akhet-Aten in the night. His brother Smenkhare hardly ever appears here, and the young Tutankhaten has been sent to Waset to continue his education with Nefertiti's uncle, Ay. There are far fewer people now than there were; those that remain are fiercely loyal to Suten – or else so greedy for profit or advantage that they will not leave.

"Tomorrow, my Lord, tomorrow. We must ask your heralds to call the people together. Come with me now, you need to eat and drink if you are to talk to your subjects. You will need your strength. I will bathe your eyes for you so that you can see again."

But, when morning comes, Suten remains blind.

"Lead me to the Window, little Shen, I must speak to my people."

There is nothing more for me to do. Finding the Vizier, I tell him that his master needs him and allow this august presence to lead the king to announce his departure to the people:

"People of Akhet-Aten. You have been with me through the long years. You set up this temple to the holy Aten, you have worshipped him, enjoyed his love and the fruits of his blessing, his face has shone down upon you. You have been our people. Now the Great High God, the Lord Aten, has called me to lead you into the desert. The ground shook, clouds veiled his face, then his ray shone out and he spoke to me."

I saw none of these things, heard nothing. Was it sunstroke, an hallucination, or does he really believe his god spoke to him?

"Our enemies draw close, he wants to preserve the people of the Aten. You must pack enough food and drink for forty revolutions of our father Aten. If you bring animals, you will need extra feed and water. Carts will be provided. Tomorrow the march will begin. My priests will take before us the Aten image from the temple. The sun-disc will be our guide."

A babble of voices drowns him out. Thank the gods he cannot see. It would break his heart. Such consternation, people are running from the square. I fear many will hide until Suten has left. His priests look undecided.

"Come, priests of Aten, you will join me in the temple for a vigil. My servants will pack all that we need. My guards will ensure we are undisturbed."

He has realized he could be abandoned by these wily servants of a new god – who may still hold allegiance to the old within their hearts.

Turning to me, he says, "Little Shen, I charge you to take word to my brother Smenkhare and my daughter Merit'aten. He is now ruler of the Land of Khemet. My daughter carries my blood and will make an excellent Queen. I command my brother to take good care of my people and to keep the faith of the Aten whom I serve. Give him the crook and flails of the Aten. They will be his symbols of authority."

Has he forgotten that his blood does not run through the veins of Merit'aten, his adopted daughter? Or has he persuaded himself that she is indeed his child? I fear my Lord has grown delusional under the Aten's gaze. But it is the people who must be convinced, and they have never known the truth. I thrust the instruments Suten hands me beneath my all-concealing robe as the old soldier Ay comes puffing up to the temple. He commands the king's guard when not elsewhere in the country. I hadn't realized he was at Akhet-Aten. Is he lodging with Queen Nefertiti? I have heard that her soldier is his son.

"My Lord, what do you wish me to do? Am I to accompany you into the desert?" From the look on his lined face he wishes most devoutly that the answer is no, and his prayers are answered.

"No, my good and faithful Lord Ay, I wish you to take young Shen here to my brother Smenkhare. She has messages for him."

"My Lord, should you not dictate them to your scribes?"

"No, my Lord Ay, I know whom I can trust. Shen-en-k'art will take my words to my brother. Go now, take the royal barge and make all speed to Waset."

"My Lord, what about your lady wife, the Queen Nefertiti and her children?"

"They shall have the choice to accompany me or to travel with you on the royal barge. Go, tell them that I would speak with them in the temple."

But, by the time I have returned to the palace, packed my small bundle of belongings, and collected Min'et, the Lady Nefertiti, her children and her entourage are already ensconced on the barge with Lord Ay. Surely she cannot have had time to speak to her husband?

"Shen-en-k'art, it has come to my notice that my husband the Suten Akhenaten, Life, Health, and Prosperity to Him, handed several objects into your care. I think the land would be better served if they are with me." Nefertiti's hand goes out imperiously.

Courage, Shen-en-k'art, do not fail your Lord now. I had not realized she knew my full name, who could have told her? It gives her a certain power, which I must block.

"I am sorry my Lady, the instruments were given into my care and I swore a sacred oath. They have been well hidden. I am charged with handing them to the Suten Smenkhare and this is what I must do."

The Lady Nefertiti and the Lord Ay are clearly furious.

"But Shen-en-k'art, the journey is long and hazardous, especially at inundation. Surely you remember your last trip up river at the flood?" Nefertiti's silken tones cannot hide their menace.

So she did know. It was she who told Akhenaten – or did she merely tell her soldier? Where is he anyway, I heard tell he was a general now, called to defend the northern boundaries.

"My lady, the power of the Aten will surely protect me. And now, if you will excuse me, I will retire to the other barge. I fear this one may be a little too crowded for you if my friend and I remain."

Fleeing across the gangplank lodged between the two barges, I feel her malevolence on my back. Why is she like this? Is it, as I fear, that she wishes to claim the throne herself? To do that, she will need the sacred instruments. It is as well that I used a ritual from the temple of Mut to hide and protect the symbols of authority. No one will find them, of that I am sure.

When I awake, someone has searched my baggage in the

night. But the crook and flails remain where I placed them, in plain view but hidden to all but the most penetrating eyes by the wings of the Lady Ma'at. Divine Justice will guard them until we reach Waset.

Inundation is gentle, the barges hardly feel Hapi's rise. A crocodile glides by, visible only as a wickedly toothed snout and two staring eyes. The Lord Sobek does not demand a sacrifice from us this time. The river spreads slowly over the fields, fishermen in their shallow boats taking the opportunity to spear the glittering silvery fish that lie stranded in shallow pools. Wildfowlers cast their nets. Their catch makes a welcome change in our monotonous diet.

Our barges proceed, the rowers lashed if the pace slows. Ay and the Queen are in a hurry to reach Waset. My Lady protect me. I must take care. The picture's fading ..."

"Did Akhenaten leave for the desert with his people?" Ronald clearly could not contain his curiosity any longer.

"I don't know for sure, I think so. When I passed the temple on the way to the barge, there were about a hundred people gathered outside with their bundles and a few animals, mostly those who had first gone to Tel el Armana to prepare the new city. They were the fanatics, the true followers of the Aten, the ones who believed in him and formed the core of the new cult. The others at Akhet-Aten merely tagged along hoping to gain Pharaoh's favor – or were forced into going – there were many of those. Once I was on the barge, I never looked back. I couldn't bear it."

"And you have no idea what happened to him?"

"No, not as far as I can remember. I'd like to see what happens when we reach Thebes, maybe there'll be news of him there."

"That should be interesting, so little is known for certain about this period."

"I am stepping out onto the bank on a dark, moonless night. We are at Thebes, moored in front of the Malakata Palace on the West Bank. The royal barge went to the East Bank, but our barge swung quickly into the palace landing stage. I am being escorted by a handful of soldiers wearing the royal livery, the barge is leaving, moving to join its twin. In the palace, the lady Sitamon greets me.

"Welcome back Shen-en-k'art. I will do my best to protect you but I'm afraid you have become more conspicuous than is wise. I fear the Queen Nefertiti has plans that would go better if you were not here. I bribed the boatmen to bring you to me, rather than to the Eastern palace. It will be safer. What have become of the crook and flail that were put into your care?"

Can I trust her? There is no one else.

"They are here, my lady."

I point to the tattered ostrich feather fan in my hand. It has cooled me during the journey exactly as it used to cool the Old Queen when she sat in her garden.

"I see no instruments of power, merely a few feathers."

"Those are the feathers of Ma'at my Lady. Divine Justice will reveal the truth when I go before the Suten Smenkhare."

"Come this way, quickly. He is staying in the palace. My spies brought me word by a faster boat than yours and I recalled him from Nubia where he was on the king's business. It is my belief that the Lady Nefertiti seeks to have herself declared Regent and to appoint her own co-Regent. That wily old jackal Ay has ranged himself on their side. He already holds young Tutankhaten hostage. He hopes it will be his son, Horemheb, who is chosen to rule with her. The symbols you bring are of vital importance."

Horemheb, that dark shadowy figure who haunts the edges of my world. Is it Nefertiti's soldier? Was he the dark heart behind the death of my child?

I am hurried through dim corridors into a part of the palace I have never visited before. These are the rooms where the royal sons lived when the Old Queen was young. This must have been where Akhenaten and Smenkhare slept and where ... no, don't think about that now.

"Well, Shen-en-k'art, we meet again. What have you brought me?"

Just as Akhenaten's light grew dim, so Smenkhare's light has flared and grown brighter. I can hardly see him for the dazzling halo that surrounds his form. Is he touched by the god? Is this a symbol of his divine right to rule? But is it the Aten or Amon Ra who lights his being? The ankh around my neck grows hot and heavy. Does my Lady Mut recognize this ruler?

"Come on, what are you waiting for?" His impatience is hot and angry, his voice raised.

"What is it, husband of mine, what troubles you? Oh, Shen, it's you."

The Lady Merit'aten is great with child. Her face lights up like the happy child she was. It seems long ago that we sat by the lily pond.

"I am glad to see you, Shen. I have missed my friend. Can you stay for the birth?" She pats her bulging belly.

"Right now, my dear wife, the lady Shen-en-k'art has more important business here. You have messages from my brother?"

"Yes, Suten asked me to tell you to take good care of his people and to keep the faith of the Aten whom he serves."

"Has he really followed the Aten into the desert?"

"As far as I know, he was preparing to when we left."

"Did he not ask Nefertiti and his children to accompany him?"

"Well, my lord, he requested that she speak with him, but she was already on the barge with the Lord Ay and her younger children when I boarded. Suten was still in the temple with his priests."

"Will they accompany him into the desert?"

"The Aten has commanded it. Suten was worried ..."

How do I say this, should I even be saying it? Anxiously I look into his eyes, will he understand?

"What? What was troubling him?"

"He was concerned that you would not keep faith with the Aten. Many of the people ran away from Akhet-Aten rather than follow him into the desert, and the inhabitants had been leaving for months before that. Rumors kept reaching him of the restoration of Amon – and of plots against him."

"My brother had nothing to fear from me. Merit'aten and I were content that I should travel the country on his behalf. Once he saw how close we became after our marriage, he withdrew his face from us and sent me to rule the land in his place. You know he swore never to leave his beloved Akhet-Aten and someone had to be his eyes and ears in the land – and bring order where anarchy and chaos threatened. The rule of law was breaking down."

"Who do you think ...?"

"I fear that the plotters were quartered closer to home. Nefertiti is determined to have the throne for her lover. I think she will declare herself Regent on behalf of my younger brother, Tutankhaten. He is young enough to be malleable – and his health has never been robust. Then they will restore the Amon temples and declare themselves beloved of Amon. Those who followed the Aten will be declared heretic."

I have to ask him.

"And what of you, my lord, will you follow the Aten as your brother commanded, or restore Amon Ra?"

"Little Shen, for I know that is what my brother called you, your secret is exposed to me. You care not for the Aten. You await the restoration of the true and rightful gods of the kingdom of Khemet. I know that my mother designated you the High Priestess of the Temple Mut."

"Shen-en-k'art, is this true?" Merit'aten's hand has flown to her mouth, "If my father the Suten had found out, he would have had you killed."

"If Nefertiti and her soldier find out who she really is, they will have her killed. Her blood poses as great a threat to them as mine."

He knows even this? Who can have told him, surely not the Old Queen, she would have kept my secret safe.

The Princess Sitamon has sat silent all this time, but now she says.

"I fear it is too late. Ay, and Horemheb too, know full well who Shen-en-k'art's parents were. Why else did they have her child killed? He could have become the heir."

"Child?" Smenkhare's gaze is intent. "My brother said there was no child?"

"My Lord, by the time Suten asked me, there was no child. He had been killed, bewitched."

I cannot help it, sobs rise up into my throat. Merit'aten jumps up and hugs me.

"Never mind, Shen. You can share my baby. You will be her mother before the gods; you will present her at the temple. And when my husband takes the throne, he will restore you to your rightful place in the temple. Is that not right, husband?"

"Is this what you want, Shen-en-k'art? To restore Temple Mut to the goddess?"

"More than anything, my lord. I have been trained for this my whole life through."

"Even though you know it will be a difficult and dangerous task that will bring you to the notice of your enemies?"

"My Lord, it is my destiny. And the will of your mother, The Great Wife. See."

Opening my robe, I show them the ankh I wear.

"The symbol since time immemorial of the High Priestess of Temple Mut."

"What other symbols do you hold? Sitamon said you had the crook and flails."

"Yes, my lord. You will recall your brother had the ancient flails destroyed and new ones dedicated to the Aten cast."

"Yes, they were smelted down by the master goldsmiths. The new ones had the Aten rays upon them."

"Like these?"

As though by a conjuring trick, I flick my fan and the flails and crook of Khemet fall to the floor.

"Shen-en-k'art, how did you do that? I saw that fan, I never dreamed it truly held the sacred instruments." The princess Sitamon has picked them up and holds them out to Smenkhare.

"Without these, Nefertiti and her soldier will find it difficult to claim power. You must go before the Council at once, brother. I will order a boat immediately and send heralds to convene the council. We have surprise on our side."

But when the boats reach the temple landing stage, Nefertiti, Ay, and the great black figure of Horemheb are waiting. The Council and priests stand shoulder to shoulder behind them. All around, the people look on, deadly quiet whilst this duel is fought. Smenkhare's glow is dimmed as he faces his adversaries. The Lady Merit'aten looks like a child beside him, except for the bulge of her belly.

"What is this, Smenkhare? Have you come to concede the Regency to me as my husband, your brother, commanded?"

Nefertiti has never looked as regal as she does at this moment. Her beauty is flawless under the unforgiving morning sun. The great double crown on her head is held high.

"No, my Lady. I have come to command the role of Suten with my wife, the Lady Merit'aten, through whose blood flows the blood of her divine father and in whose child is mingled the divine blood of her father and my father before him. We claim rulership in the name of the *per aa*."

"By what right do you claim this?"

Will she dare to reveal that his wife is not the daughter of Akhenaten but of a common soldier?

"By the right of these, the sacred instruments of power." He holds out the flails and crook. His light blazes and the Lady Merit'aten, every inch a Suten's daughter, stands proud and tall. There is no mistaking the light of the gods shining around this young couple, nor the symbols of power they hold. A great roar goes up from the people.

"All hail Sutens, long life, prosperity and health be yours."

But from the way Horemheb is glowering, there is little chance of that.

An aged priest steps forward.

"And what, Sutens, are your plans for this temple?" He gestures behind him. The huge wooden doors that Akhenaten had thrown to the ground have been restored, the gods replaced on their pedestals. Amon is in his home once more.

"My wife and I have decided that people shall be free to worship as they choose. The temples will be restored, although the Aten temples will remain for those who wish to continue to worship the One God."

A collective intake of breath, a vast sigh as it is released. Then a surge as the priests rush into their old home. Only the aged priest stands his ground.

"And who will be the High Priest? As you know, our chief priest was killed by the followers of the Aten on your brother's orders."

"Why you, of course, Ik'nari, beloved of Amon. Did you think I would not recognize you?" Smenkhare smiles. "Go, take your place, and while you are about it, you can crown my lady wife and myself. Sister-in-law, Nefertiti, your crown if you will."

His gaze is powerful. For a moment she looks him in the eye. Will she challenge him, even at this late stage? Horemheb makes as though to step forward but Ay places a cautionary hand on his arm. Bowing, Ay offers:

"Let me help you, my Lady."

Before she realizes what he is about, he has removed the crown and strides into the temple. Smenkhare and Merit'aten fall in behind, leaving the Queen standing silent.

341

"Sister-in-law, and Horemheb, this way if you please. Yours will be the first allegiance I accept at my coronation."

All they can do is follow."

"Megan, where are you? You are reporting as an eyewitness. Are you there, watching?" Ronald's voice was quiet but insistent.

"Yes, indeed. I have been cloaked and veiled. I stand on the bank until the royal party has entered the temple, then slip in behind."

"Do you want to continue?"

"Yes, please, I must know what happens."

"After the coronation, Suten withdraws into the innermost sanctuary, the holy of holies, to commune with Amon. He processes to the Aten temple at the rear. Here he and the Lady Merit'aten are crowned once more, by the leading priest of the Aten. Smenkhare is taking no chances. Again he communes with the god. Finally, he turns to the gate that leads to the Mut. Here he calls me forward and throws back the concealing veil.

"I give to you Shen-en-k'art, Beloved of Sekhmet. High Priestess of the Lady Mut. She has been well prepared by my mother, The Great God's Wife, for her role. She and her priestess will ready the temple for a festival in my mother's memory. A great feast will be prepared and beer will flow for seven days and nights in her honor."

This Suten certainly knows how to win the hearts of his people. Can he vanquish his enemies half as well?

Smenkhare escorts me to my new quarters, leaving his wife to return to the palace with the Lady Sitamon. The long coronation ceremony has tired Merit'aten, she needs to rest.

Before the Lady Mut, Smenkhare stops, turning me towards
him.

"Shen-en-k'art, I will ask you this once and never speak of it
again. To me it was as though it had never happened. I lost my
memory, until I saw you unveiled just now. It was I, was it not,
who got you with child? I remembered a night when I came upon
you in his bed, he was so tender with you, and I was so jealous I
behaved abominably. Can you forgive me?"

"Yes my Lord. I can forgive. Please do not speak of it."

His eyes are intense, he looks deep into mine.

"I will make it up to you, one day, in another lifetime, we will
be together and we will have a child. Our child. Acknowledged
and loved by both his parents. You will see, little Shen." Tenderly
his hand touches my cheek."

Sobs rose in my throat, tears scalded my cheeks. I couldn't seem to
catch my breath. The past and present were so entwined, strange
how one mirrored the other. Ramon ... How could you promise
such a thing and then leave me like that.

"Megan, you had better bring your attention back to the
present now, it's not good for you to get so upset. Let it go, move
away from it, leave it in the past, breathe in peace and love. It's
been a long session and I think you should have a break. We can
do more if you wish when you've had lunch."

I couldn't tell Ronald what was really upsetting me, so I told
myself not to think about it, to put it aside for now. And
suddenly I was aware of a rumbling in my belly and pangs that
were hunger not my baby kicking. Besides, I'd got stiff lying
there for so long.

"That sounds like a good idea to me. I'm starving and it's time

I moved, I get stiff. Would you mind putting some soup on while I gyrate around a while?"

"Fine, no problem. Oh, you really did mean gyrate, didn't you?" His eyebrows twitched, surely he wasn't laughing at me, but I suppose it did look pretty funny, a heavily pregnant woman doing such an erotic move.

"Yup. This belly dancing tones up all my muscles ready for the birth – and it helps me to remember too. It's as though my body holds the memory and this shakes it loose."

"The body is a powerful storehouse for memories of all kinds. Many spontaneous memories start during massage or some other form of hands-on treatment. Acupuncture often 'pops' memories to the surface. It's as though the body brings back memories of all that has happened to it but it can't speak them until someone stimulates the place where they are held. People can be quite overwhelmed when something like that happens and they are not expecting it."

How like Ronald, always keen to explain; he reminded me so much of Malcolm.

"You'll find some herbal bags by the kettle." I said as a gentle reminder.

"Right Megan, let yourself go forward to the next important event and we'll take it from there."

So easy to slip back in time, and I really do need to know. I fear this might be my last time – for the foreseeable future at least.

"It's the festival honoring Queen Tiye. It's being held on the land between Karnak and the Mut and out towards the riverbanks. Everyone is here, except Nefertiti and her soldier. He's rumored to have gone north to patrol the borders. No one seems to know where she is.

We have reached the sixth day of the festival. There has been non-stop singing and dancing – and feasting and drinking. So many ceremonies to honor the Queen's soul. She must be safe in Amenti by now. Smenkhare has been with his subjects night and day, Ay at his side. Both are consolidating their positions, Smenkhare as ruler, Ay as his right-hand man.

Suddenly a messenger is sent to fetch me. Merit'aten has been resting, she is near her time. Now her waters have broken. Hastily I send for Luit, she has joined the temple to teach her skills and, from the look of Merit'aten, they will be needed here. As she feels my young friend's stomach, Luit turns and looks doubtfully at me. She signs that the child is breach. She must try to turn it.

Gesturing for herbs and oils, she massages the extended belly, gently rotating the child. The Lady Merit'aten moans. She is barely conscious, Luit has administered potions to dull the pain but the royal pelvis is exceedingly small and Luit indicates that the child is large. This birth will be a struggle.

The hours pass. Suten comes to visit his wife, but Luit gestures that he should return to the people. There is nothing he can do here. Mother and child are weakening, but we do not tell him this. Eventually, with a great cry, Merit'aten pushes the child out. A boy, with a grossly distorted skull like the statues of the Suten Akhenaten, life, health, and prosperity be his wherever he may be. All the family have a somewhat extended skull, but nothing like this child. The baby is gray and pallid. I can see his *ka* is weak and no *ba* has come close to activate the body. Luit shakes her head and puts him to one side. There is nothing to be done. When children look like that and live, they are drooling imbeciles. The gods have not chosen to bless Suten and his lady this time.

What is it with this family? Are they cursed? The Old Suten had boys beyond number. Queen Tiye birthed five, three of which survived to adulthood. But after that, what happened? Mine was the only boy born healthy. Was it the curses the priests of Amon heaped upon Akhenaten's head when he destroyed their god or something handed on in tainted *per aa* blood? A living heir would have cemented Smenkhare's position. Now I fear for his life.

Somehow this Suten survives; he has strong protection around him. His sorcerers must be as powerful as those of Horemheb. But he cannot maintain it indefinitely, and within six months the royal couple are dead. Clubbed to death by robbers, so it is said, although how they evaded the royal guard is not mentioned. I retreat within my temple and await events.

Ay declares Tutankhamen, as he is now known, to be the living heir. He will be the Regent until the boy is of an age to rule. Tutankhamen has been married to Ankhesamon, the last remaining child attributed to his brother Akhenaten – to strengthen the royal bloodline, so Ay says. I fear it will weaken it beyond bearing."

"What about Nefertiti and Horemheb?" Ronald's voice was insistent. I wished he'd let me do this my way. Still at least it focused me on what I wanted to know. It was strange how I could slip in and out of this to talk to him, his voice didn't really intrude.

"I hear nothing of them in my temple. All is quiet. Time passes. I hope that I might have misjudged them. But eventually, we hear that Tutankhamen is dead. The timing is impeccable. He didn't live to see his majority."

"How did he die?" Ronald's voice was impatient again, but I didn't mind, I was as anxious as he was.

"I don't know. I only know that Ay has declared himself Suten and married Ankhesamon himself to legitimize his claim. All this before the funeral rites are completed. He has also announced that the Suten Akhenaten is dead and was buried in his capital some months previously, but I don't believe this, it is too convenient for the new ruler.

Taking my chance, I reclaim the body of my son and, weaving about myself a spell of invisibility, I slip into Tutankhamen's tomb and secrete my child within. Placing around it a magical spell, I safeguard child and young Suten. When the tomb is closed tomorrow, it will be safe for all time. Those who disturb it must face the consequences."

"Was it you who put the curse on Tutankhamen's tomb?"

This time Ronald's voice brought me right back. The picture went and I didn't think I'd get it back, but I had done what I needed to do.

"No, it was a binding spell to keep it safe. There was no curse to my knowledge – but Ay might have spread that rumor to protect the tomb. It was hastily and shoddily prepared and its defenses were few, a gas trap or two and a little magical protection. And I don't think he would have wanted anyone to see the Pharaoh's body, I suspect he was murdered. I heard from Sitamon that all the embalmers and workmen died mysteriously within days of closing the tomb – that's probably what started the rumor of the curse."

"Right, Megan, well as you appear to be back with me, I think we had better leave it there for today. I'll come back in a couple of days for another session."

So, Smenkhare ruled along with Merit'aten for those few short months but history lost sight of him. Ramon was Pharaoh twice over. Those promises he made to me, it didn't look like either of them would be fulfilled in our present life. Yes, we'd been together but not properly and he didn't even know about the child I bore. How I wished he would phone.

"Megan, my child, it is time to break the ties."
"Yes, My Lady."
"Look deep into your heart, take out the ties to the Lords of your Heart. Hand each back what is theirs and take back what is yours."
So painful, like pulling out part of myself. But as Smenkhare, Akhenaten, and Mek'an'ar's Pharaoh hand back the pieces of my heart and I place them in my chest, my heart feels whole, healed.
"Now, child, relinquish the promises and vows. Let be what will be."
"Of course, my Lady."
"And forgive them."
"I already have and I accept their forgiveness too."
And let unconditional love flow between you.
Oh Ramon ...
Now let go of the past, release yourself. Let it drop away.

Bathed in peace, I sleep on deep into the morning.

chapter 24.

sekhmet of the knives

"Megan, how are you?"

The voice was so familiar, that hint of exoticness, the words so precisely pronounced.

"Ramon? I don't believe it, it's good to hear your voice. Where are you? It's been so long ... I thought ..."

"I am in Ibiza."

Ebitha? Where was that? Never mind, there was something more important to ask him ...

"Ramon, why did you leave so suddenly? Did you remember that Smenkhare life and feel guilty? You didn't need to, I forgave you ..."

"What life is it that are you talking about?" His voice was cold. Did he really not know? And how formal he sounded, I'd forgotten that the way he spoke English had that different rhythm to it.

"Smenkhare, the Pharaoh Akhenaten's brother, you were ... I saw it all ... I thought you saw it too ... with Ronald ... surely it was the reason you left."

My tongue was all twisted, why wouldn't the words come out properly? Was I making any sense?

"Megan, I do not know what this nonsense is that you are talking. I refuse to discuss it. I was called back to my home when the father of my wife died unexpectedly, there has been an inordinate amount to ..."

"Your *wife?*"

He'd never told me he had a wife. It hadn't occurred to me he could be married. How could he do that? How could he lie to me? I was so cold, I couldn't stop shaking. My baby was heaving and tossing as though he too had heard this unbearable betrayal by his father. Bent double, hand hunched around my belly, holding in the pain, protecting this child of mine, I staggered to a chair clutching the phone. How could his father ...

"You have betrayed me. How could you? You, you ...lied ..." Sobbing so much now, I couldn't get the words out.

"Megan, I may have omitted to tell you about my wife, but I never lied to you. I did not say I was unmarried. I told you the truth. I said I had never met the woman of my dreams – until I met you. You were that woman, Megan, and I have not stopped thinking about you for a moment since I left."

His voice was soft, silkily caressing, seducing me once again. Stop it, Mecky, don't be pulled in. Think of the child. My child, my fatherless child ...

"Megan, are you still there? What is the matter? Are you not glad to hear from me?"

"Glad to hear from you? When you seduced me, left me pregnant, and went away without a word ... you betrayer ..."

"Pregnant? You are with child?"

Didn't mean to tell him, but ...

"Yes ..."

Would this make a difference? For a moment hope rose, I held my breath.

"Will you leave your wife, come to me? Marry me, be with us always? You promised to, you know, when we were together before."

"No, Megan. This I cannot do. In my religion, divorce is forbidden and I have a position here to maintain. I would like to see you – and the child, frequently. But I cannot be with you always, especially now that there is the finca to run; large estates like this take time and effort. If I am not here – my wife cannot ..."

"Oh shut up about your life with *her*. I want to know about me, and our baby. You said you loved me. What are you going to do about that?" My voice was rising but I couldn't help it.

"Well, if you do not wish to keep it, I could adopt it. My wife and I are childless, there is no one to inherit after us. My wife need not know where the child came from, we could ..."

"How dare you! Adopt my child and take him away to a foreign country? Never. And he's not an it, he's a he."

"A boy. I need an heir, he would be well cared for, we are rich ..."

Slamming down the phone, I suddenly realized ...hold on ... too late – Mecky, you idiot, you'd no way of contacting him again. No, don't. I couldn't stop sobbing and shaking, felt icy cold. My heart was breaking – cutting the ties didn't help me there, did it? Nor forgiving him, but how could I forgive in advance what he would do that day? How could I have been taken in like that? How could I have thought he loved me, cared about me – and our child? All my hopes ... Why was I so stupid? I couldn't think any more, pulverized by a terrible pain.

"Megan, whatever's the matter? I couldn't get a reply on the phone, I thought I'd come round. It's a good job you gave me that key. What are you doing in the dark?... Oh, your face, it's all puffy. What is it?"

Strong arms hugged me, Terri's warmth enfolded me.

"What's happened to you, Megan? Is it the baby?" She held me away from her to study my face more closely.

"No, he's fine. At least I hope he is, I've been so upset I didn't pay him any attention ... It's Ramon ... he phoned ... he's m, m ... married." Didn't mean to howl it like that, but I couldn't help it.

"Married? Didn't you know?" She sounded sympathetic, but she must have thought I'd been stupid.

"I had no idea, he never told me." More sobs shook my chest, I couldn't seem to breathe properly.

"Here you are, try a few drops of this rescue remedy, it'll help you calm down, and this lavender oil will soothe the pain." Her gentle fingers massaged my temples, but the pain was deep inside my heart, could anything reach it?

"We have to think of the baby, and your health. Shocks like this are not good for your immune system. Did you tell Ramon about the cancer?"

"No, I don't want him to know, especially now ... He might try to take my baby." Deep down I'd thought that if anything happened to me my child would have his father ... but now ...would I want him to be with Ramon and his *wife*? I couldn't tell her how that made me feel, but Terri seemed to understand, perhaps ...

"Here, put this cold cloth on your eyes. Suck these, ignatia's good for grief and aconite's for the shock, Breathe gently, lie still, and I'll get you some chamomile tea."

What would I have done without her? Especially now ... How could he ... No, Mecky, stop it. Think of the baby, I told myself, you need your strength for him.

"Here, Megan, drink your chamomile, then I'd better take you in to see Dr Catermoule and get you checked over. We don't want to take any chances do we?"

"It looks like you're fine, Megan. I'll see that Dr Rahim gets the results of your blood tests as soon as possible but you look pretty good to me." Fran smiled reassuringly at me. "And your baby is fine, see his little heart is beating strongly. He's a fighter this one, I'm sure he'll be alright, no damage done but try not to get too upset in future."

My baby, to have seen him like that, tiny arms and legs pumping, like a little frog. Hekat, be with him, protect him at his birth.

"His head's tucked well down. It wouldn't surprise me if he decides to make his entrance early. It's a good job you're coming in next week. Now, we'll find you a bed for the night ... I'd like to keep a check on your blood pressure." Her fingers were on my pulse again, one hand going to push her hair out of her eyes.

"Please, Fran, let me go home? I'll sleep better in my own bed and there are a few things I need to do. I'll be back here soon enough."

I didn't want to tell her about Ronald and the regression, not yet anyway. I wasn't sure how she'd take to the idea of being an ancient Egyptian healer and midwife. Dr Rahim was different. He believed in this sort of thing. But of course, I haven't seen him in any of my lives. I wondered if I knew him before?

"I can stay with her, Fran." Terri took my hand. "I'll have to get back in the morning for my patients but I'll be happy to stay overnight with Megan. I can check her blood pressure regularly and if there is any sign of a problem, I'll bring her back."

I nodded gratefully, the thought of that empty flat tore at me ... but being in the hospital would be worse. Why did Ramon have to phone then?

chapter 25.

wanderer in the wastes

"Ready for this last session Megan? Sorry I couldn't get here any sooner, that last minute call to teach was a bummer, but I had to do it. Couldn't let Bill down." Ronald very flustered that day, his usually immaculate hair was standing up in peaks and I was sure that was a coffee stain on his jumper.

"This is fine, the timing is good, I'm ready."

By now I was numb. There was only so much pain one soul could absorb, and I'd reached my limit. There was no way I could have continued my exploration until that moment; Ramon's betrayal had cut too deep. I moved like a zombie, spending most of the time hugging my bulge and reassuring my child. The pain had been locked away, it lay low, not gone, it would always remain in my memory, but I thought I was ready to move on. All I could do was concentrate on myself and my baby.

A name, I must think of a name for him, I'd intended to ask Ramon ... no, don't go there, Mecky, move on.

Ronald's voice was brisk: "I suggest you scan quickly through the period after Tutankhamen's death until you come to something significant for yourself. We can always go back to the fine detail after the baby's born."

"For a few years after Ay takes over I am left in peace at the Mut. The Princess Sitamon has died and I hear little from the Court. Suten Ay and I have certain rituals to perform but once these are over, he leaves immediately. None of them require intimate contact. The Suten looks old now, although he's still strong willed. His young wife is sent to me for instruction in her role as the Great God's Wife. Once she is ready, they will perform the Sekhmet ritual together to ensure the fertility of the land and the continuation of his dynasty. She has no child, I doubt he troubles her bed. It is Horemheb and his son who will rule after him.

Horemheb never appears on these ritual occasions but I am aware of him plotting somewhere in the background – we use far sight in the temple but the seers cannot get close to him. He has powerful protection; he has clearly been taught by a great magician and has considerable abilities of his own. It would be pointless to warn his father of his intentions. Ay knows his son better than anyone. Nefertiti has faded away, I'm not sure what happened to her."

"Is that because no one knows what happened to her, or was it just you that didn't know because of your circumstances?" Ronald was back on his quest to discover what history doesn't know.

"I don't seem to hear anything about her, no one mentions her, she seems to have disappeared, it's confusing, she might be dead, I can't seem to ..."

"Don't worry, Megan, sorry to have interrupted. Go on with the story."

"Several years later, and shortly after Ankhesamon has performed the ritual as The Great God's Wife for the first time, there is a disturbance at the gates. When I send to know what is happening, I am informed that the Suten Horemheb has arrived with his soldiers. He has flung a cordon around the temple and no one is allowed to enter or leave.

I had not known he had been made Suten and, as I would surely have heard if Ay had died, assume he has become co-ruler with his father to ensure his succession. He must be nearing sixty and has grown ever more impatient to take over, maybe he has forced the issue. I dismiss the frisson of fear that crawls up my spine. Surely my position is unassailable.

I send word that I wish an audience with Suten Ay. My messenger slips out of a side door and away to the palace. But it is Horemheb who replies. He stands before the temple gates and commands my appearance. My priestesses are fearful for me and beg me not to open the gates. I mount the wall and speak to him from above the gate. With my poor eyesight, all I see is a great black presence, but I can feel his malevolence towards me. I am certain that he knows of my royal blood. Surely he realizes that I am past the age to bear a child, even though I doubt he knew that the previous birth left me unable to bear another. I pose no threat to him.

He tells me that, as there is unrest in the country fomented by followers of the Aten, it is feared that Temple Mut is no longer safe and he has stationed a guard to protect us. Food will be allowed in, but no one can enter or leave without his express permission. His commander is charged with keeping me safe – keeping me a prisoner more like.

After Suten leaves, I seek a meeting with the commander, inviting him into the temple. A short, stocky, middle-aged man with merry brown eyes is shown into my quarters. He shows reverence for me and my Lady and my heart is calmed. This man will not harm me –

(Ronald, it's Malcolm. This is where I know him from.)

He tells me that his mother comes from the same small village as mine. All his life he has heard tell of the child who was spirited off to Temple Mut ahead of those who would kill her. All feared that she had been disposed of in The Great Upheaval and there was much rejoicing when I returned to the temple.

"But I never thought to find myself guarding you. Whilst I am sworn to obey Suten, I will do all in my power to protect you. Poison is my greatest concern. I have ordered that the wagons that fetch your food will be guarded by my most trustworthy men and you are fortunate that you have your own supply of drinking water. But that too I will test. We cannot take chances."

Does he realize he is guarding me against the risk posed by his Suten? How much can I trust this man? Should I tell him that the greatest danger comes from enchantments sent against me in the night? I have cast protective spells to keep out evil intent but my dreams are haunted by fragmentary remembrances of the creatures my enemy commands. Too many nights recently I have awoken unable to move. Now I know from whence they came. Only the rigorous training from the Great Queen has enabled me to turn away these dangers. I must never doubt that my will is strong enough, that would be sufficient to weaken the defenses.

Time passes. The commander, Ashlar, sends his young wife to the temple. She is with child and he is concerned for her, her health has always been delicate and she is suffering greatly from sickness. She is sweet-faced, with the most beautiful brown eyes –

(It's Alison, those are Alison's eyes. They were married ...no wonder I ...)

But there is nothing we can do to save her. Long before the birth is due she fades away quietly like a candle flame flickering its last. Her husband is with her at the end. As he lays her hands to her heart he tells me that this was his one true love, there can never be another. We are all weeping. Luit and I had grown to love her like a daughter.

Then we hear that Suten Ay is dead. The guard around Temple Mut is doubled. A new commander takes over. This one is harsh and cruel. His men fear him. Food no longer reaches us but fortunately Ashlar had stocked our storehouses high.

Some months later, I am awoken and pulled from my bed. Suten and the commander are there. I am dragged into a cart and covered with sacks. The smell is dreadful and I faint. When I come round, I am lying on a mortuary slab in a temple on the other side. Horemheb is issuing orders. A thin wire loops around my neck. A quick pull and my neck is sliced open, blood pouring out onto the floor. Within seconds I am dead. A dagger is thrust into my heart, a cloth into my throat. The triple death that ensures that a woman of power is extinguished.

Floating above my body, I see Horemheb slide the dagger from my heart. Slicing my chest open he plucks out my heart and feeds it to a jackal. Without my heart I cannot enter into the Duat for judgment by Osiris and Anubis. I will be condemned forever to wander. The jackal licks my blood where it has pooled on the floor. Horemheb utters the magical formula that my heart, my body, and my *ka* shall cease to exist. He curses my soul and my issue for evermore. Curses it for the sacred blood I carry and which can never be his. He commands me into the farthest reaches of the outer deep – but a hand plucks me to safety. It is the Old Queen, Tiye. "Come with me, child," she says. "I cannot undo the curse on your blood, but I can keep your soul safe until you can be reborn again."

"Right, Megan, there are several things I want you to do."

Ronald was brisk, taking control of the process.

"Your soul is safe but can you see what has happened to your body?"

"Yes, he's had it wrapped up like a mummy and slipped an amulet in similar to one I saw before, they carry the curse. He's having the body taken away."

"I want you to find a way to give the body a proper burial. Can you do that?"

"Yes. Malcolm, I mean Ashlar, has come in and taken it away to the Anubis mortuary temple. He's having it buried with his wife, there's a jackal-headed mortuary priest there performing the rites."

"Does Ashlar know about the amulet?"

"Not yet, maybe I can reach the priest. Yes, he's checking the wrappings, he's got it. Drops it like a hot coal and stamps on it. It's shattered and he's directing an assistant to carefully sweep up the pieces and put them on the incense burner."

"And what about your heart and all that blood?"

"That jackal's come in. Oh, he's Anubis. He's opened his mouth and let the heart and the blood pour into a jar that has his head on top. It's been placed inside my mummy."

"Right, now, ask that your blood be purified, that all vestiges of the curse be removed."

"There's a column of light pouring down onto the jar and all around my mummy, and the priest is making a ritual around it."

"Excellent. What about your other organs? Were the spleen and liver removed and placed in jars?"

"No, they've rotted in my body. It wasn't really mummified, only wrapped to look like one."

"Right, have the priest remove them and do a cleansing ritual over them."

"They're looking quite pink and healthy again, he's putting them in another jar – and my stomach. What about my brain?"

"The ancient Egyptians didn't pay any attention to that, they removed it and threw it away. For them, the heart was the seat of the soul and the mind. Does that bother you?"

"No, its okay."

"Good. Make sure that the priest wraps your body properly, putting the proper protective amulets in place after the mummification process. Then let Malcolm accompany it to his wife's tomb. It will be in safe hands with him.

"Now, bring your attention to your present-life body, check that there is no remnant of the curse remaining. Let healing light flow right through your blood and your heart, and into your liver, spleen, and bone marrow."

"Mmm, that feels wonderful, so warm, liquid light flowing through me. It's going through every part of my body – and into my baby too. He's purring."

Ronald's voice was soothing: "Let that process continue as long as it needs to."

"I could stay like this forever. That soft, fluffy pink light is back. It feels good – except that cold spot where the hurt from Ramon's phone call is lodged – exactly where Horemheb's dagger pierced my heart. The light can't seem to reach that. It is small though, surely it won't matter?

"Right, Megan, now I want you to let go of the patterns you have been recreating time and again in your lives and especially in your relationships. See them, and find a way to release them."

"It looks like a giant dream catcher with me and my child and Ramon – and a few other people, caught up in it. If I unpick this bit here, get this knot loose, yes, that's it, the whole thing has unraveled and we've been spun out of it. My child has run to me and climbed back into my belly. This time things are going to be different."

"Excellent, let the new possibilities open up and then, when you are ready, bring your awareness back into the room. How does that feel?"

"Much better, freer."

I wriggled luxuriantly, hands above my head I stretched my arms then pulled down until my shoulders cracked. There, that was better.

"Do you understand it all yet?"

"No, but it doesn't matter. I feel that now I've recognized the pattern and broken free I can put the past behind me. Does that make sense?"

"Of course. I've wondered all along whether you'd got stuck on a karmic treadmill, going round and round the same old path and not seeing a way to break out – that often happens, especially in relationships. We'll see how you go but I think you'll find things are different from now on. If you do need to do any more digging, it had better be after this baby has arrived in the world."

"Thanks for your patience, Ronald. You've helped me enormously."

He grinned at me:

"Where else would I have got a virtual reality tour of ancient Egypt? It has been fascinating. I should be thanking you. Now rest, I'll let myself out."

Was that it? Lives remembered, body dismembered, curses broken, ties cut, *akhar* regained, patterns dispersed, promises revoked. Surely there couldn't be anything more?

chapter 26.

MMMMM

she whose opportunity escapeth her not

Aargh, what was that? Hot knives lanced through my back, a giant fist punched me back onto the bed. I fumbled for the light, and the clock, it was three thirty a.m. for God's sake. Better go to the loo while I was awake, though, couldn't seem to hold it ...

"Yes, ambulance please, quickly. I think I'm having my baby."

Right, Mecky, I told myself, concentrate. No time for panic. You've got the case packed, it's in the bedroom, so put it by the door. Ring Terri, you'll need your birth partner standing by. What was her number, couldn't find ... hang on, she'd programmed the phone, press one, silly.

"Terri, it's Megan. Can you meet me in Maternity? Yes, I'm on my way. No, haven't told them, only rang an ambulance. Could you ... thanks. See you soon."

What else? Nothing for now. Okay, deep breaths; I'd do some gyrations till they arrived, might loosen up that tight patch in my back.

"Fran, they won't let me walk, they've put me in this chair. Tell them I can walk."

Frantically I flapped my arms, trying to propel myself out of the chair.

"Megan, calm down, please. Hospital rules state that women in labor should be brought onto the ward by wheelchair. That's why the porter insisted. As soon as we get to your room, you'll be able to walk, I promise you. Look, here we are." She pushed open the doors and gestured calmly towards the familiar bed.

"Now, could you hop on the bed for one minute? I need to see if you're dilating and have a listen to his heartbeat, just to check; nothing to worry about. Is Terri on her way?" Her hands were deftly arranging my legs.

"Yes, I rang her, she's coming from Sussex. My back hurts, it feels like I've pulled a muscle."

"Some people have their labor in the back rather than the front. I expect that's it. Hold still while I take a look, let your knees go loose. Hmm, long way to go yet, but labor has definitely started. I told you he was anxious to arrive. How often are the contractions coming?"

"I'm not sure. There was the big one that woke me. Then I had two little ones close together in the ambulance, nothing since so I can't really say."

"Okay, we'll start timing them from now – you can jot the times down on that board on the wall if no one is with you. Now, let me have a listen to this young man's heart ..."

She was peering at me from around a strange stethoscope attached to my tummy. How like Luit she was. I was so glad she was looking after us.

"That sounds fine. I'd like to get you onto a fetal monitor for an hour or so to keep a check. We can do it while you sleep."

"Is it possible to do that a little later? I'd really like to do my belly dancing. That teacher that Miranda found, Jasmine, taught me some special moves to get the muscles toned up and ready to go, she said it would help the pain. Lying here makes me feel twitchy and I don't think I'll get back to sleep now. I need to move."

"Well, take it easy, I don't want you exhausting yourself, this could be a long labor. I'd like to make yours a natural birth if possible, but I have got the theatre standing by in case."

Fran's face was creased with worry, but I thought that was more to do with me than with my baby.

"If I get tired I've got more exercises from Dr Shen-Tao to tone up my chi. He said he could help with the pain too if I need it."

"We can call Dr Shen-Tao later, we might as well let him sleep. Dr Rahim will be here later, too; he asked us to call him if you were brought in. I don't think he has the result of those last blood tests yet, but he wants to take a look at you." She patted my shoulder reassuringly and turned to go.

It was going to be a busy morning. I hoped Terri would get there soon, I needed someone to keep me calm. Right, now how did that hip move go, oh yes ...

"Terri, it's so good to see you. Thank you for coming. Sorry I had to call you in the middle of the night."

"Don't worry, Megan, my babies were night birds too – and it made the drive to town so much quicker, there being no traffic about." She planted a big kiss on my cheek and took off her jacket: "How are things going?"

"Fran says I'm dilating rather slowly but she doesn't want to give me anything to speed things up – I've been doing my belly dancing, that seems to help the contractions. The worst thing is this pain in my back."

"Would a back rub help, Megan?" She was already rolling up her sleeves.

"Oh yes, please, that would be wonderful."

"I've brought my labor kit with me. I'll talk to Fran afterwards and see if we can help things along. That's the beauty of homeopathy, it won't interfere with anything else they need to give you. Now, why don't you get comfortable on your side, here, put this pillow under your bump and roll over as far as you can. That's it. I brought some clary sage oil along, should be just the thing. It aids the contractions and will help the pain."

Mmm, that was better. Such skilful hands, it was kind of Terri to say she'd be my birth partner. It would have been awful to be all alone. Fran was there, of course, but she didn't know the full story ...

"What's this, why am I tied down? I can't sit up ..."

"Gently, Megan, you'll detach the monitor pads and set the alarm off. You dropped off to sleep while I was massaging you and Fran took the opportunity to check the baby's heartbeat – look, you can see it changing when you struggle to get up. Lie still and I'll let them know you're awake."

Terri put her head round the door and called to someone. It was only a moment before Fran came rushing in, her hair even more scraggy than usual, she must have been rushed off her feet. The poor woman must be exhausted but she still managed to smile.

"Well, Megan, things are going well. You've slept through a

number of small contractions and there's a good heart rhythm going so your baby is fine. Mind if I take a look at how you're dilating? Then you can get up and walk around ... There, better than when you first came in but these things take their own time. We'd better let Terri try her potions." She touched Terri's shoulder affectionately, it seemed they'd become firm friends.

"Come on, let me help you to sit up. There, grab hold of me and get your feet on the floor. How is that?" Fran was smiling with Luit's eyes again.

I was a bit lightheaded, it must be that sleep. I wouldn't say anything yet, I didn't want to fuss and it would probably wear off.

"I'll see you later, Megan, I've three more babies arriving. If you need anything, ring the bell and someone will be along to see you. In the meantime, I'm sure Terri here will keep you company. We're fortunate she used to be a nurse, we're short-staffed today as it's my registrar's day off. Somehow, the babies seem to know." Fran admitted wryly.

They probably preferred to have Fran around to greet them, that registrar of hers was a cold fish. Strange that he should be attracted to obstetrics, although didn't someone say most gyny surgeons were men? Perhaps he had to do his stint in Maternity first. What was that Terri was saying?

"Megan, I rang Anne while you were asleep. She's coming up to town for a workshop at the weekend and says she'll call in if that's okay? Oh yes, and I let Alison know too. She's going to ring Malcolm. From what I gathered they've been seeing quite a lot of each other since we got back. I said I'd let her know when they could come in. Is there anyone else I should notify?"

"My solicitor, Serena Webster. She's making arrangements in case anything happens ... I've signed most of the papers but she's going back to court today. Could you let her know what's happening in case she needs to see me? Her number's in my bag ... here ..."

The whine when the door opened went right through me. I must ask someone to do something about it. Perhaps Terri could...

"Megan, how are you?" Dr Rahim was beaming. "The results of those last blood tests have just come in. You are doing extremely well. At this rate, we will be able to put you down for a bone marrow transplant. All this work you have been doing seems to be paying dividends. Terri, I put some of the improvement down to your treatment."

"Well, thank you, Dr Rahim. It was nice to find a doctor who would work with me. Thank goodness you went private for this, Megan. Now, excuse me while I go and make that phone call – that is good news, Megan."

Her cheery wave lingered as she left the room.

"Would you say I'm in remission, Dr Rahim?"

"Well, perhaps not quite yet. There are still a number of cancerous cells in your blood, but nothing like the number there were. It is definitely moving in the right direction and, once this baby is delivered, we can get you onto that drug regime I recommended." He wasn't going to go on about that again, was he?

"Do you mind if I think about that later? Right now it's taking all my energy to deliver this baby."

"Of course, my dear. Whatever is that commotion? I will go and ..." His words were lost as he closed the door.

It was Greg, I could hear him from there. Who told him? ... It sounded like Dr Rahim was trying to reason with him. Always a mistake; he needed to be firm. Yes, there went Greg shouting and blustering. Who was that running, you didn't often hear that in this hospital? Greg's voice was retreating ... Ouch ... better put that one on the wall – when I could straighten up again. The pains were getting stronger now. How long would it be?

"Megan, are you alright?" Terri was looking worried.

"Only a contraction, but I heard Greg shouting ..."

"Yes, Dr Rahim called security. Some idiot let Greg on the ward when he said he was your husband. Don't they know those locks are there for a reason? Someone should have checked. Security have evicted him and told him not to come back." Teri said fiercely.

"That usually makes him all the more determined. What did he want?"

"To see his wife and baby, or so he says." She grimaced with disgust.

"Wonder how he found out?"

"When I rang Serena Webster, she said she'd been in court first thing this morning. She'd had to say you were in hospital, although of course she didn't know you were about to deliver. Apparently Greg was there and rushed out; she was about to ring to warn us. He must have come straight round. Reception probably told him where you were and he guessed the rest."

Of course he did, wouldn't miss an opportunity to get his hands on the money, and on my baby if they'd let him. I remembered how he'd shouted on and on in the past, and I'd caved in so often just to get some peace.

"But Serena said not to worry, Megan, the court appointed guardianship has gone through and the trust fund is all set up. There's no way he can get the baby now. Don't cry, it'll be alright, you'll see. Here, have a tissue, and some rescue remedy. And I'll put some oil on this door while I'm at it, I could see you wincing at that dreadful sound."

"Thanks Terri." Perhaps it would be a good time ... "Terri, can I ask you an enormous favor?"

"Yes, of course, what is it?"

"Could you fish in my bag and find a large white envelope. Yes, that's it. If anything happens to me, I want this to be my epitaph. Please read it at my funeral. It's from a stele at Tel El Armana and it sums up for me what Akhenaten stood for, and I'd like my baby to have a copy when he's old enough. It goes like this:

Follow your desire, so long as you live. Put myrrh on your head, clothe yourself in fine linen, and anoint yourself with the marvels of life.

Increase yet more the delights that you have, and let not your heart grow faint.

Follow your desire and do good to others and yourself.

Do what you must upon the earth and vex not your heart, until that day of lamentation comes to you – for He With The Quiet Heart, Great Osiris, hears not lamentations, and cries deliver no man from the underworld.

Spend the day happily and weary not thereof.

For no man can take his goods with him.

And no man that has departed can come again exactly as before.

"And, please, tell him my story – Serena Webster has my journals, he can have those when he's old enough. I want him to know he was born as the fruit of a great love affair – even though it did go horribly wrong at the end."

"Of course I'll do that, Megan. But I'm sure you will be able to tell him yourself. Personally I prefer Ptah Hotep's words:

Be merry all your life
Toil no more than is required
Nor cut short the time allotted for pleasure.

She'd got such a wicked grin, it was strange how often she reminded me of Anne.

"Now, how about that walk we were going to have before Greg interrupted us. Shall we go around the block? I could bring the wheelchair in case you get tired."

"I'll be fine. It'll do me good to stretch my legs. Aah, put this one on the wall for me before we go. Should have ten minutes or so before the next one."

I think I was a bit over-ambitious there. I was so tired, and glad to be back on my bed. I didn't want to worry Terri but I needed a rest.

"Terri, why don't you go and get a cup of coffee and a breath of fresh air. I'll doze while you're gone."

"Well, if you're sure, Megan. I missed breakfast and I am hungry. I'll only be twenty minutes or so. I'll let them know I'm going out. I'm sure someone will be in to check on you."

"Fine, see you later."

I wished the room would stop spinning, perhaps I'd better call that nurse ... Couldn't seem to ... Orange flashes pulsed through opaque eyelids drawing me out. So bright ... I was floating, effortless ...

Things look different from up here. My body is so calm and peaceful lying down there on the bed, except for the bump. That's going up and down like a football. Is he trying to trampoline his way out? Or does he want me to wake up? He will be alright, won't he ...?

"Of course he will, my child, but will you?"

Sekhmet, my Lady.

"What do you mean? Will I be alright? Dr Rahim's just told me my blood count is better."

"Yes, but see where you are."

She's gesturing towards that brilliant light coruscating over her shoulder; we seem to have moved further away from the bed now. I look tiny lying down there, a mere speck. I can see all my lives, strung out like pearls around me, and recognize the effect of every action, each decision I ever took, every thought and each emotion. I can see how they all link up. But it's much too peaceful to think about that.

"But you must face this, Megan. This is the answer to all things. See, the curses weave themselves through your lives like black shackles, and the promises like silver chains. Both tie you down, each create dis-ease. Your previous lives bond you to others; it is cause and effect. Desire is the most potent source of karma. You could not let him go and so you drag Ramon with you like a ball and chain. Relationships echo down the centuries, endlessly recreating your story. It disturbs the harmony of the whole. Energy cannot flow unimpeded, evolution is halted. You freed a part of it but it is like a hologram, it rebuilds itself from the tiniest particle."

"But what about the promises he made me? Smenkhare told me one day we would be together and have a child that would be acknowledged and loved by both his parents."

"Exactly. Karma can be very literal. The soul that is now Ramon did not promise that the two of you would be together in a lifelong, loving relationship; he promised you his child and that the child would be loved by both his parents. That is what will happen."

"I suppose so, but I thought he meant ... and what about Ibi? He promised to love me."

"Yes, child, he did. But he did not plan it properly. The way is blocked, what he promised cannot be in this life."

"What must I do to change it?"

"Choose grace my child. The power to let go of the past and create a different future. Step into grace."

Such an effort. I'd like to float here forever.

"Well, you could, this is what dying is like, you know. Entering utter peace. This is the entrance to the other world. You could choose to stay here and pass on through into Amenti. You don't have to go back to your body. But, one day, you will have to do it all over again. You will have to go through everything that brought you to this point. You will face this choice again."

"What about my baby?"

"Oh, he'll be fine. In a moment Dr Catermoule is going to come through the door. She'll rush you into theatre for an emergency caesarean. Your baby will be lifted out alive and well."

"But what about me? What if I choose to stay here?"

"You simply won't come round from the anesthetic. Your heart is only beating now because the link hasn't yet been severed."

"What if I don't die, what then?"

"Well, your baby is a special soul and you could prepare him for his task in the world – and start your own, you haven't even touched that yet. You'd be a powerful healer Megan. You understand the workings and dis-eases of the soul so well, and don't forget that the Lady Isis passed her healing girdle on to you.

But if you're going to live, we have some work to do."

"Not more work. I thought I'd done everything there was to do these last few months. Can't I just choose grace?"

"No, child. Look at yourself down there, what do you see?"

"My body lying on the bed, the door's opening ..."

"No, child, look with your spirit eyes. Now what do you see?"

"My light is dim and there's a black spot right in the middle of my heart. It seems to be blocking all my energy, no, wait, it's like a black hole sucking all my energy in and it's getting bigger all the time."

"Exactly. If it gets much bigger, there will be no life force left in your body. You'll die. Now, do you know what is causing that black hole?"

"No, unless ..."

"Unless what? Go on."

"Well, after Ramon phoned me the pain was so bad, I couldn't bear it. In the morning, it felt like it had all been rolled into a little hard, cold stone that was lodged somewhere inside me. Is this the stone?"

"It is."

"How do I release it?"

"You have to trust, child. Open your heart again. Dare to love."

"But ..."

"There can be no buts. Only love can dissolve that stone. Only love can help you let go of the past."

"Love got me into this. I loved Akhenaten and Ibi, my other Pharaoh, and Ramon, and look what happened."

"It's a different kind of love. That love was born out of your neediness. You clung to it – for all those thousands of years. The promises glued you together, but the consequences were not well thought out. When you and Ramon met in this present life, the pledges could not be honored. The love was tainted with the past – and he, of course, had a wife.

"So often people promise to be together again, but they lose sight of that intention when they incarnate. They marry and then, when they meet the soul-mate for whom they were destined, there is an impediment, it is no longer appropriate. This is what happened with you and Ramon. Can you give him up, Megan? Can you set him free?"

"I think so, but you said I needed love?"

"The love you need now is beyond human; it is generous and forgiving, you'll find it deep within your true self. Love yourself, Megan, love the divine being that you are in your heart. Therein lies grace and the power to change. With change comes new opportunities – and new love."

"Is it too late? Everything down there looks like it's in slow motion, but could I get back in time and have my baby?"

"Haven't you realized? It's never too late, but you need to hurry – look Fran has reached the side of your bed, she's taking your pulse and getting ready to move you to theatre."

"But what do I do?"

"Go into the light."

Comforting and calm, totally accepting and radiantly bright. All loving, all embracing. Now what? Oh yes, open my heart and take the stone out. Sekhmet's putting out her hand for it. It's left a big hole but the light's rushing in to fill it. So warm, such loving. It's filling me up, I'm getting as big as the universe, bigger and bigger, like Mek'an'ar and her Pharaoh, a part of creation. We are the breath of the gods. They're all here with me, the characters from my different lives and the gods flowing into me, we're all one. All parts of the same spirit, uniting at last. Only Ramon stands apart. Can I open my arms to him? Of course I can. My heart light goes out to him, wrapping him in this divine love, forgiving everything. He's ...

There was a nasty jolt. I didn't expect to go back into my body quite like that, but I'd taken that wonderful feeling with me, it was tucked inside my heart, so much love.

"Megan, Megan, wake up. Stay with me. Quick, get her into theatre." Fran's voice was frantic, her quiet composure gone.

"No, Fran, no, it's okay, I'm back and he's on his way out. You'll need to be quick to catch him. Help me squat. That's it. He's coming."

Fran's arm hooked me up into a squat and pulled up my gown:

"I can see the head. One big push and ... here he is. Alive and well. Oh Megan, you gave me such a fright, I thought ..."

"Never mind that, Fran, can I hold my baby?"

"Of course, dear." As she lowered me gently back onto the bed a warm bundle was placed on my chest.

Well, look at you. Your head's all slippery and covered in blood, but your eyes, I know those wise old eyes gazing from under those translucent lids. All those tiny veins pulsating. And look at these long curling lashes. So beautiful. You've got your father's nose, no doubt about that, and his black hair. I didn't know babies had that much hair. Welcome to this world, little soul friend. You are a shining one. I shall call you Lucian. No matter what happens now, it has been worth it just to see you safely born.

"Megan, can we take him now. We need to cut the cord and get him cleaned up and checked over. That sheet's not really keeping him warm enough. You can have him back in a few minutes. I'd like to get you into the delivery suite. Lie back and we'll push your bed across. I'll be glad when the placenta has been delivered. I don't want you hemorrhaging at this stage." Fran had that worried look again, pushing her sleeves up with her face as her hands tried to bring order to her hair.

"I know I'm going to be fine. Don't worry Fran."

"Megan, Fran, what's going on?"

"Oh hi, Terri, you've missed all the fun. He's here, arrived in the corridor, and his name is Lucian."

"We are just taking her across to the delivery suite, Terri. She gave us a bit of a fright back there, but everything is fine now. We need to get the placenta delivered though. I'm worried about postpartum hemorrhaging."

Terri's smile was huge. "Congratulations, Megan. Anne I met Dr Rahim in the corridor, he ..."

"Hold on a moment, Terri, let us get the placenta out of there. Big push now, Megan, I'll give you a hand ..." I didn't think she meant literally but her squeeze on my stomach had shifted it, I could feel it slithering out.

"... there it is. Looks good, intact, no bleeding. The nurse will tidy you up a bit and then you can go back to your room. I expect Lucian is there by now. He'll be wanting to see his mum. We'll have him in the nursery to keep an eye on him but he's not going to need an incubator. Congratulations, Megan." Her face glowed brightly.

"Yes, Megan, well done. I'm so happy for you." A warm Terri hug enveloped me.

Shouting woke me. It was impossible to sleep in that place. What was the commotion about this time? Don't tell me Greg was back.

Nurse Merryweather popped her head round the door. I hadn't realized she was on duty.

"Megan, there's a Mr Ramon Lavaries here. Do we want to see him?"

"Well, you can see him if you like. I won't, not just now. But I will, when I've had a rest, could you ask him to return later?"

"Shall I ask him to come after supper?" She was grinning so it didn't look as if my bad temper had upset her.

"Yes, please." That should give me time to decide what to say to him. "Can someone find me something to eat, please? I'm starving, and I think I'd like a cup of tea."

That felt better. Now I could think again.

Well, Lucian, what are we going to say to your father, eh? I don't want deny him his right to see you, but he certainly can't take you away to Ibiza, not until you're much older anyway. He'll have to come to England.

And what about me? Did I want any kind of relationship with him? No, not any more. Certainly not while he had a wife and I wasn't sure that without her things would be any different. As a lover he belonged in the past. I recognized that while I was in the light. Perhaps we could become friends. I'd like that for Lucian's sake, so much more civilized ...

Not again. Whatever was going on? Didn't they know this was a hospital? It sounded like both Greg and Ramon this time. Listen to them ...

"She's my wife. I have every right to see her."

"She told me you left her."

"That was before I knew about the child. He's mine, she was still married to me when she ..."

"No, the child is mine. I intend to take him back to Ibiza with me. He will become the master of a great estate."

"Oh no, you won't. He's staying here with me. Megan was a rich woman and I'll inherit. I'll be the one looking after him and dealing with Megan's finances. She was barking mad, you know, thinks she lived in some other time. The child will need a lot of care."

For God's sake, couldn't somebody remind them I was still alive? They were picking over my bones before I was dead. And nobody was taking my baby anywhere.

Serena Webster's voice intervened:

"What's all this commotion? Is it Megan and her child you're arguing over? What are you doing here, Mr. McKennar? You know there's a court order that you do not harass Megan or disturb her in any way. And you, I assume are Ramon. I'm sorry, I don't know your surname."

Maybe she could talk some sense into them.

"Neither of you has any rights over the child. Both of you deserted her. It has all been arranged by the court. Should anything happen to Megan her sister in Canada will take the child. Megan's already set up a trust fund for that purpose so there is nothing for you, Mr. McKennar. No way you can get your hands on the child or the money. And you, Ramon, what would your wife say if you were to start a custody battle?"

Ouch. She knew how to use her ammunition. Did she know I was alive? Maybe she thought this argument was because I was dead? Maybe I'd better ... no, that sounded like Nurse Merryweather. Let her sort it out. Her head came round the door again. It was an excellent technique for blocking the view.

"Megan, do you wish to see Mr. Lavaries now?" Eyes wide and gleaming, she pointed behind her.

"Yes, please let him in, and Miss Webster too."

"And what about this other, er, gentleman?" Her lips curled. Was that a grimace of distaste?

"Perhaps you could have security escort him out again?"

"With great pleasure."

I was warming to that woman. I must find out her first name.

"Ramon, this is Serena Webster, my solicitor. I'm glad she's here because there will be further arrangements to make, visitation rights and such like."

She was so slender standing there next to Ramon, but almost the same height, and fiercely protective of me. It was nice to know she was on my side.

"Does that mean you will let me have the child? My wife and I will be happy to adopt ..."

"No, you're not hearing me. I said visitation rights. I have no intention of stopping you seeing your son, but he will stay with me, at least until he's old enough to decide for himself. When he's older he may want to spend more time with you in Ibiza – if, of course, you tell your wife the truth."

"I have already done so, Megan. Miss Webster, would you mind? Do you think I could have a few minutes alone with Megan? I assure you, she has nothing to fear from me and I would like to see my son." He was particularly hawk-like that day, very commanding and not at all reassuring but Serena didn't seem too perturbed.

381

"Is that alright with you, Megan?"

"Yes, of course. Why don't I phone you tomorrow and let you know what we've decided. Thank you for all you've done."

"It's been a pleasure, Megan, glad to help. Oh, and congratulations."

"Thank you. If you find Nurse Merryweather I'm sure she'll let you have a peep at Lucian and afterwards perhaps she'll bring him in here so Ramon can meet his son."

Serena slipped out through the door, closing it gently behind her. She was well named, very serene despite her rather startling appearance. Now, time to deal with Ramon.

"Lucian, I like that. It could almost be Spanish." Smiling he repeated the name quietly to himself, pleasure softening that severe face. I'd seen him look like that after we'd made love. No, Mecky, don't go there ...

"Do you have a name you'd like to add, Ramon?"

"Yes, Azhar. It is an old Moorish name that has been in my family for centuries."

"Lucian Azhar McKennar. Quite a mouthful. I expect I'll call him Luke, Luke McKennar sounds nice."

"You will not give him my surname?" His shoulders sagged and his mouth turned down.

"No, Ramon, I can't do that. Maybe when he's older he will adopt it, but it has to be his decision. You said you'd told your wife?"

"Yes, I thought perhaps if I returned with the child she need not know where he came from. But I realized that I have too much respect for her not to tell her the truth. It has been hard for her that we could not have children. In Spain people are old-fashioned about such things. It was difficult at first for her to accept that I would have a son but Nadja has a loving heart. She would welcome him, it was she who insisted I came here."

I didn't think I could have done that in her place.

"She bears no animosity towards you. Ours was an arranged marriage between two old families who wanted to safeguard their land in a changing world. She knew that, although I grew to love her as a wife, she wasn't my passion, nor I hers. I believe there was someone she wanted to marry when she was young but her family would not allow it. We both allow each other our little peccadilloes, provided we are discreet. "

Peccadilloes. I was a peccadillo?

Careful, Megan, think of your heart. You've forgiven him so much, you can forgive this too. Yes, I suppose I can. Shine out heart light. But I won't be so quick to forget. If I'm going to change my future, I need to remember what the past was like – at least long enough to catch myself before I go down the same old rocky road.

"Megan, there is one thing. You know I am Catholic ..." Ramon shuffled uncomfortably, his poise almost gone.

"Yes."

"It possible, yes, that my son be brought up in my faith?"

"I don't think that is a very practical idea. As you know, I'm not a Catholic myself. It wouldn't feel right for me to bring my child up in a religion I do not accept. That is another thing he will have to make his own decision about when he is old enough. You can take him to church when you see him, I will have no objection to that."

Ramon raised a hand as though he was about to protest, but ...

"Here we are, here's our little gorgeous one." Nurse Merryweather inserted all of herself through the door that time. "He's ready for his supper."

"Perhaps we can introduce him to his father first."

"Lucian, meet your father. Ramon, meet your son."

Nurse Merryweather's face beamed as she held out my child to his father and formally introduced them.

"Look, Megan, he has taken hold of my finger. Do you think he knows me, he is looking a little puzzled?" Ramon's face was alight, so tender and fierce at the same time.

"Probably a touch of wind." The ever-pragmatic Nurse Merryweather lifted him and expertly rubbed his back. He rewarded her by spitting milk over her uniform.

"Never mind," she said cheerfully, mopping at herself with a tissue. "It's something you'll have to get used to. I usually put a muslin square on my shoulder – it saves on washing. If you'd like to hold him, I'll go and sponge myself down." She handed him to Ramon. "Here you are, keep a hand here, you'll find it's easy when you know how. Watch that expensive suit though, it will stink to high heaven if he spits up on that." Laughing, she left the room.

"Ramon, it looks terribly awkward standing there holding him like that, why don't you sit down?"

"I have never had anything to do with babies. But to hold my own son. I never thought it could be." His eyes were suspiciously moist as he seated himself carefully beside the bed.

"Megan, could we not come to some arrangement? I could spend a week each month with you and Lucian here in London and return to my home for the other three weeks."

"No Ramon, I'm sorry. I want more than that from a relationship. Until I find it, I shall be happy living alone with my son. But you can see him. We'll work something out with Miss Webster, put it on a proper footing."

"Miss Webster said something about a court appointed guardian?" His eyebrows lifted.

"Yes, that was to stop Greg grabbing him to get at my money. It isn't written in stone. It can be changed. My sister didn't even know she'd been appointed. I couldn't contact her, she was away her answer phone said. We haven't seen each other in years – she has her life out there, I was busy with mine. With such a big age gap, after our parents were killed there seemed nothing to hold us together. You know how it is."

This wasn't the time to tell him the way Greg had driven a wedge between us, how jealous he was, and how horrible he was to her. She always saw through him, and he couldn't stand it. I realized now how much I'd missed her. I must ring her and tell her the news, and apologize for not taking what she said about Greg seriously. Perhaps she would come over to visit us. That would be nice. She could be Lucian's godmother.

"In Ibiza we keep in touch with our families. This is why it would be terrible to lose my son now I have found him." His face was fierce again and he held Lucian tight.

A head appeared around the door. Nurse Merryweather was back.

"Megan, we really do need to feed baby now. Shall I show Mr. Lavaries out?"

"Yes please. Goodbye, Ramon. I'll be in touch. Perhaps you'd like to leave me a phone number?"

Handing Lucian to Nurse Merryweather, he reached into his pocket.

"Of course. Here is my card. This is my home number and here, this is where I am staying in London. I'll be there for a few days more. Please contact me soon. Goodbye."

He bent to kiss me on both cheeks and hurried out of the door without a backward glance.

Funny thing, I never did tell him about the cancer returning. Didn't talk about Smenkhare either ...

"Right, little man, time to get you fed."

No time for regrets with Nurse Merryweather around.

A gentle knock woke me, and a bright, bespectacled face cocked enquiringly around the door.

"Are you awake, Megan? I just had to bring you this."

Ronald waved a magazine at me. What on earth could it be that was so important? It felt like morning hadn't even begun.

"Oh, and by the way, congratulations and all that. I knew you'd be alright you know. But look, you must see this." He held out a picture. Three dusty looking mummies were spread across two pages, their nakedness plain for all the world to see. What an intrusion, how could they do this? But wait a minute. Who was that on the left, closest to the camera? That long, lustrous, curly auburn hair. I knew that hair, and that profile. It was ...

"Ronald, it's Tiye, the Old Queen, she's..."

Tears spurted from my eyes, I couldn't go on. My heart held unbearable pain, and sadness. She was my Queen, my mentor ... to see her reduced to this.

"Yes, and see, here, there's another picture of her, a close up. It says Queen Tiye was one of history's sexiest fashion icons."

That beloved face, exposed to public scrutiny so long after her death.

"How could they do this to her? She was magnificent, awesome. What the Americans would call a foxy lady. She had power and majesty, and enormous presence. There was an aura around her that you could almost touch – if you had dared. Incredibly attractive and sensual, yes, but no Egyptian would have proclaimed her sexy, it would be an act of unspeakable *lese majesty*."

Ronald was busy turning back to another picture.

"And look at this one, they say it's Nefertiti. Do you recognize her?" A bald head, a long, slender neck, and a battered face, the mouth smashed in.

"She looks nothing like I remember her. There's no trace left of her beauty."

"It says that she ruled as Smenkhare after Akhenaten's death. That the pictures of the effeminate Pharaoh are of her; that she called herself Smenkhare. What do you think about that?" He thrust the page under my nose.

"I'm certain Smenkhare was a man, although he did look rather effeminate, like his brother. I'm positive what I experienced was true; it was so real. I could not have imagined that rape, could I?"

"I wouldn't have thought you would make up something like that. No, you seemed so positive. And these Egyptologists still don't know for sure. This mummy was stripped naked and desecrated – the arm was torn off and the face smashed in – before being interred in a corner of another Pharaoh's tomb. It's still only speculation that she's Nefertiti. It's not as if she was found in her own tomb and named as Smenkhare. They'll have to find more evidence to prove she was Smenkhare. In the meantime, I prefer to believe you." His head nodded emphatically.

Good old Ronald, always so supportive and yet his keen mind assessed the evidence thoroughly. If he believed me that was a bonus, but I knew what I experienced and I'd always believe it, no matter what anyone else conjectured.

"Megan, I must go as I have a client. I only popped in to bring you this. I'll leave it here for you to read. Come and see me when you're out of here and we'll do some more delving." With a breezy wave, he was gone. The article looked interesting, but I'd read it properly when I could concentrate a bit more. I needed to sleep.

"Megan, it's good to see you. Congratulations." Alison was looking radiant, such a change in her. No longer dowdy and severe, she'd had her hair styled and colored and was wearing smart clothes. Malcolm was looking pretty good too, much younger; nothing would ever quite tame that hair but his eyes were sparkling and that looked like a new jacket. It suited him.

"And look who we met in the corridor."

Anne's face was glowing.

"Well done, Megan, I knew it would be alright. What are you going to call him?" She bent to kiss my cheek.

"Lucian, or Luke."

"Shining One, how apt. Where is he?"

"In the nursery, they're keeping him under observation but they seem pleased with his progress."

Like a conjurer bringing a rabbit out of a hat, Malcolm produced a bottle of champagne from his coat and waved it in the air.

"Pass those glasses. We have two things to celebrate. Young Luke's safe arrival, and Alison and I have some news. We're getting married." He was beaming from ear to ear as he handed me a tooth mug filled to the brim with champagne.

"That's wonderful. Such good news. Congratulations. When ...?"

"As soon as possible, we would like you to be there so we'll time the wedding for when you're out of hospital."

The other mugs were quickly filled and passed around.

"I wouldn't miss it for the world. I'm so happy for you. Cheers."

Anne smiled.

"I knew you would get together. Congratulations. This is perfect. Cheers!"

Having drained her glass, she turned to me.

"By the way, Megan, did you see that article in the *Sunday Times* magazine? The one about finding the mummies from the Akhenaten period?"

"Yes, Ronald popped in with it first thing this morning. He wanted me to see it. I recognized Queen Tiye, of course. Her hair is unmistakable – and her profile. But I'm not sure about the other one. I never saw Nefertiti without her wig and with the face all smashed in like that, it's hard to tell. But the article says there'll be more evidence in next week's edition. That will be interesting."

"Never mind that now," Alison was impatient. "I want to see this son of yours, Megan."

"Nurse Merryweather will be bringing him along for a feed in a moment. And there's something I wanted to ask you. Please, will you all be godparents? I'd like to know he's in safe hands."

"We would be delighted, my dear. It is an honor." Malcolm's face shone with pleasure and his hair was being raked into that familiar peak. It was so comforting to know they were there for us both.

chapter 27.

The Great one of Healing

I was back in the same waiting room with its awful memories. But it was looking different now – someone had painted the walls a cheerful yellow. Brightened things up no end, and there was a cold drinks machine alongside the coffee – and some newish magazines. Was this Dr Rahim's influence? I wouldn't have been surprised. It was good to have Terri with me, I knew I was fine but it felt different being here with a friend. I wished I'd known her when I was here before. Was the waiting time still as long, even though this was a private appointment? But no, someone was calling my name. And she'd got it right this time, what an improvement.

"Megan, my dear, come in. How are you feeling?" Dr Rahim shook my hand vigorously.

"Absolutely wonderful, Dr Rahim. These last six months have made such a difference."

"And you, Terri, how are you? It is very good to see you again." He smiled at her with great fondness.

"It's good to see you too, Dr Rahim. I'm very well, my practice is busy and life's wonderful." She gave him one of those special Terri smiles.

"And how is young Lucian, Megan?"

"Very well, thank you. He's such a happy child, he'll soon be walking, and he's cutting teeth. He keeps me busy, especially since I've gone back to work. It was fortunate that Emily, Nurse Merryweather, wanted a change of scene and came to look after us both."

"Yes, I heard she was with you. Dr Catermoule was sorry to lose her, she was a good nurse. I think if it had been anyone else but you, Fran would have applied pressure on her to stay." He smiled cheerfully as he settled himself behind his desk.

"It's worked out really well. She'll be able to take Luke to Ibiza to see Ramon. He and his wife keep begging me to let him visit. I've promised he can go when I am in Egypt with Anne and the others."

"More past life exploration?"

"No, this time I'm going purely as a tourist. I intend to soak up the sun and visit all the places I didn't have time to see before, plus some old favorites of course."

"And what else are you doing with your life, my dear?"

"Well, as you know, that job I took after I had to sell my father's business was never very fulfilling for me, so I never went back. I'm about to start an energy healing course based on ancient Egyptian symbols. It culminates with an initiation in the temple at Siwa Oasis so it felt right for me. And I'm going to study homoeopathy, having seen the magical effect it has. When I had that near death experience, Sekhmet told me I should do soul healing. I'll need to find a way to bring all the different approaches together. I'll probably join forces with Terri, I'd like to get out of the city."

"Well, you know I support the holistic approach. For me, all illness stems from a dis-ease of the soul. Now, I must give you the results of the latest blood tests. Are you ready for this, Megan?" His eyes were serious.

Whatever it was, I was prepared, I'd never be frightened of death again, it was such a wonderful sensation, but I knew I was okay, My Lady wouldn't have let me choose life like that if it was to be snatched away less than a year later. Dr Rahim was rather somber though, surely he couldn't have bad news? I was glad Terri reached out to hold my hand.

"Naturally with an illness as serious as this one we have to be cautious about long-term pronouncements, but I am pleased to report there is no sign of cancer in your blood and the bone marrow test was negative. It is much too early to say you are cured; we will need to do blood tests for a year or two, and we may have to consider a bone marrow transplant at some time in the future, but you are definitely in remission and your life expectancy is good." White teeth flashed against his dark skin.

A big Terri hug enveloped me.

"See, Megan, I knew it, everything is going to be okay."

Sa Sekem Sahu.

Standing in the British Museum before Sekhmet, I give thanks. Pour beer over her head. All honor to my Lady.

" 'Ere, you can't do that in 'ere," the same grumpy attendant tells me.

Too late, I already have.

A frisson of energy. A shiver up my spine. Kundalini on the move again.

Turning, I meet the sky-blue eyes of a stranger, laughter lines crinkling around their edges. My base chakra ignites and my heart opens wide. You are here, the one I've been waiting for.

The great round begins again.

This time, though, it will be different.

This time, I know, love will find the way.

characters

Megan McKennar: recently separated from her husband. Her swoon into a past life memory at Karnak forces her to confront the possibility of having lived other lives. She experiences lives as **Mek'an'ar,** a high priestess of the temple of Mut. Sister/lover to Pharaoh Ibi (Lavaries) and Shen-en-k'art, young priestess in training, servant to Queen Tiye when Akhenaten overturns the temples and moves the court to Amarna.

Ramon Lavaries: wealthy Ibizan. He experiences a life as **Ibi** (pharaonic name unknown), Pharaoh of Egypt. Megan sees him as **Smenkhare,** co-Regent of Egypt with his brother Akhenaten.

Greg McKennar: husband to Megan. Megan sees him as the nameless renegade priest who took Pharaoh's place in the ritual that killed her.

Anne Cottington: past life therapist and workshop leader.

Ronald Rollingston: past life therapist.

Malcolm Appleyard: an elderly eccentric. He briefly believes himself to be **Tutmoses.** Megan sees him as **Ashlar,** kindly leader of Horemheb's guard who oversees Shen-en-k'art's captivity.

Alison: workshop and Nile cruise participant who remembers being at the Mut temple with Mek'an'ar. Megan sees her as Malcolm/Ashlar's wife. She also shares a past life connection with Malcolm when she was mistress/harlot to a Roman soldier.

Khaled: Egyptian caleche driver.

Joseph: A Coptic, Egyptian tour guide for the party.

Beatrice: domineering, middle-aged teacher, convinced she was the female Pharaoh **Hatshepshut**.

Jane Abrams: American tour leader who also believes herself to be **Hatshepshut**.

Stephen: Beatrice's supposed 'toy boy'. Actually a gay man who remembers a life with:

Miranda, a young actress who remembers a life as **Hormose**, a young lute player.

Joan: friend of Beatrice.

Terri: a cruise participant and homoeopath, Megan's birth partner.

Dr Fran Catermoule: Megan's ante-natal consultant whom Megan recognizes as **Luit**, midwife and wise woman from the Akhenaten life.

Dr Rahim: Megan's cancer consultant who believes in an holistic approach.

Serena Webster: Megan's solicitor.

Emily Merryweather: Megan's nurse on the maternity unit.

ancient egyptian characters

Historical characters

Queen Tiye: mother to Akhenaten, wife to his father, and high priestess of the temple of Mut.

Akhenaten: so-called heretic Pharaoh who introduced monotheism to Egypt and overturned the established religion. He founded a new capital in middle Egypt. History is unaware of how he met his death, but Megan believes he took his people into the desert at the behest of his god.

Smenkhare: a shadowy figure, believed by archaeologists to be either brother or son to Akhenaten, or possibly Queen Nefertiti ruling in her own right. Megan believes him to be Akhenaten's brother and co-ruler.

Nefertiti: wife to Akhenaten, whom Megan believed was having a long-term affair with and children by:

Horemheb: a general who became a Pharaoh in succession to Ay.

Ay: Regent to Tutankhamen, who then succeeded him as Pharaoh.

Merit'aten: daughter of Akhenaten and wife of Smenkhare.

Tutankhamen: boy pharaoh of Egypt who is murdered by his uncle Ay.

Sitamon: sister to Akhenaten, and protector of Shen-en-k'art and her child.

ɴon-historical characters

Ibi: pharaoh (see Ramon Lavaries).
Mek'an'ar and **Shen-en-k'art:** priestesses of Egypt (see Megan McKennar).
Min'et: member of Sitamon's court.
Magrat: Mek'an'ar and Ibi's stepmother.
Ashlar: guard commander (see Malcolm Appleyard).
Luit: midwife and healer to Sitamon and Shen-en-k'art (see Fran Catermoule).

ᴍythic characters

Sekhmet: the lion-headed goddess of healing, death, and destruction who was sent out by her father Ra to kill humanity. Tamed by trickery, she was taken home by **Thoth**, the god of wisdom, and became a Goddess of Healing and Reconciliation. Megan relives her myth in the temple of Karnak.
Hathor: the gentle moon-goddess aspect of Sekhmet, also part of Megan's reliving of the myth.
Isis: the sister-wife to **Osiris** the god of death, birth, and resurrection. When Osiris was killed by his brother **Set**, Isis and her sister **Nepthys** searched the land. Osiris was briefly resurrected to father **Horus**.

———————— ❁ ————————

OTHER TITLES PUBLISHED BY JOHN HUNT PUBLISHING AND O BOOKS

The Soulbane Stratagem
Norman Jetmundsen

Listed by Wesley Owen as one of the Top 10 greats for Christian fiction. The author's first novel, *The Soulbane Stratagem*, was the number 2 bestseller in the Birmingham area in 2000. A thriller with supernaturaldimensions!

Endorsements received for The Soulbane Stratagem:

A rattling good read, good and unexpected twists., Church Times, London

Rewarding, perhaps even life-changing; a readable, spiritually instructive work which should find a wide market., The Anniston Star

Œ A welcome step along a route well defined by C S Lewis. I do not think the great Christian author would have been disappointed., The Oxford Times

Jetmundsen has an engaging style of writing, spins an engrossing tale, andresolves the plot with finesse... truly exhilarating, a significantcontribution to modern day theology., Birmingham Bar Magazine

Œ If you have read The Screwtape Letters by C S Lewis, you will enjoy meeting Soulbane, a devil of a character., The Apostle

Œ Imagine that The Screwtape Letters were not fiction but actual history! All familiar with the curren moral state of our society will recognise thatthese reports do not in the slightest exaggerate our present dilemma., Touchstone

For American student Cade Bryson, the opportunity to study in Oxford was a dream come true. But a chance discovery on a snowy winter solstice evening changes everything, and turns his world upside down. Who are the dark and mysterious characters whose plots threaten the downfall of the western world and the establishment of a permanent and diabolical thralldom?

292 pages
ISBN 1 903019 69 9
£6.99 $12.95
Fiction. Paperback

———————— ❁ ————————

The Soulbane Illusion
Norman Jetmundsen

A fast-paced novel of the supernatural, and the spiritual forces that try to control our destiny. A sequel to *The Soulbane Stratagem.*

Ten years ago, Magdalen student, Cade Bryson, made a stunning discovery in the ancient city of Oxford: correspondence and reports from two devils on the state of the modern world. Despite a vow to publish his discovery, Cade, now a successful lawyer in Atlanta, has left his promise unfulfilled. Instead, he has made work and success his gods, to the exclusion of everything else, including his wife Rachael and daughter Sarah.

His world begins to unravel, however, from several different directions: a marriage that is crumbling, a client who threatens blackmail, and a beautiful woman who intrigues him. Moreover, just as Cade has virtually forgotten about Foulheart and Soulbane, they are thrust unexpectedly back into his life.

In one shocking moment, Cade's life spirals out of control, and he is forced to confront his own failings and the possibility of losing the two people he loves dearly. The novel takes many strange and unexpected twists, and nothing is as it appears. The gripping plot hurtles toward a most unwelcome prospect for Cade -a climatic showdown with his two old devil nemeses.

308 pages
ISBN 1 903816 59 9
£7.99 $12.95
Fiction/Religion. Paperback

AUTHOR: Norman Jetmundsen is Attorney and Assistant General Counsel for the Vulcan Materials Company in Alabama, where he lives. He has degrees from the University of the South in Sewanee, University of Alabama and Oxford University, England.
